THE
SCARRED
MAGE OF
ROSEWARD

BOOK 2: PRISONER

© 2020 by Sylvia Mercedes
Published by FireWyrm Books
www.SylviaMercedesBooks.com

Cover design by Psycat Studios

This one is for Mutti,

the Toothless Wonder Cat

1

"Bullspit."

Nelle peered into the packet of oats and frowned. She couldn't pretend to be surprised, since it had been running low yesterday. She also knew what she'd find in the sugar, cinnamon, and salt packets: nothing, nothing, and practically nothing.

"We're in for a flavorless sort of breakfast, I'm afraid," she muttered to the creature twining around her ankles. "Don't get too excited."

The creature sat up on its haunches, raised the bright blue crest running from the crown of its head down its neck, and opened its mouth to display an impressive array of sharp teeth, flapping its one good wing. It might have been trying to grin, but the result was ghastly.

"Charming," Nelle said, brushing past the little draconian beast. It was really a wyvern, but it looked so much like how she'd always pictured dragons, complete with its scaly hide, leathery wings, and lizard-like eyes, that this was sometimes difficult to remember.

It waddled after her, chortling and dragging its bad wing behind it. It kept its distance from the fire on the hearth, eyeing the blaze with wary unease. In this respect, at least, it was most *un*-dragonish. But then, considering it was a being primarily made up of parchment and ink, it had every right to be uneasy around flames.

Nelle dumped the last of the oats into a pot of boiling water hung on a bar over the fire, sprinkled in the final few precious grains of salt, and stirred. "Not exactly appetizing," she commented, lifting the spoon to watch a sticky glop of oatmeal fall back into the pot, "but it'll stick to the ribs. You best not imagine you're getting any, neither," she added, glowering at the wyvern.

Its nostrils flared as it turned beady yellow eyes up at her, contriving to look pleading despite its fixed expression.

"Unh uh." Nelle shook her head. "There's barely enough for Mage Silveri and me as it is. And you ain't really *real*, as such, so I don't see any reason for you to gobble up my hard-earned breakfast."

The wyvern hissed and fastened its gaze back on the pot while she slowly stirred its contents. Nelle snorted ruefully. The little beast had pegged her as a soft touch days ago. It knew perfectly well she wouldn't be able to withstand its pathetic whining for long.

"Spittin' worm," she muttered, and concentrated her gaze on the pot, determined not to let what little porridge they had burn. She would need every mouthful for energy in the day ahead, for today . . . She grimaced, and a little shudder ran up the back of her neck.

Today she'd have to return to Dornrise Hall.

She'd known all along that the supplies she'd pillaged from the great house's larder three days ago wouldn't last. Unless she wanted to subsist on a diet of seagull eggs, she must return to Dornrise and scavenge whatever remained to be found in the extensive larder and cellars of the once magnificent hall.

But she'd not been back since learning about the Noswraith.

The Thorn Maiden.

A shadow seemed to pass over her eyes despite the bright morning light pouring through windows above and behind her. The flames licking at the kettle's base seemed to morph into new haunting shapes. Roses. Burning roses that blossomed from writhing, twining, living brambles.

Nelle blinked twice and refocused on the copper pot and her spoon. No good in letting her mind wander into such dark territory. The Thorn Maiden was asleep. Mage Silveri had stayed up all night binding her with his sorcery and magic. She wouldn't stalk the island again until nightfall, and many hours stretched between now and then. Plenty of time to slip into the hall, get what she needed, and slink away again.

But she couldn't deny the icy sliver of dread wedged firmly in her heart.

"Come on, girl," Nelle whispered, her voice scarcely audible above the crackling fire and the bubble of porridge. "Are you a snatcher or ain't you? Don't go losing your nerve now."

"*Prrrlt?*" the wyvern said, tilting its head up at her curiously.

"Never you mind," Nelle answered, glaring down at the little beast. "It's none of your—"

She broke off as her ear caught a horrible scraping sound, like a knife's edge dragging across stone. Startled, she stepped back three paces, the spoon clenched in her hand dripping small globs of undercooked porridge on the hard stone floor.

The scrape sounded again, worse than before. Was she mistaken or did it come from up the chimney?

A high-pitched screech split the air.

Nelle yelped and pressed her hands to her ears, nearly dropping the spoon. With a bleat, the wyvern bolted up one of the support beams and into the rafters, where it perched, hanging its head to gaze down with fearful eyes.

"Coward!" Nelle growled at it before taking a step toward the fireplace. Had some bird or squirrel taken it into its head to build a nest higher up the chimney? The only living creatures she'd seen on Roseward Isle were the wyverns, a couple of brave seagulls, and one seriously bloodthirsty unicorn, but she'd been here just a few days, and it was possible—

With another hideous scrape and piercing shriek, something fell down the chimney in a cloud of soot, hit the copper kettle, and knocked it rolling into the room, spilling porridge everywhere. A flurry of brilliant red plumage filled Nelle's vision, followed by a flash of sharp talons. She ducked, flinging her arms over her head, then spun in place to see the thing, whatever it was, hit the far wall. It struck in a burst of feathers and fell almost to the floor, but caught itself and pivoted on its wings, facing back into the room.

Shining black eyes fixed on Nelle out of a face that was bizarrely almost human.

With a shriek it launched itself straight at her. Nelle shrieked too and, hauling back her spoon, swung with everything she had. The back of the spoon connected with a small beaked head and sent the creature spinning to the floor. It landed in a pile of feathers, stunned.

Nelle didn't wait for it to recover. She rushed to the copper pot and, using her skirts to protect her fingers from the heated handle, popped it upside-down over the bird-thing's head, spilling the rest of the porridge in the process.

There was a tinny cry followed by a moment of silence.

Nelle huffed a breath, blowing a lock of hair out of her mouth.

Then the pot began to move.

It slid rapidly across the floor, dragging Nelle along with it. She struggled to hang on, to stop it from overturning. It paused, then jolted the other direction and knocked her off her feet. She was just fast enough to throw herself on top of it, using all her weight this time, and kept it firmly planted on the floor.

A terrible pounding knocked the bottom of the pot, right where her stomach pressed. "Oof!" Nelle gasped, every bone in her body jarred. A second blow knocked her rolling off to one side through a smear of spilled oatmeal. She popped her head up and saw the distinct indentation of a beak sticking up through the bottom of the pot.

A third bash, and the pot flew off, clanging like a bell as it rolled across the stone floor. A bolt of red feathers shot up into the rafters, screeching. The wyvern, which had watched events from its perch in the rafters, uttered a terrified bray and threw itself on top of Nelle, landing hard on her back and squashing her flat to the floor.

"Get off, you boggart brain!" Nelle roared, wrenching the wyvern over her shoulder and earning more than a few scratches for her pains. The wyvern brayed again and ducked its ugly head under her arm like a frightened puppy. Nelle gathered her feet under her but tripped on her skirts and sat down hard again, all the while craning her neck to search for the monster in the shadows overhead.

The sudden creak of footsteps on stair treads drew her attention. Still kneeling on the floor, arms full of quivering wyvern, she turned in time to see a robed and hooded figure descend heavily through the opening of the tower stair, one silvery hand pressed to the stone wall for support. As soon as his head came into view, he paused and threw back his hood.

A pair of pale gray eyes caught Nelle's gaze, staring down at her through strands of long white hair. Pale stubble lined a strong jaw but could not disguise the dense network of scars across his face. Recently dried blood crusted a thin cut along his right cheekbone.

"Miss Beck." The voice rumbled in a deep baritone just short of a growl.

"Mage Silveri," Nelle responded.

The wyvern chortled and flared its crest.

The mage's gaze moved slowly and steadily over her, noting the globs of oatmeal staining her gown and clumped in the loose hair hanging over her shoulder. His expression was impossible to read through the scars, but the glint in his eye might be anger or might just as easily be amusement.

"Is it possible, Miss Beck," he said in a tone of great patience, "that I might one morning wake to find you *not* threatening my wyvern's life and limbs?"

"What?" Nelle looked down at the wyvern blinking googly eyes up at her and quickly pushed it off her lap. "No, it's not the worm! Not this time." She yanked her skirts out from under her knees and, fully aware of the ungainly picture she made, scrambled to her feet. "We've got a visitor," she said, pointing to the rafters above. "Another one of your spittin' faerie beasts got through the wards and attacked me!"

"Oh?" The mage's brow rose. He peered into the rafters, then, seeking a better angle of vision, descended the last few stairs to the ground floor, head tipped back, eyes searching. "What kind of beast exactly? I see noth—"

Before he could finish, there was a flash of red and another hideous screech. "Watch out!" Nelle grabbed the mage's arm and yanked him roughly to one side just as a winged missile streaked over his head. He staggered, wrapping an arm around her waist as he strove to catch his balance. A rush of heat flooded Nelle's body, but that was simply excitement over the flying monster. Nothing to do with the mage's proximity. Nothing at all.

Silveri stood upright, and they both whirled to see the creature hit the wall and fluster about, its claws scraping deep grooves in the stone. The mage swung an arm, angling Nelle behind him as he did so.

"Back to the armoire, Miss Beck," he said, his voice tight and low. "Slowly. Don't attract its attention."

"What *is* it?" Nelle hissed as she obeyed, carefully stepping backward toward the tall armoire against the wall behind her.

"A harpen," the mage answered.

"A *what* now?"

"A har— Get down!" The mage gripped Nelle's shoulder and shoved her to the floor. Landing hard on her knees, she flung her arms over her head as he bowed over her. A series of horrible screams threatened to burst her eardrums, and Nelle's vision filled with violent red feathers and flashing talons.

The mage's silver hand seized one of the monster's legs. Its wings beat at his arm while its beak snapped at his face and the talons of its free leg shredded the thick fabric of his sleeve.

"Miss Beck!" The mage's shout was scarcely audible above the ghastly noise. "A spellbook! Quick!"

Nelle yelped acknowledgement and half crawled, half scuttled to the armoire. Flinging the doors open, she stared at the stacks of small leather-bound books crowding the bottom niches in no particular arrangement. "Which one?" she cried.

"I don't care! *Find something!*" the mage roared. The monster had ceased diving at his face and now dragged him across the room, knocking him into the table and chairs. He fell over one of the chairs, breaking it beneath him as he landed hard, but still managed to maintain his grip. The monster shrieked again and pecked at his eyes.

Frantic, Nelle snatched up the first book her hand touched. She opened it, paging through, but the words were all strange, written in some language she didn't know. A shimmering power emanated from the page, tingling her fingertips. There was definitely magic here.

"Miss Beck!"

"Coming!" Nelle leaped up and rushed toward the mage and the bird-thing. But how was he supposed to cast a spell while holding onto the monster like that?

She dropped the book on the floor near him and leaped for her cookpot. Heaving it by the handle, she swung it in a swift arc. A hard metallic clang and a cry of pain told her when the pot connected with the mage's silver hands, but it struck the monster as well.

The bird-thing uttered a pathetic gurgle and folded up, dropping to the floor beside the mage. It wouldn't stay down for long, however. Already it shook its head and gathered its wings, its angry, cruel, creepily human face turning to look at Nelle, who wielded the pot like a shield, prepared to defend herself.

Silveri reacted fast. Rolling to one side, he snatched up the spellbook and paged through quickly, his eyes searching. "What in the— Of all the options available, how did you grab *this* one?" he cried.

"You said you didn't care!" Nelle protested, but the mage was already at work. Reading the spell in a quick stream of words that flowed off his tongue, he began to shape something in one hand. She couldn't tell what it was, only that there was a brilliant glow of magic around it, and he seemed to be tossing it like a child's ball.

The monster shrieked, surged up from the floor, and launched itself at Nelle. With a squeak of terror, she raised her pot and crouched, squeezing her eyes shut. A flash of light burst through the dark behind her eyelids. She heard a squawk of surprise followed by a sticky-sounding thud.

Cringing, uncertain what she would see, Nelle peered out from behind the pot, first toward where the bird-thing had been, then swiveling her gaze to the wall.

"What in the bullspitting boggarts?" she cried, lowering the pot and staring. "Is that *slime?*"

Wings outspread, its head turned to one side, the monster, looking more pathetic than fierce, was firmly glued to the stone wall. Green ooze clung to its feathers and slid in slow, unctuous trickles to puddle on the floor. The muscles in its bird wings strained to pull free, but the goo kept it fastened in place.

Nelle turned to the mage. He rose, straightening his robes and assuming an air of great magisterial poise, his face impassive. Holding up the book, he cast Nelle a quick glance just before he shut it with a snap.

"It would seem, Miss Beck," he said in a cold, forbidding tone, "you managed to select one of the books from my earliest student days. Not, I might add, spells for which I received official instruction. These were . . . *extracurricular* experiments."

She blinked at him. "So that's a book of what? Joke spells?" She snorted, her face breaking into a grin. "How old were you exactly? Nine?"

Silveri coughed and looked down at the book, turning it in his fingers. "I was twelve years of age when I first began to create viable spells. Three years into my official training."

"Well. That explains a few things." Nelle fought the urge to laugh out loud. It wouldn't be fair to the poor mage who valued his dignity so highly.

Instead, she turned her attention to the monster-bird stuck to the wall. It had ceased struggling for the moment. Its eyes rolled wildly in its head, darting from her to the mage to the wyvern cowering under the table, and back again. Again she was struck by how dreadfully human that face was. It had a beak, large, curved, and cruel; but its eyes, framed by exposed pink skin, weren't at all birdlike, and tufty feathers formed startlingly expressive eyebrows. On closer inspection its torso looked distinctly manly, with impressive pectoral and abdominal muscles on full display. Feathered wings sprouted from the shoulders where arms should be, and the legs were distinctly avian, complete with great scaly toes and black talons. It would be an imposing specimen if it weren't covered in slimy ooze.

Nelle drew a step closer, her lip curling at the stink rising from the mage's awful spell. Apparently his twelve-year-old imagination had been ripe for all sorts of foulness. "Boggarts!" she said, waving a hand before her face. "I hope it evaporates when the spell wears out, cuz *I'm* not cleaning that mess up."

"No fear, Miss Beck," Silveri said. He moved to the armoire and crouched to search through the stacks of books within. "I wouldn't get too close if I were you. My skills at the time of that spell's invention were not altogether trustworthy. It may give out at any moment or react in ways I cannot predict."

Nelle took several hurried steps back and raised her pot again, ready to catch any stray slime-blobs that might suddenly hurtle her way. The bird-thing started at her hasty movements and strained again at its bindings, but for now at least, the spell held.

"Did you say it's a *harpy?*" Nelle asked, continuing to back away until she stood nearer to the mage.

"No." Silveri sat back on his heels, paging through a book. Satisfied with its contents, he stood and, still paging, moved toward the monster.

"Well, what *is* it then?"

He cast her a quick, distracted look. "A *harpen*, Miss Beck." He spoke as though it were the most obvious thing in the world. During the very few days she had known him, Nelle had come to hate that tone of his.

"Fine, I'll bite," she growled after an overly long silence. "What's the difference?"

He raised an eyebrow. "I should think it obvious."

"Oh, you should, should you?"

The corner of his mouth tilted, the ugly scars on his cheek puckering slightly. "A harpy is significantly larger, being the size of an eagle or greater. They are also exclusively female."

"Oh." Nelle regarded the little man-bird. It had worked its head free of the slime and turned to watch the two of them, snapping its beak viciously. "So that's a male harpy then?"

"No."

That seemed to be the end of it. Nelle half wondered if the mage simply didn't know anything more. He was certainly determined to end the conversation—opening his book and burying his nose amid the pages again. Hopefully, he would hurry up with whatever he was doing. The harpen had already pulled one of its feet free, and it looked as if both wings would break loose at any moment. Nelle kept hold of her copper pot just in case and sidled behind the mage.

"Ah!" he said at last and held the book out at arm's length. The next moment, a stream of that strange language flowed from his lips. As Nelle watched, something bright, white, and churning formed in the air just in front of the mage's forehead. It reflected in his eyes, turning the gray disks to shining mirrors, and soon the glare was too bright to look at directly. Nelle turned her head away.

A sizzle of heat sparked the air, followed by a loud crack. Nelle cried out in surprise, ducked to the floor, and pulled the pot over her head. A reverberating rumble seemed to shudder the ground under her feet.

When she dared peer out again, there was a black smear on the wall where the harpen and the ooze had been. The awful slime stink mingled with a sulfurous stench.

2

"Boggarts and brags!" Nelle groaned, standing upright and letting the kettle dangle from the end of one arm. She turned an accusing glare up at the mage, who snapped the book shut with a nod of satisfaction. "What'd you go and do that for?"

He glanced her way, one eyebrow upraised.

"Don't look at me like that! You blasted that poor little creature to oblivion, and you expect me to just tut and go about my day? And clean up your bull-stinking mess while I'm at it?"

"You are not obliged to clean up anything, Miss Beck. You are not a servant."

"Well, thanks so much, your graciousness." Nelle thunked the pot down on the tabletop and marched to the door. Flinging it open, she drew a deep breath of salty sea air, fresh with morning dew and a hint of coming rain. The ocean stretched before her all the way to an endless horizon. Only in one direction could she spy any break in that dizzying endlessness—due south, where the Evenspire loomed faint but present in the distance. The one visible mark of the mortal world, just on the edge of sight.

Nelle inhaled several more times before she could bear to turn and face the room. The wind blew her hair in her face, and she quickly tucked it back behind her ears before crossing her arms. The mage stood before the morbid smear on the wall and seemed to be muttering another spell, passing his hand over the stone as he did so. The stink was already much less potent, whether due to fresh air or magic, Nelle couldn't decide.

"I don't see why you had to *annihilate* the poor thing like that," she said. "It wasn't all that big and didn't seem particularly dangerous. Nasty, sure, but what damage could a bird-thing that size do?"

Silveri completed his spell without pause. When he was quite through, he closed the book and returned to the armoire. Nelle began to think he wouldn't answer her at all. He crouched, pushed a few books around, and tucked the volume carefully away inside. Only when he'd finished and shut the armoire doors did he turn to face her.

"Harpens," he said, "travel in flocks. They are swarmers—not unlike my wyverns, but a hundred times more malicious. You've heard that a flock of crows is known as a *murder* of crows, Miss Beck?"

She nodded slowly, not liking where this conversation was going.

"In this case it would be a *massacre* of harpens. With good reason."

Her gaze shifted almost unwillingly to the dark smear on the wall, which the mage's clearing spell had not seemed to affect. She could still see the outline of each individual pinion splayed out in exquisite detail. She shuddered again and looked away quickly.

"So, where's the rest of them then?" she asked in a rather more subdued voice. "If they always travel together, why is there only one?"

"I don't know." Silveri moved from the armoire to the broken chair lying beside the table. He set it upright, but it sagged sadly, one of its legs snapped clean off. He tilted it upside-down, resting the seat on the table, and inspected the break more closely while he spoke. "They breed in the mountains of Noxaur during the desolate months, then migrate across the Hinter Sea to the Umbrian Isles for the better part of the seasons of abundance. We are not far from Umbrian shores at this time of the cycle, and we must hope we have not drifted too close to a harpen migration route. If there was a storm at sea, it is likely this harpen was separated from its fellows and took shelter alone here on Roseward."

"And if not?" Nelle pressed. "Does this mean your protections have broken down? I mean, if one harpen got through, couldn't there be others about the island somewhere?"

Silveri's face was grim as he looked at her between the chair legs. But he said, "No need to assume the worst, Miss Beck. I will inspect the wards today and make certain they are secure."

"And what about me? I suppose I'll just have to stay inside until we know it's safe, right? I can't very well go wandering about the island if there's a *massacre* of harpens waiting to pounce."

The grim look on the mage's face deepened, the severe lines around his mouth pulling at his many scars. Nelle watched him closely, eager to see what answer he would give. This could be her chance. Since her arrival at Roseward four days ago, he had not once allowed her to stay in the lighthouse by herself. Which meant she'd not yet had opportunity to properly search the tower overhead.

If he would give her even half an hour to herself, then maybe . . . maybe . . .

"You will need something for your protection," he said at last. He left the chair upturned on the table and returned to the armoire. Nelle breathed a sigh of disappointment but hastily stifled it, watching curiously as the mage once more rooted around among the books.

When he turned to face her again, a slim volume clasped in his hands, she shot him a beaming smile. "Does this mean you're going to teach me magic after all?"

His expression hardened. "As I have told you before, Miss Beck, I am no more prepared to teach magic than you are prepared to learn it."

"Bullspit," Nelle shot back. She pulled out the unbroken chair and sat down at the table, leaning on her elbows and tilting her head at him. "I can already *see* magic. That's half the battle there, ain't it? You told me you studied for years to gain a proper sight, and I already got that part covered. How hard can the rest of it be? It's just writing."

"*Just* writing?" A red flush rose in the mage's deathly pale cheeks. "Is that what you think? And a master musician sitting down to his instrument, does he *just* pluck the strings? Is that all there is to it?"

Nelle rolled her eyes. "I didn't mean it like that. I just . . . I just think I could help a little bit. I've helped you some already, you've got to admit. You didn't take down that unicorn by yourself, you know. I did my part. I swung your spittin' fire sword around but good!"

The flush receded, replaced again by that unnatural pallor. Silveri nodded slowly, his face still grim but also thoughtful. "That you did," he said slowly. His eyes, though still focused on her, had a far-off sort of look to them. "That you did, Miss Beck."

This seemed hopeful. Nelle waited, chewing on the inside of her cheek. They'd had variations on this same conversation several times since yesterday morning, but this was the closest she'd come to convincing him. If she pushed too hard too soon, she knew he'd wall up again and be nothing but stern, foreboding denial. So she held her breath as long as she could, watching him.

Without a word, Silveri approached the table and placed the book in front of him. He stood with one hand propped to hold the pages open, the other hand clenched in a fist and planted at his waist. He cut a dramatic figure despite the shrouding robes. Those dense folds of cloth couldn't entirely block out Nelle's memory of the hard-muscled torso she'd glimpsed three days ago, when the unicorn stabbed him and she was obliged to strip him down and pry the shard of horn from his shoulder.

And there was also that dream . . .

Nelle flushed and dropped her gaze. Stupid to let her thoughts go there. It was only a dream, after all. And it wasn't even wholly her own dream, but part of a dangerous enchantment cast over her mind by the deadly Thorn Maiden. If she were smart, she would drive all memory of it out of her mind entirely and barricade against any return. No good could come from dwelling on the spells of a monster.

But . . .

The images lingered, nonetheless. Images of strong arms wrapped around her body, pulling her closer. Images of a beautiful chiseled face without scar or flaw, bent over hers. Soft sensual lips exploring her mouth, her cheek, her jaw.

Nelle cleared her throat sharply and sat back in her chair, rubbing the nape of her heated neck with one hand. The mage, concentrating on the contents of his book, seemed unaware of her, and she was glad of it. Somehow she felt that if he looked her way, he would immediately read where her mind had been. And that would be unbearable. He didn't know the contents of the Noswraith's implanted dream, after all. Did he? Of course, he didn't. He couldn't. He'd admitted that he, too, had been attacked that night, but of course the nightmare he'd experienced must have been something entirely different. People didn't *share* dreams.

Yet something about the way he firmly refused to reference the events of that attack in any detail did make her wonder . . .

Nelle clenched her jaw tight and folded both hands in her lap, twiddling her thumbs. The mage was taking much longer over the book than she would have expected. Feeling the need to fill the silence, she inquired, "So all those spellbooks you've got stashed away in there, are they from your student days?"

He raised one brow and flicked a look at her from under his lashes. "Yes." His gaze reverted to the book.

"Even that lightning bolt?" Nelle persisted. "That's something the Miphates teach to little boys?"

"Every sixth-year student of the Miphates branch of magic knows how to compose a bolt-strike spell," Silveri responded, shrugging one shoulder.

"Really?" Nelle made a quick calculation in her head. "The university's got fifteen-year-old boys wandering about the halls with the ability to blast each other with lightning at a moment's notice? *That* don't seem terribly smart, if you'll pardon my saying it."

He rolled his eyes slightly, still without looking at her. "Strict rules and regulations keep any unprincipled practice of dangerous magicks in check. Besides, a conjuring such as you witnessed just now would be beyond the skill of a sixth-year. Even if they correctly put down the spell itself, they may not correctly call it into being. The study of magic involves layers of which you are entirely ignorant."

"Yeah, well, whose fault is it if I'm ignorant?" she muttered, not quite loud enough for him to hear. She leaned forward on the table again, pressing her lips into a tight line and watching as the mage slowly turned another page. His eyes seemed to scan the lines far too quickly to justify the amount of time he spent poring over each page.

Despite her ignorance, she had over the last few days learned a thing or two about magic. She'd known before coming to Roseward that mortal magic involved the writing and storing of spells. She hadn't realized that those spells were written in a secret language, nor had she known that a written spell could be conjured only once before its power evaporated and the page on which it was written burned away to dust. At least so it seemed to be with the smaller spells she'd watched Silveri perform. He had implied that the great spells lasted longer.

The spell contained within the Rose Book, for instance. That was a great spell indeed.

But Silveri could no longer create spells. Nelle's gaze moved from studying his face to the silver-coated hand planted on the open book. It wasn't really silver; it was *nilarium*, a fae alloy. Years ago, Silveri had been cursed by a powerful fae king for magical crimes committed against Faerieland. He could still conjure old spells, but he could never again write new ones with those encrusted hands. Which meant that his magic had an ultimate limit.

No wonder he had kept and hoarded every spellbook from his student days, even from as far back as those foolish first-year spells. For the job he must do here on Roseward Isle—protecting the mortal world against the threat of the Thorn Maiden—required every bit of magic he could get.

How many of his precious spells had he been obliged to use trying to keep Nelle alive these last four days?

Nelle cupped her chin in her hands, a knot of guilt twisting in her breast. But she had no time for guilt. It wasn't as though she'd come to Roseward by choice. It wasn't as though she wanted to be here.

Papa, she thought, and the knot twisted tighter. *Papa, I'm so sorry it's taken me this long. I'll do the job, I swear. I'll save you . . .*

"Ah!" Mage Silveri's sharp voice jarred Nelle from her reverie. He picked up the book with both hands, holding it out before him. "This should do well enough."

"What?" Nelle asked, turning her head slightly to one side. "What is it?"

Instead of answering, he began reading in that strange language. It fell from his mouth, light and quick and easy, though how his throat and tongue could form some of those sounds Nelle couldn't fathom. It didn't sound entirely natural.

Magic shimmered in the air before him. He lifted one hand to make a little winding motion with one finger. A gleaming filament—almost, but not quite invisible—wrapped round and round his knuckle. It was so thin and delicate that he wound nearly a hundred times before it formed the thickness of a ring.

His words ended with a final imperative phrase followed by a small flash of golden light. Nelle looked away, blinking hard. When she peered up at the mage again, he was turning his hand this way and that, inspecting the little band of gold around his index finger. He nodded, satisfied, and pulled it over his knuckle.

"There you are, Miss Beck," he said, presenting the ring to her, bright gold against the silver of his palm.

Nelle hesitated. "What is it?"

"A summoning spell." The mage tossed the ring lightly. It turned in the air, flashing bright, and landed in his cupped palm. "Wear this on your finger, and a thread of connection will remain linked to me. If you get into trouble, you need only tug on the thread three times like so"—he demonstrated, clenching his hand in a fist and making three sharp knocking motions—"and I will know to come at once to your aid." He looked pleased with himself as he held the ring out to her once more.

Nelle's lip curled. "So, let's say I happen upon a massacre of harpens. I just tug three times, and you come running fast as you can to . . . what? Bury my picked-clean bones? Is that how this works?"

His pleased expression soured. "Roseward isn't that large of an island. So long as you take shelter at the first sign of trouble, I should reach you in plenty of time."

"*Should,*" she repeated, then nodded. "Should, yes. I'm suddenly overflowing with confidence."

His nostrils flared slightly. "Take the ring, Miss Beck. It is unlikely more than one harpen made it through the boundaries without attracting the attention of my wyverns. Otherwise, they would have brought me word. You may go about your day with confidence. This is merely a precaution."

Nelle plucked the ring from his hand. It was much too large for any of her fingers, so she slid it over her thumb instead. It was still a little loose, but if she was careful, it wouldn't slip free too easily. She spun it around, admiring the workmanship. From some angles it vanished entirely, and her mortal eyes could perceive nothing more than a faint shimmer of magic where she knew the ring ought to be. From other angles it was a perfect little gold band made up of a hundred delicate threads all wound together. Mage Silveri was a master of his craft.

"Still think it makes more sense for you to teach me how to defend myself," she said, rising from her seat at the table and crossing the room to the fireplace. The wyvern, recovered from its fright, was happily gobbling up the cold, half-cooked oatmeal strewn across the floor. "Wretched worm," Nelle muttered while fetching a flat pan, which she set atop the burning coals to heat. Seagull eggs for breakfast this morning. Not an appetizing prospect with no salt to flavor them, but better than nothing.

While Nelle watched the sizzling eggs, Silveri muttered more magic, using yet another spell to repair the broken chair leg. That task complete, he set the chair upright by the table, took a seat, and folded his arms deep into the sleeves of his robe, watching Nelle silently as she fetched two wooden plates and served up their meal.

Strange, Nelle thought, how comfortable she'd become with this little morning routine. Not the monster attacks and mayhem so much, but the somewhat odd and stilted yet undeniable companionship of sharing a meal with the stern mage. She liked to think that he had grown accustomed to her presence as well, that he might even welcome the change from his long solitude.

Fifteen years of exile Soran had endured alone here on Roseward Isle. Exile from his own world, cut adrift to float on the currents of the Hinter Sea between the many realms of Faerieland. That was a long time for any man to be totally alone. Small wonder, really, that he was such a brooding sort! All things considered, he'd been remarkably kind and gracious to his unwanted invader, agreeing to give her shelter and enduring all her teasing and her nosy questions with dignified grace.

And every night he battled for her protection. Battled to keep the Thorn Maiden from breaking through into her dreams and slaughtering her in her sleep.

Nelle shuddered as she served up the eggs. After she placed one plate before Silveri and took the other for herself, they ate in silence, Nelle using the one fork available while Soran daintily picked at his food with his fingers. His hands, while not wholly useless for basic tasks, were too clumsy to wield smaller utensils.

"What will you do with your day, Miss Beck?"

Startled by the question, Nelle looked up. It wasn't like the mage to make small talk over a meal. A warm glow of pleasure at this unexpected attention bloomed in her breast. "I thought I'd go up to Dornrise again," she said. "Fetch a few things from the larder."

"While you're there, perhaps you ought to find yourself a fresh gown."

The warm glow dimmed as Nelle looked ruefully down at her dress. Only a few days ago it had been a lovely dusty blue, fresh and clean and by far the nicest thing she'd worn in years, since Mother died. Now the original color could hardly be discerned beneath all the mud and grime and pulls and tears. Not to mention the newly added smear of oatmeal.

"You know what, sir," she said around a bite of egg, "perhaps I will."

3

Something must be wrong. Very wrong indeed if a harpen had gotten through the protective barrier of the ward stones.

His face grim, his mouth turned down in a hard line, Soran marched along the south coastline near the edge of the high sea cliffs. It was bad enough that a unicorn had made its way to Roseward's shores. But the Hinter currents always did draw Roseward near to the edges of the Dawn Kingdom where unicorns dwelt. And unicorns were such powerful beings, they could generally work their way through stronger wards than his.

Harpens, however . . . Soran shook his head, grinding his teeth. Even when flocked they didn't generate particularly powerful magic. If a single harpen got through on its own, that meant one of the island's wards must have failed.

"And if so," he muttered, "what can I possibly do about it?"

The wards had been a gift from Queen Dasyra of Aurelis at the time of Soran's cursing. King Lodírhal had wanted to set Soran adrift with no shield against all the horrors of the Hinter Sea, but his wife—a lovely mortal woman who'd taken pity on the mage— had insisted on providing him some form of protection. Lodírhal never officially gave his consent, but Queen Dasyra didn't need permission to do what she believed right.

And so, ward stones had been set in place around the circumference of Roseward Isle, the ancestral estate of the Silveri family. Dasyra herself had written powerful spells directly into the stones. In the mortal world, they would have lasted a hundred years or more.

But Roseward no longer existed in the mortal world. Not wholly, at least.

Soran approached the first ward stone. It was a large, naturally shaped pillar of basalt, weathered by the elements. The written spell spiraled from the top of the stone to its base, and Soran felt its emanating magic before he came within five feet of the stone itself. At first his heart lifted. This ward, at least, was still strong.

But the nearer he drew, the more that initial hope faded. The magic had . . . glitches. Its humming pulse shorted out now and then, leaving power gaps. Almost instantaneous, but . . . long enough for a harpen to get through?

Soran approached the stone, which was nearly his height and densely covered with spell writing. Some of the words had faded over the years, but they were still distinct enough for the magic to hold. Running a hand along its spiral pattern, he studied the intricate lines of the spell until his gaze caught a place where wind and weather had eroded the script to a dangerous level. Was this the problem?

He continued a little further, stepping around the stone to follow the words. As he came to the part facing out to sea, he stopped short, his heart thudding against his breastbone.

Here was the cause of the anomalies: A crack running up the front of the stone cut straight through three of the words. They were still legible, their power not yet broken. But the damage was well underway.

Soran bit down hard on an expletive. What was he supposed to do now? Queen Dasyra was one of the greatest mortal mages of known history, and this spell was highly specialized work. At one time he might almost have been able to equal her skill, but now . . .

He looked down at his hands, his fingers curling, straining against the restrictive nilarium. The magic inside him was as keen, as potent as ever. But he would never again be able to create new spells.

With a heavy sigh he sank to his knees, then turned to sit with his back against the boundary ward and gaze out across the sea at the Evenspire gleaming in the hazy distance. Bitter bile rose in his throat at the sight. It seemed to mock him, that symbol of his former prominence, the university where he had studied among the greatest Miphates of the age, where he had risen in the ranks until not even the oldest, most learned of their number could deny his superiority. Before he was twenty years old, rumors had abounded that he would one day ascend to the seat of Myrdin

Supreme, the highest-ranked Miphato in all Seryth. Before he was twenty-five, he had assumed the green robes of an Aubron Cleric, an unheard-of honor for one so young.

And he had brought it all crashing down into ruin with his own two, doubly cursed hands.

Shadows flitted overhead. Soran raised his gaze to the sky, half expecting to see a swarm of harpens closing in. But no, they were just his wyverns. His beautiful jewel-like creations, dancing on the ocean breezes without a care in the world. A smile pulled at his mouth. But it faded almost at once as he remembered the poor blue wyvern he had left dozing on the hearth back in the lighthouse. The unicorn had torn its wing, damaging the spell Soran had used to call the wyvern to life. All attempts to repair it had proven futile.

"If you can't fix a wyvern's wing, how will you manage the wards?" he whispered. With a groan he dropped his head forward, too despondent to watch the wyverns flitting overhead.

What if . . . What if the girl was right?

Soran's jaw tightened as the thought slipped through. He put a hand to his head, cold silver fingers rubbing at his temple as though he could scrub such foolish ideas out of his brain. But they wouldn't go.

Why not try to teach the girl magic? She had already proven herself naturally adept. Or rather, *un*naturally adept. Gods, she shouldn't be able to do half the things he'd already seen her do! She could see his spells clearly, with no prior training, and had on several occasions manipulated spells herself without realizing what she was doing. It was almost frightening.

And it could mean only one thing.

"*Ibrildian*," he whispered.

Peronelle Beck was an *ibrildian*—a cross between fae and mortal. A Hybrid. In her veins flowed a combination of red and blue blood, of fae and mortal magic, creating something wholly unique. And undeniably powerful.

Such a mingling of the races was forbidden by the Pledge, of course. In days of old, "bride snatching" had been a common practice among fae lords, particularly the kings and princes who sought to breed powerful *ibrildian* children to serve in their armies and households. Sometimes fae ladies would take mortal men as well to beget a child from them, though this practice was less common. But there once was a time when mortal-born Hybrids abounded, a deadly bane upon their full-blooded mortal cousins. The Great War between mortals and the kings of Eledria had been waged mainly to stop the practice of bride snatching and the breeding of more *ibrildians*.

Just because something is forbidden doesn't mean it ceases to exist. King Lodírhal had refused to give up his mortal bride after the signing of the Pledge, and no one knew what had become of their Hybrid child. These days, any mortal women discovered to carry the children of fae men were forced to relinquish the babies immediately upon birth. One of the less savory tasks of the higher-ranking Miphates was to gather these children. Their fate was unknown to Soran, and he did not like to speculate.

But not even the Miphates could find every *ibrildian* born in the mortal world.

Could the girl truly be of fae blood? The more he thought about it, the more it seemed not only possible but likely. And the potential power to be unlocked inside her was thrilling to contemplate. Power enough to heal the poor wounded wyvern, for certain. Power enough to fix the faltering ward stones.

But what else? What other possibilities might be explored through her?

Could she be taught the forbidden Noswraith arts?

Soran drew a long breath, tilted his head back, and gazed out to sea again. To teach the girl such magic was a crime, but that didn't bother him much. He'd committed far worse crimes. Teaching her would take time, however. No matter how much natural talent she possessed, it would take time.

"You can't keep her here," he whispered. "You can't. You shouldn't. It isn't safe."

The Thorn Maiden. She had been quiet last night, hidden in her dark realm. But that could only mean one thing: She was preparing. Readying herself, gathering her strength for a more vicious attack.

When that attack inevitably came, would he be ready?

If he had help . . . If he had a partner in these nightly battles . . .

Soran stood abruptly, shaking out his robes and pulling his hood over his head. Time to put an end to these foolish imaginings. The girl could not stay, and he could not teach her. It was as simple as that. He'd shelter her a few days more, then send her back where she came from. Before it was too late.

Resolve fixed firmly in his heart, Soran marched on along the cliff's edge, making for the next ward stone. He must inspect them all before sunset.

4

"Hullo, you big pile of rock," Nelle said, pushing hair out of her face. "I'm back."

Standing just outside the gate, she gazed along the overgrown length of the drive at Dornrise Hall, which was every bit as ugly and tragic as she remembered, its formerly graceful chimneys and gables now swallowed in a sea of dead briars and brambles.

Nelle shivered, and her stomach made a little twirl in her gut. Now that she knew about the Thorn Maiden, she couldn't help wondering if that epic snarl of thorns might be the Noswraith's doing. Mage Silveri insisted she couldn't break her bindings and manifest in the physical world. Not yet anyway. But could she be influencing this level of reality more than he realized? The mage wasn't all-knowing, after all.

Still, he'd assured her the house was safe during daylight hours. Nelle peered up at the sun, bright in the cold sky overhead. It wasn't even noon yet. She had hours of safe exploration time ahead. Besides, what else was she going to do with her day while the mage tramped around the island about his magely business? Would she prefer to stand out in the open like live bait for harpens?

Twisting the little gold band on her thumb, Nelle gave her shoulders a shake and strode forward. Several days had passed since her last visit to the great house, but she remembered the way through the snarl of briars, a narrow path leading around the side of the house to the kitchen door. The door opened easily at her touch, already used to her comings and goings.

She slipped into the shadowy kitchen, shutting the door behind her to keep out some of the cold. Strange, how familiar all this had become in just a few days. She knew the layout of the kitchen rather well. This cavernous space could easily accommodate a small army of chefs, assistant cooks, and scullery wenches.

She moved among the worktables and ovens with quick confidence, making straight for the larder. Every day, a fresh loaf of bread appeared in the breadbasket, a magic Nelle had come to depend on and appreciate. Yet . . . it was very strange.

On her first day at Roseward, she had peered into the banquet hall and seen a great feast spread out at the table, all utterly spoiled. Most of the house had given way to decay and ruin. But in this larder there was always fresh bread, and the other items stocking the shelves were like brand new. Had Silveri planted spells to keep himself well stocked before his imprisonment began? But that made no sense; he had never once come to pillage the supplies in the fifteen years before she came here. Had someone else enchanted it for him? The fae king who cursed him, perhaps?

"A mystery," Nelle whispered. "Yet another mystery."

Not that it mattered. The bread was fresh, and ultimately that's what she cared about. But before stuffing her sack with supplies, she had another job to do.

Time to see about a new gown.

Leaving the kitchens, she climbed a back stair to the main level of the house above. By rights she ought to search the servants' quarters. She was just a Draggs Street girl, after all—she shouldn't go plundering the wardrobes of the fine ladies who'd once lived in this house.

But then again, why not?

A little smile quirking her lips, Nelle hastened along sumptuous passages to the grand front entrance and stair. She'd been inside Dornrise only twice, but Mother had taught her long ago to quickly memorize the layout of any house she entered. It was almost an instinct, a trick she couldn't forget even if she tried.

She found the stairway with its newel posts carved like ugly wyverns spewing roses and vines from their mouths. Since they reminded her a little too much of the blue wyvern back at the lighthouse, she stuck her tongue out at them as she approached.

Just as she placed a foot on the lowest step, she paused. The skin down her spine prickled, fine hairs rising.

Nelle licked her dry lips. Then, slowly, she turned and looked to the dark place on the wall where she could just glimpse a pair of gold-framed portraits. There wasn't enough natural light in the hall at this time of day to see them clearly, for the briars outside choked the windows. But it didn't matter. She felt the intensity of the gray-eyed gaze looking down at her from the left-hand portrait.

Soran Silveri. As he once was.

Nelle backed away from the stair and crossed the hall, moving toward that portrait almost against her will. She peered up through the shadows, trying to discern the features of that face. In the half-light it was easier to see the similarities between this youth and the scarred man she'd come to know over the last few days. The jaw was the same shape, square and strong, and the set of the eyes above sculpted cheekbones. It was an attractive visage—beautiful, but not too beautiful to compromise the undeniable masculinity of the subject.

Of course, it might be idealized. Nelle folded her arms and raised an eyebrow. These fancy folks often paid artists to make them look better than reality. Young Silveri might have been a loutish sort with a bad complexion for all she knew, scarcely resembling the man gazing down at her from that frame.

Somehow she doubted it.

Uncomfortable under that supercilious scrutiny, she turned her attention to the second portrait. Although she had noticed it the last time she visited Dornrise, she'd been too taken up with the first painting to give it much heed. Due to the light's angle at this hour, the second portrait was better lit, though still too shadowy to offer more than an impression.

It was another young man. Very like the first young man, to be honest. So much like that at first glance they might be mistaken for one another. But the crinkles around this man's eyes indicated laughter, which should have made him appear more pleasant than the other, who looked too proud by half. Still . . . Nelle tipped her head to one side and narrowed her eyes. Something about the quirk of this man's mouth, something about the glint in his eye revealed mockery, not mirth. He was at least as proud, at least as vain as the young Soran Silveri. He might also be cruel.

Nelle took a step back, feeling she'd had enough of being stared at by both young men. Turning her back on them, she hastened to the stair and fairly ran up to the first landing. Only there, when certain she was beyond the reach of those painted gazes, did she pause to consider her next step.

She glanced up the right-hand flight of steps that eventually led to the vast library where she'd spent several fruitless hours on her first day at Roseward. But today she needed to find the family members' private chambers, so she turned left and hurried up to the next floor.

A thick green carpet rolled down the center of the wide hall before her. It smelled moldy, so Nelle walked on the cold marble floor along the edge instead. Something about this passage felt strangely familiar. She hadn't come this way before, had she? No, both times she'd followed the right-hand flight of stairs and gone to the library.

Yet she couldn't deny that sensation of familiarity. Nor the creeping sensation of thorny vines crawling on the edges of her awareness.

Shivering, she stopped. Perhaps this was a mistake. Daylight hours or no daylight hours, Dornrise was a haunted place. Haunted by its own emptiness. Haunted by the nightmares of all who once lived here.

Haunted by the Thorn Maiden, bound, yet present.

Nelle's mouth went dry, and her heart thudded in her throat. How badly did she want a new gown anyway? She took a step back. But in that moment, her eye landed on a partially open door. It, too, was familiar. Something about it called to her, beckoned her to come and look inside. The call was strong, overwhelming even her prickling fears.

Quickly crossing the moldy carpet, Nelle peered through the door into the chamber beyond. At once that sensation of familiarity intensified. The beautiful canopied bed draped in rose-colored curtains, the soft gold-tasseled rug, the walnut vanity standing along one wall, set with a mirror of flawless glass—she had certainly seen all this before. A memory lingered in her mind, though where it came from she couldn't say. A memory of this same chamber filled with a rose-hued glow, its atmosphere dense with the perfume of burning roses. And there, seated at that vanity . . .

Nelle blinked. For half an instant, while her eyelids were lowered, she thought she saw a young woman poring over her reflection in the glass. An exquisite creature, all dusky skin and silky black hair, wearing a revealing dressing gown that bared her shoulders and much of her ample bosom. A gold locket on a chain hung from her throat, the oval charm bright against her dark skin.

Nelle's eyelashes fluttered open. The room was empty again, the image fled. A faint scent of roses lingered, so faint, she might almost have imagined it.

"Bullspit," she whispered. She was letting her imagination get away with her. Mage Silveri would not have told her Dornrise was safe if it wasn't. She was too jumpy by half. What would Mother think if she saw her now?

"Come on, girl," she muttered as she entered the room. "If this ain't a place to look for dresses, then I don't know what is."

Sure enough, when she opened the doors to a huge wardrobe, she found more gowns than any one woman could possibly need. Both waistlines and necklines were lower than the current mode among fashionable ladies of Wimborne, but the fabrics were glorious. Silks and satins and velvets, all trimmed and beaded and embroidered.

"Don't need trimming and beading," Nelle muttered, studying dress after dress with a critical eye. "And I sure as boggarts don't need to be displaying everything I've got!" She held up one gown with a front so plunging, she wondered how the lady who'd worn it managed to keep herself contained. Her face heated at the thought of wearing it anywhere Mage Silveri might catch sight of her.

At last she pulled out a pale purple gown with a high, round neckline, a belted waist, and a simple cut. It was too flouncy to be wholly practical, but when compared to everything else in that wardrobe, it was positively demure. She could also get into and out of it with no assistance.

"This'll do," she said and, after a quick check to make certain no moths had nibbled at the fabric over the last fifteen years, spread the gown out on the bed. A few more minutes of rummaging produced a pair of warm, sturdy boots only slightly too large. Though hardly a match for the dress, they would serve for tramping around Roseward. She also found what looked like a waterproof cloak.

After adding these treasures to the dress on the bed, Nelle paused and considered. Somehow she didn't like to strip and change in this strange woman's room. But what other option did she have? Carry it all back to the lighthouse and change there, with Mage Silveri just upstairs? No, definitely not.

Nelle hastily pulled at the ties of her blue overdress and left it in a puddle on the floor. Her chemise was in better shape, so she kept it on as she slipped into the soft purple gown.

It was . . . *delicious.* So smooth and wonderful against her skin. Much nicer than she'd expected. Was this how high-class ladies always felt when they dressed in their beautiful gowns? Why weren't they happy all the time? Nelle arranged the folds of the skirt, feeling strangely girlish and vulnerable as she swished them this way and that. Seven gods! She felt like a five-year-old child again, dancing in a pretty new frock Mother bought for her with stolen coin.

This thought sobered her somewhat. She wasn't here to play dress-up. She had a mission, a job to do.

Dropping the skirts to fall almost to the floor, Nelle moved to the vanity and took a seat. The light from two filthy briar-shrouded windows was too poor to see her reflection beyond a hazy impression. An impression that made her frown. Her hair tumbled in a mass of snarled curls over her shoulder. Draggs-wench hair. She might put on the pretty gown and parade around like a little fool. It didn't change who and what she was.

Nelle narrowed her eyes, meeting her own gaze in the glass. She studied herself for some moments.

"Are you going to do it?" she whispered. Her voice was soft but clear in the quiet room. "Are you going to . . . kiss him?"

That was her job, after all. Mage Gaspard had sent her here for the purpose of taking Silveri by surprise with her poisoned kiss, the Sweet Dreams drug she'd inherited from her mother, which could knock a man out for up to twenty-four hours. Ample time for her to search the lighthouse tower, ample time to find the Rose Book.

The Rose Book . . . which she now knew bound the Thorn Maiden.

Why did Gaspard want that spell so badly? Didn't he understand that a being like the Thorn Maiden couldn't be controlled? He would end up like Silveri, his whole life spent trying to contain the nightmare monster before it got out and destroyed everything.

Nelle shook her head and ran a hand down her face, pulling at the skin beneath her tired eyes. What choice did she have? Gaspard had Papa. Gaspard would kill Papa if she didn't return with that book in the given time. She must do what he wanted.

Mother had charged her to take care of Papa no matter what, and she had promised. She had promised over her mother's dead, broken body.

Bowing her head, Nelle gritted her teeth. Then she looked up at her shadowy face in the mirror again, her eyes glinting bright. Of course she would do her job. Of course she would get the Rose Book and return to Wimborne. Of course she would kiss Mage Silveri, drug him, leave him gasping on the floor. She would look into his face and watch his eyes as he felt the poison course through him, as he realized what she had done.

Nelle bit down on her lip hard enough to draw a bead of blood. "Maybe it's for the best?" she whispered. "If the Rose Book is taken away, won't that spare him in the end? If the nightmare is removed, he won't have to keep fighting it. Maybe he can leave Roseward then, return to his own world. Have a life of his own."

As if the fae king who'd cursed him would ever allow that to happen.

Her fingers tightened into fists. "Anyway, why are you so concerned?" she growled. "You don't know him from anyone, and what little you know *about* him ain't exactly to his credit. He's a Miphato, after all. Sure, he's been kind to you these last few days, but what difference does that make?"

She could argue and rationalize all she liked. The truth remained: She didn't want to kiss him. That is . . . Nelle frowned and brushed the back of her hand across her nose. She didn't want to poison him. But if the opportunity arose, she must take it.

"Bullspit," she muttered again and suddenly reached for one of the vanity drawers, yanking it open so hard the mirror rattled in its frame. She fumbled around, searching for a comb or some hairpins, something she might use to tidy her snarl of hair. If she was going to pretend to be a lady, she'd best make a thorough job of it. She reached further back into the drawer.

Her fingers touched something cold, hard, smooth. And a chain.

Curious, Nelle pulled out a gold necklace that glinted even in the partial light. It was a locket, an oval locket etched with a blooming rose on the front. Nelle turned it over in her fingers several times before snapping it open to see a delicate plait of hair set inside the tiny frame: black hair braided with strands of gold. The opposite side held an inscription delicately written in a precise hand. Nelle had to bring the locket quite close to her face to make it out.

Eternally yours

SS

"SS," Nelle whispered softly. "Soran Silveri?" She touched the plait of hair with the tip of one finger.

And she wondered.

5

Hold still," Soran muttered.

The wyvern flared its crest in defiance and rolled a beady eye up at the mage. Heaving a great sigh, it settled down, its nose hanging over the edge of the table, its wounded wing spread out before Soran.

With a last stern look at the wyvern, Soran bent over its wing. He saw it as a wing, of course—the pale blue, membranous skin shot through with delicate purple veins. But he also saw the underlying spell, the parchment and ink by which the wyvern had been brought to life. By his own hand.

The wing was badly torn, pierced through by the unicorn's savage horn. And the parchment on which the spell was written was torn as well. Soran studied both closely, using his awkward silver hands to push the ripped fibers back together, reconnecting the sundered words. It would need to be properly patched, possibly rewritten, if the wyvern was ever going to fly again.

At the mage's elbow waited an inkwell and a quill. He merely needed to write the spell—write it fresh, write it clear, write it clean. Not even the entire spell, just the torn part should be sufficient. Once he could have done this in a single afternoon without breaking a sweat.

Soran's frown deepened. He'd already made several attempts to work this repair, so he knew what would happen when he tried again. His hands, clumsy and inept, would apply too much pressure or too little. The quill would wobble in his grip. The ink would run and blot. Magic would surge from him, erratic and ineffective. He might even make things worse.

"*Prrrlt?*" The wyvern raised its head again, blinking at him, its eyelids not quite synchronized.

"I know, little friend," Soran said, leaning back in the chair. "I know you want to rejoin your brethren in the air. I . . . I wish I could help you."

The wyvern tilted its head and flicked its tongue at him, snakelike. Its gaze was distinctly accusing.

Soran glared. "Do you think I haven't considered it? But there's too much risk. Besides, she might not be able to understand the magic." He pushed his hood back over his shoulders and rubbed a hand through his hair. "You'd be better off accepting your lot, accepting that you'll never be what you once were. You'll never fly so close to the sun again . . ."

The wyvern burbled and tilted its head. Then, with a snort, it twisted its neck around and started grooming the spines along its back, picking at each one in turn. In truth, it probably didn't care if it ever flew again. It wasn't exactly the brightest of the flock, and it had a nice situation here, snoozing its days away beside the hearth, growing fat on the girl's cooking.

Soran slumped over the torn wing and spell. It really wasn't for the wyvern's sake he'd pulled out the tools of his craft yet again. He wanted to prove to himself that he wasn't afraid to try and try and keep on trying until he somehow, by a sheer act of will, forced the skill back into his crippled hands, thwarting Lodírhal's curse.

It was only another vain dream. And well he knew it.

He buried his face in his hands, his fingers and palms cold against his recently shaved face. He'd spent a long day marching the shores of Roseward to check every one of the ward stones. Three of them were compromised, though none more so than that first stone nearest to the lighthouse. At this rate it would only take another few cycles through the Hinter Sea before the island was entirely at the mercy of any hungry or curious faerie beast. He would soon run out of weapons to fight them.

The situation wasn't desperate. Yet. But it wouldn't be long now.

He lifted his head, his gaze turning to the nearest window set high in the wall above. The sky had deepened in color since he returned to the lighthouse. Dusk was fast approaching.

"Where *is* she?"

Soran turned in his seat to look at the door. Realizing what he did, he muttered a curse and faced forward again to stare down at the broken wing. He shouldn't be worried. It wasn't his business how she came and went. In fact, it would be better for them both if she came to her senses and left Roseward altogether. Better still if she didn't bother to say goodbye.

And yet, here he was, watching the door again. Wondering, worrying . . . hoping . . .

The wyvern's head shot up, bright eyes fixed, crest flaring with alertness. It had heard something.

Soran refused to turn around in his seat. He plucked up his quill, dipped it in ink, and set to work writing once more. He forced his hand to be steady, forced his brain to concentrate. He managed a single fluid stroke.

But he didn't see it. His ears strained, and he held his breath.

At last, before he could blot the spell and ruin it, he lifted the nib from the page and simply sat there, waiting. Listening for the sound of her footsteps.

"You're a fool, Silveri," he whispered.

But when he heard her knock and the doorlatch turn, he couldn't stop the smile pulling at the corner of his mouth.

Dark clouds rolled in fast by the time Nelle drew within sight of the lighthouse again. Her new boots rubbed her heels, but at least they were sturdier than the little slippers she'd been wearing. As the first icy drops of rain fell, she tucked deep into the waterproof cloak, hoping it would protect the lovely purple gown she wore—it would be a shame to ruin it the very first day.

She paused on the cliff above the wyverns' beach, her breath puffing in little clouds that the wind instantly whipped away, blowing hard enough to knock the hood back across her shoulders, sting her cheeks, and tousle her hair, which she'd managed to put up with a few dozen pins. Overhead, wyverns wheeled and sang a haunting song suited to the harsh mood and landscape.

She turned away from the sight, looking to the lighthouse. Light shone through the lower windows. Mage Silveri must already have a fire going. Did he anticipate her return now that sunset approached?

Did he . . . miss her when she was away?

Nelle set her jaw. She had no business thinking such things, and she wouldn't stand for it.

With a little headshake, she strode swiftly up the path toward the lighthouse, a basket of stolen larder goods swinging from her arm. As she approached the door, she shifted the basket from her right arm to her left before knocking loudly on the door. "Oi, Mage Silveri!" she called. Then she put her hand to the latch. It gave under pressure.

"It's me, sir," she said, pushing the door open and entering the fire-lit room. "Boggarts, but there's a cold wind blowing in from somewhere! It's going to come down like hellspit tonight, or I'm much mistaken. Don't suppose you thought to put on the kettle, did you, sir? I'm that cold, right through to my bones, and I—

Seven gods above, what is *this?*"

She stopped short, the door still open at her back, and stared into the dim space. Her gaze fixed on the wyvern sprawled out across the table, its ridged nose between its webbed front claws, its long tail draped over the far edge, faintly twitching. Silveri sat in his place with an assortment of pots and quills before him. The sleeves of his rough robes were rolled up past his elbows, exposing the lines where the silver Nilarium ran over his wrists and gave way to human flesh.

At Nelle's exclamation he looked around, his face nearly as expressionless as the wyvern's. "Miss Beck," he said coolly.

Nelle grimaced and slammed the door behind her. "Don't you go Miss Beck-ing me!" she growled, striding across the room. She set her heavy basket down with a thump beside the wyvern's tail. It raised its head and rattled its tongue at her with half-hearted menace. "What is the worm doing on the *table? We eat* here. I may be a Draggs wench, but even I've got *standards.*"

Mage Silveri blinked impassively and bowed over his work once more. He held what looked like an old goose-feather quill, supporting it awkwardly in his misshapen fingers as he made marks along the rip in the wyvern's wing. "Hush, Miss Beck," he said. "This requires . . . concentration . . ."

His voice trailed away as though he couldn't quite maintain that stream of thought while simultaneously focusing on the task at hand. The wyvern laid its head back down and burbled pathetically.

"Ugh." Nelle flung up her hands, marched to her little alcove bed, and undid the clasps on her cloak. "Wretched wyvern," she muttered. Shrugging the cloak from her shoulders, she tossed it in a mound on the rug-pile bed. "You watch; I'll bet that beast is a mess of plague! Don't blame me if you end up with speckled fever or toe rot or green gripe or . . ."

She turned around. And froze.

Silveri's shoulders were still bowed over his work. But his head was up, and his eyes peered at her between fallen strands of white hair. His mouth hung partially open, his expression surprised.

Heat roared in her gut and flushed up her neck. Which was stupid, of course, so Nelle quickly masked it with a scowl. "What?" she demanded.

His hand, awkwardly holding the quill, hovered in midair above the wyvern's wing. The wyvern cast him a baleful look and heaved a sigh. The sound was enough to bestir the mage, who blinked and shook his head. "Miss Beck," he said, and cleared his throat roughly. "I, um. You look—"

"Bedraggled as a half-drowned kitten caught in the drain? Yeah, I know."

The ugly scars around his mouth pulled as though he were suppressing an urge to smile. "I was going to say *lovely*."

Nelle gaped. Her mind flailed for some sort of response. She'd been called many things in her life—lewd things, most of them. She knew the effect she had on the opposite sex. And she hated it. Mother had always known how to use her physical allure as a weapon, but Nelle always felt as though her natural attributes made her a target for all that was depraved and wicked in the hearts of men.

No man had ever looked at her quite like this.

No man had ever called her *lovely*.

"Pish!" she said and dropped her gaze. "It's just this fanciful gown I snatched from the great house is all. Look at that hem? Half ruined by the mud, I'm sure. But I don't suppose the lady what once owned it will mind overmuch."

"No. She won't mind. Not in the least."

Silveri's voice was so soft, Nelle couldn't resist stealing another look his way. He had reverted his gaze to the wyvern, but his hand remained frozen in the air. A single bead of dark liquid dripped from the end of the quill and spattered on the tabletop. Silveri grunted and moved hastily to wipe it up, but his hands were clumsy, and he dropped the blotting rag. He growled, all the softness gone from his voice, and tossed the quill, nib-first, into an open bottle of reddish ink.

"Oh here, let me!" Nelle said quickly and sprang across the room. She crouched and retrieved the rag, then hastily mopped up the spot on the table. As she did so, she noticed the wyvern's wing. The rip was much improved since three days ago. Still ragged and lumpy, certainly not serviceable for flight. But improved.

What intrigued her most, however, was the pattern of characters written in a blocky script, trailing along the scar, outlining it on both sides. She almost recognized the letters, though not quite.

But she felt a certain . . . *simmering.* A buzz of energy not unlike what she'd felt from the grimoires in Gaspard's quillary.

"Here, what's this now?" she asked, pointing at the scar. The wyvern snapped at her finger without any real menace. She flicked its nose. "Down, you!" Turning her gaze to the mage, she realized suddenly how close she stood to him, so close her arm very nearly brushed against his. She shivered and took a half step back. "Are you making magic, sir?"

He grunted and nodded, his silver eyes briefly swiveling up to her face, then focusing on the wyvern. "I am attempting to, yes."

"How does it work, exactly?"

At that he chuckled, a warm, low rumble in his chest. "I couldn't begin to explain *exactly.*"

Nelle prickled. With a sniff, she flicked his ear with the same force she'd used on the wyvern's nose. He started, but before he could protest, Nelle moved to her end of the table, grabbed her chair, and dragged it around to his side, where she plunked it down, plunked herself down on it, propped up her elbows, and cupped her chin.

"All right," she said. "Don't explain *exactly.* Explain *un*-exactly. And use very small words." She blinked at him with exaggerated doe-eyed wonder.

He had the grace to look chagrined. "Forgive me, Miss Beck. I didn't mean to give offense."

"You condescending snobbish sorts never do, do you?"

He tipped his head slightly to one side and rubbed his forehead with one silver-crusted finger. "The theory behind what I am currently attempting is complicated. But in layman's terms, if you will, the wyvern is a creature born of parchment and ink. Not to say that the beast itself is *made* of parchment and ink—only that this was the medium through which it was birthed. It is also the medium through which it can be healed."

Nelle nodded. "I . . . think I understand that."

"You do not, I assure you."

She glowered at him, then turned her glower to the wyvern's wing. The wyvern chortled and shifted uncomfortably under her gaze. "So, when you spelled this little beastie into being, was it sort of like when you created the Thorn Maiden?"

"The process was similar, yes. Unlike the rendering of nightmares into reality, the rendering of daydreams is not forbidden by the Miphates. But it is considered low magic. I learned the trick as a schoolboy, quite by accident. Not until years later did I recognize rudiments of the greater, darker magic in this foolish little hobby. Then I began to practice, producing more and more of these daydreams until their creation was like second nature to me."

"Could you see them?" Nelle asked. "Back in the mortal world, I mean?"

Silveri shrugged. "They manifest as shadowy forms in our world. But they are happier in Eledria, where the air is lighter. More conducive to magical beings."

"They seem to like it here well enough."

"Yes. The farther Roseward has drifted from our world, the

more my wyverns have flourished."

Nelle chewed the inside of her cheek thoughtfully. "You told me once the wyverns were prisoners here. Like you. Did the fae king curse them too?"

"No. I did." His voice was heavy. Shamed. "One year after my sentence began, I was . . . I feared I would fall into madness if left alone much longer. I went back to the original spellbooks in which I had crafted the wyverns and wrote bindings into their creation spells. My skills are not what they once were"—he held out his ruined hands, palms up—"but I had the drive. I forced my fingers to comply until each of my little creations was bound to me even as I am bound to Roseward." His voice sank to a lower register, barely above a whisper. "They were angry at first. Furious. Ferocious. But we have grown used to each other. And they offer much relief from the silence, from the monotony."

He bowed his head, casting only the briefest glance her way from beneath his pale lashes. "You see, Miss Beck, I am not a kind man."

Silence fell between them, broken only by the wyvern's chirruping breaths and the crackle of the fire on the hearth. Silveri's gaze remained fixedly downcast, but Nelle could see by the way his scarred cheek twitched that he was aware of her scrutiny.

How much shame could one man bear? The proud mage seemed bent beneath the weight of it. But Nelle found she could not despise him. Shame, after all, could be a virtue of sorts, if a crude one. This man had spent fifteen years staring his sin in the face every night. He could not look away, neither could he pretend blindness. The experience had changed him. Shattered him to pieces. The scars covering every inch of his skin were only the outermost signs of worse damage within.

And yet . . . Nelle frowned, squinting a little as she studied that hideous face. Was he truly so broken? Was he beyond repair? Or had the shattering been but the beginning of something new?

She cleared her throat and shook her head, looking down at the wyvern and the ink drying on its wing. "Will you be able to fix the wormling?" she asked, putting out a finger to trace beneath one of the twisted lines of writing. The thin veiny wing rippled under her touch.

"No," Silveri answered at once. "At least, not completely. Not with these hands. I'm afraid this little daydream will never fly again."

"And you won't let me help you?"

He didn't answer.

Nelle quirked an eyebrow. Maybe she was foolish to bring this up again so soon after their last argument. "Don't look at me that way. Is it really such a ridiculous idea?"

"I . . . That is to say, Miss Beck . . ." He paused and cleared his throat, his scarred brow constricting as though in pain. "What you ask is—"

"I know it ain't *easy*. I ain't stupid, you know."

"I never said you were—"

"I ain't talking about mastering great spells. I don't fancy myself a magician in the making. I just want to *help*. Surely I can learn to hold the quill, and you can show me where to make the marks? I can practice. Maybe I can . . . I don't know." She sighed, dropped her head into her hands, suddenly tired, and rubbed her eyes, shaking her head slowly.

Then she looked up again, propping her chin on her interlaced fingers. "Maybe I can make a difference."

His eyes were on her, studying her. His silence went on too long.

"I'm sorry," she whispered at last, and started to rise.

"Wait."

His hand darted out, lightning fast. Cold hard fingers latched hold of her wrist. Nelle felt the strength in that grasp, power enough to break her bones with a single twist. For the first time in days, fear of this man, this stranger, jolted through her heart. She went still in his grasp like a mouse frozen in the owl's talons.

Still holding her arm, he stood and towered over her, at least a head taller. She found herself faced with the open front of his robes, the loose ties of his undershirt . . . and the scars covering his chest in an ugly pattern of violence. Her heart thudded painfully, and she realized she wasn't breathing.

"It takes more than a little magic in the blood to make a mage." Silveri's voice was deep and dark as the night, cold as winter. "It takes a spark. The *ensildari*, as the Old Ones called it: the *inspiration*. One either possesses it or one does not. Without it, you can never hope to control the power inside you."

Nelle forced her eyes to move, to lift from his scarred chest to his throat, his chin, and up to his twisted, misshapen lips. Tilting her head farther, she still couldn't bring herself to meet his gaze. She focused instead on his forehead, on a particularly gruesome scar between his brows.

"Can you tell?" she asked, her voice tight and small. "Do I have the spark?"

He drew her toward him, forcing her to take a step closer. His other hand came up, catching her chin between finger and thumb. She trembled at the cold touch of nilarium but braced herself, firming her jaw and fixing her brow in a hard line.

"Look at me," he said.

She dropped her gaze from his forehead to his eyes. They burned into her, the dark pupils dilating to nearly eclipse the silvery irises. She could feel him searching—delving into dark, secret places inside her, places she hardly knew existed.

Could he read her other secrets as well? Could he see who she truly was? Could he unravel her purpose for coming to Roseward?

The struggle was too great. She couldn't maintain that gaze. Her eyelids fluttered, and she focused on his mouth. On the scars ringing his lips. She could still see their former shape beneath the puckered skin, the phantom of the beautiful man from the portrait. But the scars were so disfiguring, twisting the sensual mouth into something unnatural and hideous. Still . . .

She shivered as a thought passed unbidden through her mind. What would it be like to feel those lips on hers? Would the scarred mage's kisses be anything like that wild and breathless dream? Would they burn with the same intensity while simultaneously teasing her with tenderness unlike anything she'd ever felt before?

It wouldn't take much to find out. She could rise on her toes, place her mouth against his, and discover the answers to all these questions here and now.

Don't be stupid, girl!

She jerked back, pulling her chin out of his hand, wrenching her wrist against his hold. He let go at once, and she staggered several paces away from him, nearly tripping over the hem of her skirt. "Well?" she demanded, shaking her head. Several curls escaped from pins and fell across her shoulders. "What did you see?"

Silveri's hands dropped to his sides. He opened his mouth, closed it.

Then he turned from her. In a single swift motion, he scooped the wyvern from the table in a bundle of wings and limbs and tail and deposited it on the floor. He set to work corking the bottles, wiping and capping the quill, then placed all his tools into a satchel and slung it over his shoulder. Without a word he strode for the stair, the wyvern scuttling at his heels.

"No!" Nelle barked, surprising herself.

He paused, one foot on the lowest tread. He didn't look her way.

"No, no, no," Nelle said quickly, folding her arms and taking three steps toward him. "No, sir, you can't just go through all that and leave me with nothing! What did you see? Do I have the spark? The inspiration?"

Slowly he turned his head, meeting her gaze across the firelit room. "There . . . may be something there."

The words, though spoken softly, rang out in the air between them.

But before Nelle could think of a response, Silveri ducked his head and marched up the stairs. He vanished into the shadows above the ceiling, leaving her where she stood, her mouth ajar, her head spinning.

6

It's crazy. You know it is. Just crazy talk, nothing to take seriously."

Again and again, Nelle firmly muttered the words. As she sliced bread and cold meats for herself and the wyvern. While she sat before the fire, chewing thoughtfully and listening to the wyvern's grunting gorging. As she cleaned and tidied the kitchen, storing away the goods she'd brought from Dornrise. With each new task she tried to focus her attention, to concentrate, to not let her mind spin off on this new and exciting idea.

But it was there anyway, burning in her head like a newly lit fire. *Something there. You have . . . something there.*

Outside, the storm finally broke in earnest. Thunder growled like a host of dragons, and rain drove against the stone walls and pounded at the door. Overhead, the great lighthouse tower groaned, and Nelle couldn't help looking up now and then, wondering if the whole thing would come toppling down.

And still Silveri did not return.

"Not hungry enough to face me again, are you?" she muttered and put away the plate of food she'd prepared for him. Well, fine. If he'd had enough of her presumption and pestering, she'd had more than enough of his superiority and condescension. Let him brood up in his lonely tower with nothing but a wild storm for company. She'd had a long day. She'd just as happily turn in early.

But first she had a final task to accomplish.

While wind and rain rattled the door in its frame, Nelle plucked a small jar from among the other jars and packets of larder supplies arranged on the small shelf. She lifted the lid. Pungent vapors rose to burn her nostrils, and she had to turn her face away quickly. Once the first wave passed, she peered inside.

Only two doses remained of the Sweet Dreams ointment.

"Stupid," Nelle whispered. She'd often told Mother she thought the Sweet Dreams the most ridiculous poison imaginable. What was the good of a drug requiring a kiss to activate it?

But Mother always smiled and said that for a lady in their profession, it was terribly useful. She herself had made free with the kisses when she went out on snatching nights.

Nelle sighed, rolling her eyes to the rafters. The wyvern perched up there, sitting fat with its full stomach distended, and watched her through sleepy, half-lidded eyes.

Nelle shook her head ruefully. "It'd be much simpler if I could add this to his porridge in the morning and have done with it."

The wyvern burped. Which was about as intelligent a response as one could expect from a wyvern.

"Wretched worm," Nelle muttered and brought the jar to the table with her. She set it down and took a seat. For several moments she simply sat there looking at the jar, one hand tracing the grain pattern in the tabletop. Then, suddenly, she reached inside the front of her new gown. Her fingers found a delicate gold chain, and she pulled the oval locket out into view.

She hesitated. Perhaps this wasn't such a good idea. It felt . . . invasive somehow. If the message inside and the fair hair plaited with the black had indeed been given by Mage Silveri to this mystery lady, did she really have a right to take it? And to use it for her intended purpose?

"It doesn't matter," Nelle whispered. "You can't go wasting opportunities. You've only got two doses left. You have to keep it on you so when the next chance comes . . ."

She flicked open the locket. She had already taken time to carefully remove the plaited hair, leaving it behind in the lady's vanity drawer. Now, using the tip of her finger, she scooped out the last two doses of Sweet Dreams and smeared them into the locket frames. It was a bit messy but just about a perfect fit.

Snapping the locket shut, Nelle dropped the necklace back down beneath the neckline of her gown. It rested cold against her heart. She pressed a hand against her chest, pushing the locket into her skin, trying to warm it quickly. But the chill wouldn't go away.

Maybe she wouldn't have to use it. Maybe she would find some other means of getting the Rose Book to Gaspard. Maybe . . .

"Maybe you're a fool," she growled, then quickly lidded the empty jar and returned it to the shelf among the other supplies.

Thunder rolled ominously overhead, but the worst of the storm seemed to have passed. Rain came down in a steady rhythm, beating against the shutters. Runnels of water ran down cracks in the wall and pooled in patches on the floor, but Nelle decided to deal with those tomorrow.

For now, she set about removing the purple gown and draping it carefully over the back of a chair. Then, wrapping herself in the thin blanket, she crept into her alcove bed and her pile of fur rugs. The wyvern scuttled down a support beam and waddled up to her. Resting its head on the rugs, it gazed up at her with burbling entreaty.

"Not a chance," Nelle growled, pulling the corner of her blanket out from under its chin, then curled up, her back turned to the wyvern and the fire, and studied the pattern of shadowed grooves and divots in the stone wall inches from her face.

Her mouth moved, silently forming words she dared not utter out loud: "Something there . . ."

Of course, it didn't mean anything. It wasn't as though she could really expect to hone whatever potential she possessed into anything like real magic. She was a snatcher. She'd never be anything but a snatcher, no matter how hard she wished or strived.

Rolling over, she buried her head in the fur rugs and tried to will herself to sleep. The fire died down; the room darkened. The rain continued its steady beat, and the many drips within the chamber itself made a sort of chorus in the stillness. Something warm, scaly, and burbly crawled up on her bed, coiled into the curve behind her legs, and snored.

And still she lay there.

She thought of Silveri, high above in his tower chamber. Bowed over his desk, he guarded her sleep from the Thorn Maiden by reaffirming his slowly disintegrating binding spell,.

Nelle tucked in tighter, careful not to disturb the wyvern, which twitched and flapped a membranous wing.

Then, suddenly, she threw back her blanket and sat up. The wyvern rolled onto its belly, claws up, spine unnaturally twisted, and continued to snore. But Nelle stared out from her alcove, across the darkened room. Only the faintest red glow illuminated the hearth, but a thin sliver of moonlight poured through one of the high windows.

Moonlight? Strange. When had the storm passed and the moon come out?

She slid out of the alcove and slowly crossed the room; she knew the layout of the space well enough to navigate in the darkness. Her bare feet made no sound as she carefully placed one before the other, creeping to the door. Brilliant moonlight shimmered through the cracks in the panels, and not far away she heard the ocean's murmur.

She walked right up to the door. Hesitated. Leaning forward, she placed her ear against it. Her breath stilled, caught behind her pursed lips and clenched teeth.

Nothing. Only the ocean and the wind.

No creeping creak of vines, no scrape of thorns. No feather-light shushing of soft petals stirred in a breeze.

And yet Nelle stood there for some while, longer than she reasonably should.

At last she slowly released her breath and whispered, "I know you're there."

Yessss . . .

Her eyes flared open.

Nelle choked and started up onto her elbow, kicking the solid weight behind her knees. The wyvern growled, and sharp claws rested on her hip in not-so-gentle warning. Nelle couldn't react. She stared at the wall illuminated by the glow of the dying fire, her heart racing furiously, thudding against her breastbone.

She looked over her shoulder. Across the room.

The door was shut. Fast shut.

All was dark and still save for the constant drum of rain. No moonlight filtered through the windows. The storm had not yet passed.

"A dream," Nelle whispered. "Just a dream."

She rolled over to face the door, pulling her blanket up to her shoulders and under her chin. The wyvern stretched out, grumbling, its ugly snout close to her heart. It blinked at her and showed its teeth in an unconvincing hiss.

Nelle wrapped an arm around the creature and hugged it close, ignoring the discomfort of scales and knobbly limbs. When she fell asleep at last, it was to the sound of wyvern snores and the drip of rain hitting stone.

She sat on his bed. Right behind him.

Soran bowed over the open spellbook. He was already several hours into the spell. The night had grown deep and dark around him. His candlestick had burned halfway down, wax pooling thick in the base of its wooden bowl. Light glowed in his eyes.

But the light he saw wasn't candlelight. It was the light of burning words, burning magic, dancing in the air before his vision.

After all the hundreds of times he'd read this spell, conjured this magic, it never got easier. The sheer complexity required tremendous effort. Despite the open windows all around him, despite the icy blasts of air and driving rain that poured in on every side, a sheen of sweat covered Soran from head to toe. An hour ago he'd thrown off his heavy robes and loosened the ties of his shirt. Damp hair clung to his forehead, and he took care not to let beads of sweat drop onto the pages and mar the precise handwritten script.

The storm raged on for hours. At last, however, the worst of the thunder rolled away, leaving behind a gentle, steady rain. Only then did Soran feel the change in the atmosphere.

Only then did he feel her arrival.

It wasn't unexpected. Last night she'd been quiet, distant. But he knew better than to hope she'd retreat for long. He braced for battle, ready to drive her out while simultaneously maintaining the complexity of the ongoing spell. It was a battle he'd fought many times. One of these nights, his strength would give out.

But not tonight.

Not while Nelle lay on her bed down below, trusting him to protect her until dawn.

To his surprise, no sudden vicious attack came. A wave of perfume heralded the Noswraith's arrival, the dense scent of crushed and burning roses that accompanied her everywhere. No thorns crawled along the walls or wound up the legs of his chair, however. He sensed her movements behind him, even heard the creak as she took a seat on his bed. Otherwise she was quiet. Demure.

His pulse quickened with dread.

For some while he managed to maintain single-minded focus on the spell. But the sensation of her eyes watching the back of his head was too much. With a growl in his throat, Soran split his consciousness. His physical body continued to bow over the book, his eyes reading the spell, his lips soundlessly forming the words. But a piece of his awareness sat up and turned to face the room behind him.

She sat just where he expected, perched on the edge of his bed, her hands neatly folded in her lap. She was strangely human in appearance. Though he could just discern the shadowy outline of thorns and briars all around her like a dark halo, she herself was shaped in flesh and blood. She wore a white silk slip that exposed her shoulders, the laces partially opened across her bosom. The skirt was split from hem to knee, displaying her small feet, her daintily crossed ankles, her shapely calves.

Her eyes were downcast, but he knew she was aware of his scrutiny.

"What are you doing, Helenia?" Soran growled. His spirit voice was inaudible to human hearing, but her ears pricked at the sound. *"What do you want?"*

She raised her face, lifted her long dark lashes. Black eyes flashed bright in the glow of the candle.

What I've always wanted, my love.

Her lips didn't move when she spoke. This body, after all, was only an illusion.

To be yours. As you are mine. Eternally.

Soran's spirit-self flinched and recoiled. His mortal body tensed, his fists clenching tight as he continued to read the spell, winding the enchantment tight.

"I'm not a fool," he said. *"Remember, I am the one who called you to life. I know who and what you are."*

I am your Helenia.

"You are a nightmare. A Noswraith."

I am your Helenia. And you are my beloved.

She stood. The illusion was so convincing. So perfect. When she approached him, her hips swayed in just that way he remembered. The light caressed her soft curves, so tempting and so near.

Embrace me, she whispered. *Embrace me as you once did.*

"No." He stood upright, braced to meet her, and raised a hand in defense. In this realm it was not encased in a nilarium curse.

It was whole, human, able to touch and perceive all manner of sensual pleasures.

She reached out. The shadows of briars wound up and around his arm, spiraling to his shoulder, but he could scarcely see them. Instead, he saw her hand take hold of his and pull him toward her, placing his palm against her beating heart. It was so real. She was warm and soft and willing.

Stop fighting, my love, she murmured, stepping nearer. Her lovely face upturned to his, her lips plump and parted. For the moment, he couldn't see how they were truly formed of rose petals.

It would be so easy to give in. Yes, he would die for the mistake, die for his weakness. But could any death be more desirable?

Our bond is for eternity, she whispered.

Then she made her critical mistake.

What can that mortal girl possibly have over me?

Soran blinked.

With a snarl, he lifted his hand from her bosom and wrapped his fingers around her throat. "*Get out!*" he roared and, with a single brutal twist, snapped her neck.

The Noswraith screamed. Thorns erupted through her skin, tearing apart the illusion to reveal the reality. Briars and thorns swarmed up Soran's legs and around his waist, wrapping his arms and body. But his grip on her broken neck never faltered. He swung her off her feet, tearing her briars from the walls, uprooting them from the floor. Twisting fast, he hurled her straight out the nearest window. Her thorny arms scrabbled and tore, cutting into his flesh, cutting into the stone window frame.

Then she fell, dragging her multitudinous slithering limbs behind her.

With a gasp, Soran reared his head back and stared down at the page in front of him. He was seated at his desk, candlelight illuminating the text before him. The shimmering magic of the incomplete spell danced in the air before his eyes.

Good. It wasn't broken. Not yet anyway. The Thorn Maiden's distractions were powerful, but he hadn't let his focus drift too far from his task. Hastily he resumed the spell, carefully reading out the words, forming the complex patterns of magic and power.

He felt her out there in the darkness, in the rain. Crawling around the base of the tower. Her long-fingered, thorny hands scraped at the stone, and now and then she uttered a low, wordless moan. But by the time dawn tinged the edge of the horizon, she was silent.

Soran completed the spell and closed the book fast.

7

Nelle was up, dressed, and already busy flipping and stacking flapcakes when the mage came down from his tower the next morning. His footsteps echoed in the tower while he was still far overhead, and she listened to him descend until he stood just above the opening in the raftered ceiling.

There he stopped, hesitated.

She counted slowly to twenty.

Still he didn't come.

Nelle pulled the last of the flapcakes off the fire and turned her head to the opening. "You know, I really hate it when you do that," she called out.

Another few breaths, then he was in motion again, his robes dragging on the steps behind him as he appeared. His hood was up, and pale hair spilled out from beneath it in long coils. "Do what, Miss Beck?" he asked, his voice perfectly smooth and mild.

"Leave the room, all mysteriously abrupt like that, while I think we're still having a conversation. Like last night, I mean. It's rude." Nelle slid the last flapcake on top of a stack, marched across the room, and plunked the plate down on the table. "Have a seat, sir," she said, her words polite, her tone icy.

Silveri obeyed. The wyvern, which had stayed curled up in the middle of the alcove bed, rose, performed an impossible-looking stretch, then waddled across the room to curl up at its master's feet. It whined piteously until Nelle set a stack of cakes in front of it as well. While it chomped and grunted noisily, Silveri, by contrast, didn't touch his meal until Nelle had sat down opposite him and taken her first bite.

"They're not poisoned or anything," she said around a mouthful. "I ain't *that* angry with you."

He nodded and pinched off a small bite between finger and thumb. Before eating, however, he said, "I do beg your pardon. My behavior last night was indeed unbecoming. You are a guest in my home and deserve to be treated with courtesy. I am . . . somewhat out of practice."

"Mmm hmmm." Nelle took another bite. She watched him closely for several moments, even let him eat a whole flapcake before speaking again. "So. Sir."

"Yes, Miss Beck?"

"When do we begin?"

He paused. His eyes flicked to meet hers. "Begin what?"

"You know what." She chewed, swallowed. Then, turning her

fork around, she mimed writing along the table with the blunt end.

His eyes widened. The next moment his brow pulled into a knot, and he dropped his chin. "Oh. That."

"Yes, *that*." Nelle stabbed at a cake. "You said I have the spark. You said I *can* be taught. So why not teach me? Or at least give it a try. See if I've got a knack for it."

"A *knack* for it?"

"You know. A bit of talent."

He pressed his lips into a line, then opened them just enough to say, "The talent is there."

"So why not then?" She set the fork down and laced her fingers over the plate, propping her chin. "It's a miserable, cold, rainy day outside. I don't want to go tramping about in it, and I doubt you do either. What else are we going to do with the time? I'm not saying I want you to train me to Miphates proficiency—"

"That would be impossible."

"Yes. Fine. I get it." Nelle scowled darkly. "I know I ain't the stuff of mighty mages. But if you can teach me even a little, I might be able to help you."

"In what way exactly do you propose to help me, Miss Beck?"

"Well, the worm, for one thing." She waved a hand to indicate the wyvern, which had sat up on its haunches, belly swollen, and was now smacking its fleshless lips with glutted satisfaction. "I could help with that healing spell on his wing."

Very slowly, Silveri nodded. "It is . . . possible."

It was the first real acknowledgement of potential he'd uttered.

Nelle's heart jumped with surprise, and she couldn't help the smile that burst across her face. "Really?"

Another nod. "Yes. Really."

"In that case, what are we waiting for?" She leaped up, reached across the table, and snatched up his plate. "We should get started at once!"

His brow puckered. "I was still eating that."

With a huff, Nelle slammed the plate down in front of him again. He picked up the last flapcake, using extreme delicacy despite the awkwardness of his hands, rolled it, and bit into the end. He continued to take small, precise bites, chewing thoughtfully and thoroughly each time, until Nelle thought she would go mad with impatience. Just when she was ready to explode in a torrent of invective, she spied a quirk to his mouth and a glimmer in his eye. He knew exactly what he was doing.

"Bullspit!" she growled, stole the last two bites' worth of flapcake out of his hand, and crammed it into her mouth, glaring ferociously at him. "Come on," she said, her mouth still full. "Get your quills and inks while there's still some daylight left in the sky!"

Silveri blinked up at her. Then, his scarred lips twisted back, revealing his strong white teeth as he tossed back his head and laughed.

It took rather more time than Nelle liked for the mage to fetch his supplies down from the tower. The armoire held a few spare quills and sheets of parchment, but all the ink was above stairs, along with the trimming knives, pumice stones, and other items the use of which Nelle couldn't begin to guess.

She was itching to get started, but Silveri refused to be rushed. He arranged everything neatly on the table and kept rearranging by slight degrees. Perhaps this precision of display held some magical importance, but Nelle suspected it was only the mage's obsessive nature getting the better of him. She slumped in her chair, arms crossed, fingers tapping impatiently along her upper arm, and counted to twenty several times over. Somehow she managed to keep hold of her temper.

At last, when all was exactly as he liked it, Silveri turned. "Draw up your chair please, Miss Beck," he said, hastily adding in a most forbidding tone, "and touch nothing!"

"Right. Not touching," Nelle muttered, pulling her chair to her usual place at the table. The mage had set out a blank parchment beside a long white quill that her fingers itched to pick up and twiddle. Her palms were suddenly clammy. How many years was it since she'd actually written a word? Not since Mother died, that was certain. And she'd never been one for letter-writing to begin with. What if she thoroughly embarrassed herself?

But after all that pleading and arguing, she couldn't back down now, so she tucked her hands up under her arms and waited, watching the mage from under her lowered brows.

The mage took his place at the opposite end of the table, steepled his fingers, looked about him, and drew a long breath. "Where to begin?" he said softly.

As he did not seem to be addressing her, Nelle held her tongue.

"Magic," he said at last, "does not originate in this realm. Not in Eledria. Not in the mortal world. Nor any world of matter and physical reality. Magic is the stuff of the *quinsatra*—another realm altogether. A realm without matter, a non-physical dimension that lies as close to this reality as your flesh adheres to your bones."

Nelle swallowed, wide-eyed, and glanced to one side, half expecting to catch a glimmer of this near reality from the tail of her eye. But that was silly, so she focused her attention back on the mage.

After what felt like an endless silence, Silveri plucked up one of the other quills lying before him on the table and held it up by its nib, twirling it slowly first this way, then that. "Do you know what this is, Miss Beck?"

Convinced it was a trick question, Nelle nodded slowly but refused to speak. To her relief, the mage continued without prompting.

"This is the bridge between the *quinsatra* and the mortal realm. This is the instrument by which we draw the indescribable out from the ether of unreality and transform it into the physical, the graspable, the concrete. By this instrument, the sage may transcribe secret truths of the universe within volumes of holy text. By this same instrument, the mage creates what you know to be magic."

Nelle nodded. He seemed to be expecting an answer this time. She opened her mouth, hesitated, then said, "Right. Magic."

One brow slid slowly up the mage's forehead. Very neatly, very precisely, he set the quill down in front of him and steepled his fingers again.

"Mortal magic begins with the written word," he said. "The ability to take the airy nothing of ideas, feelings, and sensations, and render them into a concrete and comprehensible form, is a distinctly mortal ability. The fae, though their very veins run with liquid magic, do not understand the power of the written word, cannot be made to comprehend how markings on page or stone or wood can be made to contain words, ideas, worlds, and power."

This was not entirely new information to Nelle. Mother had explained much of this to her when she was a girl, and most folks in Wimborne understood that mortal mages used writings to channel their magic while the fae did not. It was a simple enough concept insofar as it went.

Or maybe not so simple. As Nelle sat there across from the mage, listening to him talk, she began to suspect that layers of complexity and understanding she had never before fathomed existed. The prospect was thrilling. And terrifying.

"Before writing," Silveri continued, leaning back in his chair and relaxing into his subject, "there was language. But not a single language. As you know, the mortal world boasts hundreds of languages, possibly more. Many, though not all of them, possess a written form that allows the speakers of those languages to record their ideas and beliefs for future generations. This is a magic in and of itself, though you may not realize it, Miss Beck."

Nelle kept nodding, hoping she looked intelligent and thoughtful. This was not how she'd expected magic lessons to begin. Then again, did she really think the mage would hand her a book of spells and have her conjuring slimeballs within the first fifteen minutes? She cupped her chin in her hand, elbow resting on the edge of the table, and forced herself to take in each word.

"But you must remember," the mage continued, "that there is no single pure language, no *truly* pure language, in all the known worlds. Every culture of humankind strives to the best of its ability to transfer the thoughts, ideas, realities, and beliefs that exist in the realm of the mind into communicable shape—but the transference, through the medium of articulate speech, will always be imperfect. There will always be nuances of thought that language cannot articulate. Not in its purest sense. Only one language comes close to what the Miphates have deemed true purity. And what language is that, Miss Beck?"

Nelle blinked, taken aback. She hadn't expected quizzing at this stage. "Um, it's um . . ." What was that strange word he'd used? She'd heard him say it once or twice already. "It's Old Ara . . . Araneli?" she hazarded.

"Wrong."

Naturally. Nelle barely kept from rolling her eyes. Heat flushed her cheeks, but Silveri didn't look disappointed or frustrated. He was too keen, too excited about the revelations he was sharing to notice her embarrassment.

"The only nearly pure language in all the known worlds," he

said, "is the language of mathematics. It is the one language that *every* culture, *every* race understands. A true universal. The symbols and organizations used to form the ideas expressed in mathematics are the same throughout every country in our world. Through mathematics, the men and women of science may express the inexpressible in such a way that all who have been taught the language may comprehend it with a purity of comprehension beyond debate or deniability."

Again, Nelle found herself nodding blankly. Her enthusiasm waned as the mage droned on. Was magic study going to be like writing out long arithmetic?

At length, however, Silveri's lecture took a turn for the better. "By the pre-Pledge year Eight Hundred Sixteen, the early Miphates of Corintar discovered that the language of mathematics, despite being the universal language they had always sought, was, if anything, too pure for a comprehensive study of magic. So, the great mathematician mages began a fresh search. A hunt, as it were, for a language that could achieve the same level of logical universality without compromising the importance of nuance. A nearly impossible task, a task for which all studied mortal languages were woefully inadequate.

"It was Verof Chon of the Yian School of Miphates who finally turned to the worlds beyond our own in his search for a language to serve the purposes of mortal magic. It was he who first delved into the possibilities of Old Araneli—an ancient fae tongue from the dawn of time itself, back before the paths of man and fae had wholly diverged, branching into different realms and worlds and realities."

Her first guess wasn't so entirely wrong after all. Nelle tilted her head to hide a smile in the palm of her hand.

Silveri went on about this Miphato Chon and his discoveries for what felt like an age. All the while, rain pattered steadily against the door and dripped through the cracks in the walls and windows, pooling about the floor. Since Silveri didn't seem bothered by it, Nelle decided not to be as well. She listened with as much attention as she could manage, hoping she was soaking in at least the most important parts of this lecture.

Was this truly necessary? After all, she wouldn't be here long enough to make any real progress in magic study. Gaspard had given her three weeks to find and snatch the Rose Book. She had already used six days. How many more could she afford to give to this pursuit that was ultimately a mere deflection of her true purpose?

At long last the mage's lecture wound to an end, and he told her to take up her quill. Nelle's interest quickened at once . . . but receded again when the first thing the mage told her to do was to write out her alphabet, one character at a time. Not even the Old Araneli alphabet—just the same old letters she'd learned as a child.

Feeling like a silly schoolgirl, Nelle swallowed her grumbles and set to work shaping the letters, one after another. It had been some while since she'd picked up a quill, and her penmanship left much to be desired. Still, she finished each letter, forbearing from adding any flourishes, which she knew would only irritate the mage.

Silveri picked up the sheet of parchment and studied it for rather longer than she thought necessary. It was as though each individual letter told a complete story, which he analyzed in painstaking detail. She watched his eyes slowly travel down the page, and by the time he reached the last line, she was sweating.

"Well?" she asked when he finally set the parchment down and looked at her again.

"Well." He nodded, and his twisted mouth quirked thoughtfully to one side. "You are not wholly without skill. There may be . . . something there."

"You said that already. Last night. Remember?"

"Yes, well, I'm saying it again. But don't get your hopes up." He placed another sheet of parchment in front of her. "Once more, Miss Beck."

She spent the better part of two hours writing out the alphabet over and over and over . . . By the time she was through, her hand was cramping, her head was spinning, and she was beginning to rethink the wisdom of this entire idea. When Silveri picked up the most recent sheet and studied it, she dropped her forehead to the tabletop and groaned.

"Head up, Miss Beck." His voice was sharp enough to make her tilt her head to one side and glare at him, still with her forehead against the table. "Come," he said, "you're making progress already. It's time you tried a spell."

"Really?" She bolted upright, surprise coursing a line down her spine. "Do you mean it, sir? I'm ready to try magic?"

"No." He planted another blank parchment in front of her. "You couldn't manage magic at this time even if your life depended on it."

She huffed and tossed her hands. "Then why get me excited for nothing?"

"Because, magic aside, you *are* ready to try a written spell. Don't look so crestfallen," he added, lifting a long white quill from a well of indigo ink and placing it in her unwilling hand. "I wasn't permitted to attempt any spell writing for months when I began my training. I am far more lenient than my masters before me."

"Lucky me," Nelle growled and crouched over the parchment. "What am I writing?"

"This." Silveri produced a small soft-leather volume from within the folds of his robe. He flipped through its pages, his nilarium fingers fumbling, then opened the book near the middle and held it up for Nelle's inspection.

Her brow puckered. "Here, that's not proper writing, is it?"

"You know all the letters, don't you?"

"Yes . . ." She nodded uncertainly. She did recognize most of the characters from the familiar alphabet. But the words formed were utter gibberish to her. "Is this Old Araneli?"

Though she fully expected him to snap out another "Wrong," Silveri nodded solemnly. "Indeed. It is the language still used among the High Fae of Eledria . . . or a close approximation. Fae tongues were never intended to be captured in written form. But here it is rendered down into crude mortal characters, with a few additions to the alphabet as you know it. Each word you see before you brims with magical essence, with the purity of spirit captured in physical confines, ready to be transferred from mind to mind. Can you feel it?"

She didn't. Not the way she'd felt the magic emanating from the grimoires in Gaspard's quillary. Not even as she'd felt the power vibrating in the characters Silveri had written on the wyvern's torn wing.

But she hated to admit this, so she bit her tongue.

Silveri wasn't fooled. He hummed an inscrutable, "Hmmmm," and placed the book open on the table in front of her. "Try it, Miss Beck."

She took up the pen, carefully shook out the excess ink, and held the tip poised over the fresh page. For a moment she froze, panic thickening her throat. But really, what was her issue? It wasn't as if Silveri expected anything of her. She couldn't disappoint him unless she refused to try at all.

With a shrug, she bowed to the work, copying out each letter. She thought she was careful, thought she was precise. But when she reached the end of the line, she found she'd made the letters a little too large and was obliged to break up one word and fit the rest of it on the line below. Oh well. She kept going until she reached the end of the spell.

Silveri didn't bother to pick up the page for inspection this time. He bowed over her shoulder, his breath tickling her ear, one hand planted on the table beside her resting arm. "Hmmmm," he said again in the same inscrutable tone. Then, "Again, Miss Beck.

Just there, in the space underneath." He stood up and backed away from the table, his hands clasped at the small of his back. "Precision is everything, Miss Beck. *Everything.*"

She sighed but set to with a will. This time she got the size much closer, and the shape of her letters was more precise. But if Silveri noticed he said nothing. After another quick inspection, he uttered another brisk, "Again," and she was back at it.

She copied the line seven times before running out of space on the parchment. Only then did Silveri pick it up and look at it, turning it this way and that. She watched him, the first two fingers of each hand rubbing circles into her throbbing temples. She was fairly certain her eyes would fall out of their sockets any moment now.

At long last, Silveri lowered the parchment and looked at her again. "Precision is everything," he said.

"Yeah. So you said."

"Except . . ." He held up a finger. "Except when it is not."

She slumped in her chair and made a face at him. "That ain't really helpful, you know."

He set the parchment down in front of her again. She looked at it dully, and several silent moments passed before she realized he'd placed it upside down. She reached to turn it, but he said, "Ah, ah!" so sharply, her hand froze. "Look at it again, Miss Beck. Tell me . . . what do you see?"

Nelle frowned and turned her eyes to the parchment, studying the backwards and upside-down lines of gibberish. At first there was nothing. Nothing but her own frustration weighing down on her, making her eyes cross with fatigue.

Then there was . . . something.

A shimmer. A vibration, a pull.

An energy . . .

Her breath caught. She couldn't speak, but her whole body tensed. The headache that had been pounding her skull vanished in a flash. Was she imagining things? Yes, she was, she certainly was. But maybe . . .

Maybe that was the point.

Silveri whisked the parchment out from under her, leaving her staring intently at the tabletop. She opened her mouth to utter a protest, but he placed yet another blank page in front of her, his silver hand planted firmly in the center of it

"Try it again, Miss Beck," he said. His eyes were mere inches from hers, his face down at her level. She stared at him but hardly seemed to see him. That energy still shimmered in the air, invisible, yet utterly distracting. "This time don't try to be precise. Write as fast as you can. *As fast as you can*, do you hear me?"

She didn't need to look at the book. After seven times copying, she knew the assortment of letters, or at least close enough to recall the essence of them. She took up the quill dripping with ink, shook it out, and held it poised for a moment while she gathered her wits.

Then she bowed to the work, scribbling as fast as she could, careless of the shapes, careless of the blots she left on the page, careless of everything. And as she wrote, she felt vibrations of power rise around her in shimmering streams of energy she had no words to describe. She could feel the spell wanting to work, wanting to take shape beneath her pen, and she poured into it, thrilling with the sensation of such power at her fingertips.

At the end of the parchment, she stopped and looked. A gasp caught in her throat. "What a spittin' mess!" she cried, dropping her quill into its well and clapping an ink-stained hand to her cheek.

Though it had required seven copies to fill the last page, this single copy took up the whole of the parchment. How could that be? Her vision spun, trying to chase the characters, which wouldn't quite sit where they were meant to on the page. They seemed to *flee* her gaze, shifting, scuttling, avoiding all attempts to read or follow them. They shifted and . . . and . . .

Nelle cursed and rubbed the heels of her hands into her eyes. When she looked again, the characters were still. What's more, although as sloppy as she'd originally thought, they didn't cover the entire page but stretched across only three small lines along the top.

She must be going crazy. She must be. Because she could have sworn for a moment there—a brief, infinitesimal moment—she'd glimpsed a ridged spine, an arch of wing, a long, sinuous tail.

Definitely crazy.

With a sigh, she slumped back in her chair and gave Silveri a baleful look. He watched her contemplatively, one elbow cupped in the opposite hand, silver fingers rubbing his shaved chin. She tried and failed to read the expression glittering in his eyes.

"All right, you can tell me," she said, tilting her head to stretch her sore neck. "Am I a *complete* failure or just a bit of a failure? Don't spare me, sir. I can take it."

He opened his mouth. Closed it again. Rubbed at his chin harder than before.

Then, in a voice almost too soft for her to hear, he said, "That was most impressive, Miss Beck."

8

The rain let up by the time that first lesson was complete. Soran moved to the door and flung it open, allowing a cold blast of air into the room, cooling his flushed face. He stood on the threshold, his eyes closed, simply breathing in the smell of the sea and the freshness of the world after a storm. For the space of several breaths he concentrated on these sensations.

But he couldn't block out the thoughts clamoring inside his head.

She was good. She was more than good. She was talent unlike anything he'd ever before witnessed.

Seven gods, for a moment there he'd thought she would bring a wyvern out of nothing into the air!

Any uncertainties he'd clung to vanished entirely. The girl was, beyond any shadow of a doubt, an *ibrildian*. A Hybrid. She could be nothing less. How strong the strain of fae blood in her veins was, he couldn't guess. He couldn't even know if more or less fae blood would make her more or less powerful. A little too much in either direction might tilt the scales against her.

But she could *feel* the presence of magic most mortals would never detect. He himself, though blessed with a sensitivity that had allowed him to bring small spells into existence at a young age, had required years of study and training before he could perceive the *quinsatra* with any clarity.

Years that Peronelle Beck had skipped over in a single morning.

He opened his eyes, gazing out on the ocean stretched before him. Gazing out to the Evenspire, which was more clearly visible following the thundershower. One could almost believe it existed within this very world.

A smile pulled at the corner of his mouth. What would his old masters and instructors say if they knew he'd found a Hybrid? Would they fall over themselves in their rabid eagerness to get their hands on the girl and the potential power flowing through her veins?

No. A sobering wave washed over him, leaving Soran shivering in the cold. The Pledge forbade the very existence of Hybrids. At best, Nelle would be driven into exile and obscurity, forbidden to so much as look at another quill or parchment for the rest of her born days, held prisoner in some remote location where she could do no harm to the world.

At worst, she would be killed outright.

What was he doing? Soran ran a hand down his face, nilarium-tipped fingers freezing against his already chilled skin. What business had he to put her at such risk? And without even telling her the possible consequences.

But if she knew, would she still be so eager to learn? Would she still look at him with those shining eyes, begging him to unmask the secrets of the universe as he understood them? Would she be able to throw herself into the study and practice with the same gritty determination he had observed this morning?

Or would she do what she ought to have done the very morning of her arrival at Roseward: Climb back into her boat and flee to her own world, never once looking back.

Movement behind him returned Soran to the present. He dropped his hand from his face and opened his eyes but couldn't quite bring himself to face the dim room at his back. He heard busy sounds, homey kitchen sounds, and wasn't surprised when the girl suddenly plucked at his elbow.

"Here, sir. All that writing gives one an appetite, don't it? Eat up."

Soran looked down and around into a plate of sliced bread and cold cured meats. The girl looked up at him through loose strands of red hair and offered a little smile.

He accepted the plate and somewhat unwillingly stepped back inside, leaving the door open. He noted with satisfaction that the girl had taken time to set paperweights atop all the loose parchment sheets; no stray breeze could send them flying. She'd also pulled the chairs closer to the hearth so the two of them could enjoy the fire's warmth while they ate.

For once she seemed happy to let silence linger. They took their seats, tore off small pieces of bread and meat to pop into their mouths, and chewed quietly. The few times Soran dared to glance her way, he found her studying the fire intently without really seeing it. Her eyes held a light, dancing and bright, that may have been a mere reflection of the flames. But he doubted it.

They finished eating in silence. Nelle took Soran's empty plate and carried their dishes across the room to the washbasin. Soran watched her go, watched the way the firelight played on fiery strands of her hair. The way the soft folds of her skirt fell from her narrow waist. The way her hips swayed with unconscious grace at her every step.

How could one so dainty, so lovely, be simultaneously so lethal? The strange contrast was utterly captivating.

Nelle turned. Soran quickly looked away, staring into the fire. But he knew she'd caught him watching her. For a minute she stood near the basin, silent and hesitant. Had he made her uncomfortable? Frightened her? Gods, what a beast he was! He couldn't go offering the girl shelter one moment, then eye her up like a choice piece of fruit the next.

She returned to her chair at last and perched on the edge of the seat. "So," she said.

He waited, afraid he might somehow betray his thoughts if he spoke.

"What's next?" she continued at last. "We going to try another spell?"

Soran cleared his throat and quickly shook his head. "No, Miss Beck. That was enough magic study for one morning. We . . . we both of us need time to clear our heads so we can return with fresh focus."

"Ah." She nodded slowly. He felt her eyes watching him. "A walk then?"

Was she suggesting they take a stroll together? Soran cast her a sideward glance. Surely she didn't desire his company!

"I . . ." He cleared his throat again. Why was his jaw so tight? "I must inspect the ward stones," he said and rose abruptly. With a quick nod he indicated the door. "You may go where you please, Miss Beck. Only return before sundown."

She remained in her seat for some moments, watching him from beneath her eyelashes. Slowly she stood, her mouth set in a line. "Very well, Mage Silveri," she said and moved to her alcove, where she'd left her new cloak folded neatly atop the fur rugs. She wrapped it around her shoulders, pulling the fur-trimmed hood up over her head, and walked to the door, all without another look his way.

The moment she crossed the threshold and moved beyond his sight, Soran breathed more easily. Gods above, what a fool he was! He shouldn't have agreed to these lessons in the first place, shouldn't have agreed to any scenario that obliged him to spend time in her presence. Had the encounter with the Thorn Maiden last night taught him nothing?

"You're a danger to her," he whispered. The words echoed dully inside his head like the toll of a distant dolorous bell.

Setting his jaw, he moved to the armoire and bent to rummage among the spellbooks inside. Finding the volume he sought, he tucked it into the front of his robes. The wyvern, which had spent its morning dozing in a basket by the fire, chirruped lazily at him as he straightened.

"Don't worry, my friend," Soran said, pulling his hood up and adjusting the folds of his long robes. "I know better, believe me. She's safe here for as long as she stays. I'll protect her. From myself if need be."

The wyvern blinked and dropped its head, utterly uncaring. Soran muttered a curse in the creature's general direction and strode swiftly across the room. He stepped out into the morning light, pulled the door shut behind him, and hastily secured the secret latch spell. Then he turned to face the sea.

And saw the girl standing just a few yards away.

She waited with her arms crossed, her shoulders hunched against the wind. Stray locks of red hair blew out from under her hood, framing her pale little face.

She smiled at him—a stubborn sort of smile with an edge to it.

Soran's heart gave a sharp thud. But he drew a breath, controlled his expression, and faced the girl calmly, certain he betrayed nothing of what he felt inside. Drawing his shoulders back, he stepped toward her.

"Miss Beck," he said.

"Mage Silveri," she replied.

Uncertain what else he ought to do or say, Soran simply turned left down the path that led along the cliff's edge toward the first of the ward stones. The girl fell in step beside him, taking two quick strides for each of his long ones. Her pace jostled her hood back over her shoulders, and her hair blew free.

"I haven't seen the ward stones yet," she said after a few moments of silence. "Is that one there?" She pointed to the tall pillar on the edge of the cliff.

Soran cast her a quick glance, then refocused his attention ahead. Did she truly mean to walk with him? And if so, what was he going to do about it? He ought to send her away . . . but where? Roseward wasn't that big of an island. There was nowhere for her to go except back to Dornrise or down to the little abandoned village on the harbor. Otherwise there were just overgrown forests that once had been elegant parks, and a few tumbledown ruins where once stood handsome outlying buildings, chapels, and pavilions.

He realized he'd not answered her question. By now it would seem foolish to say anything at all, so he held his tongue. They approached the first ward stone already anyway.

Carefully averting his attention from the girl, Soran approached the stone and located where the carved spell began at the top. Concentrating, he touched the spell with the tip of one finger and followed the flow of words, slowly circling the pillar to follow their spiral pattern until he reached the place on the stone's seaward side where the crack broke one of the words in two, compromising the spell. There he paused for some moments, analyzing the depth of the crack, the severity of the split.

The girl appeared at his elbow, bending toward the ward stone, her brow constricted, her gaze thoughtful as she studied the lines of the spell. "This is Old Araneli again, eh?" she said, looking up at him.

Soran nodded and drew the spellbook from the front of his robes.

The girl put out one hand and touched the stone, her palm over the split. She closed her eyes, the knot in her brow deepening. "I . . . I think I feel it," she said after a moment. "I think I feel how it went wrong."

"You can *see* where it went wrong, Miss Beck," Soran said. "The break is easily discerned." He reached out and caught her wrist, plucking her hand away from the stone.

She retracted her hand quickly, tucking it away inside the folds of her cloak. "I know. But there's more to it, ain't there?"

Soran narrowed his eyes, studying her face closely. What did she see? What did she perceive with those peculiar senses of hers?

"All right," he said slowly. "Tell me."

She turned to the stone again and almost unconsciously extended her hand. This time, however, she didn't touch the stone itself. Her fingers twined in the air in front of it, as though catching at strands of nothing and feeling how they played across her skin.

"There's magic here," she said. "I can almost . . . I think I can see it. Magic lines rising from the words, if that makes sense." She quirked an eyebrow up at him. "Is this the protection spell?"

He grunted. "Go on."

"They're broken. Not all of them. Just a few strands here and there. Like this one." She plucked at an invisible nothing, twirling it between finger and thumb. Then she sniffed and shook her head. "Oh, no. I can't quite catch it. I can't even really *see* it. But am I right?"

She looked up at him again, her face eager and possibly a little afraid.

"There is a spell, yes," Soran acknowledged. "A warding spell, part of the larger spell of protection surrounding Roseward. And yes, your method of describing it is correct. Some of the . . . of the *threads* have broken." He hesitated, almost afraid to learn the answer to his next question but unable to resist asking. "How would you go about fixing it?"

"Oh! Well." Nelle studied the air before the stone again, not seeming to see the stone itself at all anymore, concentrating instead on the invisible magic. "If I could catch 'em, I'd just tie them together. That should fix 'em well enough, at least for the time being."

Soran nodded slowly. He had brought a small healing spell with him in the book he'd tucked into the front of his robes. He'd thought to use it to mend the stone, to repair the crack splitting the words. The result would be basically the same as the girl proposed.

But it was strange—so strange and so fascinating—that she should propose fixing the magic threads themselves and not even consider the physical stone. Soran could only see the threads if he concentrated hard. How expanded was her magic sight already, after a single morning of study?

And how far might he take her, given time?

Drawing the book out from under his robes, he quickly turned to the spell he sought, near the back of the book. "Miss Beck," he said, "I am going to read this out. I want you to watch and tell me if you can see the spell taking shape. Will you do that?"

She nodded solemnly, pushing hair out of her wind-whipped face.

"Very good then." Soran raised the book and began to read off the Old Araneli script. It was more than simple reading, of course. It was rather a form of connection—a drawing of his mind into the words, and the words themselves drawing his mind beyond into the unseen and yet ever-present realm of the *quinsatra*, making it perceptible and revealing the magic he sought to grasp and pull into his own reality. He read off the words and, using his mind, scooped up the magic and drew it out.

A little shimmering ball appeared in the air above the pages of the book. It had a liquid-like quality to it as it churned and bubbled slightly. The color was not one that could be named in any mortal language and was almost beyond Soran's range of perception.

When he finished the reading, the little sphere hovered in place above his book, more solid now the spell was complete. Soran returned his gaze to the girl. "Can you see it, Miss Beck?"

Her lips were slightly parted, her eyes wide and rapt. "Yes," she said quietly. "Yes, I do see it. And . . . and I think . . ."

"Do you think you know what to do with it?"

She nodded. Then she closed her mouth into a firm line and nodded again with more conviction.

"In that case, be my guest." Closing the book, Soran took a step back and indicated the sphere with a wave of his hand. Her eyes swiveled to meet his, but only briefly, as though she feared to look away from the ball, feared it would vanish if she did so. The muscles in her jaw tightened.

She stepped forward and caught the sphere in both hands. It immediately began to run and dribble, but she didn't seem startled by this. With a few quick flicks of her wrist, she spread the liquid across each finger until they shimmered with the same magical brightness.

She turned back to the stone. Soran watched closely, wondering what she would do. He would touch the crack and begin the healing process from the physical side of reality.

But the girl had different ideas. She reached into the air, reached for the broken strands of magic. One by one she caught each little strand, the spell on her fingers enabling her to do so. She took the broken pieces and tied them together, securing the knots fast. It was ugly, awkward work. Certainly not polished magic.

A grinding sound filled the air. Soran wrenched his attention from the girl to the stone and saw that, while she worked, the crack in the stone was healing as well, closing as neatly as a sewn seam. She may have gone about the thing backwards . . . but she got it right. By the seven secret names of the gods, she got it right.

Nelle stepped back, her hands shaking. A little series of flashes like glints of sunlight on water appeared as the last of the spell evaporated, the magic returning to its own realm. The girl continued to stand there, staring at her hands, staring at her now empty fingers.

"Miss Beck?" Soran said, moving in behind her. "Miss Beck, are you—"

She started to turn to him. A moan slipped from her lips, and her knees gave out. Soran was only just quick enough to catch her before she could fall to the ground and strike her head.

With a muttered curse, Soran scooped her up, one arm behind her knees, the other around her shoulders. What a fool he was! In his eagerness to see what she might accomplish, he'd neglected to think of the physical consequences. She was unpracticed, had built up no tolerance for magic-casting. A healing spell took a great deal of energy, especially when used on a lifeless substance like stone. He shouldn't have been so careless, so reckless.

"Miss Beck, can you hear me?" he said, peering down into her face against his shoulder. She was out cold. Was she even breathing?

Panic flooding his veins, Soran turned and strode back along the path as fast as he could go. She made for an awkward burden with all her skirts and the folds of her cloak, but at least she was small. He staggered to the lighthouse door, hastily muttered the spell to open the latch, and kicked it open, slamming it so hard against the wall that the wyvern squawked and shot out of its basket bed, scrambling up the fireplace stones to perch on the mantel. There it flapped its good wing and rattled its tongue in a prolonged hiss.

Ignoring the beast, Soran carried the girl to the alcove and laid her down on the bed as gently as he could. Her lips looked blue! At least it was warm in here, out of that wind.

Rising, he hastened to the fire and added a log to the embers, hastily stoking the blaze to life. The wyvern, crest flared in concern, crawled down the fireplace stones and waddled to the alcove. It burbled and snorted and nuzzled the girl's face.

"I know. I know!" Soran growled as he grabbed the copper kettle and filled it with fresh water from the basin. "I shouldn't have let her do it. But you should have seen her! By the gods, you should have seen her at work!"

He put the kettle on to boil and returned to the girl's side, nudging the wyvern roughly out of the way. She lay very still, but her chest rose and fell with steady breathing. She might have been in deep sleep. And little wonder. She must be utterly exhausted.

The room seemed uncomfortably warm now, so Soran undid the clasp of her cloak at her throat and carefully peeled the heavy garment away. Her skin looked pale above the neckline of her lavender gown, but her cheeks and lips were pink.

"She'll be all right," Soran whispered. The wyvern popped its head up by his shoulder and chortled in his ear. "She'll be all right," he repeated firmly. Without quite realizing what he did, he reached out and took hold of one of her hands. He couldn't feel her skin through the nilarium. And yet . . .

He looked down with some surprise. Though she was still unconscious, her fingers moved, interlacing with his.

For some while he could only sit there, staring. Staring at that connection unlike anything he'd felt in . . . in such a long while. It almost didn't seem real. He felt like an outside observer watching this moment take place between two strangers. Only, that cursed hand must belong to him. So it must be true.

A sudden sputter on the hearth drew his attention. He turned and saw the kettle boil over, spitting water out into the fire.

Dropping Nelle's hand was almost physically painful. But it was for the best. He couldn't allow himself to indulge in moments like that. He clenched his teeth hard as he moved to pull the kettle from over the fire, taking no care to protect his hands from the hot handle as it made no difference. Finding a package of tea Nelle had brought from Dornrise, he busied himself spooning leaves into the hot water to brew.

"Oi! Get off me."

Soran spun round quickly, just in time to see the girl sit up and push at the wyvern, which had taken advantage of Soran's absence to curl up on her stomach. It protested with noisy hisses and flapped its good wing, but she caught it by the tail and flung it out of the alcove onto the floor. She sat up as she did so, and immediately all the blood rushed from her cheeks.

"Oh, bullspitting heavens," she moaned, and curled over, her face buried in her hands.

"Miss Beck." Soran returned to the alcove in a few strides and knelt beside her again. His hand hovered in the air above her back, but he couldn't quite bring himself to touch her again. "Miss Beck, you must remain still. You're suffering from fatigue brought on by the manipulation of magic. It's best you do not try to speak or—"

"Bullspit," she muttered again and pushed her hair out of her face, looking up at the mage. "Did I do it? I thought I did, but I can't remember. Did I fix it?" Her eyes burned into his, bright and eager.

Slowly, Soran nodded. He dared not trust himself to speak,

dared not let his voice betray his own excitement. It would not do to encourage her overmuch.

But her face broke into a brilliant smile. Then she closed her eyes and lowered her head back into her hands, muttering, "Boggarts."

Soran fetched the tea and poured it into a wooden mug. When he returned, she was upright again, turned so that her back pressed against the cold stone wall of the alcove, her legs drawn up in a crisscross beneath her silken skirts. "Drink this," Soran said.

She accepted the mug. Eyes closed, she inhaled the steam deeply, then breathed out in a sigh. Her lips pursed to blow gently before she took a tentative sip. It must have been more bitter than she expected, for she made a face, one eye squinting half shut. But she bravely took another sip before turning her gaze up to him.

"So," she said, another smile curling the corners of her mouth. "What are you going to teach me next?"

9

The days fell into something like a pattern.

Every morning, Nelle rose before the sun and prepared a hearty breakfast. Silveri joined her in time to eat and then, while she cleaned up their dishes, he would set out the writing implements.

Several hours of lettering practice and repetitive copying followed. For the first two days she spent all her time on that same line of written magic, never quite bringing it to fruition, never even getting as close as she had that first day. She grew frustrated, and her precision suffered. So Silveri gave her fresh lines to copy.

This was better. But also its own version of frustrating. Each line began as total gibberish to her and remained gibberish no matter how many times she copied it. But as the days passed, she began to *almost* feel the sense behind the senseless. As though a part of her mind she'd never known existed might be unlocking.

At the end of each session, Silveri always had her write out whatever spell she was practicing in a mad, slap-dash manner. Most of the time this resulted in nothing more than a mess on the page, but sometimes, *sometimes* she felt the energy increasing. Intuition intensified until her fingers and her mind could play along the edges of understanding that juxtaposition of precision and madness that made up magic . . .

By midday, Silveri would declare their lessons ended and send her out of the tower again. Come rain or come shine, she found herself wrapped in her purloined cloak and out in the open air, trekking along the cliffside, her face numb with cold, her mind numb with all that she'd learned or *almost* learned that morning.

Once she simply walked for hours until it was near enough to sundown that she might safely return to the tower and expect to find the door unlatched. A few times she ventured back to Dornrise to fetch spices or delicacies from the larder, and another time to find a fresh gown. Every time she offered to walk the boundaries with the mage to check the ward stones, he refused—and refused with such finality of tone that she didn't dare press him.

On the sixth day of training, Nelle threw down her pen before she'd gotten halfway through the final spell for the morning. Her eyes burned and her neck was sore, and the enthusiasm she'd felt when first setting out to learn magic had faded to almost nothing.

"I don't get it!" she groaned, pressing the heels of her hands into her eye sockets. She could feel the mage's gaze on her. Part of her was embarrassed to indulge in a sulk in front of him. But most of her didn't care anymore. "When we started a week ago, I understood better than I do now. Have I gotten stupider in the last seven days?"

Silveri approached the table. She didn't look up, but she felt his presence, tall and warm at her back, bending over her chair and observing the mess she'd made on the page. She dropped her hands into her lap and, after a quick glance at the haphazard attempt at a spell, turned her head away, fixing a glare on the wyvern instead. It was lounging belly-up by the fire, its spine twisted at an angle that shouldn't be possible. Then again, the wyvern itself shouldn't be possible, so why shouldn't it sleep however it liked?

The mage was silent for too long. Finally, Nelle threw up her hands and slid out of her chair, moving away from the table. "I wish you wouldn't hover so!" she muttered. "All looming and disapproving like that." She paced several steps toward her alcove bed before turning and glaring at him, arms crossed.

Silveri rested one silver hand on the tabletop, still bent over her empty chair, studying her work. His long pale hair hung in a sheet over one shoulder, and light from one of the upper windows gleamed on it in such a way that it almost looked gold instead of white. He had submitted again just a few evenings ago to her barbering skills, allowing her to scrape several days' growth from his cheeks. The pale stubble that had grown back in edged his sharp jaw and obscured some of the ugly scarring.

There was such unconscious power in his pose—in the set of his shoulders, the way he held his arms. For all he dressed like a crazed old hermit, in moments like this it was impossible to mistake the truth of his lordly heritage.

He looked up suddenly, and Nelle realized she'd been staring. She blinked several times and schooled her expression into a stern frown, ducking her chin. A few strands of hair fell across her face like a veil.

"Just tell me straight," she growled, "am I stupider than I was a week ago or aren't I?"

"You are not stupid, Miss Beck," he replied at once, straightening. "Your problem is certainly not stupidity."

"Oh. Thanks. That's a relief anyway." Nelle shrugged her shoulders up to her ears. "What *is* my problem then?"

"There is no problem. Not really." The mage plucked up the quill she'd tossed in her anger, moved to the other end of the table, and took his seat at his accustomed place. He twirled the quill lightly. "Magic does not come quickly for anyone. Not even the fae receive their powers or control of those powers all at once—a young bird is born with the ability to fly, to soar to the highest reaches of the heavens, yet it must wait for its feathers to grow. The more powerful the bird, the longer it takes. A little songbird may leave the nest within mere weeks. The phoenix, however, requires many months."

He stopped fiddling with the quill and turned the plumy end at her, motioning from her to her chair again. She took the hint and, with a little sigh, moved to sit once more, resting her elbows on the tabletop and propping her chin between her fists. "So. What?" she said. "My feathers need some growing time?"

"To put it bluntly, yes." Silveri set the quill down on the table. "It is my suspicion that our initial forays into magic were something of a release to your system. Since your arrival here on Roseward, you've breathed the Hinter atmosphere, which activated the long-dormant-but-nonetheless-potent potential in your blood. Those experiments of a week ago were like a burst of air escaping from overtaxed lungs. Now you must develop the strength and endurance necessary for proper magic-wielding."

Nelle sighed. Had she really thought she was going to prove herself some sort of prodigy within a week of study? Boggarts, she'd worked two years at the university, observing the Miphates students from afar. She'd seen the various stages of their educational development—the wide-eyed first-years with their youthful arrogance and great dreams. The harrowed faces of the second-years, all of them crushed with doubts, many of them unable to continue. The dogged determination of the third- and fourth-years, which, over time, grew into the arrogance of the fully fledged Miphates like Gaspard. And like Silveri himself, truth be told.

She hid her eyes in her palms again. What was she playing at anyway? She hadn't come to Roseward to learn magic. Time was passing. Already she'd been more than a week on the island. But how much time had passed back at Wimborne? How many weeks, days, or hours did she have left before Gaspard's deadline?

"Don't be discouraged, Miss Beck."

Silveri's voice and the sudden scrape of his chair startled her. She'd almost forgotten he was still there. Nelle slid her hands down her cheeks, fingers pulling at the skin under her eyes, and cast him a baleful look as he crossed the room to his armoire, which he rummaged within before returning to the table with one of his spellbooks in hand. It looked like one of the better volumes, a little larger and more impressive than most of the stash. Something from later years of study, Nelle guessed.

The mage sat and paged through the book for some moments before he looked up again. "There is a ceremony," he said, "usually performed at the end of a student's first year. An acknowledgement of his place within the Miphates. We call it quill-binding."

He plucked up her discarded quill, twirling it between finger and thumb. "No one knows if it's true or not," he continued, "but it is universally believed throughout the Miphates school that a mage may pour his magic into a favored quill, infusing it with power. Over time it becomes a channel for him, a means to more effectively access the magic inside him and direct it into the physical world. Any quill, of course, may serve the same basic purpose. But a bound quill, one that has served its one master for years, may work as a sort of . . ." Silveri paused, pursing his scarred lips thoughtfully as he sought the word. "A sort of talisman, as it were."

"Like a good luck charm?" Nelle suggested.

Silveri nodded slowly. "You may think of it as such if you wish. Unlike your typical rabbit's foot, however, there is more truth than fancy to a quill-binding."

Nelle watched the quill still turning slowly in the mage's fingers. It was a white goose feather, one of several she'd used over the last seven days. It had been trimmed three times already, and after the rough treatment she'd given it, she hardly thought it would last more than another day or two. Maybe the process of quill-binding made feathers last longer?

She thought suddenly of that dark night not so long ago . . . of that endless climb up the side of the Evenspire to the twelfth-story window. She thought of Gaspard's quillary and all the grimoires brimming with power piled on his desk and around the room. But she'd not been sent to carry off any of those.

She'd been sent for a quill. A black swan's feather. When she'd picked it out from the display of quills on the wall, she'd sensed no power inside it, no unnatural energy or essence. Nothing like the grimoires, which had hummed with potent magic.

Why had Gaspard desired the quill so specifically? And why had he feared to take it himself—why had he risked hiring a snatcher to do it for him? Was it Gaspard's own quill? Or did it belong to someone else?

"I know what you're thinking, Miss Beck."

Nelle's head shot up, and her hands dropped away from her face. For a moment her heart jolted. Was it possible the mage could perceive what went on in her mind?

But her surge of terror abated at once as he continued: "You're thinking this quill-binding is a foolish practice, a school-boy superstition. And perhaps you are right. Nevertheless."

He stood and approached her side of the table. The goose-feather quill lay across the palms of his hands, and he bowed to present it to her with solemn dignity. "If you will permit me the honor, I should like to perform the ceremony of quill-binding for you now. As a sign of my belief in your abilities and of my . . . my admiration." He stopped for a moment, cleared his throat. "My admiration for your willingness to apply yourself to this difficult work. For the humility and determination you have exhibited over the last seven days. And for the true potential I believe flows in your veins."

Nelle gaped up at him. Thunder pounded in her ears, almost deafening. If he asked her to stand at that moment, she didn't believe her legs would support her. Had he truly just said all those things? Had he truly just spoken of *admiration?* For *her?*

It was too much. Much too much. And coming from him, of all people!

A wave of emotions broke over her, bringing a hot flush of blood roaring to her cheeks. First, pride coupled with pure elation. Then, embarrassment and a nagging fear that this was all some kind of joke, that he was teasing her, telling her foolish tales to see how gullible she could be.

After all those . . . shame.

She bowed her head, unable to meet his eyes. When she opened her mouth to speak, no words would come.

"Would you allow me, Miss Beck?" Silveri pressed gently, still holding out the quill. "May I perform the binding?"

No! the voice in her head snarled viciously.

But Nelle only nodded, mute and a bit numb.

The mage knelt beside her and began to recite the words of a spell. A frisson of energy drew Nelle's eye from the book lying open on the other end of the table, and she knew he was using one of his spells. How it worked, she wasn't certain. With most of the spells she'd seen him use, she'd been able to discern some sense of the magic, been able to trace the shape or even, in many cases, see the actual spell as though it were physically manifest before her.

In this case, the magic was subtle—so subtle that it might have been nothing more than a slight change of pressure in the air. As his words flowed on, coolness—like a breeze but not quite—seemed to touch her face and slide up her nostrils. She breathed it deep into her chest, where she felt it coil in cool strands around her heart. She closed her eyes, seeking the sensation, trying to make it stronger. But the more she sought, the more it faded from her perception.

Was she doing something wrong? Was she supposed to respond to the spell in some way? He hadn't told her as much, but maybe he simply expected her to know?

Panic fluttered in her gut, and she opened her eyes, gazing at the mage before her. His eyes were closed as he concentrated on the spell, so she took the opportunity to study him. When he knelt, his head was nearly level with hers, offering her a clear view of every awful pucker and tear in his skin. Even the newest ones, which he had received the night before in his ongoing battle with the Thorn Maiden.

Nelle grimaced, no longer paying attention to the magic he spun. Her mind flitted elsewhere into dangerous thoughts, dangerous ideas.

What if she were to stay here and devote herself to this study? What if she didn't hold back but truly poured herself into these exciting possibilities, delving into the worlds of knowledge now opening before her eyes?

What if she could help him bind the Thorn Maiden?

Papa . . .

And there it was.

Every fantasy crumbled to nothing, every hope, every foolish idea.

Gaspard had Papa. Nothing else mattered.

Silveri came to the end of his spell. Nelle felt the little jolt of completed magic as the spell written in the book broke apart, never to be used again. The mage looked up at her, tipping his head back to meet her eyes. He offered the quill.

"All you must do now is claim it," he said. "If you wish to, Miss Beck."

She wished to. Oh, how she wished to! Her fingers reached out, hovered over the goose-feather with its carefully trimmed nib stained dark with blue ink.

"Will it make a difference?" she asked, her voice little more than a whisper. "Will it make me . . . better?"

He shook his head. "You and you alone can make the difference."

She pulled her lips in, biting down hard. Then, her jaw firming with resolve, she plucked up the quill, half expecting to feel another jolt, some burst of magical energy, some sensation of binding. But there was nothing. The quill felt the same as it ever had in her hands.

But Silveri rose and stepped back, a gleam of satisfaction in his eye. "Miss Beck," he said, "you are now officially on your way to becoming a true magician."

The cold coils around her heart tightened. It was all Nelle could do to offer the mage a thin smile.

Silveri sent her out from the lighthouse again for the rest of the day.

He wouldn't say much. No further words of congratulation or explanation for the strange ceremony he'd just completed. Only, "That is enough for one morning. Take some air. Clear your mind. But take these with you."

So saying, he pressed a small book into her hand as well as her newly magicked quill. This surprised her more than a little. While it wasn't unusual for the mage to carry one of his spellbooks with him on his rambles across the island, he'd never entrusted one to Nelle. What spells did it contain? And why did he think she would need them?

"What's the good of me taking this?" Nelle asked, twirling the quill in her fingers. "Or am I to stick a bottle of ink in my pocket everywhere I go?"

He smiled and shook his head. "Part of the quill-binding includes a temporary spell that enables your quill to write without ink. It will fade over time but may be reestablished at need."

More questions rose to Nelle's lips, but he gave her no chance to ask them. Scarcely allowing her time to don her cloak, he escorted her across the room and over the threshold, then shut the door behind her with a final-sounding thud. She stood on the step for some moments, staring at the latch, willing it to turn, willing the mage to open the door and speak again. She wasn't even sure what she wanted him to say. Something. Anything.

But the latch did not turn.

Nelle whirled around and faced the afternoon before her. With a little growl and a muttered, "Bullspit!" she set off walking.

She didn't go far. Just far enough that if Silveri watched from his tower window he would think she had taken the path toward Dornrise. She waited half an hour for the ruse to be convincing before creeping back to the tower again. There she crouched behind a shielding grove of trees, tucked the folds of her cloak tightly against the chill wind, and settled in to wait.

Minutes slowly slipped away, measured only by her heartbeat. At last, face numb and legs sore from sitting in an awkward position, she pulled out the book Silveri had given her. Was it one of his early spellbooks? Did he expect her to read through some of his old work while she wandered the island? It wouldn't be such a terrible way to pass the time. At least she could further familiarize herself with the Old Araneli characters.

But when she opened the book, she found blank pages. Frowning, she leafed through from beginning to end. Blank, blank, blank. Nothing but blank.

"What in the boggarts?" she whispered. Her frown deepening,

she pulled out the quill, studied it from every angle, then looked at the book again. Was she supposed to . . . practice?

"This is ridiculous." She slammed the book shut and tucked both items back under her cloak. Just as she did so, she heard the door creak. Breath quickening, she peered out from her hiding place.

Silveri appeared on the doorstep, his hood up over his head. Pulling the door fast behind him—and no doubt triggering the locking spell—he set off down the cliff path to the beach below. Nelle watched until his hood vanished from sight.

Then, with another emphatic "Bullspit," she staggered to her prickling feet, gathered her skirts, and set off after him.

Eleven days. Eleven days she had spent on Roseward. That was all. Yet it felt so much longer. She tramped down the path, keeping well enough back to avoid attracting Silveri's attention. Just eleven days ago she'd tried to land on that beach down below and been chased off by the very wyverns even now wheeling overhead. She'd been terrified nearly out of her wits, barely able to grasp the fact that such creatures really could exist. Now she accepted their presence as easily as she would accept seagulls or pelicans soaring on the air currents above the waves.

And that hooded figure picking his way across the pebbly beach . . . How could a mere eleven days have changed her entire perspective on this man? This scarred, broken, murderous, arrogant, condescending, fascinating man.

She reached the end of the path and stepped onto the hard stones of the beach strip, still trailing well behind Silveri. He walked close to the cliff, and the wyverns flocked around him. They chortled and sang, and some of them pulled at his robes. One knocked his hood back, and his long fair hair flowed free. He turned, and Nelle caught in profile the flash of his smile as he laughed at the high-spirited wyvern.

Her heart caught in her throat. It was so strange. So impossible. But undeniable.

When he smiled like that, she couldn't even see the scars.

He was too far away for her to hear his voice above the wind and the waves. She watched him reach out a hand. A smaller wyvern landed on his forearm like a hawk, its bat-like wings slapping the air as it found its balance. Silveri gently tickled its chin and stroked a nilarium-crusted finger down its throat.

Nelle took a seat behind a boulder where she could remain mostly hidden while she observed, then wrapped herself in the folds of her cloak and simply watched Silveri. Her hands were cramping and her brain was sore, and she couldn't bring herself to think about Papa or Gaspard or Cloven or Sam or any part of a life that felt literally worlds away.

She simply sat and watched the mage as he petted his wyverns, inspecting their wings and claws and crests and scales. She watched for more of those brief sunburst-like smiles, and each time found herself shocked into a secret smile of her own in response.

He knelt in front of one particularly large wyvern—a tall red fellow with a crest that trailed in ridiculous furls all the way down his spine, and a wingspan that had to be close to eight feet. It bobbed its head the same way the blue wyvern did, yet somehow managed to make the awkward stance seem dignified and noble.

Silveri reached into the front of his robes and withdrew a scroll tied with black string. He slipped the string and unrolled the single sheet of parchment. Even from a distance, Nelle could see how frail and old it was, delicate as an autumn leaf. She watched Silveri present the parchment to the wyvern, which nosed it, crest rising and falling three times in some sort of wordless communication.

Then she gasped as the wyvern suddenly snatched the parchment into its mouth and swallowed it. Gone in a single second.

The wyvern threw back its head and bugled a cry. The other wyverns chortled and sang, flocking around it in a funnel that whirled up to the clouds above. The great wyvern spread its massive wings and, with a powerful gathering of its haunch muscles, sprang into the air, pulsing upward through the center of the flock, still bugling.

Nelle craned her neck to watch that brilliant red crest and trailing tail until it vanished into the clouds overhead. Only its voice still drifted down.

Then it was gone.

The other wyverns dispersed out across the waves and up into the cliffs, their chortles no longer a harmonious song.

Silveri remained kneeling on the beach, his shoulders back, his chin up, watching the clouds where the wyvern had gone. He looked paler than before, and his scars seemed deeper, darker. Harsher. His hair blew about his face, a partial veil, but Nelle could still read his expression. The sorrow. The remorse. The resignation.

At last Silveri shook himself and stood. He looked up and down the beach again, his gaze briefly scanning the wyverns in their cliff nests above. Then he turned and started back the way he had come. Toward Nelle.

With a little gasp, Nelle tucked away behind the boulder, her heart thudding. Why she didn't want him to see her there, she couldn't say. It wasn't that she feared him. Not anymore. Perhaps eleven days was too short a time to form a just opinion of character, yet she could not *make* herself feel afraid. She trusted Soran Silveri. She knew the worst of his sins, knew the evil he had wrought upon the worlds. And she trusted him anyway. More than any other man she'd ever met.

Which doesn't say much for the quality of men in your life.

A rueful grimace pulled at her mouth as she crouched in hiding, listening to the crunch of the mage's footsteps as he passed. If he was aware of her presence, he gave no indication but marched on by without pause. She peered out from behind the rock and watched him climb the cliff path to the lighthouse again. Only when he was out of sight did she finally rise and sit on top of the stone, her arms tucked close inside the cloak.

"What's wrong with you, girl?" she whispered.

She shook her head and gazed out across the white-topped waves rolling toward the beach. Out across the hazy horizon line to where Wimborne ought to be. She searched for the tip of the Evenspire but could not see it. Her old world—her *real* world—

might almost never have existed at all.

If only she had time. *Real* time, not the bizarre approximation of time that existed in this world. If only she had months, years ahead of her. Years to spend here on Roseward, learning this strange new power she'd never realized she possessed. If only she could commit to the study, honing and perfecting these new skills under Silveri's guidance.

If only she could stay here.

With him.

Feeling a sting on her face, she lifted a hand to brush away a single hot tear. With an angry snarl, she shook it away and clenched her fingers into a tight fist. "What's *wrong* with you? You're better than this, smarter than this. You've got a mission. You know what you've got to do. You're not careless. You're not stupid. You *won't* risk Papa's life. Or yours for that matter."

She would not, under any circumstances, for any reason, fall in love with the scarred mage of Roseward.

Nelle got to her feet, staggering a little on the uneven stones. Determined to outpace her own thoughts, she set out walking along the quiet beach, heading away from the path up to the lighthouse, away from Silveri. The dispersed wyverns showed no interest in her, and she continued for some while without seeing or hearing another living creature.

Then a sound caught her ear. Distant. Not quite familiar . . .

Or was it?

Pushing hair out of her face, Nelle looked up into the sky. A flock of dark creatures wheeled overhead, so dense she couldn't pick out individual shapes. Was it the wyverns again? She'd seen them flock like this before. Only something was different about the movement, the energy of this flock. It lacked the graceful coordination. It was more frenzy than dance.

The sound reached her again—a chorus of shrieks, sharp and piercing.

Nelle's eyes widened.

"A massacre," she gasped.

Her heart leapt to her throat. The ring! Was she still wearing the summoning ring Silveri gave her? She hadn't thought about it in days, hadn't even looked to see if the spell had worn off. She felt for it now and, to her surprise, found the little gold band of spell threads still wrapped around her thumb. What had the mage said about activating it? Pull the threads three times?

Lifting her hand, she prepared to pull. But as she did so, she raised her gaze back to the approaching mass of wings above. They pivoted in the air, their strange, undulating mass moving as one entity as they altered course, veering away from the beach. She looked up along the line of cliffs, searching for whatever prey the swarm had fixed upon.

And saw Silveri standing high above.

10

Soran watched the red wyvern whirl up and away out of sight. He'd sensed for some time now the slow disintegration of that spell. It wouldn't have lasted much longer, and if he'd allowed it to fall apart entirely . . .

He shivered at the thought of his beautiful wyvern disintegrating along with the spellpaper of its original creation. The magnificent beast had served him faithfully for years now and always demonstrated loyal devotion, though Soran knew it had chafed under its binding restrictions.

The only way to free a wyvern was to present it with its own spell, to make it master of itself. Once that job was done, what became of the spellpaper didn't matter anymore. The wyvern was free to live out its life, however long or short a life it might be.

Soran sighed as the crimson wings flashed out of sight, leaving the boundaries of Roseward behind. He knew it was foolish, but a small part of him had dared hope the creature would choose to remain with him. If not for his sake, then for the sake of its brethren, whose ranks were once again depleted. Their greatest safety lay in numbers, after all.

But the lure of the wide worlds beyond the Hinter Sea was too great. Soran couldn't begrudge the poor beast its opportunity to glimpse sights beyond the confines of its prison.

What he wouldn't give for such an opportunity!

He turned his gaze from the sky to search along the horizon for the Evenspire. He had barely glimpsed its very tip in the distance when clouds rolled by, making the view intermittent. Roseward had drifted further along the Hinter Cycle, approaching the Eledrian realms furthest removed from the mortal world.

Soran narrowed his eyes, straining his vision a little harder than before. What was that line on the horizon just to the right of the Evenspire? An illusion? The first shadow of a storm rolling in? Or was it . . .

"By the seven secret names," he hissed, his nostrils flaring with realization. Through the distant haze, almost too far away to spy with mortal eyes, appeared the shore of a distant land.

Noxaur. The Kingdom of Night.

Fear shot down Soran's spine, momentarily rooting him to the spot. How was it possible? In all the cyclical journeys Roseward had made along the strange currents of the Hinter Sea, it had never come this close to Noxaur.

This was bad. This could hardly be worse. Unless he was

mistaken, unless his memory of the strange maps of Eledria was faulty, he knew whose shore he now strained to see.

His lips silently formed the name, breathing it out in the salty air: "Kyriakos."

Gathering his robes, Soran whirled about and made for the path leading up to the lighthouse. He kept his head bent, watching his footsteps beat in time with the throb of fear in his veins.

The girl. Nelle. He must find her. At once.

What a fool he'd been to give her that book and quill! What a fool he'd been, agreeing to teach her magic in the first place! All along, his reason had warned him against it. Why had he allowed himself to be persuaded, given in to her eager persistence?

He must find her. Fast. Before she suffered for his weakness.

At the top of the sea cliff, he turned toward the lighthouse. But no. She wasn't there. He'd sent her out, told her to clear her head. Foolish, foolish! She could be anywhere on the island. She could be poring over that blank spellbook, discovering the power of the spell he'd worked over her goose-feather quill.

She could even now be spinning an enchantment, sending pulses of mortal power rippling across the *quinsatra* to strike the senses of those attuned to listen for such telltale signs.

With a curse grinding through his teeth, Soran turned for the path toward Dornrise. Where else could she go? He strode swiftly, almost running, until he reached the place above the cliff's edge where, not long ago, she and he had faced the unicorn together. The place where she had saved his life.

How had he repaid her courage? He'd endangered her again and again . . . all because he couldn't bear to do what must be done. He couldn't bear to send her away.

It was too late now. They would have to wait until Roseward had progressed farther along its cycle, approaching mortal lands once more. Meanwhile, they could hunker down quietly, drawing no attention. They could—

A terrible shriek pierced the air.

Soran stopped dead in his tracks and turned slowly on the clifftop, gazing across the sea toward Noxaur's shores. He knew that sound.

The writhing swarm of harpens darkened the sky like a living cloud. Hundreds of wings and flashing talons and raptor beaks snapping on ravenous humanoid faces.

Would the wards hold? Soran watched, frozen in place, his hands clenched into fists. He had checked the ward stones again only yesterday. The repair Nelle made on the first stone had held, and he'd taken the time to strengthen weak places on three others. But that was yesterday. New weaknesses might have emerged overnight, new cracks in the rocky surfaces, new breaks in the spellwords.

And he had stayed home all morning to give magic lessons to the girl. Leaving Roseward's defenses to crumble.

"Seven gods," he whispered, almost in prayer. The massacre of harpens drew closer, their cries mingled in a hideous, cacophonic chorus. "Let the wards hold. Let them hold . . ."

There was no sudden flash of light, no brilliant break of magic. One moment, Soran clung to hope, telling himself the swarm was still too far away to know for sure.

The next moment, he knew they were within the boundaries. And they were closing in fast. On him.

For the space of three heartbeats, Soran stood in numb horror. Somewhere in the back of his brain he realized that he'd stepped out of the lighthouse today without a spellbook in hand. No weapons, no means of protection. Granted, Roseward wasn't usually a dangerous place during daylight hours. But he should have known better, should have realized they were drawing so near to Noxaur. He should have . . .

Too late now.

A surge of pure terror jerked his body into motion. He ran, making for the lighthouse. With every step he took, his heart cried out, *Nelle! She's out here! She's alone!*

He could do her no good without spells. He could do her no good if the flesh were torn from his bones and his carcass lay in bloody ruins beneath a mass of ravenous harpens.

If he could reach the lighthouse . . . If he could get through the door, slam it behind him . . .

A shadow fell over him like a cloud. He'd never make it in time.

With a despairing cry, he veered off the path. Along the cliffs there was nowhere to hide. He was a helpless target. But if he could reach the denser growth of trees, the harpens would have to disperse in their pursuit of him. Perhaps they'd even give up the hunt, swerve off to find easier prey. Like Nelle.

Spitting out every curse he knew, Soran plunged on. He could almost feel those hundreds of talons tearing into the back of his neck, those raptor beaks ripping into his clothes, his flesh. Deafening shrieks drowned out everything, even the pounding pulse of his heart.

At the last possible second, Soran reached the tree line—a grove of pines, their thick branches densely bunched together. He hurled himself into that shelter, ignoring the scrapes and cuts of those low branches across his skin. The pine boughs closed in behind him, and the harpen flock screamed in frustration. Soran staggered and fell to his knees.

There was no chance to catch his breath. Searing pain drove into his skull. He cried out, collapsing to the ground and rolling. His vision filled with feathers, bizarrely humanoid faces, snapping beaks, flashing talons. Several of the monsters had managed to squeeze through after him. He flung up his hands, covering his eyes. Talons tore uselessly at the nilarium coating, and he felt a stab of strange gratitude for Lodírhal's curse.

He struck out and managed to hit one harpen, sending it reeling against the nearest tree trunk. He caught a second one by the leg, hauled it toward him. The wings beat at his face, and the beak pecked savagely at anything it could reach. Catching it by the neck, Soran gave a quick twist. Bone snapped. The harpen fell in a dead pile of feathers.

No chance to rejoice in this one small victory. Two more harpens lunged at his head, going for his eyes again. Overhead, beyond the shielding canopy of pine boughs, the rest of the flock had re-gathered, swarming to and fro as they searched for openings. Several of them worked their way through the upper branches and sped down to join the fray.

He had to get up. He couldn't stay here. He must find a weapon of some kind, find some way back to the lighthouse. His mind spun with half ideas, but the harpens' shrieks drowned out thought. He caught another harpen and pounded it into the dirt, breaking its spine, but another slashed at his ear. Blood poured down the side of his face and neck.

The smell drove the flock mad.

Was this it then? Was this how he would meet his end? After all these years of fighting the Thorn Maiden, was he to fall prey to a massacre of harpens? What a stupid, stupid way to go! And all because he couldn't resist a pretty girl's pleading.

Nelle. What would happen to her? Would she find shelter before the harpens caught her? Even if she did, it would make no difference. When night fell, the Thorn Maiden would return. With no one to stop her, she would rend the girl to pieces.

"*No!*" Soran cried and surged to his feet. He swung his arms, beating at the five harpens now harrying him. His blows were wild, but two of them struck home, and the harpens crashed at his feet. More came at once to take their place as the flock pushed its way through the trees.

Could he run for it? He was closer to the lighthouse than he had been. Maybe he could make it. While the harpens struggled to escape from the dense forest growth, maybe he could race across the open space to the lighthouse door. Maybe . . .

What other choice did he have?

Pulling his hood up over his head, Soran forced himself to take stock through the whirl of wings. He would have one shot at this. When he broke from the trees, he must be sure he was aimed in the right direction. There would be no chance to regroup, no chance to alter course. Even a few steps off would spell disaster.

He drew a deep breath. Let it out in a gusting prayer.

Then he sprang out from the pines, trailing harpens. They tore at him, savaging his robes with every step he took, but the rest of the flock didn't seem to realize what had happened yet.

The lighthouse. It wasn't far. Maybe twenty yards at the most. He could make it. He would make it. *He must make it.*

His foot struck a stone. His arms windmilled; his hood flew back from his head.

Before he even hit the ground, he knew he was done for. He'd never rise again.

His whole skeleton seemed to clatter with the impact as his body struck the hard ground. Instinct made him roll, made him fling his arms up over his head. He heard the rip and shred of his garments as many beaks and claws tore into him, tore down to the skin. His eyes, rolling with terror, stared out between his nilarium fingers and glimpsed the flash of talons ready to rip them from their sockets.

But he also saw a flash of fire.

It couldn't be—

Before the thought could take full form in his head, the fire struck. Not in a wild blast but in a single stroke, so precise, so searing, it never touched him. It passed directly over his body, close enough that he felt the wave of heat roll by. Harpens shrieked with agony, but their cries cut off almost at once. Bodies rained down on him, wings still flapping, legs still kicking.

Soran tried to raise his head, but another flash of fire forced him to duck and roll again, burying his face in the dirt, covering his head with his arms. More bodies thudded against his back and shoulders and littered the ground around him.

A high, thin voice cried out, "Sir! Sir, are you all right?"

Soran pulled his head upright. Blood dripped from cuts across his forehead and scalp, running into his eyes. He dashed rivulets away and blinked up into that pale freckled face framed by long coils of red hair.

Nelle crouched over him. With one hand she gripped his shoulder; with the other she grasped the hilt of a flaming spell-sword.

"How—" Soran gasped.

Before he could get another word out, the harpens were upon them again. The girl sprang to her feet, her stance wide and protective. With both hands she swung the sword in a furious arc of fire, cutting through wings and bodies. A smoldering stench of death and magic filled the air, stinging Soran's nostrils.

The flock veered off and away, the shrieks no longer ravenous but terrified as the creatures made for the shelter of the pines, vanishing among their branches. Surrounded by dead harpen carcasses, Nelle watched them go, her sword still at the ready.

It was impossible. He must have gone mad. He must have lost his mind with terror, and in these last moments before death, his brain had conjured this insane image.

But though he blinked and shook his head and blinked again, the vision did not fade.

Nelle looked down at him. Sweat ran in streaks down her cheeks, and her arms shook with the effort of the magic she'd conjured. She opened her mouth as though to speak, but before any words could come, the spell-sword flickered dangerously. The spell was on the verge of breaking.

Soran pulled himself to his feet, staggering to keep from falling over again. Every part of his body hurt, and his robes hung in shreds from his limbs. "Come," he said, holding out a hand to the girl. "We must get to the lighthouse."

She nodded wordlessly but didn't hand over the sword. Instead, she let go of the hilt with her left hand and slid her fingers into his.

That was . . . not what he'd intended.

There was no time to argue. The harpens would be on them again the moment they detected a weakness in her magic. Summoning his strength, Soran set off swiftly, dragging the girl behind him. She kept the sword upright, but he could feel the trembling weakness in her arm. This spell she'd conjured was surely far beyond her strength.

They were still ten yards out from the lighthouse when the spell-sword sputtered and the enchantment broke. Immediately the harpens rose in a cloudy mass from the pines and swooped toward them.

"Hurry!" Soran cried and yanked the girl along after him. She tripped and almost fell, but his firm grip on her hand kept her upright. He threw himself at the door, barging through the magical lock. Dragging the girl inside, he shoved her so that she fell headlong onto the floor. Then he whirled and slammed the door shut.

Harpens crashed into the wood and stone on the other side in a tidal wave of screams that seemed to go on forever.

11

Nelle lay panting on the floor, unable to move. She heard the sound of crashing harpens, half expecting to hear them burst through the door and swarm the chamber. But the protections on the lighthouse were strong.

Eventually, the assault dissipated and the shrieking faded, leaving behind a ringing sort of silence.

After one small effort to raise her head, Nelle closed her eyes and simply held still, waiting for the world to stop spinning. Her veins ached. She hadn't realized it was possible for veins to ache. Apparently it was. Not a pleasant sensation.

Behind her she heard the mage approach, moving with a staggering limp quite unlike his usual purposeful stride. She couldn't quite bring herself to open her eyes, but she felt the brush of his shredded cloak as he knelt heavily.

"Miss Beck?" His voice was a rough growl. He sounded angry.

"Peronelle?"

Her lips twitched in an involuntary smile. Was that the first time he'd called her by her name? She swallowed and tried to summon the strength to answer. But it was too much effort, so she just lay there.

With a series of grunts and groans, the mage stretched out on his back beside her. For a long time they remained like that, silent. The wyvern, which had no doubt dived into hiding at the first sound of the harpens' approach, eventually crept out and waddled over to nose them both. Nelle found she possessed just energy enough to growl, "Go away, worm." Anything more was too much effort. She didn't try to resist when the little beast curled up beside her, resting its head across the small of her back.

Slowly, coherent thoughts began to take shape. Nelle grimaced as she felt the corners of the spellbook tucked into the front of her cloak press uncomfortably against her ribcage. And her quill? Was it still there as well? Or had she dropped it in her mad frenzy the moment she finished writing the spell-sword into being?

"How did you do it?"

She started at the sudden rumble of Silveri's voice. He was asking about the spell, of curse. But how was she supposed to answer?

With an aching groan, Nelle opened her eyes and propped herself up on her elbows, resting her chin on her clenched fists. Soran lay beside her, his face turned to her. She could count every new cut added to the scars across his features. Those harpen talons were vicious. His pale gray eyes gleamed at her, full of questions.

"I don't know," she said at last. "When I saw the harpens heading right for you, I knew I had to do something. You sent the book and quill with me, and I couldn't think of anything else to try."

"It was a good thought," the mage said and sat upright, grimacing and wiping blood from his face. "But I don't know how you managed it, Miss Beck," he continued. "None of the spells I have given you to practice pertained to weaponry in the least. How did you know to create that spell?"

Nelle frowned, her brows tightening into a knot. "I . . . I remembered that spell of yours. The flaming sword you used when we hunted the unicorn. It seemed to me I could recall the sort of shape of it. The . . . the energy, as it were."

"And did you write it in Old Araneli?"

That was a good question. Nelle's frown deepened. She couldn't well remember what she'd done. Not exactly.

She pushed herself up onto her knees, dislodging the wyvern in the process. It squawked and crawled to the mage, burbling irritably. Ignoring it, Nelle sat cross-legged on the cold floor, fumbled inside the folds of her cloak, slipped the little spellbook from the front pocket, and opened it to the first page.

"Bullspit," she muttered.

Of course, the used spell had burned away. Only a few charred scraps of paper still clung to the binding. A few partial letters and lines, written in such a hurried fashion she couldn't make anything of them, were all that remained of her spell.

Nelle passed the book to Silveri, who studied it by the poor light coming through the windows. "Interesting," he said after a long silence. "This is . . ." He glanced up, meeting her eyes over the top of the book. "This is quite unlike any spell I've ever seen before."

Grunting, Nelle folded her arms around her middle. "Well, it worked. Sort of. Didn't last long, but it did the trick, didn't it?"

"It certainly did." The mage closed the book and offered it back to her. Nelle didn't move to take it. She lacked the energy.

He set it aside on the floor and quietly said, "Once more, Miss Beck, I find I owe you my life."

Nelle looked at his scarred and bleeding face, then away again. Heat rushed to her cheeks, and her gut churned uncomfortably. How close had she come to losing him? It was hard to fathom, hard to believe. Mage Soran Silveri was such a powerful force, such a figure of mastery and mystery. She couldn't imagine him actually being mortal. Vulnerable.

Yet when she'd seen that flock of harpens turn in midair, making straight for him . . .

She shuddered, ducking her head. She'd scarcely thought about what she did. It was as though instinct had made her pluck the empty book from her cloak pocket, had made her grab her quill and begin to scrawl the words, letting the spell pour out of her.

Then she'd run up the narrow cliff path with everything she had, heedless of the danger a single false step would mean. Only when she'd reached the top and seen the harpens gathered in a tumultuous cloud above the grove of pines where the mage took shelter did she pause long enough to read off the spell.

It probably should have surprised her, the ease with which the sword manifested from thin air, flames bursting to life along its razor edge. But at the time she'd thought of nothing but getting to Silveri.

Perhaps that was the trick of it. Perhaps all along she'd been too focused on *making* the magic do what she wished. Perhaps if she'd concentrated instead on the goal, the intent, and not on the act itself . . .

Nelle groaned and dropped her head into her hand as another wave of exhaustion struck and her body shook with the aftereffects of creation. Who knew that magic took such a toll?

"You should lie down," Silveri said.

"You know, I think you're right," Nelle agreed and began to stretch out on the floor once more. But his big hands reached out to grip her shoulders, and he pulled them both to their feet. Then he wrapped one arm around her, holding her steady as he guided her across the room to her alcove. Nelle's fingers fumbled with the clasp of her cloak but couldn't quite seem to manage it.

"Here," said the mage. His cold fingers rested on hers, gently pulling her hands away. Unresisting, she allowed him to work the clasp, slide the cloak away from her shoulders, and drop it on the pile of rugs below.

She gazed up at him, watching the blood trickle in ribbons along the scars and grooves of his face. The wounds the harpens had dealt were already beginning to heal under the influence of Hinter air. Still, they looked raw.

Nelle reached up one trembling hand to rest her palm against his cheek. She heard the sharp intake of his breath. His lashes moved in a series of swift, surprised blinks as he met her gaze.

She wanted to say . . . something. To apologize for taking so long to reach him. To tell him she was glad she'd gotten there in time, glad she'd somehow worked a spell, even if she couldn't remember how she'd done it. To tell him how thankful she was that he was still alive.

Her mouth moved, wordless. She saw his gaze flick down to her lips and focus there. Something glimmered in his eye, some expression . . . she couldn't quite read it. She tried again to speak, but her throat closed tight.

Hardly aware of what she did, she leaned toward him just a fraction. The movement was enough to break the momentary spell.

"Lie down, Miss Beck," Silveri said. "You've had an ordeal. The harpens will not get through, I promise. You may rest easily."

Nelle nodded, swallowed, and dropped her chin. Then she sank onto the pile of rugs, drawing the blanket and folds of her cloak over her body. She was asleep almost before she'd closed her eyes.

She woke to the sound of the door opening.

Nelle started upright in the alcove bed. With a scramble of wings and scales and an irritable bleat, the wyvern tumbled off her and landed in a pile on the floor, but she paid it no heed. Her eyes, bleary with sleep, blinked across the room to see Silveri outlined by daylight as he stepped through the door.

His pale eyes met hers across the room. "Ah," he said. "You're awake."

"Did you . . ." Nelle choked on her own voice and quickly coughed to clear her throat. "Did you go *outside?* What about the harpens?"

He closed the door, crossed the room to the table, and took a seat, pulling a spellbook from the front of his shredded robes. He dropped it on the tabletop. "The harpens are dealt with," he said grimly. "Every last one of them."

Nelle swallowed hard, a little shudder running down her spine. The mage must have used a great portion of his precious spell supply to do away with that flock.

She threw back the blanket and climbed from the alcove, straightening her skirts as she staggered to the table and took her seat opposite him. Only then did she realize: He'd left her alone in the lighthouse. For the very first time, she'd been inside unsupervised. And she'd slept right through it! She could curse herself for her own exhaustion. Who knew when such an opportunity would come around again?

Feeling the mage's eyes upon her, she quickly shook her head. She couldn't very well let him guess what she was thinking. "I suppose this means we're floating in a harpen migration route," she said hastily. "Think we're gonna see more of the spitters?"

"It is likely, yes." The mage's voice was heavy, dark. "I will attend to the ward stones again to make certain they are strengthened, but . . ." He shook his head. The hood slipped back down over his shoulders, exposing his face to her view. The wounds from the harpen talons had closed, but dried blood streaked his pale skin. The effect was ghastly.

He turned away from her and studied the shimmering embers in the fireplace. There was a certain hardness to the line of his jaw. As though he knew something he didn't want to speak aloud.

"Out with it," Nelle said at last. "No use in keeping secrets from me. We're in this together now. Something worse than harpens is out there, ain't it."

The muscles of his throat constricted as he swallowed hard. "The Hinter currents have taken us dangerously close to the coast of Noxaur. The Kingdom of Night, as it is called in your world."

A pit formed in Nelle's gut. She had heard many tales of the Kingdom of Night; it featured in every scary story told to every young child of Wimborne City, be they high-born or low. Tales of a realm where the sun never rose but for three days out of the year. Tales of deadly beings born of night and shadow—demons and skin-walkers and vampires. And worse.

She drew a shaky breath and expelled it slowly. "Figures," she said. "Harpens definitely belong in a place like that." She rubbed a hand down her face. Her body was still weak after the exertion of spellcasting, but this subtle thrill of dread filled her with a nervous energy. "I'm guessing you've never come so close to . . . to this nasty place before?"

Silveri shook his head. "As the ties binding Roseward to the mortal world loosen, we drift further out into the Hinter where the stranger realms of Eledria lie." He swallowed again, and Nelle watched one of his hands clench slowly into a fist. "I should never have let you stay."

Nelle frowned, a dart of irritation interrupting the steady thrum of fear in her veins. "No use in fretting about that now. I'm here."

"Yes. Yes, you are." Silveri turned to her, fixing her with the full force of his stare. Firelight reflected in the depths of his dark pupils. "It will be several days at least until you can safely set out for the mortal world again. The Evenspire is beyond sight, and without it to serve as a guidepost, you would be in danger of ending up on dark shores. You must remain here. A little longer."

"Well, good." Nelle crossed her arms and leaned back in her chair. "I wasn't planning on going nowhere yet in any case."

When he looked as though he might argue, she set her face in a determined scowl, daring him to do his worst. His eyes moved across her face, contemplative and stern. He seemed to think better of pushing an altercation, however, and turned back to the fireplace.

"You must cease your magic studies."

Though his voice was low, his words rang out in the stillness. They struck Nelle's ears, ringing hard inside her head, and for some moments she couldn't quite believe what she'd heard.

Then she snarled, "Bullspit."

He didn't look her way. Folding his arms across his chest, he stretched his right leg out long in front of him, a pose somehow both easy and combative. "It's too dangerous. The beings of Noxaur are particularly interested in mortals. Any trace of mortal magic on the wind will draw them like flies to Roseward's shores. My wards are compromised as it is."

"What about *your* magic?" Nelle tilted her head, her jaw tight and tense. "You've got spells up all over the island. Ain't they bad enough? To attract nasties from Noxaur, I mean?"

"Yes. They are." Silveri nodded slowly and glanced her way under his brows. "But it is well known across the Eledrian realms that I am under a curse established by the king of Aurelis. Even the lords of Noxaur would hesitate to cross Lodírhal. They will keep their beasts in check if they know what is good for them."

Nelle snorted. "Didn't keep the harpens in check, did they? And if I hadn't had my spellbook and quill on me, you'd be carrion by now." She shook her head fiercely and leaned on the table, resting her weight on her elbows. "You can't take me this far, then just cut me off. I worked magic today. *Real* magic. And I saved your hide with it. You said yourself I've got the spark, the . . . the inspiration."

The scars around his mouth puckered in an ugly frown. "It's for your own good, Miss Beck."

"Yeah? Well, it's for *your* own good I refuse."

He looked at her then, straight on. And his eye held such a dangerous flash that she wanted to cower back in her seat, to crawl away to her alcove and hide her face under the blankets. Only a will of iron made her hold her position, leaning over the table and meeting his gaze straight on.

"Look," she said at last, breaking the tension in the air, "I'm not stupid. I'll promise to leave off the spell-writing and conjuring until you say we're back in safer waters. But I ain't returning to Wimborne. Not yet. And I ain't giving up the magic-studies. I won't do it, sir."

With a sudden scrape of chair legs, the mage stood. His tattered robes hung from his limbs like a ghostly shroud, and in that poor lighting he looked truly ominous. Nelle couldn't move, trapped under his gaze like a mouse pinned down by a cat.

Still silent, he turned and strode to the stair. She watched, her heart in her throat, as he climbed the treads and vanished from sight, then listened to his footsteps continue up the tower above. When even that sound had faded, she let out a gusting breath.

"Typical!" she growled, bowing her head and running trembling fingers through her hair. The exhaustion of the day returned in full force, and she couldn't find the strength to lift her head again for a long, long while.

12

What was it I said to you once, so long ago? A woman doesn't like to remain in calm waters all her life. She likes a little risk, a little peril. A little danger.

Soran bowed over the Rose Book, reasserting the binding spell. After the day he'd had, the last thing he wanted was to work this complex magic yet again. But he had no choice.

He stumbled over a word and felt the whole spell waver. A brief error, one he quickly corrected.

But the Thorn Maiden sensed the weakness and was swift to take advantage. She poured into the tower chamber, a mass of slithering vines. Then she emerged from the undulating coils, assuming her womanly, thorn-studded shape, and leaned against his desk, draping herself in the very way Helenia once did when she sought to distract Soran from his work.

You'll never be able to protect her, my love. Not if she doesn't wish to be protected. You're fighting a battle you cannot win. She reached one long-fingered hand to tickle him under the chin like a favorite pet. Her fingertips left burning scrapes along his skin. *It seems I may not have my chance at her after all.*

Soran tried to steel his concentration, to force her words out of his head. But she was far too sly. The poison of her perfume filled his nostrils, drawing his attention her way.

With a wrench, he pulled his consciousness partway free. While his mortal body continued to bow over the spell, reading off the words with careful precision, his spirit-self looked up into her face. Such a strange face. Such a strange, beautiful, terrible face. Every feature so exquisitely sculpted from twining vines and silken rose petals that one could almost mistake it for the real thing. For Helenia as he had known her years ago.

She smiled at him. And that smile was so familiar it cut him to the quick.

I see I have your attention.

"What do you know, Helenia?" Soran demanded, impatient and abrupt.

La, what a ruffian! Is this the gentlemanly Soran Silveri, son of the Lord of Roseward? She leaned over him, the vines that formed her body twisting and twining with every move she made. The dark pits that were her eyes gazed into him, beckoning and deep. She fluttered rose-petal eyelids. *But then, I always liked this ungentlemanly side of you so much the better. I liked the Soran who could make me cry out in fear as well as ecstasy. I liked—*

"*Enough of this,*" Soran snarled. His mortal body halted over the spell, the words suspended on his lips while his spirit-hand lashed out and caught her by the throat. "*What do you know? Tell me now.*"

A slow smile spread across her face. Tendril vines grew from her shoulders and wrapped around his hand and wrist, coiling up his arm. Soran squeezed, threatening to break the stems making up her neck. Thorns broke against the nilarium coating of his hand.

Kyriakos, the Thorn Maiden purred.

Soran set his jaw, squeezing harder. "*What do you know?*" he demanded again, grinding the words through his teeth.

I know what you know, my love. I know the fears spinning through your mind, the nightmares in the shadows of your soul.

She leaned toward him. More briars crawled up from the ground, wrapping up the legs of his chair, winding around his knees, around his waist.

Word must have reached Kyriakos by now. He will have heard rumor of Hybrid magic close by. He is coming—

With a strangled roar, Soran's spirit lurched out from his body, dragging the Thorn Maiden with him. While his mortal self hunched over the Rose Book, his true self, his soul-self, tore the briars and branches in half, ripped them into handfuls of roses, and scattered them on the floor. But each time, the Thorn Maiden reformed, recreated her womanly shape, seductive and vindictive, her arms always reaching out to enfold him.

He couldn't fall for her games. He couldn't let himself be

distracted. It was too easy, too natural to surrender to his violent instincts, to throw himself into this savagery. But that wasn't the way to beat the Thorn Maiden.

He had fought this battle too many times to give in now.

Soran jerked his head roughly, pulling himself upright at the desk. The images and sensations of the spirit realm faded into the depths of his mind. He still felt the vines wrapped around his body, the thorns gouging into his skin. But he knew them for what they were: dreams, nightmares. Not part of this mortal reality.

She hadn't escaped her bindings. Yet.

With an effort Soran refocused his eyes, his mind. The words took shape, the magic spilling from the pages of the spellbook. He worked them with expert care, reaffirming the restraints, the chains.

Slowly the slithering vines retreated, creeping out of his mind and back into the nightmare realm where they belonged. But the Thorn Maiden's voice lingered long, whispering in his ear:

Kyriakos is coming. He's coming for her. He'll be on your shores tomorrow . . .

Nelle slept badly that night.

She always knew when the Thorn Maiden gave Mage Silveri a particularly difficult battle. On those nights, Nelle sensed her presence as well—a dark, shivering nearness that crept into the edges of her dreams. The subtle *tap, tap, tap* at the door, eager for admittance but unable to barge through.

Every hour or so, Nelle woke with her heart in her throat, sat up in her bed, and stared across the chamber at the door. But the instant her eyes opened and consciousness returned, the presence vanished. Which meant Silveri was winning his battle. As long as he reaffirmed the binding spell, the Thorn Maiden could not manifest in physical form.

The sixth time she woke, Nelle didn't bother lying down again to sleep. It was still dark outside, but when she peered out the window, she saw a faint tinge of gray in the sky. Surely it was close enough to dawn to be safe.

Dislodging the wyvern, which snorted and twitched in its sleep, Nelle climbed out of the alcove, pulled her gown on over her flimsy chemise and, on impulse, snatched up her cloak as well. She wasn't hungry and she didn't feel like tea. She felt . . . stifled. Cramped. She felt as though she'd been entombed in this room for a year or more, though she knew it was only since yesterday afternoon.

Heaving a sigh, she glanced first at the door, then at the stairway leading to Silveri's tower. More than anything she wanted to step outside and breathe in a few deep lung-fulls of fresh air. But the mage had been clear in his warnings. What if more harpens had breached the wards last night? Or worse?

She pulled her cloak around her shivering shoulders and moved to stoke up the fire. Once she had a little blaze going, she lit two candles and set them on the table. Their flickering light shone on the cover of the blank spellbook Silveri had given her. Her enchanted quill lay beside it. Silveri must have picked them off the floor and placed them here sometime yesterday. She didn't remember when.

Taking a seat at the table, Nelle drew the spellbook toward her, sighed, and didn't open it. What was the point? Just yesterday she'd felt the surge of true power burst through her veins. And now . . .

Now she must keep her head down. Stifle all the urges teeming in her fingertips and remain quiet. Unobtrusive. Wait and hope that danger passed by without turning her way.

"Bullspit," she growled.

Was this to be her lot in life? Cowering and hiding and deceiving? She shook her head and shoved the book away, almost knocking over one of the candles. "Get your head on straight, girl! You're not here to learn magic. You've got one job to do. One!"

But why was it so hard to remember? Why did that life in Wimborne seem so far away, so . . . pointless? Even Papa's face had faded from the forefront of her mind.

Which was wrong, so wrong! Papa needed her; Papa depended on her. She'd promised Mother she would care for him. She'd promised. She'd . . .

Nelle frowned. What was that sound? Was it . . . footsteps outside?

No. It couldn't be. Maybe she was still asleep. She must be, and this must be one of the Thorn Maiden's manipulative nightmares. She would ignore it, and it would go away.

The thought had scarcely crossed her mind before the footsteps reached the door. The next moment there was a terrific pounding, loud enough to jolt her to her feet. If that was a nightmare, it was a boggart-spitting convincing one! One hand pressed to her heart, the other to the table for support, she stared across the dark chamber.

"Hullo?"

Nelle's eyes widened. Her breath caught in her throat.

"Hullo, is anyone in there?" Another round of pounding, and then, "Please, *please,* answer!"

That voice. She knew that voice. She'd know it anywhere, whether in dreams or reality.

But it couldn't be true, couldn't be real. It must be a dream, a nightmare, it must . . .

She was already moving, already crossing the chamber in quick strides. All but falling against the door, she fumbled with the latch. It resisted her pull—powerful spells held it shut.

The voice on the other side cried again, desperately, "Please, can anyone hear me?"

Grinding her teeth, Nelle yanked hard. The spell gave. The door swung open.

And Samton Rallenford fell into her arms.

She staggered as she caught him and dropped heavily to her knees, dragging him down with her. He wrapped his lanky arms around her, clinging like a child clutching hold of its mother. He was soaked to the bone and trembling like a leaf.

"Thank the gods!" he whimpered. "Thank the gods! Thank the gods, someone is here!"

"Sam?" Nelle quavered.

A jolt shot through his body. He pulled against her grasp to blink at her in the dim pre-dawn light. "Boggarts, am I dreaming?" he said and shook his head hard before looking at her again. "Is that really you, Ginger?"

She couldn't answer. Her throat closed too tight to get a word out. This was no dream. He . . . *smelled* too real. Like the Sam she'd always known. A little sooty, a little salty, yet always a little sweet as well from the sugar-grass leaves he was in the habit of chewing. No dream could recollect that smell with such exactness. It had to be him, really him.

Nelle shoved him away, slapping his hands when he reached for her again. Outside, the wind rose, driving against the cliffs, whistling into the chamber, and threatening to douse her fire. She tugged her skirts out from under her knees and regained her feet, quickly stepping around the young man to shut the door firmly, press her back against it, and stare down at him. He gazed up in return, his eyes wide and round, blinking in a daze.

"What are you doing here, Sam?" she demanded.

"I . . . I came looking for you, didn't I." His teeth chattered with each word. He was freezing as well as drenched, and his whole body quaked.

A restless huff escaped Nelle's lips as she bent, grabbed his arm, and hauled him to his feet. When he sagged, his knees ready to give out, she hastily ducked under his shoulder, offering him what support she could. "Here, quick. Sit by the fire," she said, helping him across the room.

He didn't protest. With a grateful sigh he collapsed on the floor by the hearth, not even attempting to perch on the stool she'd tried to guide him toward. When she pulled away, he made as though to hold on, but his grip wasn't strong enough to keep her by him.

"Take your clothes off," she said, her voice a gruff bark.

An altogether too familiar grin broke across his boyish features. He peered up at her through the wet strands of dark hair plastered across his forehead. "You don't know how long I've waited to hear you—"

"Stuff it." Nelle spun on her heel and marched across the room to the armoire, where Silveri stored his extra shirts. Many of them had rips and old bloodstains, but Sam was in no position to complain. She grabbed one and turned back to the fire to see him struggling with the ties of his shirt. His fingers shook too hard to be of use.

"Bullspitting baby," Nelle muttered and stomped back across the room, dropping to her knees beside him. She pushed his hands away and untied the laces herself. He watched her closely, his eyes large in hollow sockets. It was hard to look at him, so she concentrated on getting the shirt loosened. "Lift your arms," she growled.

He obeyed, and she pulled the garment up over his head. Firelight played on his body, casting a warm glow across his pale skin. Smooth, young, supple skin stretched taut across the long, lean muscles of an agile snatcher. Hard life on Wimborne's streets had only toughened him over the years, filling out his slender limbs with true strength and latent power.

Nelle didn't allow her gaze to linger. She held up the fresh shirt and, after motioning him to lift his arms again like a child, pulled it on over his head and shoulders. He snaked his arms through the sleeves and lifted his chin, allowing her to tie the laces down his chest.

"What about my trousers?" he asked meekly.

"Leave them," Nelle snapped. "They'll dry out fast enough." She unfastened the clasp of her cloak and quickly draped it over his shoulders. His eyes widened in surprise as he looked her up and down, taking in the elegant purple gown. It was the worse for wear after the events of the last few days, but it hugged her figure well and was, she knew, by far the most elegant thing he'd ever seen on her.

"Why, Nelle!" he exclaimed, his voice still trembling slightly from the cold. "No wonder you ain't been in no hurry to return to us at Draggs. Looks like you struck it rich here on the Haunted Isle!"

"Don't be stupid." Nelle shuffled back, her hand reaching for the low stool behind her. Dragging it closer, she sat on it, wrapped her arms around her middle, and stared down at him, her brow knotted in a studying frown. She'd known Sam for as long as she could remember. They'd had many adventures together, participating in daring snatches staged by Mother, venturing into the darkest, most dangerous parts of Wimborne City. She'd walked to the brink of death at his side on numerous occasions. Not once in all that time had she seen so much as a flicker of fear in his face.

But now . . . his features were harrowed in a way she didn't recognize. Even when he smiled, even when he tossed his bantering words her way, a dark line of horror underscored everything about him.

"What's happened to you, Sam?" she asked, her voice low. "You've got to tell me."

He tried to smile, but it didn't quite reach his eyes. Tucking the folds of her cloak closer, he leaned in toward the fire as though he would almost cast himself into it to get warm. "Cloven sent me," he said at last through his chattering teeth. "Or rather, that Miphato. Mage Gaspard."

An unpleasant sensation coiled in Nelle's gut. Her lip curled. "What's he want? He gave me three weeks, didn't he? I've still got half that time left."

"Three weeks?" Sam tilted his head at her, his eyes shining oddly. "Nelle, don't you know?"

That look in his eye . . . she knew what it meant as soon as she saw it. She didn't want to know, didn't want to admit it. If she tried hard enough, maybe she could deny it, pretend stupidity even for just a few more moments. If possible, she would have stopped him from saying a single word more.

But Sam continued relentlessly. "It's been two years. Two years since you set out for this gods-forsaken island. Gaspard's sent five men after you, six including me. None of them's returned. I wanted to volunteer long before now, but Cloven wouldn't stand for it. This time I insisted, threatened to—"

"Papa." Nelle gasped, struggling to draw breath, struggling to ask what she must ask. If she didn't speak now she would never find the courage. She would simply shrivel up and die. "Tell me. What's happened to my Papa?"

Sam blinked at her, his mouth opening and closing several times. "I don't know. Gods' truth, Nelle, I don't know."

She sprang up from the stool, turning her back to him. Tears filled her eyes, blinding her, and she hardly realized where she went until she was at the door. She opened it, her hands fumbling desperately to get the latch working, to escape this close dark space into fresh air.

But the cool morning wind that rushed into her face wasn't fresh. It was strange air. Hinter air. The air of a world to which she didn't belong.

She dashed tears from her eyes and stared out over the cliff's edge to the horizon where the Evenspire should be visible. Though dawn ought to be well advanced by now, it was still peculiarly dark. A heavy darkness like a curtain of living shadow pulled across the world.

"Papa," she whispered.

Gaspard had said if she did not return in three weeks, he would make her father pay for her crimes. He would take him to Master Shard in the Square of Correction. There, in front of a gawking crowd, Papa's hands would be chopped off. The price for thievery. Even though Papa had never stolen so much as a crumb in his life.

He would never survive. He would bleed out from those wounds and die.

No, he was already dead. Years ago.

Why had she stayed? She'd known, she'd bullspitting *known* all along that time moved differently here in Roseward. She'd counted days when she should have been calculating months. She should have drugged the mage, stolen the book, and made her getaway ages ago. She should have . . . she should . . .

With a moan, she sank down onto the doorstep. The freezing air blew her hair and billowed her skirts, but she didn't care. She simply stared out at that looming darkness.

"Nelle." Sam's footsteps approached behind her. He knelt, placing a hand on her shoulder. She lacked the strength to shrug him off. "I don't know if it'll make a difference," he said, "but Gaspard sent a message with me. He said if I found you I was to tell you that the terms of your agreement still stand. He'll still make the exchange if you're prepared to follow through."

Though the darkness on the horizon did not lift, Nelle felt as though light beamed suddenly across the shadows of her soul. She turned to meet Sam's strangely serious, fear-worn face. "Don't lie to me, Sam. Is that truly what he said?"

Sam nodded. "Snatcher's honor, I swear it."

Then maybe . . .

Maybe Papa was still alive after all.

Maybe Gaspard had realized or guessed at the time differences between Roseward and the rest of the world. He was a Miphato, after all. He understood more about the workings of the different worlds and realities than most men. It only made sense.

"Then there's time," Nelle whispered. She dropped her head into her hands, unable to stop the tears pouring down her face and through her fingers. "There's still time!"

For a long while she was insensible to everything. She scarcely noticed the weight of Sam's arm wrapped around her shoulder, scarcely noticed when he drew her to him. Eventually the storm of emotion subsided, and she realized her face was buried in his shoulder and his cheek pressed against the top of her head. He seemed to be murmuring something, but she couldn't hear what.

Sniffing loudly, she sat upright, pushing him away. She stood then, her legs a little shaky, and grabbed hold of the doorpost for support. Sam rose as well and reached out to take one of her hands, but she refused to give it.

"I'll help you," he said. "They never told me what they sent you for, but I'm sure I can help. I'm good for a snatch, you know," he added with a wry sidelong grin that was almost like his old self.

Nelle quickly shook her head. Despite the heavy shadow on the horizon, pink had begun to tint the sky above. Dawn came on fast now. Silveri would soon descend from his tower.

"Quick, Sam," she said, stepping back into the chamber. She hurried across to the fire where she'd dropped his soaked shirt and plucked it up. Spying her quill and empty spellbook on the table, she grabbed those as well and, since she had no pockets, hastily stuffed them into her little satchel and slung it from her shoulder. After a quick look around to make certain they'd left no signs that might betray Sam's presence, she hurried back to the door.

"We've got to get you out of here," she said. "I can't let him find you."

"Can't let who find me?" Sam looked down at her, the fear in his face intensifying to a startling degree. "Who else is here with you, Nelle?"

Nelle shook her head. There was no time to explain. She took Sam by the hand and pulled him outside, then softly shut the door. Her mind whirled with half-thought ideas. Where could she take him? Where could he go?

"Where's your boat, Sam?" she demanded, dragging him away from the lighthouse.

"On the beach below," he replied, and indicated the top of the cliff path, which he must have used to climb up to the lighthouse. He came to a hard stop, jerking Nelle's arm and turning her to face him. "I won't go back." His eyes were huge and overly bright. Strange terrors seemed to swim in the depths of his pupils. "You don't know what's out there. You can't know or you wouldn't try to send me."

Nelle stared back at him, sucking her lips in and biting down. Her journey to Roseward had been simple enough. From the mortal world, the island looked to be only a mile off the coast of Wimborne. In reality, it was much farther. She'd rowed out into the sea and passed through a veil of reality into this strange, otherworldly realm, but altogether the trip had taken no more than an hour or two.

Since then, however, the currents had carried Roseward farther on its cycle through the Hinter realms. Sam's journey must have been quite different from her own. And, as close as Roseward now was to Noxaur and all the dark beings of that realm . . .

Although a shudder rushed down Nelle's spine, she squeezed Sam's hand encouragingly. "It'll be safe to travel again in a few days," she said. "I'll have to hide you until then."

Though where she would hide him, she couldn't possibly say. Not at Dornrise, surely. The Thorn Maiden haunted those halls at night. He wouldn't be safe there after sundown. Perhaps in the old harbor village? Maybe she could establish some sort of ward spells around him to keep him safe and hidden. She'd seen enough of Silveri's ward stones, had even worked a little magic on them. Could she replicate the spell in the same way she'd replicated the flaming sword?

But first things first.

"We've got to hide your boat, Sam," she said. "If he . . . if it's found, I'm not sure I'll be able to keep you safe. The master of this island will send you away at once. Back out into that."

She waved a hand at the ocean, at the dark shadow on the horizon, turning to look as she did so. Some of the details had become clearer, revealing a forbidding shoreline that drew closer by the moment.

The Kingdom of Night itself.

13

Soran slept longer than he meant to, exhausted both from his battle with the Thorn Maiden and from the harpen hunt the previous afternoon. He couldn't remember the last time he'd used so much magic in a twenty-four-hour period. It took a toll on body and mind. The moment he closed and fastened the Rose Book, he'd stumbled across the room, collapsed on his bed, and fallen into a deep sleep, senseless to everything for many hours.

He woke with the sun in his eyes, wincing and groaning. His body was a mass of aches and cuts. The wounds from the harpens had healed over, but many of the Thorn Maiden's lacerations were still open and bleeding, leaving ugly stains on his clothes and blankets. He sat up and held out one arm, grimacing at the shredded cloth of his sleeve. He hadn't changed following the harpen attack, and the garment was more rag than shirt by now.

Rising stiffly, he plucked up his robes from where he'd left them in a pile at the foot of the bed. Lacking the energy to shrug into them, he simply draped them over his shoulder and descended the tower stair. His ears almost unconsciously pricked for sounds of movement below—the clatter of spoons and pans, the scolding chatter, the wyvern's answering burbles.

All was strangely silent.

Well, that wasn't much of a surprise. The girl must still be exhausted after the incredible work of spell-conjuring she'd performed yesterday. And the precarious situation they now found themselves in might induce a more solemn, quiet frame of mind in her, at least for the next few days.

This was going to be difficult. Soran frowned, considering. He would have to keep her inside as much as possible. He couldn't let her go rambling about Roseward on her own just now. A second flock of harpens was the least of his worries, though that would be dangerous enough. Yet he would have to check the ward stones several times each day. Which meant bringing her with him. He couldn't very well leave her alone in the lighthouse.

Then again, why not? What was it he feared exactly? The Rose Book was the only item of real peril he owned. Nelle, though curious by nature, would surely know better than to go looking for such a dangerous spellbook, especially now that she knew what it was. She'd had her own encounters with the Thorn Maiden. She would be wary.

Yes, perhaps it would be wisest to leave her behind when he tended to the ward stones. The protections on the lighthouse itself should conceal her even from more sensitive fae perceptions. And it was only for a few days. They would pass by Noxaur soon enough, and then . . .

Soran's thoughts trailed off as he emerged through the hole in the ceiling and glanced around the lower chamber. Nelle wasn't there.

He shook his head and looked again, his gaze darting first to the alcove bed. He saw the tip of the wyvern's snout emerging from the pile of blankets and furs, but no sign of the girl. His gaze turned to one place after another, to all the places he would expect to see her rifling through supplies on the shelf, sloshing water in the washbasin, crouching over the hearth, or bowing over books and parchments at the table. His mind tried to fill in some ghostly impression of her, to believe she was where she was supposed to be.

But she was gone.

A growl rumbling in his throat, Soran looked to the door. It was closed fast, but he sensed an alteration in the locks and protections he'd placed on it yesterday. Why had he not thought to lock her in? Damn his folly! He had protected her only against the monsters outside. He'd never thought to protect her from herself.

Soran sprang down the last several steps, dropped his robes on the table, and strode across the room to fling the door open. Cold air sliced through his ragged shirt and bit at his skin, but he didn't care. He stared out into the morning, hoping against hope that she would be there, standing on the edge of the cliff as he had found her several times before.

She was not. A very different sight met his eye.

A harsh shoreline loomed less than a mile off Roseward's coast. Barren, desolate, poisonous. Shrouded by a darkness deeper than night. A sharp line cut across the water, separating the morning light above Roseward from the deep shadow of that realm. A shadow that crept ever closer.

Three longboats crossed over that line from dark into light, each black sail boasting an unmistakable, unforgettable hound-skull crest.

"Kyriakos," Soran whispered.

"Do I look as ridiculous as I feel in this thing?"

Nelle glanced back at Sam, who followed her down the narrow cliff path. He was still wearing her purloined cloak. And, yes, he did look utterly ridiculous in it. For one thing, it was much too small for him, the hem flapping around his calves, and the seams didn't sit right across his shoulders. Worst of all, he'd gone and pulled the hood up.

And he batted his eyes at her through the pretty fur trim.

That was Sam for you. Even in the direst circumstances, he always found a way to make a joke. She used to find it charming.

Now it was simply exhausting. And infuriating.

"You look a right idiot," she snapped and returned her focus to the path ahead. The wind whipped through the thin fabric of her foolish, fancy gown, and she wished she hadn't been so hasty to lend

Sam her only cloak. Should have let him shiver to death instead.

A burbling cry erupted off to their right. Sam gave a startled yelp, and Nelle turned to see him pressing his back against the cliff wall. His eyes were so wide, the whites showed all the way around.

"Nelle!" he gasped, his voice quavering. "Nelle, I think I saw a dragon!"

She snorted. "It's a wyvern. And it's harmless. Hurry up."

Sam's mouth opened to protest. But the expression on her face seemed to convince him. Peeling himself back off the wall, he inched down the path after her. "What's a wyvern?" he asked after a while. "Sounds like some kind of foreign cooking utensil."

Nelle snorted again and didn't bother answering. Gods willing, Sam wouldn't be on Roseward long enough for it to matter if he could tell the difference between dragons and wyverns.

She peered up into the sky. It was so empty. Usually wyverns filled the air at this hour, performing their aerial dances from sunup to noon, when they crawled away into their cliffside caves for an afternoon snooze. The looming proximity of the Noxaur shore must have driven them into hiding.

Just as well, Nelle decided as she reached the base of the cliff path. The wyverns would likely take notice of a stranger on their land and report back to the mage. Remembering her own initial arrival at Roseward, she shivered. At the time she couldn't have imagined anything more terrifying than the swarm of claws and teeth and scales Silveri had sent to chase her along this very beach.

She hadn't known about harpens then.

"Where's your boat?" she demanded as soon as Sam set foot on level ground.

He pointed with a sweep of velvet cloak. Looking where he indicated, she spied a little craft much like her own boat on a strip of sand several yards away, looking as though the waves would reclaim it at any moment. Sam had obviously not bothered to secure it before he climbed up to the lighthouse.

Gathering her skirts with both hands, Nelle hurried across the beach. The boots she'd taken from Dornrise were much sturdier than the slippers she'd worn upon her first arrival and better able to cope with the sharp stones. She heard Sam panting behind her but didn't wait for him.

When she reached the boat, she immediately grasped the side and gave it a heave. It was heavy, but not too heavy for her to move on her own. She pulled it hard, fighting the dragging waves, and managed to haul it several feet further inland before Sam joined her.

"What were you thinking, leaving it like that?" Nelle growled when they paused to catch their breaths. "It could have floated back out to sea, and then what would have become of you? As far as you knew, you'd be trapped here for good!"

Sam passed a hand across his brow. The fur-trimmed hood had fallen back over his shoulders, and Nelle could clearly see the fear lines scoring his face. His gaze swiveled to meet hers, and he attempted a smile. "Truth be told, I wasn't thinking much by that point. The things I saw out there . . . You know I'm fae-blessed. Your mother told you about that. I can sense danger when it's near and always get myself far away before anything bad happens. But when I was out on that water . . . feeling what I was feeling . . ." He glanced out to sea, shuddered, and quickly shifted his unseeing gaze to the cliffs. "I despaired of my life."

Nelle nodded slowly. Better not let him dwell on those thoughts. Turning to study the cliffs, she searched for a spot they could carry the boat where it wouldn't be obvious. Silveri wouldn't go walking on this beach in the next few days; he'd be too busy tending the ward stones when he dared venture out at all. Still, she didn't want to risk his spying the boat by chance.

Her gaze settled on a low sea cave from which water streamed as the tide rolled out. "Maybe we could hide it there," she said, pointing.

Sam, his reverie broken, looked where she indicated and nodded slowly. "Maybe."

"I don't see a better place." Nelle grasped her side of the boat and met Sam's eye. "Let's get it over there."

He heaved up his end, and the two of them staggered several yards across the uneven ground before they were obliged to stop and breathe again. Nelle's hands smarted with cold, and painful blisters were already developing. But they were nearly halfway to the cave. They could do this.

"Come on," she said, bracing her legs. "Sam?"

His head was up. Long strands of dark hair blew across his face, whipped by the ocean breeze as he stared out to sea. Fearing he had sunk into enervating memories of his recent ordeal, she snapped, "Sam!" trying to shock him back to the present.

He blinked but didn't look at her. "Danger," he breathed. Then more loudly, "Look!"

She turned in the direction he stared. Her eyes rounded.

Three longboats approached across the channel between Roseward and the darkened shore. Their billowing sails were black save for a huge skull-like insignia. Nelle didn't need fae blessing to sense imminent peril.

"Come on!" she said and heaved the boat. Every instinct told her to drop it and run, but that would do no good. They had to hide it if they were to have any chance of hiding Sam's presence on Roseward. The dark sails were still far enough away that they might not have been spotted by lookouts, and the cave was close.

Galvanized into action by the sharpness of her voice, Sam picked up his side of the boat, and they half staggered, half ran with the weight suspended between them. Several times Nelle's grip slipped, and she winced as the keel crunched against the stony ground. It would take a miracle for the boat to be seaworthy after this treatment.

The cave, when they reached it, was smaller than she'd thought, too low for Sam to enter without stooping almost double. Now that she stood looking into the dark hole, she couldn't help wondering what else might have taken shelter inside. Some creature of Noxaur washed up on the shore in the night . . .

No! She wouldn't give way to imagination. "Hurry!" she growled and ducked inside. Sam followed, and together they hauled the boat into the cave. It was most of the way in before they ran out of space, so it should be mostly out of sight.

"We'll pile up rocks around the entrance," Nelle said as she crawled into the boat and over the rowing bench to get back to the cave opening. "Hurry, Sam . . ."

Her voice died away as she peered out.

"Bullspit," she hissed.

The boats were already drawing in toward the shore. There must have been magic in that wind blowing them across the channel. They would land at any moment. She and Sam could not make it to the cliff path without being seen.

"Bullspit!" she said again, louder this time.

"What is it? What do you see?" Sam's voice was thin at her back, wrung through with terror. That, more than anything, turned her blood to ice.

"We'll have to stay here," she said. "There's nowhere else to hide. We'll have to wait for them to go again and hope they didn't see us."

"Who is it? Who's out there?"

Since she had no idea how to answer, Nelle said nothing. She crouched low at the stern of the boat just beneath the shelter of the cave entrance, her hair pulled into a knot over one shoulder so the wind wouldn't make it fly like a signal flag, and she watched.

The prow of the first boat crunched on the gravel, and dark figures leaped into the shallows. With ropes over their shoulders, they hauled the craft further inland. They weren't far away, yet Nelle could get no solid impression of them, as though she watched from a great distance or through a filmy glass. They were all very tall, she could tell that much, taller than Sam, taller even than Mage Silveri. They seemed oddly jointed somehow, as though their arms were made up of too many elbows, their legs of too many knees. Their spines were unnaturally curved, with great humps at the shoulders and an impression of what might be spikes protruding down their backs. But they were too strange, too hazy for any clearer impression.

Nelle knew she should tear her gaze away, crawl back over the rowing bench, and huddle in the dark with Sam. However, not seeing what was going on seemed worse than seeing it, so she hunkered down further, straining to see what happened on that stretch of rocky shore.

A gangplank lowered from the side of the foremost vessel. More of the shadowy figures ran down and lined up on either side, their hunched forms relatively erect. But Nelle could not spare them any attention. Her gaze went instead to the figure at the top of the gangplank.

Once she glimpsed him, it was impossible to look anywhere else.

He was nearly seven feet tall—not as tall as the shadowy beings, perhaps, but far more commanding in pose and demeanor. Nothing about him was stooped or oddly jointed. He stood like a master, like a king, with shoulders thrown back and chin held high. From this distance it was impossible to get a clear view of his features, but Nelle did not doubt he was devastatingly handsome, far beyond the beauty of mortal men. What she could see was his strange complexion—dark, dusky, with almost a purple undertone. His hair, which flowed to his waist, was blue-black like a midnight sky. He wore a trailing silver garment that floated dreamily when he moved. It also bared his chest, revealing the powerful musculature of a warrior.

"A fae," Nelle whispered. This was her first sight of a fae— and not just any fae, but a man of Noxaur, more dreadful, more otherworldly than all other fae inhabiting the realms of Eledria.

She'd known they were beautiful. She'd known they were terrible. But she'd never imagined anything quite like this.

He strode down the gangplank to the shore, his boots crunching loud in contrast to the perfect silence of the shadowy minions whose ranks he passed through without so much as a glance, and made his way several yards inland before pausing, fists planted at his waist, to look this way and that along the beach. For a moment Nelle feared he spied her hiding place. But his gaze traveled past without pause, turning up toward the towering cliffs and the lighthouse above.

Suddenly he raised one hand, the loose sleeve sliding down to his elbow, and snapped his fingers once with a sharp sound like the crack of a whip.

A hideous series of gulping, bellowing roars erupted from the ship. Sheer terror jolted down Nelle's spine as six four-legged creatures appeared at the top of the gangplank—long, low, massive creatures that sprang down to the beach and swarmed around their master's legs. They were shadowy things like the silent minions, but more solid. She would have called them dogs by the way they moved and the sounds they made. But she'd never seen any dogs quite like these.

Their master swung his arm first to the right then to the left. The creatures, slavering and howling, obeyed at once, three tearing off in one direction, three in the opposite.

Those second three came straight toward her.

In a mad scramble, Nelle backed up to the other end of the boat where Sam waited. "Out, out!" she hissed. "We've got to block the entrance!"

She couldn't see his face. Just enough light squeezed through the cave opening to gleam in his eyes, reflecting her own terror back at her. "How do we do that?" he demanded breathlessly.

"Turn the boat!" If they could shift it, put it on its side and turn it slightly, they could block enough of the entrance that the dog-things wouldn't be able to get in.

She heaved at the boat, and Sam, seeing her intention, hurried to help. The noise of scraping and of wood grinding on stone pounded her ears, and Nelle could only hope the wind drowned it out so that it wouldn't draw the dogs' attention.

A forlorn hope. No sooner did they get the boat on its side than a hideous growling filled the air. Nelle heard Sam catch his breath. He hadn't seen what was coming, but that sound was more than enough warning. They stood, holding onto the boat as though clinging to their very lives.

Nelle watched the narrow crack of light on her side of the cave. Was it too small for the dog-things to get through? She had to hope. There was nothing else she could do. Or . . .

She felt the satchel slung across her shoulder and the weight of the little spellbook inside. How would creatures like these react to a flaming sword? Could she remember how she'd managed the spell yesterday and conjure up a weapon? These dogs were much larger and more formidable than harpens, but presumably they would cut and burn just the same.

The first of the dogs arrived at the cave. The bulky shadow flickered past the opening.

Then she saw a nose—a bone-white nose, a skull nose. Was it a mask? There was flesh farther up the snout, but it seemed half peeled away, like a partially rotted carcass. It snuffled eagerly. No lips covered the grotesquely exposed fangs, and saliva dripped freely in long, shimmering ribbons.

The snuffling turned to a growl, then an enthusiastic, roaring sort of bark. The dog lunged at the opening, and the whole boat rocked wildly. Nelle grabbed hold and felt Sam on the other side do the same as both sought to hold the boat in place. Their only chance for survival was to keep that entrance blocked, and it was a slim enough chance.

The dog lunged again and a third time. The boat creaked. Would it break? Shatter into kindling under these attacks? If she were to write a spell, it had to be now. But how could she let go of the boat? Sam couldn't hold it on his own, but if she waited even another second, there wouldn't be time, there wouldn't be—

A sudden cacophony of noise filled the air, drowning out even the bloodthirsty roars of the dog-thing.

At first, Nelle couldn't think what might make such a sound. Then she realized: the wyverns! Those were wyvern battle cries! Her heart leapt as the light streaming through the cave mouth broke up in the flickering shadows of many dozens of wings.

The dog uttered a furious roar and pulled back from the opening. A series of chilling sounds followed, rasping wyvern shrieks and bellowing howls. The tearing of flesh. The breaking of bones. Nelle's courage shattered. She collapsed to her knees in the shallow water on the cave floor, covering her ears with both hands.

But the storm of horror abated at last. Nelle pulled her hands from her ears, her limbs trembling so hard she wouldn't have been surprised if her whole skeleton rattled apart. She tried to rise but couldn't, so she remained where she was while a painful, expectant sort of silence rang in her ears.

Summoning what small dregs of courage remained to her, Nelle crawled to the cave opening and peered out. She saw a pile of . . . of something. Lying not many yards away. At first she couldn't recognize what it was, couldn't understand what her eyes saw. Then it came to her like a thunderclap: the dog-thing's carcass. A bloodied mass torn apart, bits of skeleton exposed, lumps of flesh strewn across the beach.

Her stomach heaved. Nelle pressed a hand to her mouth, only just stifling the sickness trying to rise. Trembling, she gripped the stones at her side and pulled up onto her feet. Again she peered out through the narrow opening, gazing back along the beach to where the fae man stood.

He was in exactly the same place she'd last seen him, his fists planted on his hips. The wind played through his hair, billowing the dark locks into an ominous storm around his head. He seemed to be looking at the smear that was all that remained of his dog-thing.

Then he took a step in their direction. Nelle cowered back, terrified.

"*Kyriakos!*"

A crisp, clear voice rang out across the beach, carried on the wind. Nelle's heart surged in fear, hope, and surprise commingled. "Soran," she whispered.

Peering from her hiding place, she saw the mage step from the cliff path onto the beach. He wore no robes, only a loose, tattered shirt that did nothing to protect his scarred body from the elements. His hair flowed white behind him, and he raised one arm, his finger pointing at the tall fae stranger.

"Kyriakos," he cried again, "call off your hounds!"

14

It had been many years since Soran set eyes on a Noxaur fae. He'd almost forgotten what strange and awe-inspiring beings they were. The specimen now standing on his beach was certainly impressive. Massive shoulders, flashing eyes, a mouth cruelly curved in a smile that was simultaneously amused and displeased.

The fae lord turned that smile upon Soran and raised one eyebrow in mild surprise.

Soran strode swiftly across the beach, refusing to betray hesitation or fear. He knew how the fae worked. They watched for the faintest trace of weakness to exploit. If he moved too carefully, it would be read as trepidation, a trait despised among fae nobility. He must brazen this out, threaten far more force than he could actually muster.

"Ah!" said the fae. He made no effort to speak above the wind, but his mellifluous voice carried effortlessly to Soran's ears like the thrum of a deep bass string. "A mortal. How quaint. Tell me, how is it you know my name?"

Soran halted and drew himself up straight. Instinct told him to salute, to bow, to make some form of obeisance. But that was a mortal instinct and one he hated, one he had long fought to suppress. He would not grovel to the fae.

"It is well known that Lord Kyriakos of Ninthalor governs this territory of Noxaur beneath the shadow of the Twin Peaks," he said, meeting the fae's eyes without blinking. "It is also known that he is forbidden from stepping foot beyond his lands by order of King Maeral Noxaur himself."

"Indeed," the lord responded with placid indifference. "But it would seem your island has floated into my waters. Which makes you the invader and not I." He smiled a catlike smile of subtle viciousness. "Tell me your name, mortal, and I may yet choose to treat you as a guest rather than an enemy."

Soran knew better than to give his name to a fae, and he could see by the look in Kyriakos's eye that he fully expected a refusal. Yet, if he wasn't careful, the fae lord might declare him discourteous and use it as an excuse to mount a full attack. His shadowy subjects standing on the beach behind him and lining the decks of his three boats looked ready for a fight. There were far too many of them for Soran's sadly depleted flock of wyverns to handle.

He drew himself up straighter than before. "I am a Miphato of the Evenspire, a mortal mage," he said. "And this is Roseward Isle. No doubt you have heard of it even from within the bounds of your internment."

The fae's nostrils flared slightly. "Roseward," he said slowly, almost purring the name. "Yes, I have heard of the mortal island cut loose from its world and set adrift on our Hinter Sea. You are under a curse, are you not, mortal mage?"

"I am cursed by King Lodírhal Aurelis," Soran responded. The words were bitter on his tongue, but he spoke them as a protection. "I am serving the sentence imposed by the crown of Aurelis for my crimes against Eledria."

Teeth flashed in a brief grimace, the only betrayal of feeling the fae offered. He could not provoke Lodírhal without bringing the wrath of Aurelis down on his head. His own king would make no move to protect him.

For some moments they stood in a tense, contemplative silence. Then Kyriakos waved one hand in a calculatedly dismissive gesture. "I have no interest in Lodírhal's games," he said. "I merely wished to investigate this intrusion upon my shores. And now, mortal mage, you owe me restitution."

Soran's jaw tensed. "I owe you nothing, great lord."

"Do you not? I presume these spell creatures are of your own contrivance." The fae indicated the sky above them where the wyverns circled in ominous watchfulness. "They smell of mortal magic. And you are the only mortal mage present, I trust."

Soran nodded slowly.

"It would seem," the fae continued, "your little spell beasts have amused themselves by shredding one of my hounds limb from limb." As he spoke, he dropped his hand to rest on the head of one of the five remaining monsters. They had crept back in around their master, a formidable pack of *skullars,* ugly and putrid and utterly loyal. They regarded Soran out of dark eye sockets from which gleamed pinpoints of red light.

Soran swallowed carefully, wetting his dry throat, and steadily met the fae lord's gaze. "Your hounds have invaded their nesting grounds. My wyverns have defense spells written into their essence. When threatened, they respond with force."

"And you think my hounds pose a threat?" Kyriakos shrugged and stroked the skullar's head affectionately. "They are curious beasts by nature. If they pick up an intriguing scent, they are bound to pursue it. And I believe they detected a scent most interesting indeed."

A shot of ice ran through Soran's veins. But he couldn't back down, couldn't give an inch. "In our ongoing cycle through the Eledrian realms, we encounter many interesting creatures," he said, maintaining a stoic countenance. "Just yesterday, a massacre of harpens reached our shores. Not long before, we were visited by a unicorn."

Kyriakos's smile twisted sideways into a knowing smirk. "I have no interest in harpens, still less interest in unicorns. However, word reached me within Ninthalor's cold halls that ibrildian magic has been sensed close by. Powerful magic blending the best attributes of mortal and fae gifts. As you may well imagine, such a rumor piqued my curiosity. And when your island appeared upon my horizons shortly thereafter, radiating such a profound display of mortal magic, it struck me as a likely place for an ibrildian to hide. Do you not agree, mortal?"

Soran allowed himself only a single blink. But in that blink he must decide between half-truths or an outright lie. "I have seen no *ibrildia*," he said.

A half-truth, not a lie. After all, he'd put no date on the statement, and he truthfully hadn't set eyes on Nelle yet that day.

Kyriakos opened his mouth, and a red tongue protruded, dampening his full lips. Light from the struggling sun above flashed on a wolfish fang. "But you are familiar with the term, are you not?" he said slowly. "In your own language, I believe, you call them *Hybrids*. Strange, dangerous creatures, outlawed by the Pledge itself. If one were to come within your purview, it would be your solemn duty as a servant of the Pledge to report its existence to the nearest authority." He pressed a hand to his heart, long fingers splayed across his bare skin. "As master of this region, it is *my* duty to protect Eledria. And, as I said, you owe me for the death of my hound. A single word of information, and I will consider your debt paid."

"I owe no debt," Soran answered firmly. His head spun with subtle pain, and he realized Kyriakos had been working a spell through his words. He would not fall for such a trick. With an effort of will, he persisted. "You came to my shore without invitation and set your creatures freely roaming. My wyverns, sensing a threat, defended what is theirs and their master's. There is no debt. Indeed, if you return to your ship even now, I will consider this discourteous interruption of my privacy forgiven and send no word to Lodírhal."

Kyriakos's eyes narrowed slightly as he considered the validity of this threat. How likely was it that Lodírhal had left means for his prisoner to contact him in case of invasion? The King of Aurelis was fiercely protective of all that he deemed his. How much value did he place in a single mortal prisoner serving out a curse sentence? Certainly not much, but . . . how much was Kyriakos willing to risk?

Soran waited in tense expectation, watching these questions play across the fae's stern features. The shadowy figures standing behind the lord shifted on their feet, responding perhaps to the tension in their master's spirit. A single word, a single thought from him would put them in motion.

One of the skullars snarled. Another barked and took a lunging step.

"*Zivath!*" Kyriakos snarled, and Soran's heart stopped. Then, with a gasping breath, he realized the fae had uttered a command for retreat.

The skullars backed away, hackles raised, bony spines bristling. Though every step was reluctant, they turned, one after another, and loped up the gangplank onto the deck of the foremost boat. The shuffling among the shadowy servants stilled, and at another sharp command from their master, they filed onto the boat and made ready to pull out once more.

Kyriakos remained where he stood for some moments, holding Soran's gaze. His eyes burned with frustration but not with defeat.

"Very well, mortal," he said at last. "We'll say no more about it for now. But if another report of *ibrildian* magic reaches me before you have gone from Ninthalor territory, I will not hesitate to protect my people and my realm."

Soran nodded once, slowly.

With one last flash of a sharp white fang, the fae lord turned about. His silvery garments billowed behind him as he returned to the gangplank and strode up to the deck of his boat. He assumed position at the prow, watching Soran while his servants pulled up the gangplank and the last few remaining shadow-beings hauled the boat back out into deeper water, then scrambled like bizarrely jointed monkeys up dangling ropes to the deck.

Soran took care not to drop his gaze, not to shift his stance until the three boats turned and sailed away, until Kyriakos was finally out of sight. Even then he stood for some time, watching the black sails until they disappeared beyond the line of darkness into the Kingdom of Night.

"What are they saying? Can you hear?"

Nelle started at the sound of Sam's voice so close to her ear. She hadn't realized he'd crept around the boat and behind her to peer over her shoulder.

"Hush!" she growled. For once in his life, Sam didn't argue or make a joke out of the situation. That alone was enough to tell her the danger hadn't passed yet, not by a long shot. He remained close at her back, a solid, warm presence. She had to stop her shivering body from leaning back against him for comfort. Sam could offer no real comfort, after all. He was helpless here on Roseward. It was up to her to protect him, to protect them both.

But what about Soran?

She watched the mage as he stood opposite that tall fae lord. The wind was too rough for her to discern more than a word or two here and there. She heard Soran speak the name *Lodírhal* and saw how the fae lord reacted to that name. His aggressive bearing shifted almost imperceptibly into a defensive stance. This gave Nelle hope. Soran wasn't wholly outmatched by this powerful being. She saw the fae indicate the bloody remains of the skull-dog, and he seemed to be making demands of some sort. But Soran didn't back down.

Why had the fae come here to Roseward anyway? Mere curiosity? Or had he heard rumor of the Rose Book and the Noswraith spell contained therein? No, it couldn't be that. Noswraith magic was mortal magic, which no fae could either create or control.

Perhaps he merely came to make certain Roseward posed no threat to him and his. If that was the case, the wyverns hadn't helped their cause.

Nelle grimaced but cast a grateful glance to the sky above where the wyverns circled in threatening patterns. She owed them her life. Again. That skull-dog would certainly have torn her and Sam to pieces.

At that thought, she felt almost unconsciously for the spellbook inside her satchel. Would it be wise to go ahead and create a spell now, while the fae was distracted? Those shadowy beings lurking in the shallows and along the decks looked ready for a fight. Silveri was unarmed. He would be overwhelmed in moments, slaughtered before her eyes.

Nelle's jaw hardened. She couldn't let that happen. She couldn't just quiver in terror and let him face those monsters all alone. She pushed back the satchel flap, began to slide the spellbook out.

Suddenly, the fae lord barked a strange word: "*Zivath!*"

Nelle's heart leapt, certain he'd called for attack. But no . . . first the skull-dogs, then the shadowy beings retreated up the gangplank. The fae lord stood firm a few moments longer before also turning and marching back to his craft.

"Seven gods!" Sam breathed. His hand closed on Nelle's shoulder, trembling hard. "They're going. They're really going!"

Nelle glanced back at him. "Is the danger past?"

Sam winced and clenched his teeth, momentarily undecided. Then he nodded. "We're not . . . we're not exactly *safe*. But we're not in immediate danger."

Nelle breathed a sigh of relief and looked out again, watching the longboats pull away from the shore. Her heart, which had been racing wildly since the moment she laid eyes on those wretched sails, calmed somewhat, sinking from her throat back into her breast where it belonged. Gods willing, the fae was gone for good.

Him and all his ugly dog-things.

Suddenly aware of just how cold she was, Nelle tucked her spellbook back into the satchel and wrapped her arms around her body. More than anything she wanted to get out of this wretched damp cave.

But Mage Silveri continued to stand there, apparently impervious to the icy wind, watching the boats sail back across the channel toward the darkened shore. The rising sun gleamed bright on his head, making his hair seem whiter than ever, but Nelle could not catch a glimpse of his expression from her current position.

"Who is that?" Sam asked after a little while. He was shifting and stamping uneasily, his boots splashing in the shallow water on the cave floor. "Is it the cursed fellow? The crazy Miphato everyone says lives here?"

Nelle grunted, feeling strangely reluctant to say anything more. Sam was not supposed to be part of her mission or her dealings with Mage Silveri. His question, though perfectly natural, felt intrusive.

Besides, Soran wasn't crazy. Taciturn, yes. Temperamental, undoubtedly. But not crazy. At least, not particularly so.

"He certainly sent those sinister fellows packing, didn't he?" Sam continued. "Must be one powerful magician, that's all I've got to say."

"Yes," Nelle hissed. "And he'll send you packing just as fast, so if you don't want to row back out into *that*"—she waved a hand to indicate the shadowed water of the Hinter Sea—"you'll shut your mouth."

Sam obliged her and held his peace. He also continued holding onto her shoulder, his fingers pinching harder than she liked. But she was so cold, she lacked the will to shrug him off.

They remained in that attitude until, at long last, Soran turned from the sea and walked to the cliff path leading up to the lighthouse.

"Spitting heavens, I thought he'd never leave!" Nelle breathed and sank back against the cave wall, out of Sam's grasp. She ran her hands down her face, then pushed wild locks of hair back over her shoulders. "We've got to wait a bit. The island's not that big, and I don't want to run into him as we go."

"As we go where?" Sam asked. "I hope you've got someplace with a fire in mind. And maybe a little something that'll fill an empty stomach."

Nelle peered up at his face by the light coming through the cave mouth. His tone was easier than it had been, but the hollow circles ringing his haunted eyes were still deep. They stood close together, the upturned boat taking up most of the narrow space, and Nelle felt the sudden urge to wrap protective arms around him as though he were a child. It was a strange sensation and one she quickly fought back.

She glanced around the cave, wishing she dared leave Sam here for the time being. It wouldn't be that hard to fetch food and maybe a couple of blankets from Dornrise, make him a sort of camp.

But what if Roseward remained close to Noxaur's shores for days on end? Sam couldn't stay here, exposed to that darkness. She had to spirit him away to somewhere he could hunker down until they passed back into safe waters.

She would have to take him to Dornrise.

Every cold, shivering step of their trek across the island, Nelle expected to run into Mage Silveri. She was as jumpy at the prospect of meeting him as she would be of meeting another harpen massacre or even the dark fae lord from the beach.

The most frightening moment was reaching the top of the cliff path, where she knew they stood in full view of the tower windows. If Soran was up there, one chance glimpse would be their undoing.

"Come on," Nelle urged, grasping Sam's hand. He panted from the exertion of the climb and didn't move as fast as she wanted him too. Where was the spry and boundlessly energetic Sam of the old days? His journey across the Hinter Sea had drained him.

She didn't dare take the cliffside path she ordinarily used when traveling to and from the great house. Instead, she cut into the same grove of pines where Soran had sought shelter from the harpens the day before. The moment they were under the sheltering branches, Nelle breathed more easily. Maybe they would make it after all.

Roseward wasn't big enough for her to worry about getting lost. Neither Nelle nor Sam, Wimborne children born and bred, was comfortable in forests, but they were both snatchers by training and knew how to move silently when necessary.

Only once did Nelle stop short, her heart in her throat. She tightened her grip on Sam's hand as her ears strained, listening again for the sound she had half heard: *"Miss Beck? Miss Beck, can you hear me?"*

She felt Sam's eyes on her and glanced up quickly to meet his gaze. He raised an eyebrow. "Is that the Miphato?" he whispered.

She nodded.

"He sounds . . . worried."

She could think of nothing to say, so she nodded again. Then, "Come on!" she urged, and tugged his hand.

The sound of the mage's voice faded away; he was moving away from their current position, away from Dornrise. Sam was quiet now, but he wouldn't be able to hold his tongue forever.

Sure enough: "So, exactly how friendly have the two of you become over these last two years?"

Nelle rolled her eyes and dragged him onward. "It ain't been two years. Not for me. Just a bit over a week. And Silveri ain't a bad sort, really."

Sam snorted. "High praise, coming from you. I didn't get a good look at him down on the beach. Is he handsome?"

"No," Nelle answered, maybe a little too quickly. She hastened to add, "He's cursed, you know. And scarred up real bad. Not a pretty sight."

"He must be old too," Sam mused, his fingers tightening around hers slightly. "This island's been haunted for going on twenty years if I remember the stories rightly. He's got to be ancient. All that white hair . . ."

Nelle bit her tongue to keep from pointing out the obvious: Hadn't they just acknowledged that two years for Sam had been not even two weeks for her? Soran Silveri had lived on Roseward for a long time, but what did that even mean? He'd aged, yes, and he'd changed. But he wasn't old. Not by a long shot. She couldn't pretend he was exactly *young* either. More sort of . . . ageless.

When they came within sight of Dornrise, Nelle, pushing through a curtain of low branches, breathed a sigh of relief.

Sam whistled softly behind her. "If that hulking place ain't haunted, I'm a spitting boggart," he said.

"It is haunted," Nelle answered. "Just not by ghosts. Hurry up!"

"Wait. Nelle!" Sam let her pull him along, but his feet dragged as they hastened across the open space to the tumbledown gates. "If it's haunted, why are you taking me there? Ghosts or no ghosts, I don't *do* hauntings. The idea gives me the shudders."

"Use your fae blessing," Nelle said, trudging on doggedly. "Does it feel dangerous to you?"

"Well . . ." Sam was silent for a moment before finally admitting. "Well, all right. It feels safe enough."

"It is safe. Enough. At least until sundown."

She hurried him down the path, painfully aware of how exposed they were on all sides. If Soran had returned this way, he could spot them at any moment even from a good distance.

But they reached the shelter of the overgrown brambles without impediment, and Nelle hastened along the narrow trail through the tangle to the kitchen door.

"Glad you know where you're going," Sam muttered. "It's like a bloody nightmare around here!"

His choice of words sent a shiver down her spine. Nelle glanced back at him before dropping his hand and pushing the kitchen door open. She stepped into the shadowed space and beckoned Sam in behind her. While she forced the door shut, he stood looking around the cavernous kitchen.

"Drafty, ain't it?" he said, pulling the folds of her velvet cloak around his shoulders.

"There's kindling and fuel aplenty." Nelle gave him a push toward one of the big ovens. "Go get it lit. I'll find food."

Sam looked as though he wanted to protest, but his fae blessing must have continued to reassure him, so he nodded and did as he was told. Nelle hurried to the larder, glad for a few moments to herself, however brief they would be.

She needed an excuse, something she could tell Soran to explain her absence from the lighthouse all morning. The larder made the best sense. She could tell him she'd wanted to stock up their supplies for while they barricaded themselves into the lighthouse over the next few days. It was a feeble excuse, she knew. He'd think her a right fool, running out and risking another encounter with harpens all on her own, but . . . well, he didn't think her the brightest candle as it was, now did he? She could pass it off as thoughtlessness, shrug, and bat her eyes. If she played the part well, he wouldn't ask too many questions. She hoped.

She hadn't brought anything to carry food in, but she

crammed what she could into her satchel along with the book and quill. As always, there was a fresh loaf of bread in the breadbasket, but she took that for Sam, along with a few sausage links and a handful of dates.

By the time she stepped out of the larder, Sam had managed to get a small fire going. He grinned up at her as she approached. "You look a bit ghostly in this light," he said. Then his eyes fastened on the bread in her hand.

"Here." She tossed it to him. "It ain't cursed or nothing. Eat up."

He needed no further urging. While he tore into the loaf, she built up his fire and made a flat place among the embers. Then she found a pan and set the sausages on to cook, passing Sam the dates to keep him occupied until they were ready.

Only after she'd turned the sausages did she stop to think about the smoke currently traveling up the oven chimney. Would Soran see it from the tower?

"You can't keep this fire going all day," she said, speaking over her shoulder. "But you can stay here until sundown."

"And you'll stay with me?" Sam asked around a mouthful. He was sitting on the floor close to the fire, one hand full of dates, the other still clutching the end of the loaf. "Boggarts, Nelle, you don't mean to leave me alone in this old tomb, do you?"

She cast him a quick glance. Using a fold of her skirt to protect her hand, she pulled the pan off the fire. After setting the sausages aside to cool, she started breaking the fire down. "I can't stay. He'll keep searching until he finds me, you know. He might be on his way here even now."

Sam's face hardened. He set the bread down on his knee and gave her a penetrating stare. "Didn't you once tell me you don't belong to no one?" One eyebrow slid up his forehead. "Sounds to me like this Miphato owns you."

"He ain't like that," Nelle snapped, glaring at him. "He's not Cloven or Gaspard, he's just . . . He's gonna be worried. You saw those monsters on the beach this morning. Roseward ain't safe right now."

"Is it ever safe?" Sam leaned toward her. He set aside the last of the bread and reached as though to take her hand again. "I want to help you, Ginger. I risked everything to get here, to bring you Mage Gaspard's message. And I want to help. When it's safe to travel again, you're coming with me. We'll get whatever it is you were sent for. Between the two of us we can manage one mage, I'm sure. And then we'll—"

Nelle stood and backed away from him quickly. "I'd like my cloak back, Sam."

He gaped up at her. Then, shutting his jaw with a snap, he worked the clasp at his throat, unslung the folds of velvet from around his shoulders, and passed them to her. He started shivering almost at once, but for the moment she didn't care.

"Feel free to wander about," she said as she donned the cloak. "Find a blanket or something. Get some rest. I've got to get back to the lighthouse now, but I'll return before sundown."

"And if you don't?" Sam asked, one eyebrow upraised.

Nelle drew a long breath. "If I can't get here in time, you got to get yourself out. Go down to the harbor—you'll see it from the cliff's edge. There's a bunch of old buildings there. Take whatever food you can find with you, blankets and such. And . . . and try not to go to sleep."

He frowned up at her, pale and strained in the half-light making its way through the briar-choked kitchen windows. Then he stood and reached a hand to her. His face was so unlike the old Sam she'd once known, it wrung her heart to see it.

"Don't go," he said. "Stay with me. Please."

But she shook her head. "I've got to. It's the only way."

Before he could catch hold of her, before he could utter another word of protest, she grabbed her satchel off the nearest worktable where she'd dropped it and hurried to the door. She ducked out into the tangle of brambles, pulled the door tightly shut behind her, and prayed to all seven of the gods that Sam would have the good sense to listen to her, just this once.

15

When Soran spied that wild red mane in the distance, his heart surged in his breast. He'd walked almost all the way around the island and was half convinced that Kyriakos had found the girl and spirited her away while he fruitlessly hunted high and low.

But no. No, there she was, approaching him on the cliff path with the hood of her fur-trimmed cloak blown back and her hair streaming behind her. Was she an illusion? Was she a dream conjured by the Thorn Maiden or his own half-mad mind?

"Miss Beck!" he called out.

She lifted her gaze, which had been fixed on her own feet, and offered him a wave and a smile. It was so incongruous, so ridiculous, it could only be real. He surely couldn't dream such a thing.

Biting back curses that were more like prayers of gratitude, he ran toward her up the path. He had not stopped to don his robes before leaving the lighthouse, and the wind flayed through the thin fabric of his shirt. He hardly felt it. A warm flush of relief mingling with fear and anger heated him from his core.

He sped across the stretch of ground between them, and as soon as he was close enough to see her features clearly, barked, "What do you think you're doing?"

"Well, good morning to you, too," she answered with a tilt of her head and shrugged one shoulder, indicating her satchel. "What does it look like I'm doing? I've just been up to the great house, and—Oi! What is this?"

He had grabbed her arm, rougher than he intended in his haste, and dragged her off the path into the shelter of the trees. "Have you taken leave of your senses?" he growled. "Did you not see Noxaur on our horizon? Did you not realize where we've come?"

"Yes, I saw," the girl answered, twisting her arm in a vain attempt to escape his grasp. "I saw it. Of course, I saw it. And I thought you'd probably lock us down indoors for the next few days, and I knew we was running low on tea. I don't know about you, but I don't want to be trapped in that one room with your smelly little wyvern for days on end without a proper brew to be had! So, I thought I'd nip out and—"

"It was foolish. Foolish, Miss Beck!" Soran looked back over his shoulder toward the open cliff top. Who could say whether Kyriakos had spies out on the water even now? Spies who would report back to him about a red-headed mortal girl walking in open view.

"I kept a wary eye out," she muttered, no longer protesting as he dragged her swiftly through the trees. "I didn't see sign of harpens or any other beasties."

Soran growled wordlessly. The lighthouse was not far off now. Once she was behind those doors, the protections ought to be enough to block out any trace of her. He doubled his pace, forcing her to run to keep up with him. She swore and snarled every step of the way, but he scarcely heard her. All that mattered was getting her through that door; all that mattered was keeping her safe.

All that mattered was shielding her for the next two or three days. Then he'd send her home. As he should have done ages ago. He'd send her home, back to her own world and safety. And he'd never think of her again.

A shadow as dark as the looming Noxaur landscape seemed to suffocate his heart. Shaking his head in denial, Soran hurried them both out from the trees and across the last open stretch to the lighthouse door. In a matter of moments, they were safely inside, the girl standing behind him in the middle of the room, panting hard after her run, while he slammed the door and secured the locks.

Then he turned to face the girl and found her glaring furiously up at him.

"I'll have you know, I don't appreciate being manhandled," she snarled. "I ain't a sack of flour to be hauled about."

His mouth too dry to speak properly, Soran merely ducked his head. When he tried to push past her, making for the armoire, she grabbed his arm and pulled hard. She might be small, but there was more force in her grip than he'd expected. He whirled and looked down at her, startled by the ferocity in her face.

"I mean it," she said. "Don't go all silent and broody and bullspittin' *protective* on me. Tell me what's going on! What's got this fly up your snout? Tell me, or by all the boggarts and brags, I'm marching out that door again and finding out for myself!"

Soran swallowed hard, the muscles of his throat constricting. She meant what she said. Truth blazed fiercely in her eyes. And what could he do to stop her? Toss her over his shoulder and carry her back inside again? Tie her hand and foot and gag her like some prisoner?

Her fingers trembled on his arm. He could feel the tension reverberating through her body. His gaze sank to that small hand resting on his forearm, so forceful and yet so small. She was brave— Gods above, he knew she was brave!—and she was certainly strong.

But strong enough to face Kyriakos?

"We had visitors this morning," he said slowly, lifting his gaze from her hand to meet her eyes again.

Her expression was hard, unreadable. He couldn't gauge her reaction.

"Right," she said slowly. "Visitors. More harpens?"

Soran shook his head. "The land you see beyond our shore belongs to a lord of the Noxaur realm. One Kyriakos of Ninthalor."

Nelle let go of him abruptly and wrapped her arms tight around her middle. "A fae, huh." Her voice was almost gruff enough to hide the slight quaver. "What did he want?"

Soran hesitated, his hands clenching slowly into fists. But he couldn't hide it from her. She wanted the truth, and he must give it.

"You, Miss Beck. He came to Roseward looking for you."

All color drained from her face. She blinked up at him, true surprise registering in her face, followed by a flash of real fear. It pained him to see it, yet at the same time it was good. She needed to be afraid. She needed to realize what was happening.

But he couldn't tell her all. Not about her Hybrid blood. Not if he was going to send her back to Wimborne in a few days' time. If she remained unaware, she would more likely be able to hide and blend in with humanity as she had before coming to Roseward.

No, he couldn't tell her everything. But enough. He'd tell her enough.

"Kyriakos is known throughout Eledria for his peculiar tastes," Soran said slowly. "He is a . . . collector, of sorts. It is said that within the walls of Ninthalor he has accumulated a harem made up of women from all different races across the realms. Naiads and nymphs. Faunas and centauri. Even goblins, trolls, and other, stranger creatures. He takes them as his . . . his wives."

She knew what he was going to say next. He could see understanding flare in her widening eyes. But she wanted the truth, so he would give it to her.

He met her gaze grimly, refusing to look away. "Mortals are his favorites."

She nodded. Her lashes flickered, but she stubbornly held his gaze.

"After the signing of the Pledge," Soran continued, "The King of Noxaur commanded Kyriakos to give up the mortals from his collection. He refused. The resulting conflict cost many lives, including those of Kyriakos's mortal wives and all of their children."

All his *ibrildian* children—powerful Hybrid magic-users, whom he had shaped into a lethal fighting force. It had required all the power of the five Eledrian kings and queens to bring them down. But these details Soran kept to himself.

"Since that time, Kyriakos has been curse-bound to his lands, where he will remain until his king sees fit to pardon him. But within his territory he governs uncontested, a sovereign in his own right."

Nelle's mouth opened, her lips parting softly. After some silent moments she managed a little, "Oh." Dropping her gaze, she looked around herself, blinking hard. "Oh," she said again and tottered to the table, pulling out a chair and sinking into it. Her shoulders hunched, the folds of her cloak draping heavily like leaden weights. She propped an elbow on the table and sank her head into her hand.

Soran stepped closer. He wanted to reach out to her, to take her hand. Instead, he planted a fist on the table and leaned heavily against it. "Please forgive me, Miss Beck." His voice was hoarse with emotion he could not wholly suppress. "I should never have let you stay here—"

"Will you shut your big flapping mouth?" she snarled and glared up at him over her fingers. "*I'm* the one who insisted on staying, remember? And I ain't sorry about it neither, so don't you get apologetic at me now. Just tell me what we've got to do to keep this, Kyr—Kyria—this fae fellow from coming back."

Soran blinked and withdrew from the table. He shouldn't be surprised. Did he really expect the girl to crumble in tears and terror? He had yet to see her anything but ferocious in the face of danger.

But that very ferocity could get her in trouble.

Without a word he turned and moved to the armoire. Flinging the doors open, he knelt and rummaged inside among the spellbooks, searching for a particular volume that ought to contain the work he needed. He felt the girl's gaze on his back as he crouched on his heels and flipped through a little green book, scanning the spells it contained.

"What is that?" she demanded.

He cast her a quick glance and went on turning pages. "A precaution, Miss Beck."

"What kind of precaution?"

He didn't answer. In the middle of the book he stopped and studied a spell more closely. Then with a nod he stood, shut the armoire, and moved across the room to the front door.

As though reading his intention, Nelle sprang to her feet. "What are you doing?" she growled.

He re-opened the book, lifted the spell to eye level, and began to read it off slowly. But before he'd gotten three lines in, the girl crossed the room, grabbed his arm, and yanked his concentration away. The faint spell traces, only just beginning to come to life, faltered.

Soran cursed and glowered down at the girl, who met his glare without flinching.

"Is that a lock?" she said through gritted teeth. "Are you

locking me in?"

"I am making certain that the lighthouse is secure against potential invasion."

Her fingers dug into his arm. "You've got locks and spells and enchantments running all up and down this place. I can sense them, you know. They're all as strong now as they ever were. You don't need more locks."

"I think perhaps I do."

Her mouth screwed up into a tight knot, as though she fought back the string of vicious words springing to her tongue. She drew a long breath and let it out slowly, her nostrils flaring.

When she spoke at last, her voice was low. "You can't do this. You can't make me your prisoner."

Her words were like a blow to the gut. Soran almost staggered. "That . . . is not my intention."

"You can't lock me in and call it protection," she persisted. "You can't." Fire seemed to light her pale eyes, hot enough to burn him. "I don't *belong* to you."

The little bit of magic sputtered out. Soran's hand trembled. The spell itself was compromised, but if he turned to it now he might yet be able to salvage it. It was only a temporary lock, after all. Just until Roseward had bypassed that dangerous shore, just until Nelle was safe again. It was for her own good.

But he could not ignore that look in her eye.

If he locked her in against her will, how was he any better than Kyriakos?

He must trust her. He must trust her, or else . . .

Soran snapped the book shut and yanked his arm free of her grasp. He turned to face her fully, crossing his arms over his chest. "Very well, Miss Beck," he said, his voice dangerously soft. "But know this: If you step outside this door, you risk everything. Your life, your freedom. Everything."

She opened her mouth, but he didn't wait to hear what she would say. He pushed past her, stormed across the room to the stair, and hastened on up to his solitary chamber. Anything to get away from that accusatory gaze.

Anything to hide from her an awareness of the peril he had so recklessly led her into.

Nelle simply stood there, arms wrapped around her middle, trying to keep her shivering body from breaking apart. Her ears strained after the mage's retreating footsteps until long after they'd faded from hearing. And still she stood in silence, her mind numb, her heart pounding.

After what felt like hours but was possibly only a few minutes, she whispered, "Bullspit."

What was she supposed to do now?

At least she wasn't locked in. That was something. She whirled around, her hand reaching for the doorlatch, but froze before she touched it. Was she really going to rush from the lighthouse again with Soran's warning still ringing in her ears?

He takes them as his wives.

Mortals are his favorites.

She closed her eyes. But that was no good. In the darkness behind her eyelids she saw again that powerful form she'd glimpsed on the beach—that strangely beautiful creature with his purple-tinted skin and midnight hair. To be taken by such a man, enslaved . . .

No. No, that wouldn't be her fate. Soran had driven the fae from Roseward, hadn't he? If she stayed indoors behind all these shielding spells, they would soon be safe again. It was only for a couple of days.

But what about Sam?

She clenched her teeth and opened her eyes again, staring at the grain of the wooden door. "He's safe for the time being," she whispered, trying to reassure herself.

Come sunset, however . . .

She shook her head and softly cursed as she turned to face the room. Her gaze chanced upon the wyvern perched in the rafters over the table, its long tail dangling and twitching like a snake. It blinked big eyes at her and burbled softly. She made a face at it.

"I'm gonna have to wait until nightfall." She spoke the words out loud as though to convince herself. "I'm gonna have to wait until I know he's working on the Noswraith spell, when he won't be spying out of windows at me. It's the only way."

Since coming to Roseward, she'd been outside of the lighthouse only once after sundown. On her first night. A night she could not recall without shudders of horror. The Thorn Maiden had come close to catching her in her briary snare.

Nelle set her jaw. She wasn't so helpless now. She knew what she was up against. And she had powers of her own, however untrained they might be. Besides, while Soran worked the binding spell, the Thorn Maiden could only manifest in the realm of nightmares, couldn't reach the waking world.

"So, you stay awake," she said. "You stay awake, and you don't let yourself be tricked this time. Then, once you find Sam, you get him down to the harbor and keep him awake too."

If they stayed together and kept their heads down, they might be able to avoid the Thorn Maiden throughout the night.

And the next day? When Soran discovered she'd ventured out of the lighthouse? When he started asking questions she couldn't answer?

She'd just have to deal with that when the time came.

16

It was a long, dismal day.

Around noon, the wyvern crawled down from its perch in the rafters and bullied Nelle into making it a meal. Though she grumbled through the entire process, she was grateful for something to do. She cooked up a pot of oatmeal, seasoning it with cinnamon until the aroma filled the whole dark chamber. She hoped the scent would rise to the tower above and lure Silveri back down.

But though she strained her ears for the sound of his footsteps above, he never stirred.

"Bullspit," she growled and set the whole pot of oatmeal on the floor for the wyvern. When she pulled a chair to the wall and stood on tiptoe to peer through one of the high windows, she couldn't see much. Just the dark expanse looming on the horizon.

How long would Roseward linger in proximity to the Kingdom of Night? Days? Weeks? Hours?

Too long. No matter what, too long.

"Bullspit," With another deep sigh, Nelle sank down from the window to sit on the chair, leaning her back against the cold stone wall, and dully observed the wyvern, who was hard at work licking the copper pot clean with its long, nimble tongue. At first she found the sound annoying. But as it went on and on, she found herself lulled by the rhythmic scrape, scrape, scrape. Her head nodded, sank to her chest . . .

She woke with a start, blinking hard. How long ago had she nodded off? The wyvern, bloated from its feast, lay snoring on the hearth beside the mostly dead fire. It looked contented, while Nelle was chilled to the bone.

She sat up straight, twisting her neck back and forth. Then, groaning, she stood up on the chair and peered out the window again.

Her breath caught in her throat.

The darkness had closed in since last she'd looked. The harsh foreign shore loomed so near, the narrow channel couldn't be much more than a mile wide, if that. The shadow of the Kingdom of Night swept across Roseward, blacking out the sun.

Would this darkness bring the Thorn Maiden out to prowl earlier than usual?

Was there still time to get to Sam?

Nelle sprang off the chair. Her knees shook so hard, they almost folded beneath her as she landed, but she braced herself and managed to remain upright. The wyvern started awake at her sudden movements and uncoiled from its ball of sleep, lifting its bleary-eyed head to growl at her. Nelle paid it no heed, rushing to the table where she'd dropped her satchel to hastily dump out the few things she'd taken from Dornrise's larder, the empty spellbook, and her quill. Flipping the spellbook open to the first available page, she lifted the quill . . .

And hesitated.

She'd promised Soran not to work magic while so close to Noxaur.

But spell writing wasn't the same thing as spell conjuring. She could write down the spell without calling any magic to life and have it at the ready should need arise. What else could she do? She couldn't venture into that darkness without a weapon. Not with lascivious fae lords, bloodthirsty Noswraiths, and who knew what else stalking the island.

She wrote quickly. Too quickly for precision. But she'd not been precise yesterday either when she called the spell-sword to life. Her desperation had driven her creativity, and the result had been most effective. She was just as desperate now, and she thought— she *hoped*—the spell taking shape under her pen would do the trick. Soran would sigh and lift his gaze to the heavens at the sight of her splashed ink droplets and shaky lettering. But this wasn't Soran's spell, was it?

She wrote on, ignoring her splotches, ignoring her misspellings. The deeper she went into the spell, the less she cared and the more she simply let her inner energy guide the pen. Her vision shimmered around the edges as though she peered into another world, a strange, glowing world full of possibilities. All she had to do was reach inside and capture those possibilities on the page. Not with accuracy, but with a sort of energetic clarity. Like passion, like poetry. Like the sensation of falling.

At the end of the third page she stopped, breathing hard, then sat back and looked at the messy scrawl she'd just created. With a little snort, she shook her head and pinched the bridge of her nose. Scattered throughout her crude sentences were occasional Old Araneli words—words she'd unconsciously picked up during her work with Soran. Strange that she would choose them. Yet, when she skimmed those raw, disastrous sentences, she was surprised to feel a compelling sense of truth. As though the foreign language had permitted her to express her thoughts more completely than her own language would.

Maybe she was picking up a little proper sorcery after all.

None of that mattered so much as the spell itself, however. She lifted the book and immediately felt a tingling in her fingertips. There was certainly magic here, just waiting to be set free. If the time came, she should be able to call it to life. If not . . .

She wouldn't worry about that. Not yet.

Nelle closed the spellbook and tucked it and her quill back into her satchel. The wyvern, watching her from the hearth, uttered a questioning chortle. "I know," she said, making a face at the little beast. "I know. But I don't have a choice, do I?"

When it flared its crest and lowered its head back between its two wing-claws, red embers from the low-burning fire reflected in its overlarge pupils.

Nelle slung her satchel over her shoulder and drew her cloak tight. Casting a last glance the wyvern's way, she warned, "You stay quiet now, you hear?" and stepped to the door.

Over the last week she'd become much more sensitive to magic, or at least more aware of what it was she sensed. Now she could feel how potent the protection spells on the lighthouse really were. And as the fae darkness closed in, the spells intensified.

What awaited her on the other side of that protection?

Steeling her resolve, Nelle reached for the latch, flung the door open, and stepped out into a darkening world with a strangely split sky overhead. Noxaur darkness now covered the lighthouse, as deep as nightfall. But not far off she could see the distinct line where the shadow had not yet reached, where daylight still held sway over Roseward.

Nelle pulled her hood up over her head, shut the door firmly, and set off at a run toward the nearest trees. At any moment Soran might look out his window; she must take cover as quickly as possible.

Once she gained the safety of the treeline, however, she began to regret this decision. Under the dense boughs it was intensely dark. Her eyes had always been unusually adept at absorbing whatever light was available and expanding on it to clarify her vision. Mother had told her she was fae-blessed in this way. Now she stumbled, staggered, and fumbled along, almost blind. Was this how ordinary people felt after nightfall? She'd never once thought to bring a light . . . but then, she hadn't reckoned on the depths of this unnatural Night.

At last she spotted brightness ahead—she'd caught up with the daylight! With inexpressible relief she picked up her pace, then nearly screamed when light blazed into her dark-adjusted eyes. She could only stand still and hiss curses while waiting for the bright sparks behind her eyelids to stop dancing.

But the dark crept in behind her. She couldn't delay.

A subtle slithering sensation crept down her spine. Nelle looked back over her shoulder into the nightfall forest. Were those vines she saw slinking along the forest floor? No. It must be her imagination toying with her again.

She focused ahead, clutched her skirts and her satchel strap, and ran.

Dornrise was still bathed in sunlight when she made her way through the tangle of briars. Though she refused to look back again, she knew night was closing in fast. She burst through the kitchen door, calling, "Sam!"

Something moved in the shadows beneath one of the tables. Nelle's heart jolted, then settled back into its proper place again when she heard the familiar voice answer, "Is that you, Ginger?"

"Oh, thank the seven gods you're here!" she gasped, pulling the door mostly shut behind her as though to block out the coming darkness. The kitchen was gloomy enough as it was, with only one briar-choked window admitting a single stream of sunlight.

She hurried between worktables and fell on her knees beside Sam, who was bundled up in what looked like a bit of velvet curtain, rubbing his eyes with the heel of one hand. Apparently she'd woken him. Just in time.

"Get up, Sam," she said, reaching to catch hold of his arm. "We got to get moving. There's no time to delay."

Sam's face broke in a huge yawn. "What's the rush? Didn't you say I had until sundown? It can't have been that long, I only just nodded off—"

"Use your sense, idiot! This ain't your world anymore, remember? The rules of sunup and sundown don't always apply."

He smothered his yawn and met her gaze, frowning. Then his eyes widened just a fraction. His fae blessing was at work: He sensed danger.

"Get up!" Nelle growled again and scrambled to her feet. As she turned to face the mostly shut door, she saw on the floor the little triangle of sunlight that shone through the opening.

And she watched it go out. Suddenly and completely.

"Nelle?" Sam's voice quivered in the dark beside her.

They had to get out. Now. Or they'd be trapped in the Thorn Maiden's snare.

Without a word to Sam, Nelle sprang for the door. Her hip bone struck one of the worktables, making her gasp with pain, but she staggered on. Feeling her way blindly with outstretched arms, she forced each step, expecting grasping branches to wind her in an irresistible embrace at any moment.

"Nelle?" Sam called again behind her. "Hey, Ginger, are you there?"

Her fingers touched wood paneling, and a whimper of relief burst from her lips. She felt along quickly, searching for the door, searching for the latch. But she couldn't find it. She couldn't find it!

Nelle forced herself to stop, to take several long breaths while leaning heavily against the wall. The door was there. She knew it was there. She'd left it open, and she hadn't heard it shut.

Setting her jaw, she ran her hands along the wall more slowly, more methodically than before. She found the latch. When she tried to turn it, it wouldn't budge.

Slithering movement brushed against her ankle.

Nelle staggered back into the first of the worktables. "Sam?" she said quietly. "Sam, where are you?"

Terrible silence answered. She could hear nothing but her own breathing.

Then, finally, "It's awfully dark, Nelle."

She choked on a little shuddering breath of relief. She wasn't alone. He was still there. The Thorn Maiden hadn't dragged him away. If they stayed together, they still had a chance.

"Sam, I'm going to . . . I'm going to work some magic. Don't scream, and don't ask me questions. I don't have time for that."

Another long silence followed by a meek, "Sure thing."

Flipping open her satchel, Nelle hastily pulled out her spellbook. "Boggarts," she muttered as she opened it to the hastily written sword-spell. How was she supposed to read it in this dark? She cast around and saw a faint hint of light coming from one of the great ovens. The last smoldering of the fire she'd cooked sausages on hours before? It would have to do.

Hurrying to the oven, she knelt and held out the book so that the dim glow fell upon its open pages. Something gleamed on her thumb. Surprised, she looked again more closely, then uttered a little, "Well, spit in my eye!"

It was the ring. The little spell ring Soran had made for her more than a week ago now. Though it was a little large for her thumb, it had remained in place, invisible for the most part and completely unobtrusive. But the magic in it was still good.

She pinched her dry lips between her teeth. Should she summon the mage? If the Thorn Maiden was here, he was the only one who had a hope of stopping her, of containing her.

But if she summoned him, he would find Sam. And that would be the end. Of everything.

She had to do this herself.

Pressing the book open, Nelle bowed over the pages, her vision straining to make out the words. Why, oh why had she written in such a chicken scratch? This was why precision was so important to a Miphato's art—so that when the crisis came, he could read his own bullspitting work!

Footsteps approached behind her. "Nelle?" Sam's voice quavered.

"Hush your mouth!" Nelle snapped and began to murmur the words, recalling from memory what she couldn't actually see. Within a few lines she felt the magic working, felt the connection of power between her spirit and those scrawled characters. The *belief*, for want of a better word. The conviction, even the confidence.

The hilt of a sword appeared in her hand. She grasped it tightly and read on until a spark of light flickered on the blade. The spark ignited, and flames leapt to life.

"What in the boggart blazes!" Sam cried.

Ignoring him, Nelle focused on completing the spell. The final few lines were easier to read by light of the fiery blade. She secured the magic, like tying a series of small knots to hold it in place. It wouldn't last long; she could feel how weak her bindings were. Soon they would unravel, and the spell sword would disintegrate in her hand, its shimmering essence returning to the *quinsatra* from which it came.

But maybe it would last long enough.

Nelle rose and turned to face Sam. She held the sword low, trying not to look too intimidating. Light from the flickering flames danced across Sam's features, shining in the whites of his round eyes.

"Don't be scared," she said quickly and held out her free hand to him. "I've been studying magic since I got here."

"Yeah." Sam nodded, his jaw sagging. "Yeah, so I gathered. Boggarts, Nelle, give me a little warning next time!"

She shook her extended hand. "Come on," she said. "We've got to find a way out of this house. Hold onto me, and whatever you do, don't let go."

He looked as though he would protest. His throat worked hard, his Adam's apple bobbing in a convulsive swallow. Then he reached out, threaded his fingers through hers, and allowed her to pull him around the worktables and make for the stairway at the back of the kitchen.

Nelle held the sword out before them like a lantern. Just beyond the edge of its glow, she thought she saw slithering movement in the darkness, but that may have been her imagination. The Thorn Maiden couldn't manifest in the waking world. Soran had been clear about that. Not so long as he maintained the bindings.

But why did it feel so very real?

Sam muttered and cursed behind her as she led him up the stair to the main floor above the kitchens. In the doorway, Nelle paused and swung the sword first one direction, then the other, trying to decide which way to go. Something down the righthand passage gleamed, catching her eye. She lowered the sword and peered through the gloom.

It was a light. A small red ball of fire.

A rose in flames.

"No," she whispered.

Nightmarish memories filled her head of that first night on Roseward when she'd fallen asleep in the Dornrise library. There had been burning roses then too. And when she'd followed them . . . when she'd followed them . . .

"This way!" she growled, and yanked Sam after her, turning down the left passage. "Quick!"

"Did you see that?" Sam said, his voice weirdly soft and dreamy. "I thought I was imagining things. But it was real, wasn't it?"

"No. It's just a dream." She gave his arm a tug, wrenching him around to face the way they ran. "Stay awake, Sam! Stay with me."

She hurried down the passage until suddenly she saw another

flickering light ahead. A waft of burning rose perfume drifted through the shadows, tickling her nostrils. Quick as thought, Nelle darted down another hall, dragging Sam after her. They continued this way until she saw another light and quickly made another turn to avoid it.

This turn led them to the magnificent front foyer and the stairway. Their shoes echoed hollowly against the marble floor, and Nelle raised her flaming sword higher, trying to illuminate the cavernous space. The light glittered against a gold frame.

Despite herself, Nelle's eyes were drawn to meet the pale gray gaze of that young man's portrait. For a shocking instant she thought it was real, thought he was truly alive, truly present, looking down on her with such grave disappointment. The instant passed, however. The image in the firelight resolved back into mere paint on canvas.

A shudder rolled down Nelle's spine. Something was wrong with that picture. She took several steps, letting Sam's hand slip from her grasp. Tipping her head back, she peered up, holding the spell-sword high.

A single long gash cut across the canvas, slashed across the young man's throat. In the firelight, the paint around its edges seemed to drip like blood.

"Nelle!"

Startled, Nelle turned, swinging the sword. Sam stood in the center of the foyer, pointing back the way they had come. She looked.

"Bullspit!" she growled.

The hall was full of flaming roses. Dozens and dozens of roses springing from vines that climbed the walls and crawled along the ceiling. More vines crept out into the open space of the foyer, reaching for the support pillars.

Nelle dashed back to Sam's side to grab his hand. She took three steps toward the other side of the foyer but stopped short. That passage was filled with roses as well, their flaming petals brilliantly illuminating the undulating briars creeping along the floor.

"What do we do?" Sam choked.

"This way." Nelle yanked him toward the stair, running up the center to the landing. There she tried to turn right, toward the library, only to see more vines and roses spill over the top edge of the steps like water pouring down a cliff.

She turned to the left instead, and they raced to the passage above. This was the way to the private family apartments. It was dark and silent—no roses, no sound of slithering, no creak of branches.

A partially open door caught Nelle's eye, and she dragged Sam through it. He leapt inside, and she spun around, pushing the door shut. She pressed her ear against the panels, listening.

Nothing. No slither. No insidious whispers. Nothing.

Breathing out a sigh, she turned to face Sam, holding up her flaming sword again to look at him. He stood a few paces away from her, breathing hard. Beyond him, she could just see the outline of a large four-poster bed and other shadowy hints of fine furnishings. But the light from her spell seemed to strike only his face, illuminating him in a warm glow. Dark strands of long hair fell across his forehead, and the borrowed shirt he wore was open down the front, all the ties undone, exposing the hard muscles of his chest.

The sight made Nelle's pulse throb. But not with fear.

She frowned. Something was wrong. She shouldn't be feeling this way, this rush of heat through her veins, this sudden giddy lightheadedness. She was afraid, she knew she was. Afraid of the nightmare on the other side of the door, afraid of the darkness overwhelming Roseward, afraid of . . . afraid of . . .

She couldn't remember . . .

Her hand holding the sword shook. The spell shivered.

"Nelle," Sam said. His voice was low, thick with emotion. He took a few quick steps toward her, his hand sliding around her waist. "At last," he said, his face hovering just above hers. "At last, at last."

Nelle tried to speak, tried to protest. But when his mouth lowered to hers in a hard, bruising kiss, she shivered and dropped the spell-sword, which landed with a clatter at her feet. Her arms wrapped around his neck as he pulled her against him.

The scent of roses filled her head.

17

She was coming.

He could feel the swelling power of her draw near.

Soran stood at the west window of the lighthouse, gazing out across the cliffs to the looming shadow. Night crept ever nearer, many hours sooner than it should. With a curse on his lips, he turned to his desk and took a seat.

The Rose Book lay before him, ready and waiting. Almost taunting in its perfect stillness. He rested his hands on the straps holding it shut but did not open the cover. Not yet. Not just yet.

Would he be able to survive the coming battle? It was one thing to reinforce the spell every night. He had time then between sunrise and sunset to recover before the Thorn Maiden rallied for another assault. But with the Night of Noxaur falling across Roseward, would she ever relent?

He tried not to let his mind drift to Nelle down in the chamber below. He couldn't let himself be distracted. He had to trust that she would heed his warnings. That she would remain inside the lighthouse protections.

Darkness drew a sharp, harsh line across the floor of the tower chamber. Soran recoiled at the abruptness of it and quickly shook his head to clear his thoughts. He must prepare. He must focus.

After first setting candles at the ready in their wooden bowls, he turned his attention to the Rose Book. His hands trembling, he undid the straps and flipped open the cover.

The Thorn Maiden stirred.

He felt her deep in her realm. The writhing, powerful mass of her responding to the Night. He felt her pleasure as she stretched out her many limbs, testing her strength. She sensed opportunity, and she wouldn't miss it. He must be quick and ruthless with his spell-craft if they were to have any hope of survival.

Bowing to his work, Soran called the words to life. His spirit, unbound by physicality, connected with the physical construct of those written characters, those ideas captured in ink. And in the space between, magic radiated to life, burning up from the page.

But something was wrong.

He sensed the wrongness almost immediately, before he'd made it through even the first page of the spell. The magic was there and as strong as ever. But somehow the Thorn Maiden wasn't reacting to it as she should.

He reached out with his spirit perceptions, trying to find her again. He'd felt her near when the darkness first closed in. But now that Night had fallen in earnest, he couldn't sense her. He reached further, searching through the forests of Roseward, along the cliff edges, but still felt nothing.

He reached further still, and . . .

As his awareness crept to the edge of Dornrise, he found her. A snarled knot of power concentrated around the old house.

"*Helenia!*" he called out in spirit, trying to catch her attention.

She made no response. Something had captured her interest so completely that she had no attention to spare for him.

Soran blinked, bringing his concentration back on the Rose Book spell before him. The words flared with life and power, and the magic shimmered in the air before his vision. But it wasn't working. Something was different. Something interfered with the magic.

What could he do? He felt the Thorn Maiden crawl out of her own nightmare realm, creeping into this level of reality. Not completely, but one strand at a time. If he had use of his hands, perhaps he could find a way to bind her anew, write new layers of complexity into the spell. But as he was . . .

Soran drew a deep breath, his nilarium-crusted fingers curling into fists. "I'll have to fight," he whispered.

It could work. If he took the strongest of his spell weapons with him, he could battle the Thorn Maiden's physical manifestation and drive her back into the Nightmare Realm where she belonged. Then he could complete the binding and hold her. At least for a few hours.

But once those weapon spells were used up, that was that. He would be helpless the next time she broke through.

What other choice did he have? He'd known this day was coming, sooner or later.

But why must it be now? When more than just *his* life was at stake . . .

Soran read on through the Rose Book until he reached the end of the fifth page. There was no point in trying to finish it, not yet. Not until he'd driven the Thorn Maiden out of this layer of reality. He put a temporary hold on the spell so that the magic didn't unravel. If he were quick, he should be able to pick up where he'd left off.

Closing the book, he fastened it shut, then tucked it into the front of his robe. He dared not leave it behind, for he would need to complete the binding the moment the Thorn Maiden retreated. He pushed his chair back and crouched before one of the boxes tucked away under the desk. Inside were books—beautiful books, exquisitely bound in tooled leather, not the schoolboy's volumes he kept stashed away in the armoire down below. These were his greater spells.

Many of them were already used up, spent, but there remained a handful of spells he'd been saving for just such a time.

He picked up one volume and quickly paged through it. He knew which spells he wanted. How many times had he reviewed this scenario in his head, trying to mentally prepare for the battles he knew would come? Using great care, he tore two strong spells free of the binding. Folding these, he tucked them into his robes alongside the Rose Book.

Then, pulling his hood over his head, Soran rose and made for the stair. The weight of coming battle on his spirit bowed his shoulders as he descended with quick steps. He didn't even think about Nelle until he neared the opening in the ceiling. There he paused for a moment, one hand pressed against the curved tower wall, and listened. He expected to hear sounds from the chamber below, some indication of her presence.

All was silent.

His heartbeat quickened. His nostrils flared.

Lunging down the last stretch of the stair, Soran emerged through the ceiling and peered into the chamber. The wyvern sat by the door, its wings slumped dejectedly, its long neck coiled back, and its beady little eyes fixed on the latch. It looked around at Soran, uttering a miserable bleat.

"Seven gods damn!" Soran sprang down the last steps into the room. What was she thinking? What was she damned well *thinking?* Had she heard nothing of the warnings he'd given her? What could possibly have possessed her to venture out into that Night?

Something was wrong. He couldn't put his finger on it, but neither could he deny it. She was up to something. What, exactly, he couldn't begin to guess. But she wasn't stupid, he knew that well enough. She might sometimes play the flighty-headed waif, but he had seen through that act long ago. He knew how keen, how sharp a mind she possessed. She wouldn't act rashly without some motivation.

She was out there. Alone.

While the Thorn Maiden inched her way into this reality.

"Get back," Soran snarled as he shoved the wyvern away from the door. It scurried away to hide under the table, burbling miserably. Soran pulled the door open and gasped at the blast of pure Night waiting outside. Darker than the darkest midnight, all but impenetrable.

Cursing, he shut the door again and hastily crossed to the armoire. He needed a seeing spell to help him navigate that darkness. He grabbed a book and hastily paged through until he found the spell he needed, then held it up and forced his voice to be steady as he read it off: "*Ilrune petmenor. Mythanar prey sarlenna sior . . .*"

Reaching the end of the spell, he let his eyes close. There, behind his eyelids, he saw the Nightmare overlaying Roseward. It was dark, but with a different kind of darkness than the Night of Noxaur. This was a cold, shimmering darkness, full of energy and dread. There was no color, no life. But he wasn't blind here. He could navigate this world.

Keeping his physical eyes shut, Soran placed the little book inside his robes alongside the Rose Book and the two weapon spells. The wyvern uttered a sad little bray as Soran moved to the door. Pausing with his hand on the latch, he looked back to meet the creature's eyes.

"I'll do what I can," he said. "I promise. I'll bring her back."

Then he stepped outside and faced the world.

Seen through the rippling nightmare vision, Noxaur's shore

looked dangerously close. The waters of the channel were harsh and lethal. But even with his eyes lit with spell vision, Soran could perceive no detail on that landscape—no cities, no towns, no indication of life. It was nothing but darkness. A realm of monsters.

Monsters like Kyriakos.

Repressing a curse, Soran hastened along the cliff path. Harsh winds blasted his robes, whipping his hood back across his shoulders and snarling through his hair. He tucked his head down and ran all-out. Around him the nightmarish semidarkness of the Noswraith's world simmered with malice, but he wasn't *in* that world. He could perceive it, but nothing dwelling within could perceive him save as a faint, flickering shadow. He took care not to look too closely at any slithering, crawling thing on the edges of his vision, focusing instead on his destination—on Dornrise, high on its promontory above the sea.

Would Nelle be there?

He reached the ruinous gates of the great house and plunged on up the drive. The labyrinthine brambles of the overgrown roses seemed to shiver and hiss and tremble as he passed through them, but they made no move against him, and he saw no active sign of the Thorn Maiden.

She was near, though—he felt her presence, awake and eager.

He navigated the narrow path through the brambles to the kitchen door. When he tried the latch, it wouldn't give. Living vines had grown around the latch and hinges, fastening it shut with a force like stone.

Soran stepped back, studying the vines. He couldn't break through them in his own strength. He'd have to use one of his spells.

Reaching into the front of his robes, he withdrew one of the folded pages torn from his book, unfolded it, and studied the words in the weird half-lit gloom of the nightmare realm. It was a powerful incantation and should be enough for the purpose he required.

"*Dilaren vamnal,*" he read softly. "*Rel arrea nomot malar.*"

The words burned to life on the page, brilliant, almost blinding. He flinched but kept reading through to the end, his mind and soul melding with the written words to draw magic into physical reality and shape it according to his will.

Long, curved, razor-sharp claws sprang from the tips of his nilarium fingers. He nearly cried out at the sudden shooting pain, but that might break the spell before it was complete. With an effort of will he read on to the end, finishing the spell. It should last—for a little while, it should last.

The spellpaper crumbled and fell to the ground in a pile of drifting dust.

Facing the door, Soran drew himself up straight. Pain throbbed up his fingers beneath the nilarium coating, pulsing along his arms and through his shoulders and neck to burst in the back of his head. But transformational spells were always painful. Pain simply meant the spell was working.

With a snarl, he ripped through the vines as if they were cobwebs. At first the briars hissed and shivered and tried to fight back, fresh tendrils shooting out to replace those torn apart, but soon enough they retreated under the assault, skittering away along the wall.

Soran grabbed the doorlatch again and entered the kitchen.

Nelle lay in a mound of skirts in the middle of the floor.

His heart lurched to his throat and lodged there, unable to beat. He stood in the open doorway as though turned to stone, all life, will, and strength drained out of him. Then, with a flooding surge of energy, he sprang forward, leaving the door open behind him, and rushed to her, collapsing to his knees. He reached for her, only just remembering his spell claws in time to pull back before they tore into her soft flesh.

"Peronelle?" His voice was almost inaudible. Was she breathing? He couldn't tell. Placing his hands on either side of her, he lowered his head to her chest, listening for a heartbeat. At first he couldn't feel one, but . . . there! There it was! Thin, but present. She was still alive.

He drew back. His fingers gripped the floor, claws tearing into the stone. "Peronelle," he said again. "Can you hear me? You must wake up!"

She wasn't there. Her body might still be alive, but she herself was not present.

She walked somewhere in the Noswraith world.

But the Thorn Maiden hadn't gotten to her yet. A quick inspection of her limbs told Soran as much. He found no wounds, no slicing cuts. She was whole, for the moment at least. He had to find her. Quickly.

Gathering his courage, Soran rose. As he turned toward the door, he spied something lying on the ground not far away. A book. One he recognized.

"No," he breathed. "Please, no!"

He lurched across the room and crouched over the little volume lying beside one of the big empty ovens as though dropped there. It was the blank spellbook. When he turned it over and paged through it, he saw the used-up remnants of a spell.

Maybe it wasn't what he thought. Maybe she hadn't done it, hadn't foolishly used her magic despite all his warnings.

He looked back at the girl lying several feet away. She probably didn't realize she was dreaming, didn't realize she'd left her physical body behind.

Soran stood, flexing his claw-tipped fingers. It was already too late. The minute Nelle began to work that spell, the ripples of Hybrid magic would have carried across the *quinsatra*, striking the senses of all those on alert to detect such a peculiar strain. Kyriakos would be on his way already. He might even now approach Roseward's shore, coming to claim his prize.

But none of that mattered if the Thorn Maiden got to her first.

Swallowing a snarl, Soran left Nelle behind on the floor and headed for the stairs.

18

This is wrong! This is not what you want!

The voice exploded deep in the back of her mind, demanding attention. Nelle heard and understood but . . .

But she couldn't quite bring herself to believe it. Not with Sam's arms wrapped around her, not with his lips pressed hungrily against hers, not with her fingers tangled in his dark hair. Everything in her body responded to his touch like fire racing through her limbs. Her heart pounded wildly in time to his as she tilted her face to kiss him again and again. His hands moved to the clasp of her cloak, unfastening it and slipping the folds of velvet from her shoulders to land in a pile on the floor. Her fingers reached under his loose shirt, exploring the hard muscles of his chest and abdomen.

Sam uttered a groan and, before Nelle could brace herself, scooped her up off her feet. Her head spun wildly, and she clasped her arms around his neck as he carried her to the bed. The world around them was all shadows, darkness.

This is wrong! her mind shouted again, deep down inside. *This is wrong, this is wrong! You're in danger!*

Danger . . .

Her heart jolted, and she tried to struggle. But Sam laid her down on the bed and climbed on top of her, the weight of his body pressing her down. He kissed her again, and his hands moved, caressing her body, exploring the shape of her waist, her hips, hiking her skirts. She felt his cold fingers slip along her knee, her thigh.

"Sam!" she gasped and pushed him away, desperately trying to catch her breath. "Sam, what are you doing?"

"You want me," he breathed. His voice was rough and strange. It hardly sounded like the Sam she knew. And his face, was that truly Sam's face hovering above hers in the dark?

"No, Sam," she said firmly. Her fingers tightened on his shoulders. "Not like this. Not like . . ."

She shook her head, looking past him, looking around the room. Where were they? This wasn't the lighthouse. This wasn't . . . were they in Dornrise? She couldn't remember. It was all a blur, a strange, nightmarish blur. She tried to draw a steadying breath. Her head swam with the stink of roses.

Roses . . .

He lowered his head, kissing her jaw, kissing her throat. His hand moved further up her thigh, fingers eager and icy against her skin. "I see into your mind," he whispered. "You want me. And I will claim you—"

With a cry, Nelle grabbed hold of his head, her fingers digging into his skull. She gave a sharp wrench.

Something cracked like dry sticks.

With a quake that rattled the whole bed, Sam collapsed on top of her. He was lighter than he should be, not at all the sturdy, muscular frame she'd just been admiring. With a shuddering cry of terror, Nelle pushed him away, scrambled free, tried to climb off the bed, to find her feet. Thorns tore at her dress, at her skin. She fell backward onto the floor, staring at the mounded body sprawled on the bed above her.

It was a mass of twisted limbs. Living, twining thorns, swiftly gathering. The body twitched, jerked. Pushed upright.

Sam's face turned to look down at her. Only it was a face not of flesh and blood but of rose petals.

False! Faithless!

The voice hissed from the dark slash of his mouth, not Sam's voice anymore but a woman's, husky and soft and full of poison.

I know what you are. A pretty liar who will turn his head, turn his heart, and leave him broken when you are through!

Fear tried to paralyze her limbs, but a brush of slithering vines against one hand was enough to jolt Nelle into action. She wrenched around, searching desperately. Her spell-sword. Did it break? Did the magic fall to pieces when she dropped it, or . . . no! There it lay by the door. Pushing onto her hands and knees, she lunged for her weapon, but her knee caught on her skirt, and she fell flat on her face, one arm outstretched.

Something slithered up her ankle, bit into the flesh of her calf.

With a scream, Nelle made another lunge for the spell-sword. Her fingertips brushed the hilt, and she stretched her arm so far the joints strained. Perhaps her very will pulled it toward her, for somehow, miraculously, her fingers wrapped around the grip. The blade, which had dulled to a mere shimmering glow, flamed brilliantly to life, the spell revived.

Another cry, harsher than the last, burst from her throat. She rolled around and sliced down hard, cutting into the branch clutching her leg. There was a hiss, a shriek, and the thing that was shaped like Sam fell back against the bed, its many-fingered hands grasping the bedclothes, shredding the old embroidery.

Overhead, roses bloomed in clusters and burst into flame, illuminating the chamber in a hellish red glow. By that strange light, the figure of Sam contorted, the branch limbs pulling and constricting, the petals of the face undulating until it was no longer Sam who stood up to full, towering height.

It was the woman—the beautiful woman who had once lived in this room. The woman whose dress Nelle even now wore.

Nelle pulled her feet under her, pressing her back to the wall and holding the sword out in front of her with one hand. Her other hand scrambled for the doorlatch, but she touched thorns and quickly pulled away. More branches crawled along the floor, reaching for her. She swung the sword and sliced through several limbs, but more poured in to take their place.

The Thorn Maiden approached, hips swaying gently beneath

her blossoming gown. The bizarre, beautiful face twisted in a cruel smile as she lifted one hand, her finger pointing. From the tip of that finger a twining vine shot out, stretching toward Nelle. Nelle swung the sword, but the vine twisted away and continued to wind through the air straight for her.

It slid around her neck, pulling a delicate chain out from where it was hidden under the bodice of her gown.

Thief, the Thorn Maiden said, holding the gold locket up at the end of the chain. The clasp dug into the back of Nelle's neck. *Do you truly think you can steal a love like his as easily as you steal these trinkets?*

Nelle's gaze fixed on that little locket, bright as a star in the light of those burning roses. She'd almost forgotten about it in the madness of the last few days. Her secret poison, her deadly weapon nestled close to her heart.

The Thorn Maiden's vine toyed with the chain, coiling around it. Nelle feared she would yank it free. But could she? Surely this was a nightmare, and if so, the chain was merely an image, not a reality. The physical necklace was somewhere else, somewhere with her unconscious body . . . wherever that was . . .

Eternity is a long time, the Thorn Maiden whispered in a voice of shushing leaves and dry branches. *He may be yours for a moment, but he will be mine forever. And there's nothing you can do to change that, little mortal.*

Nelle gasped as thorns climbed out from the wall and wrapped around her waist, tore into the fabric of her gown, dug into her flesh. She pulled away and slashed with the spell-sword, but the Thorn Maiden reached for her from behind.

Come into my arms. Embrace me.

"Bullspit, you hag!" Nelle cried and spun about, swinging the sword hard. The blade sliced through branches and blossoms and flames alike. Sliced through the thin neck holding up that strange rose-petal face.

The head toppled and fell in a mass of writhing vines. The body stood for a moment, swaying, headless.

Then it erupted in a mass of branches shooting out at Nelle like tentacle arms. They wrapped up her limbs, grasped her waist and torso, and tore into her flesh. She lost the spell-sword somewhere in that swarm, but it didn't matter. In an instant, she was too tightly bound to use it. Blood streamed from every part of her body, and her bones cried out as the thorny branches began to pull, pull, pull, stretching her out into a star shape, ready to rip her apart.

It was only a dream. A nightmare.

But it was too real.

Nelle screamed, her voice cut off as roses stuffed into her mouth, down her throat, choking her.

Suddenly, a crash shook the whole room. The door fell from its frame, crushing thorns and roses beneath it. Something stepped through, a shadow that flashed with crackling magic.

It seemed to look directly at Nelle.

The next moment, magic flashed in curving strokes, tearing at the branches and vines, ripping the roses out from her mouth.

Nelle sank to the floor, suddenly released. Her body was a mass of bleeding wounds, and every bone had strained to the point of breaking. She staggered and nearly fell.

The shadow caught her. For a moment she pressed her face into Soran's strong chest and breathed in the smell of him—parchment and ink and salty sea air. Fresh and clean and totally blocking out the stink of roses.

His voice rumbled in her ear: "Peronelle, you're asleep. Go, find your living body. You left it behind you down in the kitchens. You've got to find it and wake up. Quickly!"

Nelle pulled back and saw only shimmering shadow again. But it was Soran. She was sure of it. Soran, but in the waking world. Her arms, which had wrapped around him tightly just a moment before, now couldn't hold onto him.

Peronelle! It was his voice again, but so far away, echoing across worlds. *Peronelle, find your body! Go!*

Movement writhed across the floor around her. Jolting upright, Nelle saw the many limbs of the Thorn Maiden reassembling in the darkness. Here and there, roses bloomed and burned again.

She fled. Out through the door, out into the hall. Briars crawled across the walls, but she raced through them, her footsteps pounding hard.

Soran stood in the bedchamber, his eyes closed, seeing with spell vision.

He knew this room. He knew it all too well. That bed with which he had become so familiar on many dark, furtive nights of stolen embraces. That vanity where he had watched his paramour sit and arrange her hair across her bare shoulders, sending him teasing smiles in the mirror until he could not resist climbing out from the bed and catching her in his arms once more.

The Thorn Maiden gathered her broken parts, reassuming her womanly shape, and took her seat at that same vanity. *My love,* she whispered, her voice a soft, stirring breeze. *How close we are tonight. Another few steps and I will be in your world. Then what wonders we will create together!*

As she spoke, her thorny limbs melted away, becoming soft supple flesh. She sat naked on the stool, her shapely legs crossed, her bosom covered only by a large bouquet of roses clutched in her arms. Hair fell in a black curtain down her back, rippling softly as she turned to look at him over her shoulder.

"Do you not prefer me this way?" she said, her eyes flashing at him from beneath thick dark lashes. "Is this not how you first envisioned me?"

The heady perfume in the chamber played upon his senses, luring him to believe the dream that had too quickly become reality. Soran braced himself and raised his hands, spellclaws flashing.

"I've not come to play, Helenia," he growled, taking a step toward her. "I've come to send you back where you belong."

She did not flinch at his approach. She lifted her chin, exposing her long throat even as he reached out for her. The razor claws flashed, but he hesitated to tear into her. It was one thing to rip apart the briars of the Thorn Maiden, but this . . . she . . . she looked so like that image in his memory. The image of perfection he had so long treasured and abhorred.

Dropping the cluster of roses to fall at her feet, she stood facing him. Her voluptuous body shimmered in the light of burning roses.

"I belong with you, my love," she said. "In this world, together. Eternally yours." She reached for him, her hands gently cupping his cheeks, drawing his face down toward her lips.

If he didn't act now, he would lose all will.

With a savage cry he ripped into her chest, claws tearing down through flesh, through branches, through thorns, down to the burning-rose heart. He wrenched it out and crushed the blossom in his fist until black, ink-like blood dripped through his fingers.

She stared up at him, her mouth parted in anticipation of a kiss.

Then, without a word, she melted away, the dream, the reality, the thorns. All turned to smoke and gossamer, fading out of this reality and retreating into the deeper Nightmare where she belonged.

Soran opened his eyes.

It was dark in the chamber, shrouded in Noxaur's Night. But he remembered where Helenia had once kept her candles. Feeling his way along the furniture, he found the drawer, withdrew a candle and a box of matches, and struck a light. Holding it high, he searched the room for any sign of the Nightmare intruding upon reality. But all was as it should be. The bed was perhaps a little mussed, and there might be a few new gouges in the walls and floor. No vines. No roses.

Soran found a candleholder and set the candle in place. Then, drawing the Rose Book from his robes, he opened to the place where he'd left off the binding spell. There was no time to waste. The Noswraith would soon recover and start looking for another opening. He had to finish the binding now.

The thorns and roses vanished before Nelle reached the kitchen.

She breathed a sigh of relief and allowed her pace to slow somewhat. Soran must have somehow stopped the Thorn Maiden, must have bound her back again. Otherwise, surely those horrifying vines would already have caught her and resumed tearing her apart.

She trembled and staggered, blood flowing down her arms and legs and chest. Which was strange. Why should she bleed if she was, in fact, disembodied? Hadn't she experienced a dream something like this before? But it had gone very differently. Her first night at Roseward, she'd floated through these very halls in a shapeless, bodiless state, and though the Thorn Maiden tried to catch her many times, she had been uncatchable.

Why was it different this time? It was as though the dream had seeped into reality, making even her dream-self more solid than it ought to have been.

Nelle shook her head fiercely. None of that mattered. She *wasn't* truly bleeding. And she wouldn't accept it.

She closed her eyes, bowed her head, and concentrated with everything she had—concentrated on forcing the hundreds and hundreds of cuts lacing her body to disappear, for the blood to dry and flake away to nothing. At first, her spirit-self resisted. Then, like a cramped muscle suddenly relaxing, it gave up. The pain eased and finally ended entirely.

Nelle opened her eyes, looked down at her body, and saw everything as it should be—her lacerated limbs whole, her shredded gown mended. Even the gold necklace was hidden back under her bodice where it ought to be.

She breathed out a sigh and continued along the dark passages of Dornrise. She still needed to find her physical body and somehow wake it up. Then she needed to find . . . to find . . .

"Sam!" she gasped and pressed a hand to her jolting heart. Where was Sam? If that hadn't been him in the bedchamber, when had he gone, and when had the Thorn Maiden taken his place? Was that him she'd found sleeping under the table in the kitchens? Or had he somehow vanished when the light first went out?

Was he already dead?

Clutching her skirts, she ran as hard as she could, almost losing physical shape in her haste. She darted down the passage into the narrow stair leading to the kitchens, then burst into that cavernous space.

A mounded shape lay on the floor near the middle of the room between two long tables. Was that her body?

Nelle hurried to kneel beside the shadowy thing. She could hardly see it—no wonder she'd missed it earlier when she stepped into the Nightmare. If Soran hadn't told her that her body was down here, she wouldn't believe it even now. But it must be herself. Unless . . . unless it was Sam?

She reached to take hold of what seemed to be a shoulder. Her hands went through it like it was nothing. Strange that she'd been able to hold onto Soran for those few moments. The line between Nightmare and physical reality must still be badly blurred.

Nelle sat back on her heels, resting her elbows on her knees. What was she supposed to do? She had no idea how to wake herself up. How had Soran done it last time?

Popping up onto her feet, Nelle moved to the larder, thinking to grab a bottle of vinegar or some other strong-smelling liquid and pour it over the shadowy mound. Before she'd taken more than a few paces, she heard an echoing sound of footsteps in the stairwell. She turned.

For a fleeting instant, she saw Soran standing in the doorway, robed and white-haired and solid. The instant passed, and he again became nothing but shadow to her perceptions, though perhaps a little more distinct of a shadow than before.

He crossed to the sleeping mound on the floor and crouched beside it. She got the impression he was checking her breathing.

That weirdly echoing voice sounded in her ears again: *Can you not wake?*

"Sorry," Nelle said, moving to stand at his back. "I don't know how to wake up on my own. You did it last time."

What looked like the shadow's head seemed to tilt to one side. Did he hear her? That was encouraging. Maybe. She hurried on: "If you've got something disgusting for me to drink, maybe we could—"

The stillness of the night ripped apart, her voice swallowed in a hideous, ululating howl. Nelle choked and recoiled from the two shadowy forms, staring into the darkness.

That sound hadn't come from inside Dornrise but from out there, out on the island somewhere. Not far off. A sound she'd heard before.

When it sounded again, memory shook her to the core: the skull-dogs.

She looked down at the shadow of Soran, her heart beating wildly. He'd warned her. He'd told her that daring to use her mortal magic would draw the dark fae lord back to Roseward's shores. Yet she'd defied his will, ignored his warnings. And now . . .

What would Soran do? What would he say? Would he curse her for her folly and leave her where she lay? Even as the thought crossed her mind, she watched his shadowy form scoop up the shadow on the floor, seeming to cradle it in his arms. Such a gentle act, though rather peculiar to observe from this layer of reality.

A stab of guilt shot to Nelle's core. Guilt at the lies she had told this man, the danger she had put him through. Shame that he would still try so hard, risk so much to help her.

"Please," she whispered, stepping behind him to rest a hand in the space where his shoulder ought to be. "I'm so sorry. I can't explain it, you see. There's . . . there's things I can't tell you, and I—"

She broke off abruptly as his shadowy form bowed again over the still figure in his arms. A shock went through her body and spirit. She jumped, stepped back, sensation sparking through every limb . . .

. . . and blinked open heavy eyes.

19

Soran staggered down the passages of Dornrise, leaning heavily against the walls for support. His battle with the Thorn Maiden hadn't taken long—mere minutes unless he missed his guess. But the amount of magic it had required was far more than he was used to expending in a single day. And completion of the Rose Book spell had sapped whatever strength remained.

More than anything, he longed to collapse on his knees and slump into a pile of senseless limbs right there on the floor. To sleep for twelve hours without interruption as he'd not slept in . . . he couldn't even begin to guess how long.

"Nelle," he whispered, wrenching upright again, the spelled claws on his hand digging through the plaster on the wall to the wood beneath. He couldn't sleep. Not yet. Not until he found her. Not until he made certain she was safe.

Since the spell-sight had faded, he walked with his physical eyes open. It hardly mattered. Even with the candle he'd taken from Helenia's room, the Night of Noxaur was too intense for him to see anything beyond a few inches in front of his nose. He made his way by feel and memory down the passages to the great front stair, then nearly fell several times during his descent. The candle flame wavered wildly.

Had Nelle found her body? Had her dream-walking spirit made it back through the tangle of the Thorn Maiden's briars to the kitchen? He could only hope the Thorn Maiden had been too distracted by his presence to bother with one flitting little spirit. Had the girl managed to wake herself and flee Dornrise? And if so, had she returned to the lighthouse and its protections or . . .

Or had Kyriakos already found her?

Soran clenched his jaw and pressed on, fear rejuvenating his shaking limbs. He made his way at last to the stairwell leading to the kitchens and staggered down the treads, gasping for breath, his shoulder slumped against the wall. At the end of the stair, he hung for a moment from the doorpost, his chin sagging to his breast.

A flitting something in the darkness caught his eye. A flash of red in the candlelight, a shimmer of pale skirts.

Blinking, Soran looked up, his breath trapped in his throat. Was it the Thorn Maiden? No, it couldn't be. Her bindings would hold for hours yet. Was it Nelle? Was she awake? Holding the candle before him, little caring how the hot wax ran down over his nilarium fingers, he made his way between the work-station tables. Even with the light to guide him, he nearly stumbled over the girl's prone body.

"Miss Beck?" he whispered and knelt beside her, setting the candle on a flagstone to one side. Its light shimmered on her pale face. Still asleep? Or . . . no. She must be alive—she must be! That flickering image he'd glimpsed must have been her spirit-self hovering close. If she were dead, surely her spirit would have sped on its way by now.

He bowed over her just as he had when he first found her here, pressing his ear to her breast. Her heart beat faintly, a distant pulse but stronger than before. He sat up again with a sigh. Her spirit was close.

"Can you not wake?" he asked, looking around the dark room beyond the gleam of the candle. It felt so empty, but he knew it wasn't. Almost he thought he heard an answer. Or not *heard* so much as *felt*. A faint plucking at his mind. Frustrated. Frightened. Irritable.

It was Nelle. Definitely Nelle.

And she obviously had no idea how to reenter her body on her own.

Well, they'd done this before. If he could get her back to the lighthouse, he should be able to wake her safely enough. He bent to scoop her up, taking care not to cut her with his terrible claws.

In that moment, the howl of the skullars ripped the night.

While freezing terror shot through his veins, Soran lifted his head to stare at the partially open door at the end of the kitchen, not really seeing it. His mind's eye carried his vision much farther, out to the stony beach, the dark ocean surf, the narrow channel.

And the looming nearness of Noxaur's shores.

He could almost see the hulls of the black boats propped up on the sand, could almost see dark figures work the ropes and rigging.

He could almost see Kyriakos descend the gangplank, his deadly hounds slavering at his heels, eager for the command to hunt, to harry, to destroy.

They would cut off the way to the lighthouse.

Soran couldn't breathe. His mind went still, the awful stillness of overwhelming horror. There was nowhere safe, nowhere they could run, no place they could hide anywhere on Roseward Isle. They were trapped.

With a snarl he flexed the cruelly sharpened fingers of his left hand, gouging the stone floor. The exhaustion of his recent battle fled in a surge of sudden rage. He wasn't helpless. Not yet.

He reached for the girl, lifting her into his arms so that her head rested against his shoulder. His claws caught in the soft fabric of her gown, but he took care not to touch or cut her skin. Candlelight flickered across her sleep-softened features.

Sitting back on his heels, he hesitated just for a breath. It felt wrong, what he was about to do. As though . . . as though he took advantage of her.

But the cry of the skullars sounded again. Still distant but drawing nearer. He couldn't dither a second longer.

Soran bowed his head and shifted his arm, drawing Nelle's face up to his. Carefully using the back of one clawed finger, he tilted her chin so that her lips parted softly beneath his.

They were icy to the touch. So still, so lifeless. So unlike the softness and warmth he had desperately tried not to imagine over the past excruciating week. But he felt the flutter inside her, a hint of life returning.

He deepened the kiss, gently easing her mouth open. His own mouth felt strange to him, his lips so scarred by the Thorn Maiden's brutal caresses over the years. Once he'd known exactly what to do, how to pull and tease and tempt with sensuous experience. But that was a different life, a different world. A different man entirely.

And it didn't matter. All that mattered was waking the girl.

Her body jolted in his arms. A cold hand fluttered and caught the side of his face, fingers digging into his skin and hair.

Soran pulled back, but she held on tight, keeping his mouth close to hers. For a thrilling, terrifying instant, he wondered if she would draw him back for another kiss. Candlelight gleamed in her eyes, which blinked with startled incomprehension as she stared up at him. Her breath caught sharply, and her lips moved several times before she finally breathed out.

"S-Sam?"

Soran frowned. He tried to pull back further, but her fingers dug in, catching hold of his ear. "Miss Beck," he said, his voice rougher than he meant it to be. "Miss Beck, it's me. Silveri. Can you sit up on your own?"

She gaped at him, her brows drawing together tight, her eyelashes fluttering. Then he saw recognition stir in her eyes. She gasped, let go of his ear, and grabbed his shoulder instead, pushing and pulling by turns in her effort to get out of his arms. He hastily let her go. Almost too hastily. She nearly fell flat, and only her grip on his shoulder saved her.

Who had she thought held her just now? Sam . . . A lover? From Wimborne?

Soran ground his teeth and placed his cold palm atop her hand. A shudder ran along her arm. "Miss Beck—"

The baying of skullars shocked the night, rolling through the air in threatening echoes.

Nelle's eyes flashed to meet his. Her whole body trembled violently. "Is that . . . is that . . .?"

"Kyriakos," Soran confirmed.

She swallowed hard. Her fingers tightened around the handful of fabric at his shoulder. "I . . . I wrote a spell. Called it to life."

"I know." Soran indicated her spellbook lying where he'd dropped it beside her earlier. "And now he's coming. For you."

He rose to his feet, drawing her up with him, one hand resting lightly on her elbow, careful of his claws. She snatched up the spellbook and stuffed it into the satchel at her side. Her eyes flashed to meet his again, frightened, and full of questions she dared not ask.

She wasn't the only one; a whole storm of questions clamored in his head, demanding to be heard. Why had she ventured out to Dornrise against all his warnings? Why had she brought that book with her, obviously prepared to work a spell? What could possibly have driven her to risk so much?

But there was no time.

"Quickly, Miss Beck," he said. "We must barricade the doors."

"We . . . We're staying here?" she quavered. When he let go of her and moved to grab the nearest of the worktables, she swayed heavily, and he feared she would collapse. But she braced herself and moved to help him. "What about the lighthouse?"

"We'd never make it," Soran replied as he hauled the table over to the door, its legs scraping loudly on the floor stones. "The skullars are already between there and us. We'll make a stand here. I will go out and face them. I want you to block the door behind me. The rest of Dornrise is shut down fast. You should make your way deeper into the house, find somewhere to hide. Not the banquet hall—the smell of death will draw the skullars like flies. Perhaps the library or, if you can find your way, the attics. Put as many doors as possible between you and them."

She listened to him in silence until they reached the door. As he moved to step out into the yard, her hand caught his sleeve. "I want to fight," she said. He could hardly see her face, for the candle was behind her, but her voice was tense and trembling, and he could just discern the gleam of her eyes. "I don't want to cower inside like a mouse. I'll stand with you."

He shook his head, tried to shake her hand off his arm. "You are no match for Kyriakos."

She held on fast. "And you are?"

His claw-tipped fingers tensed. That spell was still strong, for the moment at least. How much longer it would last, he couldn't say. The second weapon spell waited inside his robes, ready to be summoned to life. They might be enough. They must be.

But he was weak. So weak. The battle with the Thorn Maiden had taken so much out of him. Would he even be able to manage the second spell?

Soran vehemently shook his head. "As you value your life, you will do as I say. Bar the door behind me. Hide as deep in Dornrise as you can. The Thorn Maiden is bound for the time being, so you will be safe in here. There are old protections on these doors to keep the fae out."

She opened her mouth, prepared to protest. With a quick, lunging step, he caught hold of her shoulder, the edges of his claws just pressing into her skin, sharp enough to make her gasp. He stared down into her face, trying to see her features, trying to get one last look at her. But it was too dark for more than a vague impression.

"Please, Miss Beck," he said. "Please . . . Nelle. For my sake."

Before she could say or do anything more, he forced her back several paces, turned, and sprang through the door. He pulled it hard shut behind him, hoping against hope that she would, just this once, listen to him.

The skullars bayed again. They were close now, sniffing out his scent. They would be at the ruined gates in moments.

Squaring his shoulders and reaching inside his robes for the second of his two great spells, Soran strode through the snarling brambles, out to clearer ground where he could make his stand.

Nelle stared at the door, its slam still ringing in her ears. A faint flicker of candlelight danced on the wood slats but only made the darkness around her feel that much heavier, that much closer.

She lifted one hand, her fingertips unconsciously brushing her lips. They still felt warm. Warm where Silveri's mouth had pressed against hers.

Or was that even real?

She shook her head, blinking hard. It was all so strange, so hazy in her head. Images of thorns and flaming roses danced behind her eyelids but faded swiftly like a dream . . .

The horrifying cry of those skull-dogs shot through her senses again. She clapped her hands to her ears and almost collapsed to her knees. But she wouldn't. She wouldn't fold, she wouldn't cower and quake. Not when Soran was out there, alone against those monsters.

He would be safe if it weren't for her. And now . . . and now . . .

The echo of his warnings resounding in her ears, Nelle shoved her hand into her satchel and pulled out her spellbook and the ensorcelled quill. She wouldn't leave Soran to face those monsters alone. He must think her useless. A petty, foolish girl without a lick of sense in her head. The gods knew she'd given him reason enough!

But if this was the night she died, she spitting sure wasn't going to do it cowering in some attic.

Using the light of the candle to guide her hand, she set to work crafting the spell she had twice successfully recreated. It came more easily this time, even with the baying of those skull-dogs jolting her concentration every so often. Cursing bitterly, she channeled her fear into energy, pulled raw magic from the *quinsatra,* and trapped it in written form.

The baying outside turned into snarling. Vicious, bloodthirsty snarls followed by yowls of pain and rage. Nelle looked back over her shoulder at the partially blocked door. The battle had begun: Soran was fighting for his life even now.

She couldn't hesitate.

Nelle bowed over the spell, jaw clenched, sweat streaming down her forehead with the effort of creation. She dashed off the end of it, her handwriting so imprecise it would surely make any trained Miphato weep. But the energy, the magic—she felt it teeming within those words.

Stuffing her quill back into her satchel, she began to read what she'd written. She spoke aloud, but the hideous sounds from the yard beyond nearly drowned out her voice, and several times she came close to dropping the fragile spell before it could solidify. With an effort of will, she forced her way on until she felt a solid hilt form in her right hand, then continued reading out the strange words until they melded with the magic she'd summoned and became reality.

Bright flame flickered along the spell-sword's keen blade.

Stuffing the book back in her satchel, Nelle turned to the door.

The flaming spell felt oddly comfortable in her hand as she tested its weight. Dread hammered in her temples, but a fierce grin slashed across her face. With quick strides she hastened to the door, yanked the heavy table back, and turned the latch.

The sounds of battle intensified, almost enough to make her rethink her plan. But she had already summoned the spell. She couldn't very well drop it now.

Nelle sprang out into the snarling brambles, her path illuminated by the sword's flames. The briar seemed denser, darker than it had been when she arrived, as though the Night of Noxaur had strengthened its half-rotten roots. She pushed through, yanking her cloak and skirts free of thorns every few steps. Here and there she was obliged to use the sword to cut a path for herself. Its sharp blade hewed through the snarling branches as if they were nothing, and she made better progress. Finally reaching the end of the snarl, she peered out to the clear space between the ruined gates and Dornrise's courtyard.

Soran was there.

Soran, but . . . not Soran.

An aura of magic surrounded him, engulfing his limbs. And the shadowy thing in that shining center hardly looked like the man she knew. His claw-tipped fingers arched in savage silhouette, and blue flames sparked like bolts of lightning from his eyes, from his mouth, from the palms of his hands, sizzling with pent-up energy.

Even as she watched, he pointed one hand at an approaching skull-dog and let off a blast. This was nothing like the bolt-strike he'd used against the harpen a week before. It was more like a scythe of pure magic energy that swung down at the dog and cleaved it in two so quickly, so cleanly that the monster howled and writhed for some while before succumbing to death.

This was sorcery—true sorcery such as Nelle had never seen before.

A spell wrought by a mage with power enough at his command to create a Noswraith.

Nelle hung back among the briars, feeling suddenly very foolish. What use was her meager spell compared to the power she saw before her? Perhaps she should retreat after all, drop the spell, let the magic die, and sneak back through the thorns before he saw her.

Her hand trembled, and the flaming sword flickered and faltered in her grasp, the spell ready to dissipate.

Another skull-dog sprang at Soran from behind. In a single fluid motion, he spun around, slashing with the claws of his left hand. Horrible gashes opened across the monster's throat, but its momentum carried it on until it crashed into him, knocking him off his feet.

The dog wasn't dead. It snarled, choked, gagged, and tore at Soran's chest, trying to get through the folds of his robes down to his throat. Soran thrust a nilarium hand up into the dog's mouth, pushing it back as the savage teeth tore the air mere inches from his face. A swell of magic gathered in the palm of Soran's other hand, but it faltered, faded. Worse still, the claws on his fingertips began to retract slowly, and Soran cried out in pain, either from the skull-dog's teeth or the agony of the spell coming undone.

Two long, low shadows closed in, eyes bright pinpoints of fire, faces gleaming white in the reflected glow of magic. They lunged at the fallen mage, grabbing at his arm, his legs. Nelle gagged on a scream, adjusted her grip on her sword, and took three long strides through the brambles, intending to throw herself into the fray.

"*Zivath!*"

The command rang out in the darkness.

The dogs responded at once, swallowing their growls and backing away from the ragged, bloodied figure lying on the broken paving stones. Nelle recoiled among the brambles, lowering her sword. She didn't mean to . . . She'd meant to rush out into the open, to stand over Soran's crumpled form and brandish her spell in wild defiance.

But something in that voice—something in that shadowy figure approaching through the gloom of night, striding down the center of the long Dornrise driveway—made her knees turn to water. She sank to the ground. The flames of her sword died back, the spell nearly flickering out.

The fae lord moved with smooth unhurried grace, his silvery garments wafting gently behind him. A glow like moonlight seemed to wrap his body, making his every feature perfectly visible even in that deep night. Nelle, much closer to him now than she had been that morning, saw the details of a face perfectly chiseled into an extreme archetype of male beauty.

"Well, well, mortal mage," the fae said as he approached Soran and the crouching hounds. "It seems you have been lying to me, after the fashion of mortals. I shouldn't be surprised, but . . ." He tilted his head, and a long sweep of midnight-blue hair fell across his shoulder. "But I am disappointed."

Soran forced himself up onto one elbow, gasping as he raised his head to peer at the fae lord's face. Nelle's heart lurched at the sight. She covered her mouth to choke back a sob. But he was alive! And his magic wasn't entirely used up. Faint traces of the deadly blue spell shimmered in his hands and eyes.

He spat out a glob of blood and grimaced, his teeth stained with blood. "I've warned you, Kyriakos," he panted. "I've warned you. King Lodírhal will not take kindly to your invasion of his lawful property, nor to your assault upon one who owes him a lifetime Obligation."

The fae lord chuckled darkly and waved a dismissive hand. "I have no interest in meddling with Lodírhal or his playthings. I am here for the *ibrildian*. Don't try to pretend ignorance. I sensed a spark—a very keen spark, I might add—of *ibrildian* magic mere moments ago. It's somewhere near, isn't it?"

Soran coughed again. With a tremendous effort he pushed up onto his knees and sat back on his heels, his shoulders slumped but his head high. "The denizens of Roseward are protected by the laws of Obliga—" he began.

Before he could finish, Kyriakos took three strides, caught him by the hair atop his head, and yanked his chin back. A knife appeared in the fae's other hand, a shimmering, magical thing not quite corporeal but deadly sharp. He touched it against Soran's throat. His smile was cruel and brilliant in the shimmering light of his own illuminated body.

"Enough of this," he said, his voice smooth as music. "I don't care for mortals or mortal games. Tell me where the girl is, or I'll kill you here and now. Let Lodírhal do his worst. Something tells me he won't care about the loss of one petty mortal magician."

Quick as thought, Soran raised one hand, the accumulation of magic suddenly gleaming bright. He aimed it at the fae lord's face. But even as the deadly light bolted from inside him, Kyriakos neatly deflected with one arm, knocking Soran's aim to one side. The blast shot uselessly up into the sky and disintegrated in a shimmer like a thousand tiny falling stars.

Soran sagged and would have fallen to one side if not for the fae lord's grip on his hair.

Kyriakos chuckled darkly and trailed the tip of his knife along his captive's jaw. "You mortals. Such power and yet such weakness. You command more magic in a single spell than most of my folk can imagine . . . but your bodies are too frail to support it! What a curse it must be merely to exist as one such as you." He bent, bringing his beautiful smile close to Soran's face. "You'll thank me, I think, for putting you out of your misery. Then I'll find the *ibrildian* at my leisure. If Lodírhal complains, I'll tell him t'was you who invaded my shore."

Soran's mouth worked, the muscles of his jaw tightening. Then, with a sudden spasm, he spat in the fae lord's face. Kyriakos dropped his hold and withdrew a step, snarling. Then, eyes flashing, he raised his knife, ready to plunge it into Soran's throat.

Nelle was already in motion.

With a roar she lunged from the briars, and flames erupted brilliant and red across the spell-sword blade. Two of the crouching skull-dogs lurched to their feet and threw themselves in her way, but she swung at them wildly, cutting deep into the shoulder of one, knocking the other along the side of the head. Both withdrew with startled yelps, and Nelle charged on, straight for Kyriakos.

She saw the fae lord's eyes widen, flashing like a cat's in the light of her spell. She raised the sword, ready to bring it hewing down straight into his head. Her heart pulsed with a wild, bloodthirsty energy, and she was more fully alive in that one terrible instant than she had ever been before.

Kyriakos's hand darted out, swift as a snake. Even as she brought her sword swinging down, he caught hold of the hilt, his long fingers wrapped around both her hands. The strength of his arm was vastly greater than all the weight she could put into her blow.

For a moment they stood there, frozen. Nelle stared up into eyes blacker and deeper than the night around them.

Then, with a single flick of his wrist, the fae lord wrenched the sword out of her hand. He swung it in a lazy circle of trailing fire. "What is this?" He turned his gaze from the blade to Nelle and back again. "A pretty piece of spell work, though not very . . . convincing."

He did something with his hand—a flick, a squeeze. She didn't see what. But she gasped in sudden sharp pain as her spell dispersed in a single burst of red light. Kyriakos held up his fist, slowly uncurling his long, long fingers. A stream of dust fell from his palm to the stones at his feet.

He looked down at Nelle, and his smile this time was as serene as moonlight. "Well met, lovely maid." To her surprise and horror, he swept a graceful bow, like a dancer. "I have been most eager to meet you. Rumors spread even into Ninthalor of your presence among the realms. When first I heard them, I knew you and I were destined to cross paths."

Nelle stood still, her hands empty, her arms upraised and useless, her mouth slack. His words washed over her, but she scarcely heard them through the thrumming of her own pulse. What a fool she was! What a fool to believe she could stand up to a being like this! What a fool she was to even think about gainsaying his wishes! The thoughts poured through her head, rhythmic and terrible, and a small part of her brain recognized them as a sort of spell, a beguilement.

It didn't matter. She was already lost.

"Kyriakos!" Soran barked, struggling to get to his feet. Two of the dogs lunged at him, grabbing hold of his arms with their massive jaws, restraining him without breaking his skin. "If you take her, you'll breach the bonds of the Pledge. Do you think your king will forgive you this time? Do you think he'll settle for mere exile? You'll bring the wrath of all Eledria down on your head! You'll—"

"Silence." The fae lord reached out one long arm and placed his hand over Soran's mouth, his fingers splayed across his face.

Turning, Nelle watched in horror as the mage's eyes rolled back and he slumped to the ground in an insensible heap.

"No!" she cried, her mind bursting through the coiling strands of beguilement. She tried to throw herself down beside the mage, but Kyriakos caught her arm and whirled her toward him. She landed with her hand against his bare, muscular chest, her head tipped back to stare into those void-like eyes.

"No more of that, pretty maid." The fae trailed a gentle finger along her cheek, her jaw, down under her chin. "You don't belong to him anymore. You're mine."

With that, he pressed two fingers between her brows. Nelle tried to struggle, tried to resist, but darkness overwhelmed her with inexorable finality.

Her knees gave out, and she sank against the tall fae's chest— her last awareness, the eager beat of his heart against her cheek.

20

The coils of Kyriakos's spell wound around Soran's spirit, pulling him down, down, down. He resisted, holding on with everything he had, clinging to consciousness. His body lay in a numb stupor, but he did not fall asleep.

He gazed through dull, ensorcelled eyes and watched Nelle collapse against the fae lord as though all life and will had been suddenly sucked from her body. He watched Kyriakos scoop her up in his arms as easily as though she were made of straw. For a moment, the fae turned and contemplated Soran where he lay, his gaze considering.

A low growl rumbled in Soran's ear. He was too numb even to shiver when the cold bone muzzle of a skullar snuffled along the back of his neck. The beast whined, hungry for blood.

Kyriakos raised an eyebrow, then uttered a short, sharp command. At once the surviving skullars backed away from their intended victim and loped up the drive toward the ruined gate.

The fae lord cast Soran one last look. "My regards to Lodírhal."

The voice echoed strangely in Soran's head, throbbing against his temples. Though he tried to resist, his eyelids pulled like lead weights, and he couldn't support them a moment longer. When at last he managed to wrench his eyes open again, Kyriakos was gone. Kyriakos, the skullars . . . and Nelle.

No!

Soran tried to move, to writhe where he lay. But it wasn't only the Noxaur spell paralyzing his limbs. It was the abuse he'd dealt himself, the extreme overexertion of magic far beyond his ability to sustain. Cramped and strained, his muscles throbbed, and his spirit cried out for rest, for relief.

But he couldn't rest. He mustn't! Once Kyriakos took her from the island, once he crossed to Ninthalor, once she was inside his walls . . .

The boundaries of Soran's prison closed in around him like iron bars clanging shut. His soul cried out in fury and despair, but his sagging mouth could utter nothing more than a faint gurgling groan. He closed his eyes again and sank into the darkness, the oblivion. Maybe Kyriakos's spell was stronger than he'd thought. Maybe it would kill him, take him out of this world.

Soft fingers touched his cheek, caressing.

My poor, poor love.

His soul tensed. He tried to open his eyes again but couldn't. He was truly asleep now.

Instead he raised his spirit, looking up from the prone mortal body to face the Nightmare reality around him, the simmering overlay spread across all Roseward.

The Thorn Maiden knelt beside him. Small, frail. Still bound by the Rose Book spell but present here in the realm of the unconscious. Her thorny fingers were covered in rose petals to soften their abrasive touch. Her face was weirdly almost-human, and perfume surrounded her in a dense cloud.

She looked down at Soran and offered a wan smile so like one of Helenia's smiles that it nearly stopped his heart.

She's deserted you at last. As you knew she would. Deserted you for another man.

Her fingertips caressed his face again, his spirit face this time as opposed to the figure lying in the dirt. She blinked dark leaf eyelids across the empty holes of her eye sockets.

All women are faithless. Is that not the truth you wrote into the core of my being? All women are faithless, save one.

Your perfect dream.

Soran wrenched away from her, stood upright, and strode away from his physical body, making his way to the gate. There he stopped, gazing out over the cliff's edge to the dark shore of Noxaur. Already it looked farther off than it had been. Were the currents of the Hinter drawing Roseward onward and away?

He didn't have much time.

The dense perfume cloud reached out to him from behind. A soft susurrus of rose petals and leaves whispered in his ear. The

Thorn Maiden stood at his back, her lips hovering beside his ear.

It will all go back to the way it was. The way it was always meant to be. You and I. Together for eternity.

Her hand slid up his arm, crept to his neck, toyed with the hair at the base of his skull.

You'll forget her soon enough. You'll forget all these unpleasant things she's stirred inside you. And when that cursed book of yours finally breaks—

Soran turned sharply to face the apparition. With a snarl, he clutched her head in both hands and crushed, crushed, crushed it until rose petals burst through his fingers. She was bound. The Rose Book spell still held fast. She could not fight him, could not resist.

She broke apart into a thousand pieces, bits of broken stem and leaf and petal, drifting away on the breeze.

Wiping his hands on the front of his robes, Soran strode back to his sleeping body. He must wake up. There was no time to be lost. An idea was forming, one he hated to acknowledge, hated to face head-on. But if it was the only way Nelle could be saved . . .

Moving with deft experience, Soran lay back down inside his body. It was an agony to feel those paralyzed limbs close in upon his spirit, an agony to strain against the enchantment and his own physical frailty. With a groan, he wrenched his eyes open and stared at the world around him.

It wasn't the same pitch-dark world he had left behind. The shadows of Noxaur were already on the retreat, leaving Roseward in deep but not utter gloom. How long had he slept? It could have been hours; it could have been days.

Tentatively he tested his limbs. The skullars had savaged his garments but only occasionally managed to penetrate to his skin. He'd suffered worse from the Thorn Maiden and, recently, from the unicorn's horn. The air of Roseward had already hastened his healing, and a few more disfiguring scars made no difference.

He pushed upright into a kneeling position. Everything hurt, but it was the kind of hurt that assured of life and vitality, not brokenness. The stink of death surrounded him, and when he dared look around, he saw the battered corpses of three skullars, victims of his own magic.

Shuddering, he bowed his head. For some moments he could do no more than remain where he was, breathing in and out, his chin dropped to his chest.

Then he looked up, nostrils flaring.

Somehow he got to his feet; somehow he stumbled into motion. Avoiding the grisly remains of a skullar cut cleanly in half, he passed through the gate and strode along the cliffside path until he reached the road leading down to the ruins of the harbor town below.

The boundaries of his prison were not impenetrable. He could get through, for a short while at least. Lodírhal would find out, of course. But whatever consequences the King of Aurelis dealt him would be worth it if he could just get to Noxaur in time.

Soran slid a hand into the front of his robes to touch the Rose Book's leather binding. He'd already used the two great spells, and the small book of schoolboy scribblings would be utterly useless where he was going. But this spell . . . this one mighty spell . . .

Reaching the end of the cliff path, Soran picked his way between the ruinous buildings. He thought he heard something inside one of the tumbledown cottages—some shuffling of feet, a hastily closed door. He frowned, half turning. Had some other creature of Noxaur made its way across the narrow channel and taken up residence?

No. He shook his head firmly and continued on his way. If by some miracle he should return from this expedition, he would deal with invaders then.

Nelle's little boat waited on the shore, well out of reach of even the capricious Hinter tides. Soran picked bits of seaweed and debris from its hull and made certain it was still seaworthy. To his inexpert eye it seemed solid enough. He didn't have far to go, after all.

His arms quivered, threatening to give out on him as he dragged the boat down to the water. How could he ever find the strength for what he was about to do? Firming his jaw, he slid the boat out into the water, swiftly climbed inside, and took up the oars.

Perhaps he lacked the strength he needed. But he would do it anyway. Somehow.

Not even Kyriakos was prepared to battle an unleashed Noswraith.

21

A sensation of perfect softness greeted Nelle as she slowly returned to consciousness. A softness like clouds. Airy, floating, wispy clouds, tender against her tired body. She leaned into the feeling, her eyes still closed, and thought perhaps she wouldn't wake up. Not yet.

When she drew a deep, long breath, some spicy scent she didn't recognize tingled her nose, not at all unpleasantly. It wasn't the smell of roses, she knew that much, though she couldn't remember why it mattered just then. She breathed again, letting the spice tingle her nostrils and throat, then coil in her chest. Combined with the softness, it was pure bliss.

Soft, lilting music caressed her ear, a trilling of pure silver and moonlight underscored by deep bass strings. It was unlike any music she'd heard before—complex in a way she couldn't understand. If she concentrated on it too hard, it jarred her head.

But this music didn't require concentration. It was more like the background hum of nature itself, the slow spinning dance of the spheres. Always present, never fully acknowledged. She let her mind relax, let the music play on her senses, soothing and arousing by turns.

Fingers touched her face. Cold, hard fingers that didn't fit with the softness or the smells or the music. They pried at her cheek, pulled at the skin around her eyes. Nelle frowned and turned her head away. A deep, rough voice growled a string of strange words.

Nelle's eyes flared open.

A face carved from flaking white stone loomed over hers. A hideous face chiseled by some inexpert hand, with protruding cheekbones and exaggerated jaw and beady little eyes set deep beneath a prominent brow. Nelle sucked in a breath, trying to scream, but her chest constricted too tight to allow any air to escape her lungs.

"Step back, *Grork*," a mellifluous voice spoke from the space beyond that ugly head. "You'll frighten the poor thing."

The stone face shifted, and a new face floated into Nelle's range of vision, hardly less strange than the last. Instead of stone, it seemed to be carved from wood, polished so that the grain stood out in distinct swirls across each cheek. The nose was merely a faint bump and two slitted holes like nostrils. But it had a delicate little mouth and huge luminous eyes framed by long frond-like white lashes. The mouth twisted, revealing sharp pale-green teeth.

"Oh, my dear, dear sister," the green-eyed person said, its voice gentle and distinctly womanly. "We are so glad you have come. It's been so long since someone new joined our family, we were becoming quite desolate."

She backed up a few paces, giving Nelle a better view of her. Definitely a woman—a shapely woman of living wood, utterly naked and yet utterly unconscious of her nakedness. She had four long, twining arms that branched into more hands than Nelle liked to count. The overall effect should have been horrifying but was, in fact, strangely elegant and graceful.

"Allow me to introduce myself," the wood-woman continued. Only then did Nelle realize that she wasn't hearing a language she recognized. The actual sounds striking her ear were more like stirring leaves and creaking boughs, with an undercurrent of deep, churning earth. But somehow they transformed inside her head, becoming perfectly understandable. "I am Dirsdaliradeladi, the Second Sister. And here," she swept two of her four arms, extending multiple hands to indicate the looming pile of rock just behind her, "is *Grork*"—the word came out as a harsh bark—"the Fifth Sister. To your left, you have Merledrune, the Fourteenth Sister, and behind you is Valsatra. She is Sister Seventeen."

Nelle turned her head, first to the left, where stood a tall, slender woman with pinkish skin and brilliant magenta hair, clad in a loose wine-colored gown. The woman did not meet Nelle's questioning gaze but stared into the space over her head. She seemed less lifelike than the stony *Grork*. Nelle twisted where she lay to look behind her and glimpsed a flicker of something shadow-like, there and gone again. Whether or not it was the Seventeenth Sister, she couldn't guess.

"Wh-where am I?" Nelle gasped.

The wood-woman's smile grew, revealing more sharp teeth. As she tilted her head to one side, leaf-grown hair of white gold wafted over her shoulder in voluminous waves. "You are in Ninthalor," she said, blinking her strange eyelashes. "The mighty fortress of our renowned husband. Welcome, sister!"

With these words, she extended all four of her arms, clasping Nelle in an embrace. Nelle felt the profound strength of those limbs, which, though they held her gently, could have ripped her to pieces with no strain. She pulled back as soon as the wood-woman gave her a chance and stared around the room, beyond the surrounding figures.

She seemed to be lying on a huge bed. Red curtains hung from polished black bedposts, and the softness she lay on turned out to be an enormous red blanket made from the plushy fur of some animal Nelle had never seen or heard of before. A huge fireplace took up one wall, its blaze warming even the darkest corners with raw red light. The bed itself stood in the center of the room, surrounded by eight angled walls, all painted crimson with intricate patterns of leaves and flowers and . . . and Nelle blinked and looked again. Among those leaves and flowers were strange, fantastical figures in various stages of undress.

A third look brought a blush roaring to her cheeks.

Nelle buried her face in her hands. Everything was confused in her head, and that alluring music always playing in the background made it harder to concentrate. She saw flashes, moments in her mind's eye: Soran, his arm swinging in an arc of terrible blue magic that cut straight through the body of a monster . . . a huge figure emerging from the darkness, his skin faintly glowing with its own natural radiance . . . powerful arms cradling her body . . . the sway and dip of a boat on water . . . fear, fear, fear.

Nelle groaned and closed her eyes tight as memory clarified. Kyriakos. The Noxaur fae lord. He'd found her, taken her.

Tightness squeezed her chest, and she almost gagged on the sudden bile rising in her throat. It all began to make sense: the red room, the soft blanket, the curtains, the images on the walls.

He takes them as his wives.

Mortals are his favorites.

Yanking her hands away from her face, Nelle gazed up at the strange figures surrounding her. "You are . . . sisters," she said softly. "Sister-wives?"

The wood-woman nodded and smiled again, clasping six pairs of hands together in delight. "We are, indeed! I," she placed one of her unclasped hands against her bare bosom, "am a dryad of the Nesterin Woods of Solira, while *Grork* here," she waved three more hands at the rock-person, "comes from the Umbrian Isles and is trollkind. Merledrune," she nodded to the pink woman standing across the bed from her, "was born and raised in Cylhana, an Aurelian vila. And Valsatra is . . . well . . ." Her huge eyes flashed sideways, momentarily uneasy. "None of us are entirely certain, to be honest. We think she may be vampyri."

Nelle swallowed several times. "You . . . Were you all . . ." She couldn't quite form the words, wasn't even entirely certain what question she meant to ask.

But the dryad happily continued, her branch arms rustling as she reached out to take Nelle's hands in two of hers. "Though we may originate from different realms, we have been brought together in sisterhood by our shared love of Kyriakos, our most beautiful and benevolent lord."

Nelle gaped at the woman. Her memories of Kyriakos were hazy to be sure, but she was quite certain *benevolent* wasn't a word that applied to the imposing fae lord. *Beautiful*, yes. *Benevolent*, definitely no.

She pulled her hands free and, not liking to meet the dryad's gaze, looked down. With a startled gasp, she realized that she wore only her chemise—a torn, ratty, stained, and entirely inadequate covering in a room like this. The front ties were partially undone, and she hastily fumbled to tie them, casting about as she did so for some sign of her lavender gown.

"Oh no, my sweet!" the dryad trilled, hastily pulling Nelle's hands away again. There was no resisting the force of that wooden grip. Nelle could only sit wide-eyed as two more of the dryad's hands untied the laces. "You cannot wear something like this. Not tonight! We have something much nicer for you."

As though taking her cue from the dryad, the massive stone-woman—the trollkind—held up something in her blunt, craggy fingers. Nelle took one look and nearly choked on her own tongue. It was a garment of some sort—certainly not a gown. Black, shimmering, and long, with deep slits up the front of the skirt almost to the waist. And the rest of it . . .

"I'm not wearing that." Nelle turned back to the dryad, who blinked at her with gentle confusion. Hoping for some sign of sympathy, she turned to the pink woman but was met with an expression so studiously blank, she could almost believe she beheld a wax figure.

The dryad *shhhed* softly and plucked at the black gown with one hand. "Is black not the traditional wedding color of your world? I seem to remember one or two of my other mortal sisters claiming they preferred white for such an occasion. I may be able to find one of their old gowns, but . . . well, it would be such a shame! Valsatra made this up for you special, and you don't want to hurt her feelings."

A shadowy waft shuddered along the back of Nelle's head. She twisted in place, trying but failing to get an impression of whoever was—or wasn't—behind her. "I don't mean to hurt anyone's feelings," she said quickly. "I just . . . I ain't getting married."

The dryad made a strange sound at this, a rough barking, blowing sort of noise that somehow translated in Nelle's ears as a tinkling laugh. "Oh, sweet sister, you are *already* married!"

"No." Nelle shook her head fiercely and managed to free her wrists from the dryad's grip to pull her open gown shut across her cold bosom. "I'm pretty sure I'd remember something like that."

The dryad blinked at her slowly, the frondy lashes falling in a gentle sweep. When they rose again, her expression was much harder than it had been. "Our lord has claimed you," she said with an edge to her voice. "You are his bride. And tonight, your sister-wives must make you ready to receive him."

With those words, she lifted her head, raised several pairs of hands, and clapped smartly. "Come, sisters! Let us begin our work!"

Many hands pulled Nelle out of the bed and stripped off her chemise before she had a chance to think. She tried to fight back, but the dryad swiftly pinned her arms and legs while the pink woman sidled in close and efficiently washed her skin with a rough sponge. Nelle's mind whirled. The perfume in the air made her dizzy.

Soran, she thought wildly as someone—the unseen Valsatra, perhaps—dragged a comb through the tangles of her hair. What had become of Soran? Her memories were vague, but she was fairly certain Kyriakos had done something to him, had left him collapsed on the ground. Alive? Oh, please the gods, let him still be alive!

The pink woman standing before Nelle to sponge her shoulders and neck stopped suddenly and lifted one slender hand. Shivering, Nelle looked down to see the cold chain around her neck.

The oval locket lay between her breasts.

The pink woman cast a quick glance to one side, where the dryad was busy talking and plucking at the folds of the black wedding garment. Then, quick as a flash, she flicked the locket open. Her nostrils flared slightly as the pungent, burning smell of the Sweet Dreams ointment filled the room.

Her eyes met Nelle's. For a moment, her expressionless face was alive, bright. Amused?

Nelle stared back, her heart beating in an agony of suspense.

The pink woman flicked the locket shut just as the dryad appeared at her shoulder. "What is that, Merledrune?" she trilled.

The pink woman shrugged, her face once more impassive, and held the locket up for inspection.

"Take it off," the dryad said, resting two hands on the woman's shoulder. She smiled her pointy-tooth smile at Nelle once more. "A bride must be made new the night she receives her husband."

Nelle's stomach lurched. But the pink woman met her gaze again and . . . Was that a slight shake of her head? A warning? Her hands slid around to the back of Nelle's neck, working the clasp, and she pulled the necklace free.

"You're trembling, poor dear." Three branching hands pushed the pink woman to one side, and the dryad stepped in to take her place, applying oils and creams to Nelle's pale skin. "Have no fear. Our husband values each of his wives as a pure, perfect flower to be nurtured in his garden. You will know for yourself soon enough."

Nelle hardly heard her. Her gaze fixed on the pink woman through the branches of the dryad's shoulder. She saw the woman move back to the huge red bed. Her long hair covered the side of her face, but she flicked it back for just a moment, catching Nelle's eye.

Then she tucked the necklace under one of the huge, plump pillows.

Pulse quickening, Nelle sucked in her lips and bit down hard. Her knees buckled, and she would have fallen if the troll-woman hadn't caught her shoulders from behind and held her upright. She forced herself to take several long breaths, ignoring how the spicy air now seemed to burn in her throat.

She wasn't defenseless. Not entirely.

They dressed her in the black garment almost before she quite realized what they'd done. She came to herself with a gasp as the dryad pulled the corset laces tight. Only then did she look down and get a view of her so-called wedding gown. The slits in the skirt reached all the way to her waist, exposing her hipbones, with only a narrow shimmering panel of fabric providing anything like modesty. The corseted bodice pushed up her small breasts, making them seem much fuller than they truly were. Little beaded flowers lined the edge, twinkling in the firelight. Two loose straps fell across her upper arms, framing her shoulders—sleeves by name if not by function. It was entirely fashioned of the most sumptuous fabric, softer even than the gowns Nelle had explored in the lady's chamber at Dornrise.

It was a garment that served a single purpose.

"There." The dryad stepped back, her green eyes gleaming. "You are so lovely, my dear." She reached out to chuck Nelle under the chin. "Oh, it has been an age since we had any mortal sisters! I have missed them so. But you . . . yes, you bring back those old days, don't you? I look forward to learning of your quaint mortal ways again. Now!"

She clapped one pair of hands briskly, and the other wives—including the shadowy thing that might have been Valsatra—congregated behind her. "We shall take our leave," the dryad said. "In the morning we will come to you again and introduce you to the ways of Ninthalor. Your dwelling chambers are so charming, so very charming, I know you will love them. Meanwhile, good night, sweet sister!"

She lifted three different hands to her mouth in turn, blowing kisses. The troll raised one large hand, fingers moving in something like a slow, creaking wave. The shadowy nothingness flickered momentarily, almost visible.

Then the four of them proceeded to one of the walls and opened a door Nelle had hitherto not seen. They stepped through, but the pink woman hung back and cast Nelle a last look. Her gaze flicked to the pillows on the bed.

The next moment she was gone, shutting the door behind her.

22

Nelle sprang into motion, leaping for the bed. How long did she have before Kyriakos made his appearance? He could be outside the chamber even now, just waiting for his other wives to vacate it. It could be moments. Less than moments.

She grabbed the chain and whipped the necklace out, almost flinging it across the room in her haste. Seated on the edge of the bed, her hands trembling so hard she could barely work the clasp, she flicked the locket open. The pungent stink of the Sweet Dreams nearly overwhelmed even the spicy perfume, yet Nelle breathed it in like heavenly incense.

She had only two doses left. Well, one should be enough. She dabbed a fingertip to one half of the open locket and quickly smeared the ointment across her chapped lips. It soaked in at once, and the smell evaporated on contact.

Clicking the locket shut, Nelle glanced around, wondering

where she should stash it. Back under the pillows? No, if it worked as she hoped, she would want to make a swift getaway. Better to have it on her. But what if Kyriakos noticed the chain? What if he asked questions? It was too great a risk.

Having no other option available, she stuffed the trinket down the front of her corset. The laces were tight enough to hold it in place. It coiled uncomfortably against her stomach, secure and safe. It would be found only if . . . if . . .

"It won't be found," Nelle muttered, clenching her fists. "It won't."

She sprang up and paced across the room, her heart bounding with fear-spiked adrenaline. When she reached the huge fireplace, she paused to gaze into the fire. Strange, how it blazed so huge and bright yet did not seem to heat the room, at least no more than was pleasant. The spicy smell seemed to emanate from the logs.

Everything about this chamber was calculated for seduction. She felt it work on her senses, lulling her gently.

But she wouldn't be lulled. Fear was her friend in a moment like this.

She turned from the fire, faced the bed again, and looked away quickly. Her gaze lit upon a collection of tools held upright in an elegant stand. She would have called them fireirons, only she knew they wouldn't be made of iron here in Eledria. Gripping the handle of a long poker, she drew it like drawing a sword from its sheath. The firelight played on the sharp point. Nilarium, she guessed. It seemed sturdy enough.

She balanced it in her grip, then bit out a bitter curse. "Bullspit, girl, you're not thinking straight!"

She couldn't face Kyriakos with such open hostility. The Sweet Dreams was her best defense. Better to kiss him at once and get it over with.

But what if it didn't work? He was fae. What if he was immune to fae poisons?

Nelle swallowed hard. Then she carried the poker back to the bed and tucked it under the pillows. Knowing it was there bolstered her courage.

When she faced the room again, the heavy curtains draping one of the eight walls caught her eye, and she dashed over to fling them open. Window glass reflected the red room back at her, offering no impression of the world outside. She put her face to the glass, cupping her hands around her eyes, but gained no more than a faint impression of many peaked rooftops and chimneys below and the occasional gleam of light from long, narrow windows.

"Bullspit," she whispered again. Could she use the poker to smash through the panes? Possibly. But where would she go from there? It looked like a sheer drop below. Unless she missed her guess, she was a good twelve stories high, maybe more.

Nelle drew the curtains back together. Maybe her best bet was to wait on the bed. Arrange herself charmingly and tempt the fae lord in for that poisoned first kiss. Her stomach churned, but it was the safest plan. She would be in position to grab the poker then too.

Her bare feet padding silently on the red-carpeted floor, she returned to the bed and crawled onto the gorgeously soft blanket. She turned, sitting upright to arrange what there was of the black skirts to cover her legs, but still felt far too exposed. Perhaps that was for the best. If the plan was to lure the fae in, she'd better be spitting-well alluring. Propping one elbow on the pillows behind her, she draped her other arm along her hip.

And she waited.

The fire blazed, its crackle and snap mingling with the distant flutelike music. Nelle's heart slowly calmed its frantic beating, and she breathed more easily. She felt a bit dizzy and so, so tired. How long had it been since she'd properly slept? Not an enchanted sleep, but real, restful sleep? Not since her uncomfortable doze on the chair back at the lighthouse.

The lighthouse.

Soran . . .

What had become of him? Did he lie dead on the broken paving stones of the Dornrise drive? No, she couldn't believe it. He simply couldn't be dead. Not yet. Not until she had a chance to see him again, to speak to him, to tell him . . . what? The truth? About Gaspard and Papa and her mission? About Sam? About all the ways she'd lied and tricked him, all the ways she'd subtly laid the groundwork for betrayal?

No. All that wasn't what she would tell him if she could speak to him now. Those weren't the confessions that would spill from her heart if she had the chance.

She closed her eyes, letting the strange music and spicy scent from the logs roll over her. Was she asleep? The question came to her dully, creeping through her senses. Surely she wouldn't have dozed off! She'd only just shut her eyes to rest them for a moment. But they felt so heavy, and the blankets were so soft, and her head was pillowed so comfortably as the sweet music played in the back of her head.

Someone breathed. Deep, heavy breaths.

A spike of awareness shot through Nelle's brain. Her eyes flared open, and she stared up into the finely cut face of Kyriakos, hovering mere inches above hers.

His black eyes crinkled around the edges as his mouth curled into a slow smile. "Ah! The sleeping beauty awakens."

Nelle brought one hand up sharply, the heel of her palm connecting with his jaw in a sharp thrust, clunking his teeth together. He recoiled, and she used the opportunity to bring her knee up hard into his stomach, eliciting a loud grunt. He pulled further back, his arms wrapped around his midsection, and she hastily rolled, making for the edge of her bed. Her hands slipped under the pillows and found the grip of the nilarium poker, drawing it after her. She hit the ground, aware that her legs were fully exposed, her skirts trapped beneath the seated fae lord. With a sharp jerk, she pulled them out from under him and sprang to her feet, holding the poker with its point aimed between his eyes.

He observed the poker, his expression almost comically cross-eyed. Then he lifted his gaze to meet hers.

She'd hesitated an instant too long.

When she struck, he was already in motion, ducking to one side, springing up from the bed. Firelight played off his huge shirtless torso, making the dark skin gleam with a deep purplish undertone. She thought he would leap at her, but he merely turned, lowering his arms, leaving his chest fully exposed and vulnerable.

Nelle braced her back leg and lunged, aiming straight for his heart. She put all the force of her weight into that lunge, and the nilarium flashed bright and quick. But he stepped easily to one side, catching the poker as it passed him. He wrenched it hard and, when she wouldn't let go, used it to back her up five paces until she hit the wall.

He leaned in, pressing the cold bar against her bare, heaving chest. He was so tall, she had to crane her neck to look up at him, to meet those shining black eyes.

"My little wife is full of surprises, I see," he said, his voice a throaty chuckle.

Her stomach quivered at the sound but not quite with fear. Something about his voice mingled with the perfume she'd been breathing to elicit a dull throb in her gut, strange and thrilling.

She grimaced. Whatever this feeling was, she had to fight it!

No, wait. What about the Sweet Dreams? In her shock she'd forgotten. She shouldn't be fighting; she shouldn't be resisting. She should reach up, catch hold of his head even now, and draw his lips down to hers. But her hands were pinned under the nilarium bar.

Kyriakos leaned down. She thought he would kiss her, which would certainly simplify matters, but instead, he buried his nose in the mass of her hair piled up over her shoulder and breathed in deep.

"Ah," he sighed, and her spine quivered again at the growl in his voice. "How long it has been since I smelled true *ibrildian* blood! I had not realized how I missed it, how I longed for it."

Ibrildian? Some dull part of her mind, behind the clamor of her pulse, recognized the word. He'd said it before, back at Dornrise. Was it an Eledrian word for *human?*

The fae lord drew back, his mouth curved in that slow, dangerous smile. Then he raised one eyebrow. "You are frightened, little one." To her surprise, he let go of the poker and took several steps back. Deprived of his support, she nearly slid to the floor, only just catching herself in time.

He shook his head, still smiling, and his midnight hair flowed silkily across his broad, bare shoulders. "Don't be afraid. Contrary to rumor, I like my wives willing. Just now I have other purposes in mind for you."

So saying, he turned his back—obviously aware she'd lost the strength and will for another attack—and left her holding the poker while he approached a table she hadn't noticed before, near the wall opposite the fireplace. Murmuring words she couldn't hear, he snapped once, and light appeared at his fingertips. He held the flickering glow to two candle wicks, which caught and burned brightly.

Much to her surprise, Nelle saw her satchel lying slumped on the table, and beside it her quill and spellbook.

Kyriakos waved a hand, indicating a chair beside the table. "We must talk, my pretty wife," he said. "I am keen to learn more of your magic, having had an eyeful of it already. That cunning spell-sword of yours! So delightful. Do come. Sit. You have nothing to fear."

The fae might not lie outright, but Nelle suspected this statement wasn't entirely true. Still, she couldn't just stand there with her back against the wall. If he'd wanted to hurt her, he could have easily done so already.

Lowering the poker, Nelle crossed the room, uncomfortably aware of how the splits in her skirt exposed her knees and thighs with every step she took. Kyriakos noticed as well, judging by the appreciative looks traveling up and down her body. But he held the chair for her and, when she was seated, took the place opposite hers. He was much too large for both chair and table, but he contrived to look relaxed and graceful, nonetheless.

"Now," he said, planting one long finger on the cover of her book, "tell me about this."

"Um." Nelle coughed to clear the rasp from her voice. The Sweet Dreams burned on her lips, potent and ready. But it wasn't as though she could lunge across the table and try to catch him in a kiss. She might as well talk as not. "It's a spellbook."

"Yes." The fae lord chuckled again and moved his finger to flip the cover open, turning the blank pages slowly, one after another. "I am familiar with the concept. But are not mortal spellbooks meant to be filled with written spells? Or has the process changed sometime in the last three hundred years?"

"Oh. No." Nelle coughed again. "I'm still new at the . . . at the craft. I've only written a few proper spells. And I've used them up already."

"Indeed?" One eyebrow slid upward. "But you *have* begun your training. That is fortunate. Once the spring of magic has been tapped, it is easy enough to increase the flow. Especially in an *ibrildian*."

She glanced at him and away again, unsure what to say to this.

"That mortal mage," Kyriakos continued, "back on the drifting island. He was your teacher? Your"—he leaned in a little, candlelight gleaming on his sharp-toothed smile—"lover?"

"Teacher," Nelle answered quickly and rubbed a hand across her face, pushing loose strands of hair out of her eyes. "We had, uh, only just begun lessons. A week ago."

"And yet so far advanced!" Kyriakos shook his head gently, trying to catch her eye. "You don't realize the truth, do you? You don't know how far you've come in so short a while. It is my understanding that it takes years for a mortal mage to develop even the ability to properly perceive the *quinsatra*, much less to draw forth magic from that realm. A few years more or less seem but little to my kind. To your kind, however, I believe the time is more significant." He leaned back in his chair and waved a graceful hand her way, causing the candle flames to waver briefly. "For one such as you to come as far as you have in a mere week is, to Eledrians, like a babe dancing and singing within an hour of its birth. A miracle!"

Nelle frowned. One such as her? He spoke the words with such weight, such significance. She cast him a hasty, bewildered look before dropping her gaze.

"Oh." Kyriakos nodded slowly, folding his arms across his wide chest. "I see. You don't know what you are, do you?"

Before she could think of an answer, he stood and strode across the room to touch a place in the apparently seamless wall. When it swung out, revealing a casement of beautiful decanters, he fetched a decanter and two glasses, then returned to the table and set one glass before Nelle, another at his place. The cut-crystal stopper chinked musically as he lifted the decanter and swirled the deep red liquid inside before pouring. A sweet scent rose from the glass, mingling with the spice in the air.

"A little fortification, my dear," the fae said before stoppering the bottle and resuming his seat. He lifted his glass in a silent toast and sipped daintily from the rim.

Nelle eyed her glass uneasily. What exactly was in it? Another layer of beguilement? Her tongue felt like sandpaper, her throat terribly parched. She glanced up at Kyriakos, catching his eye.

"It's wine," he answered her unspoken question. "Aurelian wine from the coastal region of Mylaela. Said to be well suited to mortal palates. Have a taste, my dear. You'll need it for what I am about to tell you."

She picked up the glass and swirled it slightly. Then quickly, before she could change her mind, put it to her lips and sipped. A sweet tang filled her mouth, bright as dawn light. It enlivened and enlightened all at once and left behind a faintly bitter burn.

It was delightful. A far cry from Soran's horrid *qeiese*, that was certain! She took a second and a third sip before forcing herself to set the glass down.

Kyriakos toyed thoughtfully with the stem of his glass. "Your teacher never told you that you are *ibrildian*, did he."

Nelle shook her head. When her brain made a pleasant *whoosh*, she held carefully still. "Wh-what's that word?" she said, stumbling a little over the words. "*Ibrildian*. You keep saying it, but I ain't heard it before."

The fae lord smiled, turning his glass in a gentle rotation, making the wine whirl. "In your tongue, I believe, the word is *Hybrid*. It is a term used to describe fae-human crossbreeds. Such as yourself."

Nelle blinked at him vacuously. Then she frowned and sat up a little straighter. "What? What are you talking about?"

"It's the reason you are adept at magic. Your blood is a mingling of fae and human strains. Not quite half and half, I should think. Unless I miss my guess, one of your parents was also *ibrildian*, most likely your mother. Strange that she should have survived long enough to procreate. *Ibrildian* offspring were outlawed at the signing of the Pledge, you understand, and very few are yet alive to this day. My own *ibrildian* children were hunted down ages ago and killed before my eyes." Bitterness laced his words, yet he continued to smile. The contrast was unnerving. "So you see, my dear, why it is so fortunate that I should meet you."

Her heart constricted into a tighter and tighter knot with every phrase he uttered. Hybrid . . . fae and human crossbreed . . .

Mother.

Of course.

Of course. She should have known it long ago.

Of course Mother was part fae. How else could she have been so beautiful, so wild, so reckless? Only a fae could dance through life in lower Wimborne with such devil-may-care élan. Only a fae would think it a lark to snatch a handsome mortal husband and keep him like some sort of a pet all those years, helpless and utterly enthralled. It made perfect sense.

And how else had she come by all those fae treasures of hers?

But that meant . . . What did it mean? Nelle's head churned with questions she couldn't fully form. Unthinking, she lifted her glass to her lips and took another sip. She wasn't human. Not really, not fully. All right then. She could deal with that, couldn't she? She was still herself.

"Did . . . did *he* know?" she blurted suddenly, remembering at the last not to give away Soran's name.

"Your teacher, you mean?" Kyriakos drained his glass and set it down hard. "He had to know. He is familiar with the intricacies of magic; he knows how it ebbs and flows through even the strongest of mortal magicians. He could not have taught you for more than a day without realizing the truth."

"Why . . . why didn't he . . . ?"

"Why didn't he tell you? Fear, most likely. Fear of what you could do, what you could become. Mortal mages are all alike, you know—

arrogant bastards, eager to suppress and surmount all others in their climb to the top. It's a wonder he didn't kill you at once. It was mortals who urged the outlawing of *ibrildians* back when the Pledge was signed. They couldn't bear the competition, as it were. They couldn't bear the idea of beings who could simultaneously command both mortal and fae magic."

Nelle slumped in her seat, resting her elbow on the table and her forehead on the tips of her fingers. It was too much. Far too much.

Then again, it wasn't as though she had any real right to resent Soran for keeping such a secret from her. How many dangerous secrets had she withheld from him in turn?

But this secret encompassed her very nature, who she was as a person. Surely she had a right to such knowledge! Or was it better to not know? To be unaware that her very existence was a crime.

She groaned and closed her eyes, her fingers rubbing hard circles into her forehead.

Kyriakos rose. "My poor sweet little wife," he said, slipping around to her side of the table. Before she realized what was happening, he had an arm around her, one hand gripping her elbow, the other holding her opposite hand. He eased her up from her chair, and she staggered back a step, leaning into him. The sudden heat and proximity of his body awakened something inside her, something sharp and searing. Her breath caught, and she knew he heard it.

"Come, you are tired," he murmured directly into her ear. "Rest is in order, I think. A nice long rest. We can discuss these weighty subjects further once you have slept. Come, come. A few steps only. The bed is waiting."

He guided her across the floor, and she couldn't resist him. When they neared the bed, she caught hold of the bedpost with one hand. Pulling away from his grip, she turned and faced him, her back against the post.

The fae lord smiled down at her, the firelight softening his strange, beautiful features. Or perhaps it was the influence of the wine? "I told you, did I not, that I have no wish to hurt you?" he murmured, lifting one hand to trace a finger along the line of her jaw.

She nodded, swallowed.

He bowed his head, bringing his eyes level with hers, dark and intent. "There is a tradition here in my country," he said. "A wedding-night tradition. The bridegroom is free to give his bride three kisses. Just three. If she desires no more, then he will at once retire from the room. A fourth kiss is only given if requested."

The room was very warm and seemed to spin softly around her. How many sips of the wine had she taken? And when did the strange music swell with such depth, growling in the pit of her chest? She dug her hands into the bedpost behind her, using it to hold her up.

Three kisses. That should be enough.

Enough for . . . for what?

The Sweet Dreams! Her mind roared behind the throbbing

music. *The Sweet Dreams, you spittin' idiot!*

This was her chance. Possibly her only chance. If she didn't use it now, the Sweet Dreams would wear away.

She stared up into the fae lord's dark eyes, feeling so small, so vulnerable. Would her mother's trick be enough to take him down? If so, then what would she do?

And if not . . .

Kyriakos bowed his face toward hers. The corners of his mouth curved in a smile, flashing white, pointed canines. He leaned in, and she could almost feel the shape of his lips against hers. But they didn't quite touch. They hovered in the air just above her mouth so that she tipped her head back and lifted her face, her lips puckering in an almost unconscious effort to close the space between them.

He retreated mere inches away, teasing. A long-fingered hand rested on her bare shoulder. Her skin burned at his touch as he trailed his fingers down her arm, toyed with the flimsy nothing-sleeve, then followed her arm back to where her hand gripped the bedpost at her back. When his fingers closed around her hand, she tried to resist. But only for a breath. He drew her arm up between them, slender and white against his bare chest.

He uncurled her tense fingers, one after another, then turned her palm up and pressed his lips against the delicate skin of her wrist. "One," he said, his voice a low rumble.

Nelle snatched her hand back and gripped the bedpost again, certain she'd sink to the floor if she didn't hold fast. Her chest felt tight, and she was all too conscious of how her exposed bosom rose and fell with short, shallow breaths.

Kyriakos slid his hands along her shoulders and up her neck, his long, claw-like nails prickling her flesh with a subtle edge of danger not yet unleashed. He cupped her face with gentle firmness.

Now, she thought. *Now!*

But though his mouth once more hovered over hers, he shifted her head at the last and planted his second kiss on her brow.

"Two," he said.

Nelle blinked quickly. His face seemed to swim before her vision. A little whimper vibrated in her throat. He smiled, well aware of the fire he stirred, of the effect of his voice and touch combined with the music and perfume.

"One last kiss," he said, still holding her face. "Where shall it go?"

His gaze flitted to her mouth. His lashes were long and thick, too lush to be a man's. Everything about him was perfect, treacherously perfect.

This was why the lyrics of so many old songs spoke of mortals succumbing to fae seducers despite all warnings, wisdom, and common sense. An intoxicating energy shimmered in those few inches of space between their bodies. One wrong move would set the air on fire.

His right hand slid around the back of her head. His fingers coiled in her hair, and he drew her head back further, tilting her face up to his. For a moment his eyes held hers, his mouth lingering just over her lips. But then he drifted down farther, farther. Her eyes closed as she felt the barest hint of teeth scraping along the skin of her neck, and her back arched in response.

The fingers of his left hand toyed with her shoulder, drifted to play with the beaded flowers along the upper edge of her corset. He planted his third kiss at the hollow of her throat.

Her blood boiled, ready to burst her throbbing veins.

"Three," he murmured against her flesh.

Then he stepped back, his hands dropping to his sides, leaving her to grasp the bedpost desperately. His mouth still curved in that knowing, terrifying smile. She couldn't bear to look at it, so she dropped her gaze to his broad chest. Firelight played across its contours, highlighting the powerful muscles.

"Well, sweet wife?" His voice was smooth and dark as midnight. "Would you like more kisses?"

With an effort of will, Nelle raised her gaze to meet his. A mistake. She was a mouse caught in the hypnotic stare of the viper.

She let go of the bedpost, stepped to one side, then sat on the edge of the bed and leaned back, biting her lower lip for dread of what she might say.

But she didn't need to speak. He understood.

With a single step, he crossed to the bed. His arms were around her the next moment, drawing her down onto her back. He caressed her cheek, her neck, slid his hand along her shoulder, her bare arm, and down her waist to the exposed skin of her thigh.

"You have to say it," he murmured, his face buried in her hair, his teeth toying with her earlobe. "You have to say you want more. It's tradition."

Nelle whimpered again and turned to him. His eyes were so close to hers, his breath hot on her face. His hand pressed to the small of her back, drawing her toward him, and she quickly planted her palm and spread her fingers across his bare chest. He hesitated, a flash of uncertainty in his eyes.

"I want more," she said.

With a rumbling growl he rolled on top of her, planting a kiss hard against her mouth. She responded in kind, wrapping her arms around his neck, and let herself sink under his embrace. Her head whirled with danger, like leaping from a high cliff just to feel the rush of wind, the thrilling terror spiking through every limb, the plunge into darkness. For a moment, she forgot.

Then she felt the poison take effect.

The reaction was sharp—harsh enough to make her gasp and recoil, her lips burning with suddenly activated magic. She'd never felt the Sweet Dreams react like this before. But then, she'd never kissed a fae before.

Kyriakos pushed away, his hands pressed into the bed on either side of her, his long hair framing his face. Light from the red fire gleamed against the black disks of his widening eyes, which stared down at her, filled with shock and mounting horror. His mouth twisted into a grimace, a hideous mutation of his smile.

"*Rishva!*" he spat. With a gargled cry choking in his throat, he grabbed for her neck, his fingers closing fast. "You little witch!"

But his words slurred and his grip weakened almost at once, much faster than Gaspard had reacted in the Evenspire. Nelle caught hold of his wrists and pried his hands away without effort. His powerful arms trembled like a straw doll's, and his eyes rolled back in his head.

With a sinking sigh, he collapsed on top of her, his great weight pressing her into the bed.

23

Sweat dripped into Soran's eyes, but he couldn't stop long enough to wipe it away. His arms heaved in rhythm, pulling at the oars, and his body shuddered in protest as what remained of his strength threatened to fail.

The water was rough. The channel, which had looked smooth enough from Roseward's shore, had become brutal and unyielding. Waves tossed the little boat like a toy, threatening to overturn it at any moment.

No matter how hard he pulled, he made no progress. The harbor at Roseward grew no smaller. The ramshackle buildings of the ruined town taunted him with their gaping ghostly windows and empty doorways.

But he would not be beaten. He wouldn't give in. Kyriakos would not triumph, not today.

The Rose Book's weight in the front of his robes filled him

with terrifying confidence.

Soran twisted on the rower's bench, looking over his shoulder toward the Noxaur shore. But wait . . . no. He wasn't aimed correctly at the shore. Somehow, despite all his efforts, the little craft was headed toward the open Hinter Sea.

Swearing bitterly, Soran wrenched at one oar, fighting the waves and current to correct his course. He lined the little boat up as best he could and again put his back into the work, heaving, pulling, every muscle running up and down his spine and along his shoulders screaming in protest. He felt those screams gather in his lungs, and finally let them burst from his throat in a savage yell.

Only one, however. He wouldn't scream again, no matter how urgent the need. He must save his breath.

After what felt like hours he turned and looked again, expecting to see the shore much closer. Again, his course was thwarted. The prow of his little craft, which he had been so certain was aimed true, again pointed out to the waiting, ravenous sea.

"It's a curse." The words ground through his teeth, and spittle flecked his lips. Kyriakos had left a curse in his wake to throw Soran off his trail.

Soran closed his eyes, reached out with his senses, and felt the magic shimmering in the air. It wasn't a particularly powerful curse—a simple deflection. Child's play for a being of Kyriakos's magical prowess.

But without a counter-spell on hand, Soran was helpless against it. The moment he shipped his dripping oars, the waves relented. The boat bobbed on the water, drifting slowly farther and farther off course.

He could go back. The curse wouldn't stop him from returning to Roseward. He could go back and hasten to the lighthouse, dig through his spellbooks, and find something to counteract that deflection curse.

But dared he risk it? He didn't know how long he'd lain unconscious, how many hours had been wasted. Every moment was too precious if he was to reach Nelle before . . . before . . .

A growl rumbling in his breast, Soran put his back to Noxaur's shore, lowered his oars, and pulled again. He wouldn't go back. Not yet. He would not let Kyriakos beat him. If sheer will could break a curse, he would find a way through.

The Rose Book thudded against his heart in rhythmic time to his rowing.

At first Nelle couldn't move, couldn't think. She could scarcely breathe, crushed under that huge, senseless fae. It was all she could do to lie there and force her mind back into focus, wondering all the while if she too would fall prey to the poison that burned on her lips and made her whole face ache with powerfully ignited magic.

Eventually the pain was enough to bring her back to her senses. With a snarl, she shoved at the unconscious lord's shoulder and rolled him away. He slid off the bed and collapsed in an ungainly heap on the floor.

Nelle sat up, dizzy, and gripped the edge of the bed, her fingers digging into the lush blanket. Closing her eyes, she wiped a hand down her face, then pushed hair back from her forehead.

Had she really forgotten the Sweet Dreams? Would she really have submitted to this fae's seductions? Just like that?

He must have enchanted her somehow—the wine, the perfume, his voice. But when she searched down inside, she could find no signs of enchantment. Nothing but her own pulsing lust, wildly and unexpectedly awakened. Her whole body ached with longing she hardly understood, and she shuddered and wrapped her arms around herself, wishing, foolishly wishing she'd not applied the Sweet Dreams at all.

After a few long, careful breaths, her shuddering passed. Drawing a steadying breath, she let it out in a low growl. She couldn't stay here and wait for this dangerous being to wake. How long would the Sweet Dreams work on him? The dose she'd applied would knock out a mortal man for a full day at least. But while the poison had acted faster on a fae, it might wear off sooner.

Nelle grimaced and shot up from the bed, hastily arranging her split skirts around her bare legs. She stepped over the fae lord and crossed quickly to the little table where her satchel, quill, and spellbook lay. Part of her wanted to stop and write a spell. Another flame-sword, perhaps. Something to hold onto in case any of those skull-dogs lurked just outside the room.

But . . . she glanced back at the heap of limbs that was Kyriakos. Though he lay perfectly still, he might be playing some sort of cat-and-mouse game with her. Any moment now, he might spring up, and her chance of escape would be lost.

She stuffed the quill and book inside the satchel. On afterthought, she looked around the room, spotted the nilarium poker lying where she'd dropped it, and fetched that as well. It was better than nothing.

With her legs trembling with terror and her spine stiffly determined, she marched to the wall that had earlier let the four sister-wives out through a doorway and felt along the lurid mural, searching frantically for any crack or hidden latch. It was perfectly smooth to the touch.

A knot of panic tightened in her gut. Nelle glanced back at the fallen Kyriakos again. Now that the moment was past, all lust had drained away, leaving behind only dread. She would not be taken in by a fae! She would not be lured and twisted and seduced beyond her reason! She was her own bullspitting person, and she would get out of this place if it killed her.

Raising the poker, she hacked at the wall, once, twice—but before the third blow fell, it opened suddenly, swinging outward. Nelle swallowed a yelp and jumped back, brandishing the poker in a defensive stance.

The pink woman with the brilliant hair appeared in the doorway, her face glowing in the firelight. She didn't look at Nelle. Instead, she peered past her into the room, her eyes lighting on the crumpled form of her lordly husband. For an instant, her face maintained its expressionless mask.

Then a smile slowly spread across her face and crinkled her eyes.

She turned to Nelle and touched a finger to her own smiling lips. "*Rishva*," she said.

Nelle lifted a hand to her mouth. "Is . . . is that what you call it?" she asked, her voice tight. "The Sweet Dreams?"

The woman nodded, and her smile widened. "It is . . . of my people," she said slowly. The words sounded odd, as if her tongue might be unsuited to speaking mortal languages. For a moment Nelle didn't understand. Then it dawned on her: This was how the sister-wife had immediately recognized the potent substance hidden in her locket. It was a concoction created in her kind's corner of Eledria.

Was this a clue to Mother's origins? The dryad had said this pink woman was a vila. Did that mean Mother was part vila herself?

But this was no time to puzzle out mysteries. At the pink woman's beckoning, Nelle stepped through the door. Almost at once she realized her mistake. For a terrifying, gut-plunging instant, her foot found no floor and she pivoted forward. While the red room had been brightly, almost garishly lit by the blazing fire, the world outside that room was dark with impenetrable Night. The moment she crossed the threshold, she was utterly blind.

Her foot landed, and she staggered, her arm flailing in search of support. A many-fingered hand caught hold of her elbow, steadying her. The pink woman? Nelle strained her eyes, which had always so effortlessly adapted to darkness. Here, they betrayed her entirely. Even when she turned, trying to catch a glimpse of the red room, she saw nothing. Panic rippled through her veins.

The cool voice of the pink woman spoke in the darkness near her ear. "Why stop?"

"My eyes," Nelle whispered. "I can't see!"

A pause. Then the soft voice murmured a string of words that seemed to ignite the very air. Nelle blinked in wonder as she somehow *saw* those words take shape before her eyes . . . not as words or written letters, but as movements, vibrations of energy. With a gasp, Nelle blinked again. She was no longer blind. Magic shimmered on the edges of her vision, and she peered at the dark world around her as it slowly clarified.

They stood in a narrow passage at the top of a winding stair. One more staggering step, and she would surely have fallen and broken her neck. She squeezed the pink woman's hand hard.

"Come," the pink woman said and led the way.

Each step was perfectly smooth, polished to perfection, even the edges rounded. Strange etchings decorated the close walls of the stairwell, along the same theme as the risqué mural in the red room. Ye gods, was this whole tower devoted to the sole purpose of seduction? Nelle shivered.

Then she shivered again, this time with cold. The air was bitter against her exposed skin, the stones icy beneath her unshod feet. It wasn't exactly a cold like winter; it was the cold of a world where the sun never shone. How did anything live or grow in this place?

At the base of the stair they faced another blank wall. Nelle drew up short, frowning, but the pink woman approached the wall without pause, placed one hand in its center, and murmured. Magic again sprang to life, drawn out from the *quinsatra*, and a door opened, revealing an arched passage lined with tall pillars.

"There," the pink woman said, stepping back and sweeping an arm to indicate the doorway. "You go."

Nelle nodded but didn't release her hold on the pink woman. The vila's unblinking eyes glowed like two silvery globes, highlighting the sharp contours of her cheekbones. "Will you come with me?" Nelle asked. She repeated the question twice and added several expressive hand gestures to indicate flight before the woman seemed to understand.

The pink woman shook her head firmly and took a step back, putting distance between them. "No," she said. "No. I stay . . . with . . . with husband."

She meant it. There was no point in arguing with that set face. Whether the sentiment stemmed from fear of Kyriakos or loyalty, Nelle couldn't guess. If loyalty, then why would the pink woman betray her husband by helping his newest plaything escape? Unless she simply didn't want to share him with yet another wife.

Or maybe she knew what Nelle was—*Ibrildian*.

Nelle shook her head. She could work the puzzle from every angle for an age and be no closer to an answer. Meanwhile, Kyriakos might wake at any moment. "All right then," she said, and raised the nilarium poker in an awkward sort of salute. "Thank you."

"Gods be for you," the pink woman whispered. With those words, she clasped her hands, bowed her head, and let the curtain of her hair fall like a veil over her face. Her task was done.

Feeling strangely bereft, Nelle stepped through the doorway. She'd only taken a few paces before she felt movement in the air. Turning, she saw the doorway shut.

She was alone now. Totally alone.

The hall before her was twice as broad as the entry foyer in Dornrise and much, much longer. Even with her magically opened eyes, she couldn't see its far end. Windows lined the walls on either side, but they were set too high for her to see anything but darkness beyond them.

Surely the nymph wouldn't send her this way if there was no possibility of escape. Or was she walking into a trap?

Bereft of options, Nelle slipped to the nearest pillar, feeling safer with something at her back. It was enormous, reaching to the arched ceiling overhead. She peered up, narrowing her eyes. Was that a pattern of clouds painted across the ceiling? And were they . . . moving?

Her pursed mouth twisting to one side, she studied the pillar itself. It wasn't stone as she'd first thought, or if it was, its surface had been perfectly carved to look like the rough bark of a pine tree. And at its base there appeared to be roots plunging into the stone floor.

It was all so strange. So otherworldly. So impossible. She might be a city girl through and through, but even she knew trees couldn't grow without sunlight.

Then again, this was Eledria. Maybe everything in this world thrived on pure magic.

Adjusting her grip on the poker, Nelle peeked out from behind the pillar. The long hall appeared to be empty. But she was a snatcher. She knew better than to trust appearances. Some sixth sense warned her that not all was as it seemed.

She hurried on to the next pillar, paused, and continued to the next. In this way, scurrying like a mouse from shelter to shelter, she crossed what felt like miles of stone before finally coming within sight of the hall's far end.

It was another blank wall. Nelle left the shelter of the final pillar and approached the wall slowly. It was at least thirty feet high and seemed to be a single slab of stone. Polished flat stone—no etchings or decoration other than natural veining.

"There's got to be a way out," Nelle whispered. She'd now twice seen doors appear where there'd seemed to be no door at all. Magical doorways must be the norm in Noxaur.

Reaching out a tentative hand, she rested her palm against the stone. It was so cold that at first she felt nothing but icy chill straight to her bones. Rather than pull back, she leaned into it, closed her eyes, and sent her senses searching for what lay beneath the surface of the stone.

A faint, tingling buzz responded to her search—magical energy lay under her palm, much like the sensation she got from Soran's spellbooks. This whole wall was laced with magic just waiting to be commanded.

Nelle opened her eyes and let her hand drop again. She didn't know a spell for opening secret doors. And though she'd heard the pink woman speak a command, she couldn't for the life of her recall the words used. But maybe . . . maybe . . .

Magic originated in the *quinsatra*. To be used, it must first be drawn into this world. Mages used the written form to summon it into physical reality; only then could they join their minds to it and begin the manipulation.

But this magic had already been drawn into this world and trapped in stone. How was that any different, really, than magic trapped in words or paper? The ward stones around Roseward contained spell writing, didn't they?

Nelle bowed her head, placed her hand back on the stone, and leaned heavily into the wall. Magic simmered under her touch, gathering in intensity. If she knew the Old Araneli words, she could certainly call it to life. But ultimately, what was Old Araneli? Just a language like any other. A way to make the incomprehensible realm of thought and mind and soul perceivable in a physical manifestation. Araneli may be more *perfect* than her own language, but . . . how much did perfection really matter?

"*Precision is everything, Miss Beck . . . except when it is not.*"

A smile slid across her face. She understood. In that heat-seared moment of clarity, she understood.

"Open," she commanded through clenched teeth.

The door in the wall swung out beneath her hand, so swiftly, so silently that she almost fell through. She stumbled, caught herself, and looked out.

Her eyes widened. A broad courtyard stretched before her, paved with smooth dark stones and surrounded by huge walls and towering, sharp-peaked buildings. But she hardly saw those.

Instead, her gaze fixed on the heaps and bundles spread out across the courtyard, piled on top of each other in unnatural tangles of limbs. Dozens upon dozens of skull-dogs.

24

Nelle couldn't move, couldn't breathe, couldn't even blink. A wind picked up and blew at her filmy skirts, whispered across her exposed skin, and played through her hair. At last, finished with its exploration of her, it whisked away and darted off among the sleeping monsters.

Not ten yards away, one of the skull-dogs snorted in its sleep. Its body twitched, shivered. Its snout slowly rose from where it had rested between massive paws.

A rush of hot terror flooded Nelle's limbs. She leapt back from the doorway, staggering several paces into the massive hall at her back.

Then, hardly knowing what she did, she slammed her hand against the wall beside the opening and gasped, "Close! Close, close!"

The magic in the stone whirled under her hand, but the opening remained. The wind returned, whisking between her skirts, and whistled off among the tree-pillars.

The skull-dog lifted its head, snorting and snuffling. A flash of red flickered in the depths of its gaping eye-sockets. It cocked its head and, had it possessed ears, they would certainly have pricked as it turned toward the door.

In another moment it would see her for sure.

"Close!" Nelle commanded, and pounded the wall with the flat of her hand.

The magic shivered as though startled. Then the door swung slowly, slowly inward. Nelle caught one last glimpse of the skull-dog just pushing up onto its haunches.

The door clicked blessedly shut. The stone wall before her was solid again.

"Oh!" Nelle turned and sagged, only just bracing her legs to keep from sliding down in a heap on the floor. Her mind whirled with panic. What in the spitting hells was she supposed to do next? The huge pillared hall stretched before her with the door to the tower at its far end. The tower where, presumably, Kyriakos still lay in drugged sleep. She couldn't go back that way.

But if there was a hidden door in this wall, surely there were other doors as well?

She grimaced, glancing up at the expanse of wall at her back. That courtyard . . . she'd not seen much of it. Her vision had been all but overwhelmed by the sight of those awful dogs. She'd seen a gate on the far side . . . or not? If she closed her eyes and forced herself to remember, she was fairly sure she'd seen a huge arched opening leading out into the darkened landscape beyond. And was she wrong to think there'd been a glimpse of shoreline and sea?

Brandishing the poker, Nelle hastened back down the hall. She'd scarcely taken ten paces before a warning frisson ran up the back of her neck. Without pausing to question the sensation, she ducked for the nearest of the tree pillars and put her back against it.

Something was here. Here in this huge, supposedly empty space. What's more, it had been here all along. She'd known somehow . . . or suspected, anyway. The cavernous emptiness had been a little too good to be true.

Heart ramming in her throat, Nelle held her breath and strained her ears, searching for the sound of a footstep or low breaths or . . . anything.

All was silent, still.

She had to look. If she stayed where she was, that *something* would creep up on her in the darkness and catch her where she stood. Kill her? Or drag her back to Kyriakos? She couldn't say which she dreaded more.

Peeling away from the pillar, she cautiously peered around the stone-hard trunk. At first she saw only more of those sentinel trees extending beyond sight down that huge hall. She let her breath out through her teeth, very slowly so as not to make a sound. Then—

There. She saw it.

A shadow stepped from the deeper shadow cast by a pillar five rows down from her current position. It stood in the empty space between pillars, a towering, multi-jointed being with no discernible features.

Did it see her? Could it see her? It had no eyes as far as she could tell. What kind of senses did a being like that possess?

The being swayed on its bowed legs. The shadowy protrusion that must serve as its head seemed to turn this way and that. It gave off an air of uncertainty and even faint anxiety.

Moving as slowly as possible so as not to draw attention, Nelle retreated behind the pillar. She strained her ears again, listening for some indication that it had sensed her, that it was even now approaching.

Up.

The word popped unbidden into her head.

Up. Get up. Get higher.

That was snatcher's sense talking. And she'd do well to listen.

Nelle looked up the trunk of the tree-pillar she leaned against and let her gaze travel from it to the window on the nearest wall. Could she somehow climb this pillar and make her way to that window? But there were no branches.

An idea took shape in her mind.

Aware that the shadow-being might even now be lurching toward her, Nelle placed a hand on the trunk. She hated to speak aloud but didn't know if the magic would work any other way. In a low hiss of a whisper, she breathed, "*Grow!*"

Something bulged under her hand, a hard knot springing suddenly to life. She pulled her hand back and saw a little branch unfurl before her eyes. It wasn't much, but it felt sturdy enough to hold her weight. Other branches sprang out higher up, running the height of the pillar. Stifling the glad cry in her throat, Nelle prepared to climb.

Something heavy landed on her shoulder.

A stink like sulfur filled her nose.

Nelle whirled, eyes widening as she stared up into a featureless shadow of a face. Only . . . it wasn't featureless anymore. Even as she looked, a mouth gaped open—side-to-side rather than up-and-down. A billow of white-hot fire mounded up inside and rippled beneath the dark exterior, lighting up features that were horribly almost human but simultaneously utterly inhuman. Two burning moon eyes blazed into hers, and an unnatural shriek broke the silence, drowning out Nelle's scream.

Instinct took over. Nelle swung her arm, still gripping the poker, and drove the nilarium spike straight into that gaping mouth.

The moon eyes goggled.

Then, in a burst of heat and darkness that knocked Nelle back against the tree-pillar, the being exploded. Nelle flung up her arms to protect her face but felt only specks of moisture against her skin. When she lowered her arms and dared look again, she was covered in little beads of black liquid. The shadow-thing was gone. Where it had stood lay the nilarium poker, bent and twisted like a limp noodle.

Pain brought Nelle to her senses. Trying to swallow back a whimper, she looked down and saw that one of the branches had torn into her torso. Her corset bodice was stained dark with blood. How bad the wound was she couldn't tell, but it hurt. She knew that much.

The hairs on the back of her neck prickled, and she knew other shadowy beings were manifesting in the darkness on the other side of her pillar. Slow-witted but curious, disturbed by the sudden demise of one of their brothers. They would be on her in a moment.

She didn't have a second poker.

Simultaneously pivoting and pushing her satchel aside to bounce against the small of her back, Nelle grabbed the nearest branch and pulled. She got her foot onto the branch that had stabbed her. It was broken but still solid enough to support her weight. Pain knifed through her side, but fear and adrenaline pulsed thunderously through her limbs, and she climbed quickly. Some distant part of her mind admired the way the magically summoned branches had grown at such even and convenient intervals.

Only when she was halfway up the pillar and on a level with the window did she dare look down. Three shadow-beings shambled along the floor beneath her, so silent that she wouldn't know they were there had her eyes not magically opened. They seemed confused, aimless. One of them stumbled over the twisted nilarium poker and bent to examine it. Its whole body folded neatly in half to bring the head-like protrusion down to the floor.

Then it looked up.

She felt those non-eyes searching for her among the branches. Could it see her? Sense her? Could it climb?

She looked to the window again. It was tall, broad, and peaked, with a sill big enough for her to stand on, and it appeared to be open, though she couldn't tell for certain.

She glanced down again. All three shadow-beings had gathered around the base of her tree. They were looking up. At her. She was sure of it. At any moment they would start to climb. She had to get across to that window. But how?

Nelle looked down at the branch her left hand gripped. She tightened her hold, feeling the magic inside it, ready and waiting. "Grow," she said. "Grow now!"

The branch wriggled in her grasp. The instant she let go, the branch twisted, writhed, and began to sprout from the tree-pillar, thickening as it went. The tree groaned at the suddenness of growth, and the whole structure trembled. She was abusing the magic, forcing it to grow so big, so fast. What's more, she felt it taking a toll on her body. The effort of creation was enough to make her head spin.

Clinging to the other branches, she rested her head against the stone-like trunk, breathing deeply. When she could bear to look again, the newly grown branch was as thick around as her waist and stretched all the way to the windowsill.

The tree shuddered again. Then it swayed.

Her heart jumping, Nelle looked down and, to her horror, saw the three shadow-beings climbing slowly, ever so slowly, their long, many-jointed limbs reaching and searching for each handhold as they came.

She had to move. Now.

Nelle swung up onto the new branch. She stood, finding her

balance, her bare toes clinging to the twisted, knotted contours of that limb. She'd walked many a narrow ridgepole in her day—but ridgepoles weren't known for swaying so sickeningly. And it was a long way down.

Nelle looked. Just once more. Like Mother had taught her.

Looked and accepted the distance, the bone-crushing drop.

Then, once accepted, she locked the knowledge up in the back of her mind, faced ahead to the windowsill. Stepped out.

One step.

Two steps.

Three.

The shadow-beings were climbing faster now.

Four steps.

Five.

She reached the middle of the branch. Her arms extended to either side, her gaze fixed on her goal.

Six steps.

Seven.

Eight.

The tree uttered a terrible growl. Magic surged through the branch, under Nelle's soles. The branch swayed dangerously, ready to send her flying.

With a gasping prayer, Nelle bent her knees and sprang for the windowsill just as the branch cracked and gave out beneath her. Just as the tree splintered at its core and collapsed with a horrible, ear-splitting roar, shattering the stone floor below and crushing the shadow-beings beneath it.

The whole hall quaked.

Nelle hung suspended from the windowsill with her upper arms and elbows hooked on the ledge, her body and legs kicking wildly over the drop. With a gasping sob, she heaved herself up onto the sill. It was narrower than she'd thought, but she managed to poise there. Though she didn't want to, she peered back down at the wreckage of the poor tree-pillar.

The shadow-beings oozed out from broken lumps of stone and pulled themselves upright, shaking back into almost-human shapes.

"Bullspit!" Nelle hissed.

She sidled along the sill until she reached the frame, where she could stand and look out. The roof of a side building sloped not five feet below her. It was steep, but she should be able to scramble to its peak. She reached out, feeling for glass or some sort of resistance, but found only an enchantment of some kind, perhaps intended to keep out the wind. She could get through, no problem.

Crouching on the ledge, Nelle readied and sprang to the roof below. She landed too hard, her bones jarring at the impact. The rough roofing material—tile? stone?—tore at her hands and feet, her knees and elbows. The gash in her side flared with pain. But she didn't fall. She kept her balance, suppressing the pain behind her clenched jaw.

Moving swiftly, she climbed on hands and knees, momentarily grateful for the huge slits in the skirt which afforded easy range of movement. An ugly chorus of baying filled her ears as she gained the peak of the roof and peered down into the courtyard below.

The pack of skull-dogs was up and milling around, howling their ugly heads off. Disturbed by the crash inside the hall, no doubt. The whole palace had probably heard it.

Great. Just great.

Nelle stood to hasten along the ridgepole, reached a twisted outcropping that might be a chimney of sorts, and took shelter behind it. Breathing hard, she took stock of her surroundings. The building she was currently on stood close to another that appeared to be near the boundary wall. Could she jump from one building to the next, then use the wall to reach the gate? Not without exposing herself to view on many sides.

What other choice did she have?

Edging out from behind the chimney, she eased her way down the steep roof slope to the very edge. No more than five feet of space separated this roof from the next. That wouldn't be a problem ordinarily. But with this bleeding wound in her side . . .

Nelle grimaced and lowered her chin, trying to glimpse the ground below, but the darkness between the two buildings was too deep even for her magicked eyes. For all she knew, skull-dogs prowled there as well as in the open courtyard. Or more shadow-beings, mute but dogged in their search.

Probably wouldn't make no difference, she thought grimly. *A drop that far'll kill you.*

Nelle pressed a hand to her bleeding side. Then, inching back up the roof several feet, she stood, ran down the slope, and sprang, using the momentum to propel her. She landed with a solid, painful thud, managing to catch her balance and not roll down over the edge.

Biting back curses, she climbed to the peak of the roof, keeping her body low and close to the slats. Were those shouts that she heard mingling with the dog's howls down below? Not animal voices, but not human either. Those shadow-beings didn't talk, which meant the voices she heard must belong to some of the fae denizens of Ninthalor. They were on the alert now.

Had Kyriakos awakened? Or had they simply come running in response to the crash in the hall?

A little tower stood at the peak of this roof. A bell tower, perhaps. She couldn't see or sense anyone inside, so she climbed up to it, thinking it might work for a temporary shelter. As she climbed higher, however, she saw a walkway leading along the top of the roof to the tower, which meant others could easily run out to catch her. Not good. But if she didn't find a place to hunker down and catch her breath, she would end up light-headed. Hardly ideal for rooftop rambling.

She reached the little tower and caught hold of the rail, intending to pull herself up inside. Just as she started to heave her body up, she stopped short.

A bell hung in the tower, just as she'd suspected. Bright, silver. Silent.

And all around it, clinging to the rafters, were small, warm bodies suspended upside-down by long, taloned toes. Feathered wings wrapped bat-like around weirdly humanoid torsos and half covered strange, beaked, mannish faces.

Harpens.

A whole roosting massacre.

Nelle eased away from the tower and back down onto the roof slats, scarcely daring to breathe. The last thing, the very last thing she wanted was to wake those monsters—

"*Atradir!*"

Startled, Nelle turned, whipping long hair out of her face. Five figures, armed and helmeted, appeared at the end of the walkway, the last just emerging from a trap-door hatch. Spiked weapons bristled in their hands.

One of them gestured her way. The other four lunged forward, racing along that high walkway straight for her.

For a heartbeat, indecision held her captive.

Then, with a curse bursting from her lips, she leapt up, scrambled over the railing into the bell tower, and, not daring to hesitate even a second, shoved the bell with both hands. It swung heavily on its hinges, swung back again, then uttered a low, dull: *Boooom.*

Hundreds of wicked little eyes opened.

The air split with the cacophonous screaming of harpens, nearly drowning out the second toll of the bell as it swung back. Nelle's eardrums threatened to burst as she flung herself over the far rail and fell from the tower to the slanted roof, where she hit hard and rolled and rolled and kept rolling, unable to stop, unable to hear or feel anything except her too rapid descent. She expected the roof to give out, the fall to claim her.

But she came to an abrupt stop with her back against a wall, stunned but whole. She blinked hard, gasping at the pain in her side, and looked wildly up the way she'd just come.

Harpens swarmed the air overhead like a storm descending on the five armored figures. The bell tolled one last time, a deep underscore to the shouting and screaming and ripping and mayhem. The harpens couldn't penetrate armor, but they went for the faces behind the faceplates, screeching with the delight of bloodlust.

Nelle picked herself up. The roof seemed to be built against the surrounding courtyard wall, which was too high for her to spring atop. But, turning frantically, she spied what might be a drainage pipe not far from her current position.

Running at an awkward tilt along the slanted roof with one hand pressed to her ribcage, the other using the wall for support, Nelle made her way to the pipe, hoping and praying the harpens wouldn't notice her. Gods above knew she didn't have any bodily protection!

Reaching the pipe, she scrambled nimbly up the side of the wall and slipped between crenellations to drop onto a parapet broad enough for three large men to walk abreast. Rushing to the far side, Nelle peered over the edge.

"Seven gods!" she breathed, her eyes widening.

It was much, much farther down on the outside—a dizzying drop along smooth wall and ragged stone slopes to a brutal landing she could scarcely see. One narrow winding road made its way up to the gate, and there the drop was only three stories high. Still too great.

The gate. Her head snapped to her left. There had to be a lever or wheel or something that would open the gate. There had to be. Maybe she could . . .

"*Atradir!*"

Nelle started, turning. Armed figures swarmed up to the wall from various access points and marched toward her, lances readied. She cast one last look down the wall, trying to believe there could be handholds and footholds, trying to believe she could scramble down that sheer surface like a scuttling spider. It was useless.

Swallowing a cry of despair, she turned and ran for the gate arch, her thin skirts billowing behind her, her legs bare, and her unprotected feet screaming in protest as they slapped on the harsh stones. Before she'd taken more than twenty paces, she saw more armed figures approach from the opposite end, cutting her off. She stopped, sagging against a crenellation.

This was it then. Her mad getaway was over. Kyriakos would never be caught off guard again.

Would he drag her back to the tower and that red room? Or lock her deep in a dungeon somewhere, shackled and helpless?

With a sob caught in her throat, Nelle turned away from the oncoming figures and gazed out across the darkness-stricken landscape. There was the shore, the sea, not half a mile away. And was that the outline of Roseward her magicked eyes spied through the dense gloom? Or was it only her wishful thinking?

Wind from the sea blew in her face and, when she lifted a hand to push hair from her eyes, something flashed—a little band of gold threads wrapped around her thumb. A spell-band, almost invisible, almost forgotten.

"Wear this on your finger, and a thread of connection will remain linked to me."

Nelle clenched her fist, her thumb and the ring pressed tight against her curled fingers. It was useless, hopeless.

But what did she have to lose?

Pounding feet drew near. Lances gleamed in her peripheral vision. Harsh voices barked words she did not understand.

Nelle closed her eyes and felt the thread of connection stretching from the ring out into the darkness. Out to that churning sea. She flicked her wrist three times, tugging the thread. The ring burned hot against her skin.

Then hard hands took hold of her arms and shoulders, and the rod of a lance struck the backs of her legs, collapsing her to her knees. She bowed her head and, for the moment at least, did not attempt to fight.

25

Now that he knew it was there, Soran felt the shimmering curse, a pliable but unrelenting wall of resistance. It wasn't particularly strong, but in that moment, neither was he. His powers, both physical and mental, were stretched to the limit, and he lacked the strength to break through. Every time he thought he found a weakness, the spell concentrated in that area and pushed him back again.

The last push was hard enough to knock him off the rower's bench. He dropped one oar and scrambled only just fast enough to plunge his arm into the waves and catch it before it was carried off. He hauled it back into the boat and collapsed, soaked and gasping.

He felt like a fly desperately buzzing to break through the spider's web. Only he was much stupider than any fly. After all, he wasn't trapped. He could turn away whenever he liked. As soon as he was ready to admit defeat.

Raising his heavy head, Soran gazed out to the Noxaur shore. It looked closer. His efforts to push through the curse weren't entirely in vain. But even if he succeeded, it had already taken too long.

There was no chance he would reach Nelle before . . . before . . .

Spitting expletives through clenched teeth, Soran clambered back up onto the bench, fixed the oar into position, and set to rowing. Again his senses probed the curse, searching for the next thin place where he might push through.

Something tugged at his heart.

Soran stopped, surprised, and blinked down at his chest. But there was nothing to be seen. At least, not with mortal eyes.

A second tug followed, harder than the first. He gasped out loud at the sensation of . . . not quite *pain* but similar.

At the third tug, he realized what it was.

Lifting his head, he turned and looked back at Noxaur. Only now he saw not only the dark, forbidding shore, the obscuring darkness of a night-shrouded landscape, but also something that gleamed with the bright luminosity of the *quinsatra*.

A spell thread. A connection.

Seven gods! He'd almost forgotten about that ring.

The thread brightened by the moment, a line of fire through the air. It cut straight through the invisible deflection curse, and Soran felt the curse fray on the edges, giving way before the stronger magic.

"Nelle," he whispered.

His strength revived. Since the spell wasn't something that

could be seen with physical eyes, he turned in his seat without hesitation and rowed hard, with the thread's burning pull leading him straight and true.

Within minutes, the last of the deflection curse melted away.

As soon as it was gone, the Night of Noxaur deepened. Soran had thought it couldn't get any darker than it already was, but he swiftly discovered his error. Total blindness held him captive. He had to turn around, row back to where the dark was not quite so complete, and, still mostly blind, withdraw the smaller book of spells he'd brought with him and find a vision spell. He read it off quickly and breathed a sigh of relief as he felt his pupils dilate, taking in and amplifying even the smallest traces of light.

When he crossed the line again, the Night was no longer so absolute. He pressed on, following the summoning spell, and soon the little boat's hull crunched into gritty shoreline. Soran sprang out, dragged it up onto the shore, and faced what lay before him.

Ninthalor.

The infamous seaside palace sat high on sheer crags above the shoreline, looming over the landscape. Its many peaked rooftops and spiraling towers looked as though they had been carved out of the cliffs themselves, which truly might be the case. Some said Ninthalor had been a troll citadel long ago, before the fae came and populated Noxaur. Many strange stories and dark legends abounded in both Eledria and the realms of mortals. Kyriakos was neither the first nor the most dreadful lord to rule this citadel.

But he was certainly bad enough.

The spell thread glittered through the darkness, leading straight across that bare landscape to where the ground began to rise in rocky formations. A single road wound up to the fortress gates. No one could approach those gates without being spotted from the many watch towers. Sentries may have already announced Soran's arrival to their lord.

Let them.

His hand trembled more than he liked as he reached for the Rose Book. For a moment he simply stood with the waves of the Hinter lapping at his feet and gazed at the once-beautiful binding. The gold-leaf decoration on the cover had peeled away over time, and the spine was frayed on the edges, the red leather battered, the creases nearly white with wear. He felt the volume's frailty as he had never felt it before . . . and the futility of attempting to contain so much magic, so much power, in a mere physical form.

What he was about to do, would it be more than the book could survive? He had only ever worked the spell in this way once before—on the night of its creation. Since then he had only bound and re-bound the power within. Would unleashing it mean the end? Would the Rose Book disintegrate under the strain?

Soran drew a slow breath. Then he unbuckled the straps, opened the book across his forearm, and held it up before his magicked eyes. He could only just discern the words.

Yes. Yes, yes, yes.

She was there. At his side, her lips close to his ear. Invisible but ever-present.

Oh, my love, my love! Let me out. Let me loose. Let me be what I was always meant to be.

He must take care. He must maintain control. It was a balance, a treacherous balance. One word read inaccurately, one little slip of tongue or mind, and all would be lost.

Don't hold back! I am ready. I am ready to do all that you send me to do!

He felt her hands grasping his shoulders, eager and tense. Her thirst for blood was terrifying.

Soran closed his eyes. Then, firming his stance, he opened his eyes and stared intently at those words. Let them burn into his mind, let the power burst forth from the page as it had not done in all the years of his imprisonment! He began to read aloud, letting the words fill the air around him, and under the influence of his voice they changed, twisted, became true to their nature.

Not a binding. An unleashing.

The realm of Nightmares opened wide, and the Thorn Maiden spilled through to manifest in physical reality.

26

Two armored guards dragged Nelle back to the pillared hall where the broken tree lay across a deeply cracked floor. The doors gaped much wider than the small opening Nelle had made when she bade it open. These were twelve feet tall or more, and she could easily see beyond them into the hall itself.

Kyriakos stood before the ruins of the pillar-tree, flanked by shadow-beings. Skull-dogs milled around his feet, snarling and salivating as the armored guards dragged Nelle up the flight of steps and through the doorway. The guards raised their lances in salute, then brought them down in a sharp synchronized crack against the stone. Nelle hung suspended between them, her feet barely touching the floor.

The lord of Ninthalor wore a long open vest-robe of brilliant red. Funny how she could see the color even in this darkness. Though the nymph's spell had opened her eyes, the world had remained primarily colorless throughout her escape. But that red was unmistakable. It flowed like living heat from the fae lord's powerful shoulders.

He took a step toward her but stumbled. One of the shadow-beings hastily moved forward to offer an arm, but he waved it away. Nelle dared to sneak a glance up through her tangled hair and saw that the left side of his face sagged as though still paralyzed. The Sweet Dreams had worn off sooner than it did on mortals, but it wasn't completely gone from his system, not yet.

"Little wife," Kyriakos said. Although the words slurred badly, his voice was no less sinister. "It would seem you are a woman of more than one secret. *Rishva* . . . ha!" He lifted one hand and rubbed his numb face, pulled at his sagging lip. "Never thought I'd see the day when I'd be taken down by a vila whore's trick. And from mortal lips, no less!"

Nelle met his gaze. Her breath came in hard, panting gusts, not entirely due to her recent exertions. She wanted to quiver, to fold up on herself, to hide. But that wasn't the way Mother had taught her.

Instead, she smiled. "La, my lord!" Her voice came out in a bright trill. "Tell these goons of yours to unhand me, and I'll show you another trick or two."

The half of Kyriakos's mouth that still worked twisted into a snarl. He stepped toward her, leaning heavily on an assisting shadow-being and pushing skull-dogs out of his way. Catching her chin in his hand, he ruthlessly yanked her face up to his. She fixed her smile in place, refusing to look away even as he ran his thumb across her lips, smearing whatever traces remained of the Sweet Dreams. The sharp edge of his nail trailed over her skin.

"I told you," he said, spitting the words out, "I prefer my wives willing. But that doesn't mean I won't take them however they come."

With those words, he pressed his sagging, numb lips to hers while a doglike growl rumbled in his throat. There was nothing seductive about that kiss, none of the lethal fae subtlety. It was not a promise but a threat. A threat he fully intended to see through to completion.

The moment his lips left hers, Nelle spat in his face. Her spittle slid unheeded down his senseless cheek. His grip on her chin tightened, fingernails digging in, ready to draw blood.

But then, with a groan, he heaved himself upright, gripping the shadow-being's arm. "Back to the tower with her," he barked, gesturing to the guards. "Strip her down and bind her to the bed. See that she has no more such tricks hidden about her person. I'll be along . . . presently."

"Bastard!" Nelle cried. Whatever remained of her mother's bravado melted away, replaced by pure fury and fear. "Are you so afraid to fight me that you gotta tie me down like an animal? Coward, bullspitting coward!"

The guards picked her off her feet and carried her between them back along the pillared hall. Nelle writhed in their viselike hands, hurling insults and expletives back over her shoulder. Before they'd carried her more than twenty paces, however, they froze in place. Voices erupted in the courtyard behind them. Terrified voices.

"*Khilseith yesphyra! Yesphyra, yesphyra!*

The strange words echoed off the courtyard buildings and walls, magnified as others took up the cry.

Then came a word Nelle recognized: "*Noswraith!*"

Her eyes widened.

The shouts turned to screams. Kyriakos, standing at the head of the hall, recoiled from the open doorway, shouting, "Close it! Close it now!" Nelle saw him stagger and nearly fall, only just caught by his shadowy servant. As the tall doors began to close, she glimpsed armored men lining up just outside, and right before the doors snapped shut she saw . . . she saw . . .

She saw three of them lifted into the air by massive, tentacle-like vines. Enormous thorns pierced through armor. Blood spurted.

The doors shut with an echoing thud. The wall stood blank and solid, without even the barest crack to indicate where the doors had been.

And then . . .

Cracks. Hundreds and hundreds of cracks running through the wall as if it were fragile crockery.

Kyriakos screamed; the skull-dogs howled. The shadow-beings bodily picked up their master and carried him along the arched hall, making for the far end.

The wall shattered. Dust filled the air, choking, blinding.

When Nelle's vision cleared, she lay beside a fallen pillar-tree, covered in dust and bits of rubble. Her ears thudded dully, the throb of her pulse almost drowning out the other sounds—

screaming, snarling, crushing. She rubbed dust from her blinking eyes and briefly feared the pink woman's magic was wearing off already, leaving her blind in the Noxaur darkness. But then her vision slowly cleared.

The Thorn Maiden approached.

Standing eight feet tall or more—a creature of thorns and roses, but altogether womanly, altogether beautiful and sensual— she strolled along the ruins of that hall, savage briars sprouting from her body in thick masses. More thorns and briars crawled up the pillar-trees, tearing them apart and dragging them down one after another. Much of the roof had caved in, and one whole wall had collapsed.

All around, guards in armor hacked at the writhing branches with swords that flashed with brilliant, blinding magic. But for every limb they struck down, another grew in its place. The guards themselves were caught and yanked from their feet into a constrictor embrace that drove blade-like thorns deep through their armor into their writhing bodies.

Kyriakos? Where was he? Nelle thought she caught a glimpse of fluttering red, but before she could determine whether it was her fae captor, something slithered around her ankle. She just had time to look down, to see the briar catch hold of her.

To realize she was about to be crushed, impaled.

The next instant she was dragged across harsh rubble, kicking and screaming. She tried uselessly to catch hold of something, to stop or at least slow her progress, but then she was lifted upside down by her leg. The long slitted skirts flapped down around her face, and she pushed them wildly aside, her arms thrashing at random.

An exquisite face of rose petals appeared before her vision.

There, little mortal, the Thorn Maiden said, her voice a hiss of deadly perfume. *I've found you.* Her strange mouth broke into an even stranger smile. *Much as I'd like to play, I'll have to save you for later. For now, my master compels me elsewhere.*

Nelle tried to open her mouth, tried to scream. But before any sound could emerge from her throat, she was half carried, half flung from the rubble by that clinging vine. Her head spun with whirling, violent flashes. Then she collapsed in a bundle of limbs, and the briar was gone.

At first she could only lie there, convinced that she must be dead. But she was breathing. And when she tried to move, she still had possession of her body. She pushed up onto her elbows, taking stock of her injuries. Her wounded side spasmed, and her arms and legs and bare shoulders and bosom were a mass of small cuts. But she wasn't dead.

Struggling to her feet, she stood swaying, staring at the horrors in the darkness. The vine had dropped her in the center of the courtyard outside the ruinous hall. Dead bodies littered the stones—fae guardsmen mutilated almost beyond recognition, skull-dogs torn to pieces, remnants of shadow-beings shredded and discarded like rags.

Nelle turned around. The gate. The gate was broken. Shattered. Along with most of the wall.

With a whimpering cry, Nelle staggered for the opening. With each footfall, her will to live revived. She increased her pace until she was running faster than she'd ever run before. She climbed over the rubble, which heaved dangerously under her weight, and all but fell out into the open road beyond.

Behind her, screams and the sounds of crushing stone continued to fill the air. She stopped up her ears and simply ran.

Soran stood with the Rose Book on his arm, his legs braced and his shoulders back. The spell poured out from the pages in which it had been captured, channeled through his mouth and his mind and into this world.

When he reached the end of the spell, he felt the surging thrill of power *almost* beyond his ability to control. It wanted to tear out from him, to split him in two and leave him behind, like a butterfly crawling from its chrysalis.

No! He firmed his stance and held on to his sanity, to his mastery. This was *his* spell. The Thorn Maiden was great and dreadful, but for as long as the Rose Book lasted, she belonged to *him*.

He blinked down at the volume. The spell was spoken now, complete. And the book? It held together. He could feel the weakness, the frailty of the paper that wanted to erupt in flames as the energy of the *quinsatra* seared across the precisely inked lines of spell. But it held. For the time being.

Soran closed the book and looked up, lifting his gaze to see what he had done. Ninthalor still stood on its craggy heights, but smoke rose from it in a cloud. Smoke, or debris. Walls were toppled, towers teetered. And even here, with the murmur of the ocean at his back and the Hinter winds teasing through his hair and robes, he heard screams.

"What have I done?" he whispered.

How many lives lost?

How many deaths now added to the long ledger seared into his conscience?

This was an act of war. Nothing less. Word would get back to Lodírhal. News of this attack would spread throughout Eledria like wildfire. And how would the King of Aurelis respond?

Swiftly, that's how. And with finality.

Soran's jaw clenched. His hand holding the closed Rose Book trembled. Perhaps he ought to begin the binding now. Try to rein her back in before this horror got any worse.

But he couldn't yet. Not until he knew . . . Not until he saw . . . Not until . . .

Did his eyes deceive him? He shook his head, rubbed at his face with his free hand. Then he looked again, desperate hope swelling in his heart. Was that the slim figure of a young woman running along the empty stretch of land between Ninthalor's road and the desolate beach? Was that long hair flowing behind her as red as fire, even here in Noxaur's gloom? Was that . . . ?

He didn't wait to know for sure. Shoving the Rose Book inside his robes, he set out at a run. He hadn't realized he had strength enough left in his limbs to move so fast. His long legs tore up the space, sending up spurts of sand, and his robes billowed out behind him.

It was Nelle! Staggering, bleeding. But alive.

"*Soran!*"

Her voice reached out to him like a dream. And perhaps it was a dream. Perhaps he'd miscalculated the spell, perhaps he'd let something slip. Perhaps this was nothing more than an illusion planted in his mind by the Thorn Maiden. A worthy punishment for his crime, if so.

He didn't care.

"Nelle!" he shouted back. His eyes drank in the sight of her fear-stricken face streaked with blood. Then she was in his arms, pressed close to his heart. Her body quaked, wracked with sobs, shivering so hard that she might shatter in his grasp and disperse like a cloud of rose petals. He held her tighter, tighter, refusing to let this moment be a dream.

"Nelle," he gasped, one hand holding the back of her head, pressing her to his breast. But that wasn't enough. He had to see her, had to look into her eyes. More roughly than he intended, he pushed her back a pace, gripping her by the shoulders. Her very bare shoulders.

For the first time he took in her attire—and how little of it there was.

"Soran!" Nelle caught hold of the front of his robes. Tears

streaked through the grime on her cheeks, and her hair hung in snarls over her forehead, in her eyes. "The Thorn Maiden! The Thorn Maiden is free!"

"I know," he said grimly. Though reluctant to let her go for fear she would dissolve into nothing, he wrenched his hands from her shoulders, hastily shrugged out of his outer robe, and slung it around her, its folds covering her naked flesh. She looked down at herself and seemed to realize what she wore. A hot flush of shame stained her cheeks before she clutched the folds of his robe together at her throat and looked up into Soran's eyes.

"What can we do?" she said. "What can we do? We've got to stop her!"

Soran looked into her face but hardly saw her now. Red flashes burst on the edges of his vision.

That dress . . . Like something a brothel worker would wear.

It was Kyriakos's doing.

She didn't have to tell him. He knew what had been done to her. How she had been used.

He raised his gaze to Ninthalor just as another of the high walls crumbled and fell under the Thorn Maiden's assault. Good. Let it fall. Let it all fall to the ground and bury the denizens in a ruinous tomb.

"Soran!" Nelle's fingers dug into his arm. When he didn't turn, she caught his face, yanking it down, forcing him to look at her. "You've got to stop this! You've got to!"

He shook his head. "No, I don't. Not after . . . what he's done . . ." His heart was a hot, seething stone in his breast.

She blinked up at him, her face deathly pale behind the grime and streaks of blood. Slowly her eyes rounded in growing horror, as though she watched him transform into something ravenous and hideous right there in front of her. But that was also good. Let her see him for what he truly was, once and for all.

Let her see the beast. The monster.

"I escaped." Nelle shook her head, her mouth hardening, her teeth flashing. "I escaped! Do you hear me? Someone helped me get out before . . . before anything happened. Someone who's still up there, Soran! Someone who needs your help."

Her words rolled over him, unable to penetrate the hardness of his mind or the burning of his heart. He shook his head and began to turn, prepared to lead the way back to the waiting boat, to leave the Thorn Maiden to her pleasures.

But Nelle released his arm. "Bullspitting hell! Mage Silveri, if you don't do something, so help me, I'll do it myself!"

He looked sharply down at her in time to see her pull her satchel around from her back where it hung beneath the folds of his robe. She flipped it open and drew out her own blank spellbook and quill. Her eyes flashed to meet his for just an instant before she turned, opened the book, and faced Ninthalor. She hesitated, her quill poised over the empty page.

She didn't know what she was doing. She didn't have the first idea how to bind a Noswraith. And yet . . .

And yet there was something brimming in her spirit, some force to be reckoned with. That *ibrildian* magic, so uncanny, so unnatural. So undeniable.

She couldn't succeed. But in her failure she might accomplish more than many a powerful Miphato ever managed in all his lifetime.

Soran reached out, caught hold of her wrist. She jerked away with a snarl, staggered away from him, and made as though to begin again. "Miss Beck," he said sharply. "Stop. You may cause more harm than help." She looked round at him, her expression fierce, and he sighed. "I will do it. I will bind her."

"Do it then," Nelle growled, her voice hard, her breathing labored.

Soran nodded and drew the Rose Book from his robes. He saw her eyes fasten on the book with an intensity of interest he didn't fully understand. Perhaps she sensed the magic pulsing through that fragile binding.

He undid the straps and opened the book to the first page. The magic of the Noswraith spell flared out at him, ready to melt the skin from his face. The book was already strained. Could it withstand the pressure if he read the spell again so soon? For that matter, could he endure it? Every night he labored long to reassert the binding on the Thorn Maiden before she escaped. Every night it was a battle he wasn't sure he could win.

But now she was free. Manifest and physical. And he? Weakness rippled through his exhausted body. He'd pushed his limits already beyond anything he'd believed possible.

And what of Nelle? She was protected at the moment, for as he'd read the unleashing, he'd woven in a command for her preservation. But if he failed now . . .

He wouldn't fail. He couldn't.

Aware of Nelle's eyes fixed on his face, Soran began to read the spell. Silently this time, and with different emphasis. The same spell, channeled to new purpose. Magic blazed from the page and poured into his mind, poured out from his soul. He sent it racing, scorching through the *quinsatra* up to Ninthalor's ruined walls, and his awareness went with it.

He saw the Thorn Maiden amid her hellish work, glorying in gory delights. He saw the fae and faekind throw themselves at her, hurling weapons and magic to no avail. They could not stop a living nightmare. Nothing could stop her except . . .

"*Helenia*," he called out.

Even as her many arms tore into her foes and ripped into the tall buildings, the figure standing at her core paused. The womanly face and form turned, the gaping holes where her eyes should be, searched. And she saw him.

Well met, my love. Her voice lilted through the screams of her prey, bright and sweet as birdsong. *Have you come to stop me already? But I've only just begun!*

"*You've done enough, Helenia,*" Soran said. He saw himself standing in the ruinous courtyard, surrounded by death and destruction. His physical body still stood down on the road, reading the spell, but that body scarcely mattered.

The Thorn Maiden approached. While her many limbs continued to tear and destroy, she fixed him with her eyeless stare and moved with a murmuring grace of leaves and petals, her form becoming more like the Helenia he remembered with every step. She drew close enough to reach out with one thorny hand for his face, but her fingers slid right through the image, for she was physical here and he was not.

"*It's time to return,*" Soran said. "*Come back to me. Now.*"

She smiled, her face lovely and dreadful. He saw the human face of Helenia flicker briefly across her features. *I think I will not.*

She lashed out at him. This time her fingers, long and branched and claw-like, streaked through both the mortal and the spiritual worlds. But Soran was prepared. Though his physical body shuddered on the verge of collapse, in spirit he sprang nimbly aside and drew from the *quinsatra* realm a noose of brilliant, burning magic. With a deft flick of his wrist, he sent it flying over her head, down around her neck and shoulders. Catching hold with both hands, he yanked it tight and pulled the Thorn Maiden off her feet.

She crashed to the ground. All her various limbs jolted and dropped hold of the bodies and stones and walls they'd clutched. They undulated wildly, smashing into rocks and knocking rooftops in. The Thorn Maiden twisted where she lay, her neck breaking and reforming but unable to escape that shining snare.

She snarled up at him, and her face was horribly human amid the briars. She spat rotten leaves from her tongue.

Beware, my love! she hissed. *I will find you! I will find you!*

Soran yanked the noose one last time, testing to make certain it was secure. Then he took a single step back . . . far back, out of that ruined yard, out of that death and destruction and gore . . .

. . . back to where his physical body stood, still reading the spellbook.

The words glowed blindingly from the page, and sweat poured down his face, through his hair. Had his hands not been coated in nilarium, he might not have been able to hold onto that pulsing volume.

A roar tore through the pulsating magic, striking his senses with a bolt of pure, almost childlike terror. Soran choked and nearly lost the flow of the spell. Hastily he caught hold and fixed it in a temporary stay. Only then did he look up from the page. Up to Ninthalor.

Up to where a writhing storm of briars poured out from the broken walls and slithered and crawled and mounded down the narrow road. Straight toward them.

"Soran?" Nelle stood beside him. Her hand clutched his arm. "She's coming!"

He nodded. Then, keeping a finger between the pages so as not to lose his place in the book, he turned, gripped Nelle's hand, and started to run. "Back to the boat," he barked, dragging her along behind him. "She cannot cross running water, not in her physical form. Hurry!"

Nelle panted, and an occasional whimper burst from her throat. But she kept pace with him down to the dark shore, down to where the boat waited. Behind them the Thorn Maiden ripped into the landscape, trailing a noxious cloud of rose perfume in her wake.

Nearly falling as they approached the boat, Nelle caught its gunwale, braced herself, and helped Soran push it out into the waves. "Get in!" Soran cried, and she obeyed him at once. He pushed a little farther, then jumped in. He reached for the oars, but Nelle got there first.

"Read the spell," she said grimly and tossed back the folds of his robe to free her arms for movement. She set to work rowing, pulling hard, putting space between them and the shore. Her gaze fixed beyond him, back the way they had come. He could tell by the waxing horror of her expression that the Thorn Maiden drew nearer, nearer.

Soran bowed over the book, pressing it open on his knees. He flinched and smothered a cry as the violent magic struck him again, body and soul. But he must continue. Though his whole body threatened to collapse, he must. Taking up the spell where he'd left off, he read on and on, words rolling through his head, joining with the magic, consummating and creating.

He felt her presence—physically at his back, lurching and shrieking and tearing along the shoreline, stretching out her great arms in desperate, furious need—but also in his mind, in his soul. She was a nightmare. Even when manifest, she was still a thing of spirit.

You won't bind me! she hissed in his mind. Her arms coiled around his soul, thick and dark and crushing. *You won't imprison me! Never again!*

She ripped into him, and he bled and bled. Soran tried to concentrate on his physical form, to force himself to realize that she could not truly touch him. But his body responded to the assault on his mind, and dark rivulets coursed down his skin.

The words on the page before him blurred, ran together. He thought he heard Nelle's voice crying out his name, but that might be no more than wishful thinking.

My love, snarled the Thorn Maiden in his mind. *My love, my love . . .*

27

S oran!" Nelle screamed. The battering sea wind ripped her voice from her throat and sent it crashing out into the waves. She watched in horror as the mage, who'd been crouched in the boat's stern, slowly crumpled over and collapsed. Blood seeped through his shirt in multiple places, ruby red even in the Noxaur darkness.

The Thorn Maiden writhed and roiled along the shore. She was massive—as tall as the highest peak of Dornrise's roof and twice as broad. A nightmarish mass of coiling evil that never belonged to this world. And in its center stood the womanly form of the maiden herself, small compared to the span of her hundreds upon hundreds of lashing limbs, yet still towering and terrible.

She walked down to the very edge of the water, where the surface lapped at her feet. Her arms stretched long and lethal over the dark waves, eager to catch her prey.

The pain in Nelle's side where the tree branch had punctured her skin sharpened with every stroke she made, and the oars were heavy in her trembling hands. But the sight of the Thorn Maiden fueled strength she hadn't known she possessed. She rowed with frantic rhythm, putting distance between the little boat and that shore.

Only when she was positive they were beyond the Noswraith's reach did she ship the oars and, half falling from the bench, reach out to the mage lying in the shallow water at the bottom of the boat.

"Soran," she breathed, catching hold of his shoulder and rolling him a little to see his face. It was a mass of bloody streaks. She'd watched those cuts appearing on his skin, one after another, as he read out the spell. The Thorn Maiden might currently inhabit a physical shape, but she'd not lost any of her power over minds and souls.

Nelle rolled Soran a little further, the boat rocking dangerously with each move she made. Gods above, she'd better not capsize them out here in the channel! She could swim well enough, but where would she swim to? Back to Noxaur and the waiting arms of the Noswraith?

Taking a little more care, she slid her hand along his neck, pressing her fingers hard against the blood-slick skin. "Be alive," she whispered. "Be alive, be alive, be alive, you bullspitting idiot!"

She found a pulse at last, faint but present. For a moment her heart lifted.

But then another horrible gash opened along his cheek, as though cut by an invisible knife. Nelle choked on a scream. And she realized: Soran was unconscious. Passed into the Nightmare Realm where the Thorn Maiden could prey upon him at will. He had no means to protect himself.

Nelle lifted her head, pushing hair out of her eyes, and stared out across the water to that dancing mass of briars along the shore. Enough distance lay between them now that she could not see the woman's face, could not read her expression. But she *felt* the smile, the knowing, triumphant smile.

"Not today, you spittin' brag!" Nelle snarled.

She bowed over the mage again, carefully rolling him to one side, reaching beneath his heavy, inert body. She felt around in the blood and the shallow water until her questing fingers found what she sought—a leather volume.

With a glad cry, Nelle pulled the red book out from under Soran, but the cry died on her lips at once. The book was soaked with blood and sagged miserably in her grasp. Would it fall apart when she opened it? Had the written spell words all leaked out into the briny water?

"No, no, no." Nelle rose from her knees a little too fast, the boat rocking dangerously at her shifting weight. Sitting back on the rowing bench, she held the book in her lap. Her filmy skirts were still dry in places, and she used them to dab futilely at the soaked cover. Was it all over already? Was it too late? Inarticulate prayers crowding her lips, Nelle opened the cover.

A blast of raw magical energy burst in her face. Screaming, she nearly fell off the bench again. Only some desperate instinct made her hands clasp down harder on the cover rather than throw the whole thing as far from her as she could. Brilliant lights and colors for which she had no name filled her head.

This was magic. True magic. All the other spells she'd witnessed or even had a hand in making, they were nothing, absolutely nothing in comparison. This spell was as though Silveri had broken down the gates to the *quinsatra* to let all the raw magic roll through in a devastating storm.

Yet she sensed order in the pages and written lines. And where there was order, there could be control.

Nelle blinked and peered through the glare, peered down into the physical reality underlying the greater magical reality, down to the pulsating words brilliantly illuminated across the soaked, crinkled parchment. The magic wasn't as wild and uncontained as she'd first thought. There was reason here, rhythm and rhyme.

She carefully peeled each sodden page apart from the next and turned it with care. Her mind stretched painfully yet eagerly as she took in the hugeness of all that her wide eyes beheld. The words were written in Old Araneli, but it didn't matter. She understood them with an understanding entirely outside mortal reason.

She turned one more page and reached the place where the spell left off—the moment when Soran collapsed. The magic was unfinished but hadn't unraveled yet.

Dared she try to complete it? Sudden awareness of her own

inadequacy nearly sickened her. Scarcely a week of magical training, a week of dabbling, of playing around on the edges of this vast abyss of power. Who was she to think she could control such a spell? This was the work of a master mage, a true genius. Soran's work.

But Soran was unconscious. Dying. Bleeding out in the bottom of the boat.

Let him die.

The words whispered in the back of her brain, subtle and dangerous. The Thorn Maiden? Or was it her own conscious awareness?

Let him die. Close the book and take it. It's what you came all this way for. Take it and return to Wimborne. Deliver it to Gaspard. Save your father.

You must.

You must.

You must—

"No!" Nelle cried, shaking her head and gnashing her teeth. She crouched over the page, over the unfinished spell, letting her eyes and mind fill with the brilliance of the *quinsatra*, letting it pour into her.

She read the Rose Book spell.

The moment the words took shape in her head, she realized her mistake. She was not ready for this. How could she be? How could anyone? Darkness closed in—not like the darkness of Noxaur, but a darkness of the soul. A heavy, oppressive, unrelenting knowledge of the evil that lurked in her own heart and in the heart of the man who wrote this spell. At first it was too much and threatened to break her in two.

But then she saw it—a gleam as though at the end of a narrow tunnel. The climax, the conclusion of the binding spell.

She started to run. She wasn't even certain how to run in this place of souls where she had no body, but somehow she ran anyway, faster and faster. The tunnel was longer than she'd realized, and the walls crawled with invisible undulations that she felt rather than saw, filling the darkness on either side of her until writhing pervaded her mind.

You don't belong here, the Thorn Maiden whispered. *This is no place for you.*

Unseen thorns lashed from either side, cutting her legs, cutting her arms, her face. But though they tried to grab and restrain her, they weren't quick enough. She refused to let fear distract her. There was pain, but she could deal with pain. Her goal glowed ahead, at the far end of the tunnel, and she ran, ran, *ran.*

The Thorn Maiden roared, and a horrific crash filled Nelle's senses. The tunnel behind her was caving in, demolished by the Noswraith's fury. Great stone blocks dropped on all sides, and the roof of the tunnel ahead sagged.

Terror surged, and in that terror, realization blazed: She knew exactly what to do. It was just as Mother taught her all those years ago.

Look at the drop.

Accept the danger, the reality of the fall.

The reality of the stones waiting to catch you, to pulverize your bones.

Accept it and lock it down and don't look again.

Nelle redoubled her speed, fairly flying through that darkness. Suddenly, the tunnel wasn't a tunnel anymore. It became a vast, formless space full of light, full of strange colors and churning clouds—a space she had only ever glimpsed before as though in the reflection of a dark mirror.

The *quinsatra.*

It was almost too much. Her mind strained, and she knew it would break.

But she knew the reason she was here: The end of the spell— half drawn out into the physical world yet forever rooted in this one—writhed like a brilliant ribbon of light, dangling before her.

With both hands Nelle reached out and caught the thread. Pure magic surged through her, and her physical body lurched on the bench of the rowing boat, nearly dropping the spellbook. Tears of pain streamed from her eyes, dropping toward the pages open in her lap but evaporating well before they struck.

She wound the burning thread around her fingers and wrists, shaping it as she knew it ought to be shaped. The spell was already written, after all—a brilliant composition from a brilliant mind. She only needed to follow the pattern Soran had already created.

With a cry, she spun in place and saw the roiling mass of the Thorn Maiden bearing down upon her, more enormous than reason could comprehend. Hundreds of arms reached out, thousands of thorns aimed straight for her heart.

Nelle flung the thread—such a thin, delicate little thing—while keeping one end wrapped firmly around her wrist. Shimmering in stark contrast with the hideous black mass of the Noswraith, the thread shot directly at the womanly shape lurking in the darkness, circled the Thorn Maiden's head, and settled around her throat.

With a twist of her wrists, Nelle pulled the noose tight.

An agonized gasp tore through her lungs as she lurched upright on the rowing bench. Her white-knuckled fingers still grasped the Rose Book in her lap as the last of the spell-words burned bright before her eyes, then faded, faded, and settled into mere ink on a page.

Was it done?

It had to be.

Nelle slammed the book shut, clutched it against her stomach, and bent over it, certain she would be sick. Her head swam and her bones quaked so hard she could almost swear she heard them rattling. Cuts riddled her body, up and down her legs, but she didn't think they were deep. Not dangerously deep, anyway. Bullspit, she'd end up as scarred as the mage if she wasn't careful!

With that thought, she jerked her head upright, looking for Soran. Perhaps it was the afterburn of the spell, or maybe the magic the pink woman had worked on her eyes was already fading. Either way, the world was much, much darker than it had been before she opened the book. She could only just discern the mage's bulk in the bottom of the boat.

And the Thorn Maiden?

Nelle turned her gaze outward, seeking the Noxaur shore, searching for some sign of the Noswraith. But the shore was gone. The darkness was so deep, she couldn't see beyond a foot or two around the boat.

How far out into the Hinter Sea had they floated? And how long had she been reading? Soran spent all night every night working this same magic. Had it been hours for her as well?

Nelle shuddered violently and couldn't stop shaking even when she forced her limbs to relax, forced herself to lower the book to her lap and look at it again. Part of the binding was badly torn, and it looked burned all around the edges. "That's no good," she whispered.

Not liking to hold onto it any longer, she tucked the book under Soran's limp arm as the safest place she could think to stow it. She checked the mage's pulse again, just to make certain he still lived, and thought it seemed a little stronger than before. Hopefully, she nudged his shoulder and said, "Soran?" a few times, her mouth close to his ear.

He made no response.

Heaving a sigh that was almost a sob, Nelle sat back on the bench. Though she no longer felt cold, she still trembled uncontrollably. Wrapping the mage's borrowed robe back around her bare shoulders, she huddled down in the rough fabric. It smelled of him—parchment, ink, dust, and always, always the sea, as wild and unknowable as the man himself. She breathed in the scent, comforted even as the darkness deepened.

Should she try to row? But where in the seven gods' names would she row *to*? No stars lit the sky, no beacon light gleamed in the distance. All was dreadfully still, the only sounds her own tense breathing and the lap of water against the sides of her boat. She could be miles out into open Hinter Sea by now.

This was probably the end. Or the beginning of the end. It might be an end that dragged out for a long, excruciating while. Her tired mind accepted the possibility, the reality. But she saw no way out of it. She couldn't even feel afraid, not yet. At least she wasn't naked and tied down to that bed in the red room. If she must meet her fate, she'd rather it was here, in the darkness. Beside Soran Silveri.

If only he would wake. Even just for a moment. If only he would speak to her one last time. If only she had the chance to say to him all that she'd left unsaid . . .

Well. Why not?

Shifting from the bench, Nelle knelt in the sloshing bottom of the boat and reached out in the near blindness until she found the mage's head. She rested her hand there, letting her fingers toy with his long, tangled hair. He was so still, and his skin was icy cold. Perhaps he was already dead. She didn't have the courage to check.

"You're an idiot, you know," she said. Her voice sounded loud in her own ears, but simultaneously small in that huge expanse of darkness. "You're an idiot to come after me like that. And to let the Thorn Maiden out! Bullspit, sir. I mean, just, bull-scatting-*spit*."

This wasn't right. Her heart was heavy, burdened with words that must be spoken. But even now she was afraid. Once she admitted the truth out loud, there could be no going back, no denial.

If this was her end though, what did it matter?

"I never thought . . ." Nelle bit her lip, struggling against the sudden prickle of tears burning in her eyes, choking her throat. She stopped playing with Soran's hair and simply rested her hand on his blood-crusted cheek.

"I never thought I would find you," she said at last, softly. "When I set out from Wimborne, I mean. Finding you was the last thing on my mind. I wasn't convinced there was a 'you' to find, if I'm altogether truthful."

She stroked his cheek gently, feeling the line of his jaw, tracing the shape of his ear. Too bad she couldn't see him. Just one more time. She tried to make herself feel at least a little guilt for the thought, tried to make herself think of Papa or Mother. Even of Sam. But no. She loved them, all of them, dearly.

But the only face she wanted to see was scarred and hideous and so . . . so . . .

"You'd think I'm stupid," she said, sniffing hard to keep back a sob. "Very stupid, I'm sure! It ain't been long, after all. At least it ain't *felt* that long. And you're such a beast! Such an arrogant ass with your know-better airs and your 'Miss Becks,' and really I ought to hate you, but the truth is . . . the truth is, sir . . . Well, in fact, the truth is . . ."

Somewhere far away, a chortling voice sang out in the darkness. Nelle froze. Then her head slowly raised, her eyes slowly widened.

Had she mistaken it? Had she dreamed it? Had she—

The song repeated. A little louder, an answer to the first call.

"Wyverns!" she gasped.

The next moment, she scrambled back onto the bench and grabbed hold of the oars. Guessing at the direction, she stuck one oar into the water, heaved the boat around, and rowed. The splash was too loud, too frenetic. She forced herself to slow, to pause, to listen again.

There it was. A third song. Faint but distinct.

Adjusting course slightly, Nelle set to with a will. She ignored the pain in her side, the many lacerations across her skin, even the panic rising inside her, telling her not to believe it, not to hope. She couldn't help herself. She *did* hope. Desperately, fiercely.

Soon the air was full of wyvern song, and she spied flitting shapes overhead. "I see you!" she cried, her voice frenetic with sudden joy. "I see you, you spittin' beauties, you! I see you!"

Had the little spell beasts ventured out into the Hinter, straining against their bindings in search of their master? Or perhaps the terms of their imprisonment bound them to him and not to Roseward!

Either way, they had come. She followed them, followed their song while the dreadful blindness of Noxaur gave way to the darkness of an overcast night. Now and then the clouds parted, offering her glimpses of stars and even a little sliver of moonlight.

Then it wasn't dark at all. Dawn broke on the horizon, spilling light out across the water in ripples of pink and gold almost too beautiful to bear. Shading her eyes, Nelle turned on her seat. There was Roseward, much closer than she'd realized. She saw the lighthouse high on its cliff and the little stretch of beach where she'd first met the scarred mage. Dozens of wyverns circled overhead, singing and chortling and burbling the most beautiful song she had ever, ever heard.

Strength revived, Nelle guided the boat up onto the beach, glorying in the moment the prow crunched against sand and stone. She leaped out and dragged the boat as far she could, which wasn't far at all due to Soran's added weight and her own exhaustion. Then she staggered a few paces until her legs simply folded up, and she collapsed in the surf. Water lapped around her knees and calves, drenching the folds of Soran's borrowed robe. She sat for some while, breathing, shivering, weeping perhaps, and laughing as well.

At last she forced herself upright and staggered to her feet. Soran. She couldn't leave him in that boat, wounded and unconscious. She had to get him out. Maybe she could run up to the lighthouse, find a bottle of *qeiese* stashed away somewhere? That ought to be strong enough to revive him. Or maybe she could—

"Ginger?"

Nelle whirled, staring along the stretch of beach. The rising sun cast a harsh glare off the water and into her eyes, so she raised a shading hand and squinted. A shadowy outline approached—tall, rangy, and familiar.

"Ginger, is that you? I've been looking for you everywhere."

"Sam!" she cried.

28

S oran lay in blood-soaked darkness. This was the end. It must be. He'd collapsed before completing the spell, and the Thorn Maiden would be swift to finish him off.

So why did this not quite feel like death?

Granted, he didn't know exactly what to expect from death. The darkness felt about right, and it made sense that pain would follow him into the afterlife. If the seven gods were just, as theologians claimed, his eternal end ought to be one of pain. His crimes were numerous enough.

She's clever.

Soran stiffened. The sickly-sweet redolence of the Thorn Maiden filled his nostrils. He couldn't see her in this darkness, but her nearness, her hovering presence, oppressed him. Had she followed him into this pain-filled afterlife? Would she be his eternal torment? Could he never escape her, even in death? His soul quailed at the thought. If this was hell, it was a just hell . . . cruelly just.

Don't whimper so. Her voice hissed in his ear like the sound of a hundred leaves slithering against one another. *You're not dead. You're asleep. And I am bound yet again.*

What? No. No, this must be some strange form of torment. He knew better than to grasp at such a foolish hope. He had failed to complete the binding; of that he was sure. And there was no other way to . . . no other . . . no . . .

"*Nelle?*" The name whispered through his cut and bleeding lips.

The Thorn Maiden hissed again. He felt a soft hand brush his cheek, felt the fingers stick in his fresh and oozing blood.

It won't be long now, my love. Your spell is weakened. I will soon be free . . . free . . . free . . .

The echoes of her voice died away, replaced by other sounds. Waves lapping against a boat. Oars creaking. Wind sighing and . . . and was that Nelle's voice?

"Oh, you lovely, lovely beasties!" Her words came in a sort of rhythm, panting in time to the sound of the oars. "I take back every nasty thing I ever said about you. You just keep on singing!"

Another sound touched his ear: wyvern song. It flowed down from high above into the darkness behind his eyes, and his soul lifted despite every effort to prevent it. He wasn't dead. Not yet anyway.

He sank into a numb, trance-like state, his eyes still closed, his body cold, paralyzed. Every other sense stirred with life, his ears full of wind and wyvern song, his nose with the scent of the salty ocean, his tongue with the iron tang of blood. Each of these sensations, pleasant and unpleasant alike, was cause for joy. He was alive. There may yet be time to right at least some of the wrongs he'd committed.

He allowed this thought to float around in his mind, sloshing like the waves. Other sensations floated along with it, vague and oddly comfortable.

The boat crunched onto the sandy beach, jarring his body. He winced, the first actual move he'd made since regaining consciousness. With that one small act, wakefulness began to return to his body, creeping and slow, but determined. He heard the oars clatter inside the boat as Nelle dropped them, listened to her splash and puff as she leaped out and hauled the little craft farther up the shore. He ought to rise, ought to get up and help her. One hand twitched, but he couldn't quite manage more than that, not yet. He exhaled slowly, preparing to gather his strength for another, more concentrated effort.

"Ginger!"

A dart of surprise shot through Soran's awareness. His eyelids fluttered and flared open, and he found himself staring at the nilarium-crusted fingers of his own left hand, close to his nose. He turned his head slightly, trying to get his face out of the bilgewater.

"Ginger, is that you! I've been looking for you everywhere."

"Sam!"

That was unmistakably Nelle's voice. Her answer was sharp, surprised, a little confused.

Sam . . . why did he know that name? Had she spoken it before?

Oh. Yes.

When he'd held her in his arms and gently called her wandering spirit back to her body with a kiss. When she'd pressed her hand to his cheek and he'd thought she might draw him in for another kiss, one of her own initiation. When she'd looked up at him, still half asleep, half dazed, her lovely eyes blinking fast in confusion.

That's when she'd said it. *Sam.*

Wait. What did this mean? Soran's head ached with confusion, and pain roared through his limbs as he tried to pull himself together, to push himself upright. But when he heard Nelle speak again, he stilled, closed his eyes, and strained his ears, trying to catch her words.

"What are you doing here? I thought . . . Where were you last night?"

"Where was I?" answered the stranger's voice. "Where were *you?* You said you'd come before sunset, but it got darker and darker, and you were nowhere to be seen! Then I caught a . . . a sense of something. Something dangerous, getting nearer by the moment. I remembered what you'd said about not staying at the house after dark, so I got out of there as quick as I could and ran down to the harbor. I thought you'd meet me there. I waited all night and didn't sleep, just like you said. I heard all kinds of awful racket, more of those skull-dogs, I think, and I was afraid something had happened to you. I wanted to search for you, but it was black as pitch by then, and I couldn't see my hand before my face. I sat there in the dark forever. Soon as it was light again, I went searching for you and found some of those skull-dogs all torn to pieces. Was that your little dragons' work again?"

Through all this talk, Nelle occasionally made little sounds and half words, but didn't seem able to produce anything coherent. When the stranger's voice finally trailed off, she stammered, "So you didn't see the Thorn Maiden at all?"

"The what? There wasn't any maiden; I'm sure I would have noticed. Just those skull-dog corpses." Soran heard footsteps on sand, then, "I'm glad to see you all right. I was that worried. I've been imagining all sorts of horrors that might have stopped you from coming."

Nelle barked a bitter sort of laugh. "You couldn't imagine the half of it!"

Soran swallowed, a lump of blood and salt rolling down his thickened throat. So. She'd hidden a stranger on Roseward Isle. This was why she'd left the safety of the lighthouse. This was why she'd risked working magic despite every warning he'd given, despite the imminent threat of Kyriakos. For this friend, this . . . this lover?

A knot of rage tightened in Soran's heart. He shifted where he lay, rolling onto his side, ignoring the shooting pain from his many cuts and wounds. His hand caught the side of the boat, and he started to rise.

"There's no time to explain now," Nelle continued in a rush. "You've got to go, Sam. I mean it. You can't stay here. We're far enough away from Noxaur now, you should be safe enough returning. I'll help you get your boat, but you can't—"

"Are you mad?" The young man's voice snapped like a whip. "After all I've seen of this cursed place? I'm not going anywhere without you. I don't care what bargains you made or what you came here for—"

"Shut your mouth, idiot. For once in your spittin' life, will you—"

Both voices, running over the top of each other in anger and earnestness, cut off abruptly as Soran stood. He straightened to his full height, uncertain even as he did so that his legs would support him. His knees buckled, and the boat rocked on the sand until he almost toppled over in an undignified heap. But he steadied himself, tossed snarls of white hair from his eyes, and stared at the two figures a little way up the beach.

They stood quite close to each other. The stranger had caught hold of Nelle's hand and seemed to be trying to draw her to him. But now he stared, startled by Soran's sudden rise, and provided a clear view of his handsome young face, deep-set eyes, strong jaw darkened by stubble, and long black hair pulled back in a messy queue. The lad wore a familiar loose-fitting, bloodstained shirt.

Who but Nelle could have given it to him?

Drawn by the trajectory of the young man's gaze, Nelle had turned sharply, her eyes widening. For a moment—a moment so brief, Soran thought he must have imagined it—a look of pure joy washed over her expression, and she even took a half step toward him.

Then the joy vanished. All color drained from her face, and she shifted her gaze from Soran to the stranger and back again, her mouth opening and closing.

"Sir!" she gasped at last. "Sir, I can explain."

"Yes." Soran's voice was as cold as the lump of ice that seemed to have replaced his beating heart. "Yes, I'm sure you can."

His tone knocked her back a pace. Then she shook her hand loose from the stranger's grip and hurried toward Soran, stopping between the two men. Soran couldn't bear to look at her. He fixed his gaze on the stranger instead, who responded with a fierce expression that almost disguised the fear in his eyes.

"This . . . this is my friend." Nelle squared her shoulders as though trying to turn herself into a living shield. "Sam . . . his name is Sam. Samton Rallenford . . . but . . . yeah, that don't matter. Um. He's come searching for me, you see. He knew I'd run away from Wimborne, knew I'd got myself into trouble. I, uh, I always told him I'd go to Roseward if I ever needed to lie low, so he thought he'd come and find me. Then he got caught in the Hinter currents, you see, and pulled close to Noxaur. He's had a bad time of it, and he came to the lighthouse for help."

"Indeed." Soran yanked his gaze away from the young man's to study Nelle. "If that is so, why did you not tell me?"

Again her jaw gaped. "He was that upset, you see," she said at last. "The Hinter Sea was rough between Wimborne and the Noxaur shore. I wanted to give him a chance to recover a little before he tried to make his way home again. I thought . . . I thought if you knew he was here, you'd send him back right away."

"Did you?"

She blinked, frowned, and shut her mouth tight as though

afraid of what she might say next. But she needn't have worried. Her actions spoke loudly enough. They clearly proclaimed exactly what she thought of him: uncaring, unfeeling. A monster.

And did he deserve higher regard from her? He, who had knowingly allowed her to be led into the very path of Kyriakos? He, who had deliberately unleashed the most horrific monster on people wholly unable to defend themselves? Every scar marring his face bore testimony to the far more hideous scarring of his soul.

She knew. He couldn't disguise the truth from her.

In truth, he couldn't say whether he would have given the stranger shelter had she asked him. He might have taken one look at that handsome face, might have observed one moment of the interactions between the two of them—both so fresh, so unspoiled, so unconsciously beautiful and full of promise, a perfect match in every possible way—and find it more than he could bear. Even now, if he had a spell lethal enough remaining on his person, he would be far too tempted to use it. To hurl a bolt straight at that handsome, youthful face.

"S-Sam?" Nelle had whispered when waking to Soran's kiss.

What further confirmation did he need of the relationship between them?

Soran looked down at his feet where the Rose Book lay, battered but still miraculously whole, one edge of its cover touching the shallow bilgewater. He bent, picked it up, tucked it under his arm. Then he climbed out of the boat. His body roared in pain with every move he made. He welcomed that pain. It was far less than he deserved. And already the air of Roseward worked its healing magic. He would have a new collection of scars across his person to commemorate his most recent sins.

Nelle drew herself up a little straighter as he limped toward her up the beach, her chin set, her throat constricting as she tried to swallow. He did not meet her eyes but looked ahead, beyond the young man.

When he drew alongside her, Nelle reached out, almost but not quite touching his arm. "Sir?" she said quietly.

Soran stopped. "Your friend must go. Now." He dared let his eyes flick sideways, seeking her face, but couldn't bear to look at her for more than an instant. "And you should go with him."

He faced forward again. "Take care that you practice no magic when you return to the city. The Miphates won't like it. They will track you down. You would be wise to quit Wimborne altogether."

With those words and nothing more, he picked up his pace, ignoring the agony in his stiffened limbs, and hastened up the beach, past the young man. Overhead, the wyverns danced and sang, joyous at his return. But he could scarcely hear them.

Blood pulsed in his ears, and he thought he heard instead the Thorn Maiden's voice whisper in the back of his head: *My love . . . my love . . . you were always meant to be mine . . .*

29

Nelle faced out to sea while listening to Soran's retreating footsteps. At first she beheld only a swimming haze of dawn light and indistinct shadows, but eventually she realized that the shore of Noxaur was no longer in sight. Instead, she faced open Hinter waters and even glimpsed the Evenspire through filmy clouds.

Tears stung her eyes. She hastily blinked them back—it was the salt-laden wind in her face, nothing more. Sniffing hard, she shook her head, struggling to gather her thoughts.

"Nelle?" Sam's voice quavered as he approached behind her. "Are you all right?" His hand rested on her shoulder, warm and heavy through the rough fabric of the mage's borrowed robe.

"Fine, Sam." Nelle shook off his hand, took a step or two away, and turned to face him. "I'm fine," she said. "And Mage Silveri is right. You've got to go. Now."

Sam's dark eyes scanned her face, full of questions she feared he would ask. "Yes," he said slowly. "He is right. And you should come with me."

A sharp, stabbing longing filled her. A desire to reach out, to take Sam's hand, to let him lead her to the boat and away from here. Away from all the terror and frustration and hurt and sorrow that Roseward and this strange, awful, beautiful world had come to mean to her. She didn't belong here. Regardless of any deadly whispers or lies Kyriakos may have spoken about her heritage. None of that changed reality.

She was just Nelle. Peronelle Beck of Draggs Street. She wasn't fit for this world of magic and frighteningly enormous possibility. She belonged with ordinary people—the worst, the roughest, the most degraded, the most altogether *human* of people. She belonged in a world where possibilities were as narrow as the next fetid alley, where magic was the stuff of stories and unlived dreams. Although there was a certain deadness in her heart at the prospect of returning, there was craving as well.

She was like a songbird suddenly liberated from its cage, discovering that the sky is just too huge and full of hawks.

"Nelle?" Sam said softly, taking another half step toward her.

"I can't."

Papa.

Amid everything else, the fear, the darkness, the mad frenzy of fight and flight and despair, she'd almost forgotten. Papa still needed her, still depended on her. How could she go back without accomplishing what she had set out to do? If, after all this time, she returned to Wimborne empty-handed, Gaspard would be swift to unleash his vengeance.

She might deserve Master Shard's ax blade, but Papa did not.

"I can't," she repeated more firmly and drew away from Sam, pulling her shoulders back to face him without blinking or hesitation. "I've still got a job to do."

"Then, let me help," Sam said at once. In that moment he looked exactly like the old Sam, the boy for whom she had harbored such a passion. Her partner in rebellion and madcap scheming. He smiled at her, his teeth flashing in the roguish expression she knew too well. "We'll do it together. Between the two of us we can steal anything. We can outsmart one old mage."

"No." The word came out as a sharp bark. Nelle quickly shook her head, softening her tone. "It's too dangerous. I won't put your life at risk."

"If it's dangerous, then surely you need—"

"Soran . . . that is, Mage Silveri won't stand for you to stay. There's nowhere you can hide on an island this small. No, Sam. No." She shook her head again, her jaw tight. "You've got to go."

"What about you?" Sam reached for her hand, but she retreated. "I heard what he said. He told you to go as well."

"He's told me as much before. I'll manage."

"Ginger—"

"I've got options. I've got powers at my disposal you haven't got. It's just a matter of opportunity."

His eyes flared. She could see at once what *powers* he thought she meant, having nothing to do with magic. His face went grim, and he looked suddenly much older.

"I don't like it," he stated.

"Yeah, well, you don't gotta like it, do you?" Nelle folded her arms and, with a toss of her head, indicated the boat on the shore. "You taking this one, or are we dragging your boat back out of that cave? I ain't got all day, so decide fast."

She could see further protests simmering in his eyes. But he did not voice them, and after a brief discussion they agreed that, as the two boats were practically identical, he would take the one near at hand.

He was fearful to return to the open waters of the Hinter, and Nelle couldn't blame him. But she pointed out the Evenspire and explained in a garbled fashion about the bridge connecting Roseward to the mortal world. She could tell he understood not a word of it, but when she said, "If you just follow the Evenspire, you'll get there before you know it. It's closer than it looks, I promise," he seemed to accept her authority on the subject. She hoped she was right.

As soon as they maneuvered the boat back into the water, Nelle backed up on the shore, wary of Sam, half afraid he would try to drag her off to Wimborne, bound or unconscious. He regarded her sadly from the far side of the boat, grasping the gunwale with steadying hands.

"Well, Ginger," he said, his voice almost too soft to be heard over the wyverns' chortling songs. "I . . ." He swallowed, dropped his gaze, then looked up to flash her one of his bright, careless smiles. "Take care of yourself. And come home soon."

She nodded shortly, wrapping her arms around her body, pressing the folds of Soran's robes tight. "Tell Mage Gaspard I'll get what he sent me for. And find my papa, Sam. Please. Make sure he's all right."

"I will." With a nod, Sam gave the boat a final heave, leaped nimbly inside, and settled on the rowing bench. Sharp sea breezes played through his hair and the thin fabric of the borrowed shirt as he looked back over his shoulder, checking the angle of the prow, making certain he pointed for the Evenspire. Then Sam set to rowing with a will that would soon drive off any cold.

Nelle stood on the shore and watched until the hazy veil surrounding Roseward abruptly swallowed him from sight.

Nelle slowly climbed the cliff path up to the lighthouse. She was so tired, so very tired that several times she stopped, leaned her shoulder against the stones, and closed her eyes, breathing deep. But the air of Roseward had a reviving effect, and by the time she reached the top of the path, she felt better. Better than she reasonably ought to, under the circumstances.

Was Soran watching her? Lifting her face, she shaded her eyes to peer up at the gaping windows of the tower above. He had to know that she'd not left with Sam. How would he respond to her stubborn disobedience?

A thousand questions tried to pile into her brain at once as she walked the short distance from the cliff's edge to the door. The Rose Book . . . She'd now seen the Rose Book, held it in her hands, and even worked some of the bullspitting spell it contained! Would it last much longer? Would she be able to get it away from Roseward and into Gaspard's keeping before it fell to pieces?

Then there was Gaspard to consider. He was a powerful Miphato. He had studied forbidden magicks alongside Soran back in the day. Could he create the fresh binding required to restrain the Noswraith? He would know how, if anyone could.

She had to do it. For Papa. For Soran.

She pressed her hand against the fabric of the mage's robe, over the boning of her uncomfortable, corseted garment where the golden locket lay hidden, pressed against her skin. One last dose remained. She couldn't be squeamish now. If she had to grab Soran by the ears and take him utterly by surprise, the same way she surprised Gaspard on that dark night that felt so long ago, so be it.

And sooner rather than later.

She reached the door, touched the latch, and found it unlocked, to her surprise. The instant she pushed it open, a raucous, rattling bray greeted her, and a bundle of scales and wings threw itself at her knees, nearly knocking her flat. The blue wyvern leaped on its haunches, snapping its jaws and lashing its tongue. It should have seemed ferocious . . . only she couldn't help comparing it to an overgrown and overly enthusiastic puppy.

"Hullo, worm," Nelle growled, trying at first to nudge the beast out of her way. She soon gave up and knelt on the threshold as the wyvern flung itself joyfully into her arms, nuzzling her with its great rigid nostrils and whimpering with joy. "I know, I know. You want porridge, don't you? Well, I can't say but that I could use a little stick-to-the-ribs sustenance myself. Now if you'll just let me through the door . . ."

She tried several times to rise but was obliged to accept the wyvern's somewhat painful demonstrations of affection for several minutes before it finally relented enough for her to climb to her feet. Even then it pressed against her shins, rolled adoring eyes up at her, rattled its tongue, and generally contrived to get under her feet.

Soran was nowhere in sight, but then, she hadn't expected him to be. Had he heard the wyvern's ear-shattering greeting from up in his tower? Was he ignoring her?

Nelle moved to her alcove bed and slipped her arms out of the mage's robes, leaving it in a pile on the floor. Looking down at the copious amounts of bare skin on display, she shuddered. Tomorrow she'd have to pillage the wardrobes at Dornrise again. If she didn't freeze to death first.

"Bullspitting sister-wives," she growled, heading for the armoire. Soran's stash of shirts and trousers would serve until she had a chance to—

Footsteps sounded on the stairs. Nelle turned sharply, one

hand on the armoire door, just as the mage appeared through the hole in the ceiling, descending quickly. His head was down, his gaze on his feet, and only when he reached the bottom of the stair did he look up.

His eyes fixed hard upon her. Then they slowly dropped, taking in her exposed flesh. The seductive black garment was rather the worse for wear after her wild flight through Ninthalor. But it still served its purpose, displaying every womanly attribute to its most desirable advantage.

A rush of heat flooded Nelle's face. Her heart caught in her throat.

Without a word, Soran turned and started up the stair again. He would be gone in a moment.

"Wait!"

The word burst from her lips. It rang sharply in the room, so sharp that the wyvern darted outside through the open door, muttering complaints.

Soran paused, one hand resting on the wall. He still wore only the trousers and loose, bloodstained shirt he'd been wearing down at the shore. He'd probably come down in search of fresh clothes.

"Please," Nelle said softly. Leaving the armoire, she stepped across the room toward him. Blood pounded in her throat, and she felt dizzy. Dizzy, yet somehow purposeful. "Please, sir, don't . . ."

"I saw the boat." Soran didn't look at her. His head bent, his silvery hair falling to cover the side of his scarred, ugly face. "I saw it pass through the veil. I thought you'd . . . I thought . . ." He drew a long breath. "You should not have stayed, Miss Beck."

"I know," she answered softly. She was just behind him now, her foot on the lowest step. She hesitated, pinching both lips between her teeth. "Please."

Partial thoughts, schemes, and half-baked plans drained from her brain to run off like so much rainwater, leaving behind only this heat in her breast. Distantly she recalled the gold locket hidden in her corset, but she couldn't think about it or the poison it contained. Not now. Not in this moment.

"Please," she said again, climbed the second step, lifted one hand. Rested it on his shoulder. "Soran."

He turned. His face was worse than it had been, the old scars carved over with fresh cuts which the Hinter air had only just begun to heal. His eyes blazed with what might be fury or might be something else entirely. Something hot, searing. Dangerous.

When she took another step, they stood on the same tread. Her hands slid around his waist as she leaned into him. He stood like solid granite, but she didn't care. Resting her head against his chest, she closed her eyes, listened to the wild beat of his heart, and simply stood there holding him for a long, long moment. The stench of blood filled her nostrils, but she smelled life as well, thunderous life simmering with vital energy.

"I'm not going," she said, her voice soft but firm. "I'm not going anywhere."

She felt the power in him surge and knew that it must soon erupt. Was she ready for whatever violent, impassioned reaction would follow?

Perhaps not. But she wanted it even so.

Her arms tightened around him, bracing against any force that might seek to tear her away. And suddenly his arms moved in response, folding around her body. One cold nilarium-crusted hand rested on her bare shoulder, then slid up her neck, making her tremble at the chill. He tangled his fingers in her long, snarled hair. Then his head bent, and she felt . . . was that his mouth? Pressing against the top of her head as he inhaled deeply?

She lifted her face, fighting a little against the pressure of his hand on the back of her head, and looked up at him. His face hovered close to hers, his scarred, misshapen lips slightly parted, mere inches from her own. He was so unlike Kyriakos—so ugly, so broken. Frail and mortal compared to that glorious immortal fae.

But the feelings swelling inside her were also unlike anything she'd experienced amid the seductions of the red room. No fear underscored her desire. This was Soran. She knew him. The good and the terrible. The disgraced mage. The patient teacher. The arrogant ass. The courageous rescuer. The tender caregiver with the gentle touch, who had once longed to create beauty and who had watched his longings crumble into ruin.

She knew him. And maybe she was a fool, but . . . she trusted him. She wanted him.

Rising on her toes, Nelle closed the distance between them. Her lips softly brushed his in an invitation as delicate as a butterfly's wings.

"Nelle," he whispered, his voice low, ragged.

"Yes," she answered and lifted her hand to press her palm

against his cheek. "Yes, Soran—"

A shock like lightning shot through his spine. The mage drew a horrible gasping breath, and his arms pulled away, his hands closing over her bare shoulders as he pushed her roughly from him. She staggered down two steps, nearly fell, and backed against the wall to brace herself. "Soran!" she cried.

He had already turned away, already staggered several more paces up the stairway, his shoulders bent, his breathing labored. "I won't do it," he said. "I won't fall prey to your illusions. And I won't hurt her. I won't."

Nelle stared at him. Then she realized. "No, Soran!" She tried to gather herself, to follow him. "It's me! I swear! I'm not a dream or an illusion! I'm—"

"No." He glared at her, his face half wild behind long strands of white hair. "Don't toy with me, Helenia." He drew a strained breath between clenched teeth, his nostrils flaring. "I won't be the monster. Not anymore."

He wrenched away and fled up the stairs, two treads at a time. Nelle tried to follow, but her knees gave out, and she sank heavily on the cold stone, her hands grasping for anything she might hold onto for support. "Soran!" she called one more time.

He didn't respond. She listened to his footsteps climb the tower until she heard the distant door of his upper chamber slam. Then she bowed over, pressed her face into her hands, and wept.

30

If ever she had earned the right to a fit of uncontrollable weeping, now was that time. What with being kidnapped by a dark fae, chased by shadow-monsters, skull-dogs, and harpens, nearly killed by a Noswraith, and set adrift on an otherworldly ocean without hope of help . . . if all that wasn't reason enough for a girl to shed a few tears, she didn't know what was.

Nelle eventually pulled herself together, feeling hollow, tired, and no better at all. Her head throbbed. *Should have considered that before you gave way to all that tearfulness,* she thought bitterly, wiping her damp cheeks, then rubbing her temples ruefully.

A cold breeze through the open door danced across her bare skin, raising gooseflesh in its wake and shocking her back to herself. Sitting upright, Nelle rubbed her arms, muttered a curse through her lips, then rose stiffly and returned to the armoire to rummage through Soran's garments. Most were covered with rips and old bloodstains, but she found one shirt and pair of trousers a little better off than the others.

Her fingers fumbled for some while, trying to discover how to get out of her corset garment, but she managed it at last. She let the whole ghastly contraption fall to the floor at her feet and stepped out of it with a shudder.

Looking down, she caught a glimmer of gold amid the dark silk. Swiftly she bent to pick up the locket, then looped it around her neck. For a long moment she simply stood there, holding it tight in her fist, breathing deeply.

Then, with another quick shake of her head, she began to dress, pausing to inspect the wound in her side where the tree branch had partially impaled her. Dried blood crusted her skin, but the wound itself was already mostly healed. It ached when she reached her arms up to pull Soran's shirt over her head. But only a little.

The mage's trousers were much too big. She found a bit of rope to fashion a crude belt, tied the billowing shirt comfortably around her waist, then rolled up two fat cuffs around her ankles. Far from fashionable, but it felt good to be clothed again.

Regarding the pile of dark fabric on the floor, Nelle curled her lip in distaste. She stoked up a blaze in the fireplace and, as soon as it was hot enough, added the corset and silks. Perched on the stool, using the poker to stir up the embers, she watched the garment burn down. The stink of burnt silk filled the air.

If only she could as easily rid herself of all memory of Kyriakos and the darkness of Ninthalor.

Ibrildian . . .

Hybrid . . .

Had the fae lord told her the truth? Or were his strange proclamations merely another layer of his pervasive seduction? Had he been attempting to drive a wedge of doubt into her heart, to make her distrust Soran and draw her more firmly toward himself?

Or was it real?

Nelle wrapped her arms around her middle. Her physical eyes watched flames eat away the last of the silk and blacken the corset boning. But in her mind's eye, she fled from the Thorn Maiden through the dark tunnel and into the brilliance of the *quinsatra*. She felt again the power flowing through her as she worked Soran's incredible spell—a spell she had no business even looking at, much less attempting.

"*Ibrildian,*" she whispered, and drew a long, careful breath. What other explanation could there be?

But why had Soran kept the truth from her?

"Because he ain't to be trusted." The words slipped out softly, laced with bitterness. "Because he's a Miphato. A crazed, lunatic Miphato. And you . . . you should know better than to trust a man like him. You should know better than to . . . than to . . ."

She closed her eyes, feeling once more the sensation of his lips pressed against the top of her head. And that moment—a moment of heat and sweetness beyond anything she'd ever before experienced—when she let her lips touch his and thought, truly thought he would respond with the passion she'd felt stirring in his limbs, stirring in his soul.

Foolishness. Pure idiocy. Her terrifying experiences had made her vulnerable, even desperate, and she'd reached out to him without thinking. She wouldn't make that mistake again.

Her hand moved to the locket hidden beneath Soran's borrowed shirt. It was cold and smooth under her fingertips. "One dose," she whispered. "Only one."

She wouldn't waste it. And she wouldn't waste time either. The next time she heard Soran's footsteps on the stair, the next time he showed his face, she would do what she had come to do.

Nelle stood up. The fire was too hot, and the stink of burning corset boning made her feel sick. She hastened across the chamber to the open doorway and stood there, looking out across the cliff, across the sweep of sky, across the Hinter Sea. The blue wyvern, which had been sunbathing belly-up on the doorstep, twisted around, chirruped, and scuttled to her, rubbing around her shins. She ignored it.

Instead, she fixed her gaze on the Evenspire, feeling almost as though she could see Gaspard's face looming in the distance. Almost as though she sensed his hand beckoning her to him.

"Soon," she whispered. "I'll do what I came for. I swear."

THE SCARRED MAGE OF ROSEWARD

Refocused and determined, Nelle plans to snatch the spellbook and escape Roseward Isle once and for all. But when a powerful magic storm blows in—bringing with it a small castaway of mysterious origins—Nelle and Soran are obliged to lie low inside the lighthouse until it passes. Trapped in close quarters, they cannot hide from their deepening attraction.

But fate is against them. Soran knows the nightmare he created will not remain bound much longer. He must convince Nelle to leave him, to escape Roseward before she becomes the Thorn Maiden's newest victim. And Nelle sees the moment fast approaching when she will betray Soran. He will never forgive her, but how can she do otherwise? Papa's life depends on her mission's fulfillment.

Will two lost souls find their way through the tangled briar of lies and mistrust? Or will shadowy thorns tear them apart forever?

Don't miss the finale of this romantic "Beauty and the Beast" retelling.

ABOUT THE AUTHOR

SYLVIA MERCEDES makes her home in the idyllic North Carolina countryside with her handsome husband, numerous small children, and a menagerie of rescue dogs and cats. When she's not writing she's . . . okay, let's be honest. When she's not writing, she's running around after her kids, cleaning up glitter, trying to plan healthy-ish meals, and wondering where she left her phone. In between, she reads a steady diet of fantasy novels.

But mostly she's writing.

A hybrid author, Sylvia publishes both traditionally and independantly, and enjoys the exciting pace. She's the author of more than twenty bestselling romantic fantasies, including the acclaimed Bride of the Shadow King trilogy.

Visit her website to discover more titles:
www.SylviaMercedesBooks.com

ALSO BY SYLVIA MERCEDES

BRIDE OF THE SHADOW KING

Bride of the Shadow King

Vow of the Shadow King

Heart of the Shadow King

WARBRIDE

WarBride

HeartTorn

CurseBound

SoulFire

OF CANDLELIGHT AND SHADOWS

The Moonfire Bride

The Sunfire King

Of Wolves and Wardens

PRINCE OF THE DOOMED CITY

Entranced

Entangled

Ensorcelled

Enslaved

Enthralled

THE DRAGON QUEEN DUOLOGY

The Seventh Champion

The Last Dragon Queen

THE SCARRED MAGE OF ROSEWARD

Thief

Prisoner

Wraith

THE VENATRIX CHRONICLES

Daughter of Shades

Visions of Fate

Paths of Malice

Dance of Souls

Tears of Dust

Queen of Poison

Crown of Nightmares

NOVELLAS

Of Silver and Secrets

Carabosse and the Spindle Spell

www.ingramcontent.com/pod-product-compliance
Lightning Source LLC
Chambersburg PA
CBHW031054260626
47172CB00001B/63